THE STORY OF A LIFETIME

DORIS LEMCKE

THE STORY OF A LIFETIME

ISBN: 978-1-68046-911-0

Published by Satin Romance
An Imprint of Melange Books, LLC
White Bear Lake, MN 55110
www.satinromance.com

Published in the United States of America.

Cover Design by Caroline Andrus

PRAISE FOR DORIS LEMCKE

Doris Lemcke has given me generations of Langesfords to love—this may be the best one yet.

— *KERRYN REID – CHANTICLEER AWARD WINNER FOR BEST REGENCY ROMANCE.*

A wild and fascinating read mixing a Boston Journalist and a Southern Politician during 1964's Freedom Summer. I couldn't put it down.

— *KAREN DEAN BENSON, AUTHOR OF "THE LADIES OF MISCHIEF" SERIES.*

With an evocative and fresh writing style, Ms. Lemcke weaves a complex story, pulling her reader into the tumultuous South of the 60's.

— *LYNNETTE AUSTIN, MULTI-PUBLISHED AUTHOR.*

This book is a product of my growing awareness that civilization seems destined to perpetually re-live history. I began this series in the Post-Civil War South during Reconstruction. A century later in, "The Story of a Lifetime" we see both how far we've come—and how far we have to go to achieve, "Liberty for all."

I dedicate this book to those 'rebels" on both sides of the Mason-Dixon Line who won't give up on America's hard-fought rights to freedom of speech, suffrage, and the open exchange of viewpoints. A special thanks to the League of Women Voters Ann Arbor Area President Joan Sampieri for encouraging me to study and write about an era none of us should forget. Writing this book from a Yankee woman's evolving perspective in the South has been enlightening for me. I hope it will be an entertaining—and thought-provoking—reading experience for my readers.

"Choices are made in brief seconds and paid for in the time that remains."

— PAOLO GIORDANO, *THE SOLITUDE OF PRIME NUMBERS: A NOVEL*

CHAPTER 1

On New Year's Day 1964, I left my hard-won byline and the distinction of being the *Boston Globe*'s only female investigative journalist, for a staff writer job at the *Atlanta Constitution.* I told myself it was only temporary, certain I'd be writing Pulitzer-Prize winning articles about the escalating Civil Rights Movement in no time. But I was a twenty-six-year-old, *divorced woman*—and a Yankee.

By the end of June, I was still writing household hints and editing Adeline Grossbeck's weekly "Cotillions and Courtships" society column—while Negroes were being beaten for wanting to ride at the front of the bus or eat at a drugstore lunch counter just a few blocks from the paper's office. It was time to take a stand.

Though people had been fired for less, I walked into the office of the most fearsome Managing Editor in Atlanta without knocking. Despite the ceiling fan circulating hot, humid air from the open window, I was assaulted by the smell of old cigars, body odor, and stale coffee. David Winkler raised his head from the morning issue of the *Atlanta Constitution.* He peered at me above half-glasses balanced on the end of his bulldog nose and growled, "You want somethin' Missy?"

I sat in the battered captain's chair opposite him without an invitation and cleared my throat. "Yes, I do. It's important."

"It better be." He folded his big hands over the headline announcing

President Johnson's upcoming signature on the Civil Rights Act. "You got sixty seconds."

I checked the wall clock and plowed ahead. "When you put Arty Benton's byline on my money laundering article last month, you promised me a shot at Civil Rights. While we say *The Constitution* 'covers Dixie like the dew,' Northern papers are scooping us in our own backyard. I…we… can't wait any longer. I have a master's degree in journalism and worked five years under Bob Healy at the *Boston Globe* I can…"

"Success takes time, girl," cut me off.

"Laura. My name is Laura. Stainsby."

Black eyes fixed on mine as he pointed a thick, ink-stained finger at my nose. "I know who you are, your fancy degree in journalism and your father, the famous Boston Senator. I also know more than I care to about that hack Healy at the *Globe.* You may have got this job because my publisher is a crony of your daddy's, but you work for me. And *while* you work for me, you do what *I* tell you."

Crap, the Damn Yankee thing. A century after Sherman's March to the Sea, Atlanta still didn't take well to Northerners. But I couldn't back down. Sitting at my desk across the hall from Winkler's office, I'd watched seasoned reporters go in swaggering and come out like beaten puppies. Only those who fought back survived. Winkler lied to me and stole my story. If I didn't stand up to him, I'd never get a byline.

I pointed a finger tipped with English Rose polish at him. "I *have* earned my way. The money-laundering article about Lou's Wash-Mart brought in the FBI and two indictments. And people trust a skinny brunette with a face that says, 'tell me your life story'. I can get reactions about the Civil Rights Act from the street that none of your good old boys can. Reactions that sell papers. Lots of papers."

His scowl made it clear he wasn't about to let a Yankee woman report on Atlanta's peacekeepers beating people trying to use a public bathroom instead of a bucket in the back of an alley. His thick fingers splayed over the newspaper's front page, pushing his aging, line-backer body up to tower over me.

"You got some balls, Missy!"

Dropping heavily back into his chair, he raised the wood lid of a smuggled box of Cuban Partagas Maduros cigars—easily ten bucks a piece. He seemed to be an expert at using the simple act of lighting a cigar as both an intimidating and powerful diversion. Focused on the hand-rolled tobacco, he clipped the end and tilted it at an angle above a match he lit with his thumb. Raising the cigar to his lips, he drew the flame inside, savoring it for my last ten seconds before exhaling directly at my face.

"The Wash-Mart was a lucky break. But luck don't make you a reporter."

My eyes watered, but instead of pulling back and blinking, I leaned toward him. "Lucky break? Of all the newspapers in town, and fifteen TV networks in Atlanta, I was the only reporter who noticed that Lou's Wash Mart had sporadic hours of operation, broken equipment, and customers who came and went *without* laundry. I spent six weeks pretending to be a late-shift waitress, convincing Lou to trust me alone in the building. But you know that. And we both know why you really won't give me a chance."

Raised salt-and-pepper eyebrows dared me to enlighten him and he suddenly became all the men in my life—my father, brothers, teachers—even my ex-husband during our short, unfortunate marriage. They all told me what I *couldn't* do. And what I *should* do—because I was a 'girl'.

Without considering the consequences, I again pointed at him. "You're afraid a woman will out-scoop your pet, 'good ole boy' reporters."

Ignoring the fury in his bulging eyes, I pushed on, "Six months ago, Adeline Grossbeck was mixing sodas at Woolworth's lunch counter. What are *her* qualifications besides a set of double-D cups?"

The back of my dress stuck to the old wood captain's chair and my legs felt like sausages stuffed inside my hose. I took a deep breath in the suffocating room, pushing back fine wisps of sticky brown hair, expecting him to throw me out of his office. Probably the building. Maybe even Atlanta.

Instead, a sly smile curved his colorless lips and he puffed two smoke rings into the air. We both watched them rise toward the ceiling to be chopped up by the fan. I nodded when he said, rather than asked, "You done?"

"Good. Now let me set you straight on a couple things *Miss* Stainsby. First, my reporters grew up on Atlanta's streets. They can get in where it counts for the story."

By that he meant locker rooms in men-only athletic clubs.

"And Adeline's a widow with kids. The downtown crowd likes what she says about their needy little girls lookin' for boys with options." He pointed the cigar at me. "Except for society pages and recipes, girls don't belong in a newsroom. But I'll admit you got a fire in your gut. And an eye for an angle that could make you a reporter someday—somewhere else."

"Then you'll give me an assignment?"

"No."

"But you just said…"

"I know what I said, goddammit."

The cigar smoldered between his fingers as he walked to the front of his desk and rested a hip on the corner, glaring down at me with bloodshot eyes. "You been a thorn in my side for six months. Too big for your britches if you ask me. Reckless. Think you can go off on your own and break the rules to get a story. I'd have fired you after the Wash-Mart article, but you got my boss wrapped around your little *Yankee* finger."

Thin, tobacco-stained lips rose slightly into more of a sneer than a smile and I braced for the worst. *He's going to fire me. Will Healy take me back? Or am I doomed to beg for a job at some small weekly paper in Kansas?* I stared back until my eyes burned, but he blinked first.

"So, I'll tell you what," he said as if he'd just gotten a brilliant idea. "I got a call the other day from a lawyer Southeast o' here. Near the coast. He's lookin' for somebody to verify incriminating evidence about a candidate in a grudge-match election. Since you think so highly of yourself, I'll give you a chance—a last chance—to show me you're a professional."

I'd been a professional for four years and had learned from the best that sometimes you need to push the boundaries to get a story. In Boston, I'd posed as an unmarried woman trying to adopt a baby on the black-market. The exposé brought down the ring and put two people in prison.

And I didn't trust his sudden generosity. "What's the story?"

He stuffed the expensive cigar into an overflowing ashtray. "A Congressional election is comin' up in District One. A Southern Democrat by the name of Edward O'Grady held the seat for years, his daddy too, and granddaddy before him. Comin' home from a fund-raiser back in February, Ed and his wife drove ass-over-tea-kettle off a bluff, landin' upside down on their own property." He shook his head. "A terrible tragedy. Thelma O'Grady was a fine lookin' woman."

My heart raced at the possibility of investigating the mysterious death of a Congressman. "Do you suspect foul play?"

"I just told you it was an accident," he snapped. "Try to stay on track." He ambled back to his chair, tugging on the sticky center drawer of his desk.

"Governor Sanders is waiting for the general election in November to replace him. Ed's son, Patrick O'Grady II, stepped up to run for his seat and was unopposed until a few weeks ago."

He slapped an over-sized campaign button into my hand. "This is his opponent."

The open pin bit my palm and I looked down at the face of a man in his early forties, with a toothy grin and a hungry look in his eyes. 'NEW BLOOD' circled the top half with, 'William Berens III,' below.

"You Southerners sure like your Roman numerals," I commented. "It looks like the Republican has one up on the Southern Democrat already."

An eyebrow raised. "Don't sass. You want the assignment or not?"

I fought the urge to shout, *Hell, yes!* and lowered my voice. "Perhaps. Tell me more—please."

He dropped back into his chair, swatting a lazy fly strolling the rim of his stained coffee cup. "The O'Grady boy's a widowed farmer and horse breeder with a young kid. Nothin' more than a Democratic puppet running on his dead daddy's reputation. Billy came from the other side of the tracks. Pulled himself up from nothing to become the biggest Cadillac dealer in the state. There's bad blood between the families, including accusations of murder goin' back generations.

There it was. He was throwing me into the middle of a political mud-slinging fight. Nothing good came from those. But that car accident interested me. "So, it's personal," I said. "And personal politics sell papers."

"Isn't that what you said you do?" he taunted me.

Still, there had to be something in it for him besides selling papers and getting me out of his hair for a few weeks. "Which candidate has the incriminating evidence? And what's that about murder?"

He waved a hand. "Nobody cares about century-old murders. But Berens' attorney says they have something on the O'Gradys that could finish 'em in politics for good. Like any good lawyer, he needs somebody from the outside to verify it. He'll pay you for the work and give us exclusive rights to publish."

The plot just thickened. Winkler was using me to discredit the Democrat, O'Grady, and win the seat for his new buddies, the Goldwater Republicans. I'd heard him on the phone, complaining about Publisher, Ralph McGill's, liberal, Southern Democrat editorials. Perhaps that was an ace I could hold for later.

For now, Winkler's evil dark eyes challenged me. "You got the stones to dig up the dirt *and* dish it out—gir—Laura?"

I considered politicians, Democrat or Republican, Yankee or Cracker, to be much the same. They all start out with good intentions and big talk, until the gray areas take over, boundaries blur, and campaign promises get lost in party politics and cronyism. The sense of entitlement I'd seen in children from prominent political families, including my own, disgusted me. If O'Grady was covering up his family's crimes for a free ride to Washington, I was more than happy to expose them.

"So, what's Billy Three's angle?" gave him my answer.

His smug smile made me a little sick to my stomach—or was it the cigar? Or the stale body odor that seemed to cling to him like the smoke of a bonfire does to a wool jacket?

"You're the hot-shot reporter. Figure it out. If you pass muster, and the story's good, I'll pay you standard column rates. Maybe a byline."

I opened my mouth to protest, but he beat me to it. "One more thing. Nobody comes into my office without an invite, and nobody demands anything from me. If JoEllen wasn't leavin' to have her baby next month you'd have been on the street before this. But I'm a generous man, so startin' now, you're on spec for the Berens story. Take it or leave it."

'On speculation," meant that if he didn't like it, I'd be unemployed. But exposing the ugly underbelly of Southern politics—on both sides of the fence—could land me a Pulitzer. Or it could be a complete bust.

I sacrificed my ace in the hole to keep my job. "It's a big risk. Even if the story's good, McGill might not be keen on siding with your new Goldwater Republican buddies. And if Billy's allegations are false and there's no story...."

Both eyebrows raised at my mention of McGill's reaction to his affiliation with the new, ultra-conservative wing of the Republican Party. And his jaw dropped just enough to let me know I'd blind-sided him.

I smiled. "Well, a girl's gotta make a living."

"I'll give you Adeline's job," acknowledged my thinly veiled threat.

Adeline and I rarely exchanged more than a nod every week when she handed me her pathetic columns to re-write. I had no idea she was a widow with children. And even if she didn't, I felt guilty for the tacky comment about her bra size. It wasn't her fault men were pigs.

"No. I don't want a widow with kids to lose her job."

"No, she isn't."

"What?"

"Divorced, no kids." Nicotine-stained teeth peeked through a grotesque imitation of a smile. "Forget the girly sympathies and listen to your gut. Adeline got the job because of the double-Ds."

He frowned at my mousey ponytail and small chest before reaching under the paper and handing me a coffee-stained napkin with a phone number scrawled across it. "This is the attorney's name and number," he grunted and leaned toward me. "You'll be dealin' with powerful men here. You might want to do somethin' with yourself."

As I warily took the grimy napkin between my thumb and forefinger, I knew I should be dancing with joy at investigating criminal allegations in a South Georgia Congressional election. If the charges by Republican Billy Berens III against the state's most powerful Democratic dynasty were true, it could make my dream of a Pulitzer Prize a reality. So why did it feel like I'd just struck a deal with the Devil?

CHAPTER 2

The lawyer's name was Jeremy Berens. It didn't surprise me. Southern families are tight. Still, he sounded young to be an attorney and seemed nervous when I asked for details about the position. "Billy will be in town on Friday, the third," he rushed. "Can you meet us at four o'clock at the Pickrick Cafeteria on Hemphill?"

Since I didn't trust Winkler as far as I could throw him, I took heart that at least it was a well-known, public restaurant near the Georgia Tech campus, not some dive bar. I'd never been there, but Adeline touted it as the best family restaurant in Atlanta for Southern Whites.

Jeremy rambled, "The owner is a well-known Christian businessman. Even though it's closed at that time, he'll be there with his staff. You won't be disappointed. Lester Maddox serves the best skillet-fried chicken and chicken-fried steak in the South. Just knock. I'll let you in."

Fried anything made my insides cramp, but Atlanta was home to everything skillet-fried, deep-fried, and chicken-fried. I assured him I was looking forward to meeting the candidate as well as the early supper. Or was it dinner? Other than the label, neither of those occasions mattered much to me, hence my lack of womanly curves.

Winkler's suggestion to do something with myself, rankled. I'd never cared much about appearances, and after my painfully public divorce, I focused on my career instead of fashion. After the call, I turned to the mirror on the back of my apartment door and released the rubber band from my ponytail. Hair the color of wet sand fell limp past my shoulders. How did that happen? I was blonde as a kid. Maybe it was time for a change after all.

While President Johnson was signing a law that would change the course of history, I was getting a cut, color, manicure, and facial. By the time all the souvenir pens were handed out, and photos of men in gray flannel suits were taken, I was a blonde again. The clean lines of the chin-length cut emphasized my father's strong New England jaw and my mother's high cheekbones. The added body made it bounce like Grace Kelly's and a hint of plum eyeshadow complemented what I'd always considered dull gray eyes too large for my face.

I hoped it was worth the cost as I fought heavy holiday traffic, arriving at the sprawling restaurant fifteen minutes late. Noting that it was still within southern margins for punctuality, I knocked on the glass door and peered at a card table flanked by both the Confederate Stars and Bars flag and the National Stars and Stripes. A ceramic wishing well sat in the middle, surrounded by leaflets.

A black boy in a white coat mopped the floor near the door. He looked up at me and shook his head, stepping back when a young white man in a gray suit appeared from the shadows inside.

"Miss Stainsby?" he asked through the glass.

"Yes," I answered. "Are you Jeremy Berens?" He nodded, fumbled with the latch, and pushed the door open for me to step inside the shotgun-style diner. It was warm inside, but two window air conditioners and several ceiling fans dispersing the aromas of chicken and gravy kept it from being oppressive.

"Thank you for coming," he said. "Please call me Jeremy."

As I'd thought, he was young. Fresh out of law school. Maybe twenty-two, if he finished early. I reached out my hand. "My pleasure…Jeremy."

He looked surprised at my forwardness, giving my hand a feeble shake and glancing over my shoulder at the door.

"Expecting someone else?"

"No!" sounded sharp. "I mean, well, Billy's in the back. I'll get him."

Jeremy stepped through the double swinging doors to the kitchen and I glimpsed two black cooks in stained aprons chopping vegetables under the watchful gaze of a white chef in a clean uniform. When the doors closed, my gaze drifted toward the sign by the little wishing well. "Make a wish, and a gift for Segregation," encouraged patrons to support the cause.

"Give it up," I muttered to the few wet quarters in the bowl, then patted the back of my new French twist and straightened the silk skirt of my sheath with a hemline ending just above my knees. I'd have preferred a comfortable A-line dress from Rich's Department Store, but instinct told me a combination of Doris Day charm and Kathryn Hepburn class would be more effective. Dipping into my emergency-only fund, I went to Ensminger's, where all the customers were white, and the only Negro employee was the alteration lady.

"Be careful," came from behind me, and I turned to face the mop-boy's wide, frightened eyes. At the sound of approaching footsteps, he ducked his head to roll his bucket past me. "Wet floor."

The floor looked dry to me as I turned to meet William Berens III, aka, "The Cadillac King of Georgia". He looked younger than on his campaign posters. Late thirties, I guessed.

Eyes the color of warm honey assessed me from my neckline to my ankles, and back again, before meeting mine. I should have been angry at how he'd undressed me with his eyes, but I'd done the same with him, noting his broad shoulders, trim waistline, and jaw like Rock Hudson. His tailor had to love him.

"Ah, Laura," he said with a smile that, like Jack Kennedy's, made me feel I was the most important person in the world. "You don't disappoint."

Neither did he. I regained *some* of my New England composure to respond politely, "Why, thank you, Mr. Berens."

"Please, call me Big Billy. Or Billy, if you prefer. I don't stand on formality."

I assumed he liked to keep his status as South Georgia's biggest Caddy dealer up front, but Judging by his trim physique, "Big" sent my mind in directions it shouldn't go. "Of course…Billy."

He patted Jeremy on the back. "And you've met my lawyer and campaign manager. He's young, but I believe in keeping family close." The politician's smile faded. "Interviewing you was his idea."

Interviewing me? I was under the impression my assignment was a done deal.

Jeremy stepped into the awkward silence. "Miss Stainsby, I was very impressed by your work at the *Boston Globe*, particularly the adoption ring scandal."

I was about to ask how this small-town law student knew about my work at the *Boston Globe,* when Billy cleared his throat. "Yes, very impressive." He checked his watch and cupped my elbow in his palm, applying just the right pressure to make me move. "You're late. Shall we get started?"

"The Pickrick opens at five," Jeremy explained, checking his watch. "In thirty minutes."

Thinking it wasn't much time to be briefed on what my editor said could be the story of a lifetime, I let Billy lead me to the end of the long dining room, stopping at a red, Formica-top table set with a metal napkin dispenser, a glass ashtray, and the standard condiments. I sat in the chrome chair he pulled out and he took the bench seat under the window, facing the entrance. While he lit a Marlboro cigarette, Jeremy sat opposite him, squinting into the afternoon sun streaming through the parking lot windows.

Fortunately, Billy introduced me as a person, not a trout. "Lester, this is Laura."

Then to me, "Lester Maddox is the owner of this fine establishment and former candidate for lieutenant governor. Mark my words, one day he'll be governor of the Great State of Georgia."

Wondering how Billy, a Goldwater Republican, could be so tight with a Southern Democrat. I pretended to be impressed when the older man reached for my hand, exposing a holster attached to his belt. But then, the ink was barely dry on the Civil Rights Act. Given the segregationist flyers on the table, did he expect trouble?

Adjusting his coat, he glanced out the front window at two young men approaching the door. His smile seemed forced when he told Billy, "My boys prepared your favorite, son. Skillet fried chicken, chickpeas, homemade cornbread, and mashed potatoes. I'll send it out."

He quick-stepped to open the door and the men followed him back to the kitchen. I took off my Doris Day gloves and carefully smoothed a tiny paper napkin over the straight skirt that had crept to a scandalous level above my knees. Moments later, a server appeared with three heaping plates, each covered with thick, lumpy gravy.

"Be careful," he repeated the mop-boy's warning when he set my plate down.

"Plates is hot," he added when Billy and Jeremy looked up.

Billy watched him leave, then touched his plate. "The boy's right. For good, hot food, you need good hot plates."

He and Jeremy wolfed down their food while I washed my batter-covered chicken breast down with iceless water. Between bites, Billy fired a barrage of questions about my family, my education, and experience. Assuming he already knew the answers, I confessed to coming from a family of Yankee Democrats and previously working for the solidly Democratic, *Boston Globe.* He didn't seem concerned.

"I hear you're divorced," startled me and I silently cursed David Winkler's big mouth.

Smoke from a second Marlboro drifted toward me while Billy waited for the sordid details, but I'd be damned if I'd tell a stranger in a diner—or anywhere else—about my daughter's death, my disastrous marriage, and my ugly divorce. Tired of playing the vapid ingénue, I met his gaze. "I have some questions about the assignment."

"What sort of questions?" He dropped his third napkin onto his empty plate, lit another cigarette and leaned toward me.

"Well, I'd like to review your evidence against Mr. O'Grady before I commit."

After a bone-chilling glare at Jeremy, he answered, "Pardon me, I thought you understood that this investigation will make your career."

My stomach tightened at having to grovel for what could turn out to be a campaign ploy instead of the exposé on Southern politics I'd hoped for.

"I apologize," I back-pedaled. "Attention to detail is often my best—and worst, trait."

His smile was patient. "David said you were feisty. And ambitious. Good traits in an investigator—but I don't like to be pushed."

David? Did he know Winkler personally? His amber stare unnerved me too much to ask.

"Suffice it to say," he continued. "I have damaging information about the O'Grady family that goes back to their forebears, the Langesfords. I think of it as insurance, so to speak, in case the public needs a little persuading before the election."

He cast a mean glance at Jeremy. "While I hope I don't need to use it, I'm told I need to verify it before going public. And *if* I decide you're right for the job, you'll have all the details you'll need."

He touched my hand. It was warm, but dry. Strong. And his eyes seemed to glow with passion when he said, "It's time for new blood to represent Georgia in Washington, Laura. A time for honesty—finally—in Georgia's leadership. The truth is long overdue."

I wanted to believe him, but as the daughter of a long line of Boston politicians, I'd heard the word 'truth' abused too often. It seemed to be the magic word in every election everywhere. Every candidate stood for the truth —according to their own definition of the word.

"I'm afraid I'll need more than your word on that."

His jaw set and Jeremy took a sharp breath while I prepared to be rejected, Doris Day outfit and Katharine Hepburn sophistication notwithstanding.

"But you will have to take my word," Billy answered. "This story will make your career. I only want justice." He looked at Jeremy. "Give it to her."

The young lawyer looked surprised. "Yes, Billy. I mean, Sir. Then to me, "Well, we recently confirmed that the O'Gradys and their ancestors, the Langesfords, are not who they've led the public to believe. They have secrets…and have well…done things…over the years that..."

"Crimes," Billy interrupted. "Over two centuries."

Crap! All old families had skeletons in their closets. And while the public loved to see dirt on famous people, it most certainly did *not* make careers. "What crimes?"

"You name it!" Billy's voice bounced off the tile floor in the cavernous room and he leaned toward me to growl, they're goddamned crooks, liars, thieves—and murderers!"

"Murder?" Heat spread from my cheeks to the toes pinched in my spike heels.

Billy wasn't nearly as handsome without the smile, but he recovered quickly and touched my hand. "Pardon my vehemence, Miss Laura, and my rare obscenity, but since founding the colony of Georgia, the Langesfords and their progeny, the *O'Grady's,* have run this state like their kingdom, getting away with doing whatever they want—at any cost."

"But murder? Who? When?"

Leaving the cigarette to burn down in the ashtray, his big hand covered both of mine. "These are troubled times. This country needs strong, *honest* leadership. The O'Grady family has lived a lie for more than a century. It's time to expose them for what they really are."

Perspiration beaded beneath the three coats of lacquer hairspray along my forehead. I wanted to shout, what lie? What crimes? *What murder*? Instead, I said, "I understand your opponent's parents recently died in a car accident, and his wife died three years ago, leaving him with a young daughter. What can you tell me about either of those events?"

Billy's lips pressed into a thin line and gooseflesh rose on my arms when he leaned toward me, gold eyes glittering with...hatred?

"Not much to tell. Congressman O'Grady was drunk and drove off a bluff, landing upside down on his own property, killing both him and his wife Thelma. But Barbara O'Grady's death remains a mystery only her husband can explain."

He relaxed against the Naugahyde back of the bench seat. "I see both incidents as signs that the veil of lies they've been hiding behind for two centuries is lifting. It's time for them to be exposed for the traitors they are. It's time for *me* to make a difference in this state. And as Georgia goes, so goes the South."

I tried to hide my disappointment at hearing yet again how Georgia, like the mythical Phoenix, was risen from the ashes, destined for greatness. It was the mantra for segregationists as well as the battle cry for those demanding a new era of true equality. I wondered if anyone noticed the dichotomy.

Voices raised in the kitchen and Billy stood. "I trust Winkler's judgement —and I'm late for an important meeting."

"But…"

"Laura, darlin'," he drawled. "I'd rather discuss your questions alone, maybe over a nice glass of wine. But not to worry, I knew you were right for the job the moment I saw you."

What sounded like a frying pan hitting a wall came from the kitchen and he rushed, "You're hired. Meet us at my dealership in Jeffers Monday morning. Eight o'clock."

At my nod, he leaned toward me, his lips close to my ear. "It's time for the idols to fall, Laura." Then to Jeremy, "Give her the envelope and TripTik."

I couldn't argue with falling idols, but still had questions—hundreds of them.

Jeremy pushed a manila envelope toward me. "O'Grady's secretary/nanny recently married and he's looking for a new one. Since your name is well-known, I got you a new driver's license and a letter of reference. I'm sure you can take it from there."

A false identity? This was taking on a James Bond feel, but it made sense. The Stainsby name was indeed well known, especially in Democratic circles. And what better way to investigate the O'Grady crimes than as the candidate's secretary? But nanny? Two years after Rose's death, I still couldn't think of caring for a child.

A teenage boy in jeans burst through the now-unlocked front door and bolted back to the kitchen. I left my gloves, purse, and the unopened envelope on the table to follow him, but Jeremy caught my arm. My heel slipped and I fell, my skirt hiking up to expose the garters on my hose.

"I...I'm...so sorry," he stammered, trying to pull me up.

"What is wrong with you?" I grunted, shaking him off to get up on my own, ripping the dress halfway up my thigh in the process. But he was staring over my shoulder at the window and I turned to kneel on the bench seat for a closer look.

Three black men wearing clerical collars had stepped out of an old Pontiac sedan and approached the front entrance. The kitchen doors banged against the walls and Lester Maddox rushed out to face them, shouting, "You no good dirty devils! Dirty Communists. You'll never eat here. Get away from my door!"

I tried to push my way through the kitchen help blocking the door behind Maddox until I heard, "Leave it, Missy. Please. It's not your fight."

It was the cook who'd brought our food. The plea in his dark eyes and tired slump of his shoulders told me that an interfering Yankee would only make it worse. I returned to the window as Maddox lurched toward the ministers, gun drawn, threatening to close his restaurant and fire all his 'colored' help if they took another step. The sea of dark faces at the door parted when a half-dozen white men followed him from the kitchen, waving ax handles they used to smash the car's hood and windows.

I pounded the window from the bench, ineffectively screaming for them to stop while reporters beat the police to the scene. Microphones on, camera's flashing, they followed Maddox back to the door just as Billy scooped me off the bench, dragging me into the shadows.

I pushed him away. "Where were you? Why didn't you stop them?"

"It's over. No one was hurt," he repeated two more times, until he was sure I understood. "Those men came by while the restaurant was closed and threatened to come back. Lester had a few men here in case they caused trouble."

"A few men with ax handles! Why didn't you stop it?"

"There was nothing I could do."

Hair mussed, tie loosened, sweat beading along his forehead, he looked genuinely distressed.

"I was trying to talk them down when Lester's son ran in saying they were outside. I called the police after the kitchen emptied out,"

I couldn't respond. I'd joined the march on Washington to hear Dr. Martin Luther King Jr. speak, singing, *We Shall Overcome,* and crying when Odetta Holmes sang, *I'm on My Way.* Still grieving for my dead child, Dr. King's words filled my heart with hope. But in Atlanta, I'd stood behind the barricades at the Toddle House Restaurant sit-in as police carried out protesters beaten until they were limp as rags. And now I'd watched a Christian businessman point a gun at unresisting black ministers while his friends bullied them with ax handles—and bystanders cheered them on.

Then I told myself that Billy was different. He hadn't joined the madness. He'd called the police. Now, he scooped the envelope, my gloves, and purse from the table, handing them to me. "Give Jeremy your car key. Where do you live?"

My hands shook as I found my keys and tossed them to Jeremy. "It's the powder blue Beetle out front. I live on Edgewood Avenue, in Midtown. Above Dengler's Drug Store."

I followed Billy out the back door to a red Cadillac De Ville convertible. "She can go from zero-to-sixty in nine seconds," he boasted before revving the Caddy's powerful engine and hitting the gas. The spray of gravel hit the Pickrick's back door like bullets.

CHAPTER 3

It took nearly an hour to negotiate traffic across town to the drug store's busy parking lot. Billy raised an eyebrow at the rundown neighborhood. "I live upstairs," I told him, then rambled, "I normally go up through the store, but don't want anyone to see me…like this. My car was blocked by the police. It'll take Jeremy a while to get here. I'll use the back stairs behind the alley… and change…before he comes."

Billy cocked his head toward the narrow, brick-walled passage between the drugstore and the Old-Town Liquor Store. "That alley?"

I felt conspicuous in the expensive car in a parking lot filled with old Ford pickups and even older Chevy sedans. Lester Maddox's hateful words were still fresh in my mind and I wanted to put the whole thing behind me. I pulled my ripped skirt together. "Well yes, but it's not far. I'll see you Monday?"

Or did he have second thoughts about putting the investigation crucial to his election in the hands of a screaming shrew?

Without answering the question, the car-salesman smile returned. "What kind of gentleman would I be if I let such a beautiful and brave young lady walk alone through a liquor store alley, especially after what you've been through?"

He was lucky. The big car glided through the alley without a scratch, stopping behind the buildings, under an old oak dripping with Spanish

Moss. After the trauma at the Pickrick and waiting for the expensive car to be scraped from end to end, I shivered in the humid air. His right arm brushed my shoulder to rest on the back of my seat. "Come closer."

I shook my head, raining bobby pins from the collapsed French twist. "I'm a mess."

"Well I think you're beautiful. You just need to relax."

Relax? I was traumatized, but I wasn't stupid. I knew what 'relax' meant to men. But for now, I wasn't sure I'd make it up the fire escape. I stayed on my side and rested my head against the back of the seat. "Well maybe just a minute."

"I'm in no hurry."

A gentle hand touched a tangle of hair along my cheek. I wanted to lean into it, but still had a shred of dignity. The man was at least ten years my senior and the lack of a wedding ring didn't mean he was single. And technically, he was my boss. He took the hint when I tipped my head away and we sat quietly under the canopy of whispering leaves.

While I'd never felt unsafe in the old neighborhood of lower middle-class whites with a sprinkling of Negroes, after the Pickrick, I also knew the hatred and violence wouldn't stop there. Civil Rights Act or not, the South wouldn't give up the Jim Crow laws without a fight.

It was the argument my father, Senator Arthur Stainsby Jr., had used in Boston to dissuade me from coming to Atlanta. On New Year's Eve, after his guests had stumbled into their chauffeured Limousines and we'd both had too much eggnog spiked with Haiti's finest Barbancourt rum, he lectured me on my family's political legacy, my ivy league education, even my sex, to illustrate how the South would chew me up and spit me out.

When he said, "They don't need naïve little Yankee do-gooders meddling in their affairs. Let things take their course," I went cold inside. Then he added, "The powers that be will handle it,"

It was the last straw. "You mean the *Powers That Be* who sit in leather chairs, drinking aged scotch and smoking illegal Cuban cigars while American citizens live in poverty because their skin is brown instead of white?"

Ice-blue eyes that had cowed more than one political opponent, fixed on mine. "Don't test me, girl," he said. "I have the power to revoke your trust fund. And believe me without it, you won't last six months in the South."

It was an old tune that Father had played too many times. First, when I was nearly expelled for smoking pot at St. Elizabeth's Preparatory School. Then again at Smith, when I wrote a scathing political commentary under a fake name for *The Sophian.* The closest he came to doing it was after my gay best friend, Ricky Hamilton—only son of THE Hamiltons—got me pregnant while trying to prove his masculinity. Father backed off when I agreed to marry his buddy's son. The painful charade lasted until I divorced him on the second anniversary of our daughter's death.

Ricky moved to Hollywood where they accepted him for who he was, and I stayed in Boston and tried to keep a stiff upper lip, using my job at the *Globe* to keep my sanity. But everything reminded me of Rose—her short little life, and her stupid, tragic death.

This time, I told Father to shove his beloved 'Stainsby Legacy" where the sun didn't shine. On the first day of 1964, I packed my know-it-all attitude, hopped into my Beetle and left the mansion where cellars had once held slaves destined for auction, and headed South to save the day.

Today, after waiting six months for a story, the simmering pot of Civil Rights had spilled into my lap. And what did I do? I screamed like a little girl, clinging to the first man who reached out to me. I could say there was nothing I could do, but my conscience didn't agree. Something can always be done. And pounding on a window isn't it.

I was so ashamed I wanted to disappear. Since I couldn't, I vowed it would never happen again. I looked at Billy's strong profile, wondering exactly where he stood on Civil Rights. It was hard to tell. While he'd seemed genuinely shocked by the day's violence, he now looked relaxed in the massive automobile only a few people—white people—could afford.

He reached across me for the glovebox, offering me a Marlboro. My mother died of lung cancer after smoking two packs of Marlboros a day for most of her adult life. I shook my head and he lit an engraved silver lighter.

"You want some company tonight?" he asked after exhaling into the soft evening breeze.

It shouldn't have surprised me. Men seemed to think cigarettes, alcohol, and sex cured everything. I scooted closer to the door. "What? No! I mean, I'm fine."

I took a deep breath. "It's going to get worse, isn't it?"

He nodded and took another drag.

"Why did Maddox do it?" I asked, watching the cigarette burn down between his fingers. "They were ministers. Old men and a teenaged boy.

They just wanted to eat for God's sake. *And* they had a legal right to be there. The ax handles weren't necessary. Or the gun. Maddox could have closed the restaurant for the weekend and waited until things cooled off."

Billy crushed the spent cigarette out in the ashtray and turned to me. "It isn't that simple, Laura. The Yank—I mean the Federal Government—doesn't understand that when we, the South, surrendered our arms at Appomattox, it meant the end of a war, not the end of a culture. You don't end a way of life more than two centuries old with a signature on a piece of paper, no matter how many pens you use."

I argued, "What about the Declaration of Independence? The Emancipation Proclamation? More than even the French Revolution, they changed the world's view of freedom and equality."

"Words, just words," followed his sigh. "Your family goes back to the Revolution. You know the Declaration of Independence was primarily a way for wealthy landowners—slaveholders—to avoid taxes. And even your sainted Abraham Lincoln was politically motivated to draft the Emancipation Proclamation. Changing a way of life takes time."

"Longer than a century?"

"A millennium won't be enough. Presidents can sign all the laws they want, but people will always judge other people. By their color, their ancestry, and their profession, just to name a few."

"And sex," I added. My mother was a gifted political strategist and virtually ran my father's career as a US Senator. If she'd been a man, she'd have stood behind the podium instead of at the back of the stage listening to her husband read the words she'd written. His speeches never carried the same punch after she died.

"Yes, I suppose that will be next," he conceded. "But probably not in our lifetime. One cultural upheaval per generation is about all this poor country can handle. We need to keep our family structure stable. We need our women in our homes and schools."

I stiffened at the condescension in his voice but was too drained from my first personal encounter with racial hatred to argue that women had brains as well as breasts. "I should go."

But before I went upstairs, I had to know exactly where my new boss stood on Civil Rights. I couldn't work for a racist. "Is Maddox your friend? Do you agree with him?"

"Maddox is a hothead and the law was just signed. It's too soon to test it. What happened today was a fiasco but there's always a silver lining."

His gold eyes flashed in the light of the lowering sun. "I have strong beliefs about what's right and wrong, or I wouldn't have hired you to expose the O'Gradys. I didn't want this, but it happened. I…we…need to make the best of it."

Not the answer I wanted, but it could have been worse. "The best of it," I repeated. "So where do I fit in?"

His hand covered mine. "You're the key to my success, Laura. You're a scrapper and believe in the truth. And as a Yankee, you don't have a dog in the fight. Once you expose O'Grady's lies, I'll be able to do the things that really matter for District One."

"But why me? Why not a hotshot Atlanta reporter or a private detective?"

"I don't need a hotshot reporter with a household name, or some clumsy private eye. I need someone who can keep their head low and get the truth. According to Jeremy, you fooled those fake adoption people into getting sloppy, and then you buried them. You're clever, non-threatening, and you'll do anything for the truth—even lie."

He winked. "Tell me I'm wrong."

I couldn't. I *had* lied to get information on both the adoption ring and Lou's money laundering. And as a political brat, I'd learned from the best how to manipulate people with a half-truth. I wasn't proud of it, but I told myself I was using my power for good, and that sometimes, the end did justify the means. Now, holding an envelope with a false identity inside, I hoped I'd picked the right team. "What do you mean?"

"That we're not so different, you and I, *Miss Tucker.* We both have big dreams and are limited by stereotypes. Me as the Cracker car dealer, and you as the WASP princess. It's time we proved everyone wrong."

We both jumped at my Beetle's horn coming from the other end of the alley. I stepped out of the Cadillac holding the side of my dress together with one hand and waving my purse and the envelope with the other.

Jeremy stalked toward us, shaking a fist at my beautiful car. "The darn contraption kept stalling out. German cars," he said as if it was Volkswagen's fault that he couldn't handle a clutch.

His disrespect irked me. My great-aunt, Lily Winfield, gave me that car when my divorce was final. I hoped he hadn't stripped the gears, leaving me with a repair bill to further deplete my emergency-only fund. "It's okay, just give me the keys," I said, then repeated to Billy, "I'll see you Monday?"

At his nod, I slid inside the Beetle, slipped it effortlessly into gear, and rolled past the Caddy to park by the fire escape. I was halfway up the stairs when I heard Jeremy say, "I can't believe you're going through with this."

Billy's answer was lost in the sound of gravel spinning from the big car's tires.

CHAPTER 4

Hot water from the shower washed the lacquer from my hair and flushed the heavy makeup from my pores. I let the stream of warm, watery fingers massage the tension from my neck and shoulders until it ran cold, then wrapped myself in a beach towel

"Welcome back," I whispered to my reflection in the chipped, mirror/medicine cabinet. It was good to see my own face again, despite the unfamiliar hair color and cut. Me, not the princess I was raised to be—or the screaming shrew I'd become at the Pickrick.

While my mind still ran full tilt, my body felt like it had done a cycle in one of the Wash-Mart's large-load dryers. It was still early, not quite full dark, but I'd barely slept the night before. I slipped into a tropical print Muumuu, my tired muscles begging me to pull down the Murphy bed and let sleep dull the emotions of the day. Instead, I put a pot of coffee on and called my best friend.

Gloria LaBelle (Glory to me and her brother) was my rock. A Negro Scholarship winner from Atlanta, we were roommates for four years at Smith College. When she left for her JD degree at Columbia, I stayed in Boston to finish my MA at Emmerson. She'd just moved to New Orleans for a job at the District Attorney's office.

I gave up after five rings and moved to the folding card table/desk where a stack of white, erasable bond paper sat next to my grandfather's old Royal typewriter. I pulled off the worn leather cover and said, "Hello baby. Have I got a story for you."

"YOU'LL NEVER EAT HERE!" The worn metal keys branded the page as fast as I could type. With no thought about word count, I relived the scene; from the flyers by the wishing well, to car windows shattering under ax handles and the terror on Maddox's employees' faces. I ended it with the arrival of the police, who did little to stop the violence beyond forcing Maddox to put his gun away. While the incident would be on the TV news before the *Constitution* went to print, it would be news for days. And my story was from inside the Pickrick.

After finishing it, I buried my face in my hands, too drained to cry at the realization that I'd witnessed segregated Atlanta's declaration of war against the Civil Rights Act. Maddox hadn't fired his gun, but I wondered how long it would take before the violence in Selma, Montgomery, and Birmingham reached the Gate City of the New South—in full force.

I gave the pages a final read. It was the most powerful thing I'd ever written. I knew Winkler wouldn't approve it because it would jeopardize his alliance with the segregationist Republicans, but Ralph McGill, the *Constitution's* publisher, supported the Act. He came to the office on weekends and holidays and might be more receptive. I'd drop it off to him in the morning, on my way to Jeffers.

It was almost midnight before I'd edited and retyped the article, making a carbon copy for my file and one to mail to Glory. Eventually, even strong, black coffee couldn't keep my eyelids from drooping. The phone rang just as I pulled down the Murphy bed.

I knew it was Glory. We were as close as sisters, despite our backgrounds —and races. I was a rich, pure-bred White Anglo-Saxon Princess with a pedigree going back to King Henry I. She was working-class-poor and one-eighth Negro, going back to a house slave in Haiti. Like most Southern states, Georgia still held that any Negro blood defined you as one and clung to the antiquated anti-miscegenation laws to invalidate inter-racial marriages, denying children of mixed marriages their legal rights of inheritance.

Glory would have been called an octoroon a century ago, but she honored her mixed heritage, proudly referring to herself as a, "Free Woman of Color".

"Hey, girl," my friend breathed when I answered. "Did you call? I been thinkin' 'bout you all night."

Her laugh made me smile. It's a rare thing, a real laugh. I missed it.

"Glory," I scolded. "You moved three weeks ago. I had to call information for your number."

We both knew I'd have been settled and sent my new address and phone number to everyone who cared within a week, but for Glory, work and entertainment came before personal organization. Still, my brilliant friend could find a specific document in a stack of papers a foot deep, and rarely forgot anything she read. I had no doubt she'd be named a District Attorney within a few years—Lester Maddox and his ilk notwithstanding.

"Girl, this is Naw-lins." The southern drawl, so carefully hidden during her time in New England, returned with a vengeance now she was in the Big Easy. It also slipped back when she drank. I pictured her long red fingernails stabbing the air like Stella in *Streetcar Named Desire* and blamed the night on the town when she said, "Tahm is diff'rent heah."

Normally I'd laugh too, sliding into my own Boston twang saying, "Glahwee, I'm tahd an' wonna sleep." Instead, I demanded, "How much have you had to drink?"

"Jus' 'nuff, Chère, but not too much to shame the family name. Tell me you tol' that Cracker boss o' yours to fuck off an' are comin' down here where Cajuns, Creoles, Coloreds, and Caucasians mix in sinful but productive ways."

"You're too much," I laughed. "Stop talking so I can tell you what happened today at the Pickrick Cafeteria."

"The Pickrick?" she shrieked. "No! Don't tell me you were there."

The alarm in her voice chilled me in the stuffy room. "What's the matter?"

"First, tell me your version."

"Version? Gloria Eileen LaBelle, what are you talking about?"

"Laura baby, didn't you watch the news tonight? I caught the end of Walter Cronkite's report. It had to be on all your local stations. OH, MY GOD!" she gasped. "Were you the white girl pounding on the window, screaming at the ministers? How could you? After all we've been to each other? Tell me it wasn't you!"

"What? Yes, it was me. But it wasn't like that. I was meeting…a lead…at the Pickrick. For work. I was screaming for the bullies to leave the men alone. How could you think I'd support that madman? I spent all evening writing about how horrible it was."

It dawned on me then that anyone watching could have thought I supported Lester's madness, while everyone *inside* the restaurant knew the opposite. Neither perspective worked well for me. I lowered my voice. "Did they say my name?"

Silence.

"Glory?"

"I'm here," she said, all business now. "And I'm sorry for doubting you. Nice French twist by the way. I always knew you'd make a great blonde. Anyway, they're calling her, 'The Woman in The Window'. Lester's touting her as the voice of Southern white women."

My stomach lurched. "It makes sense he'd take advantage of my reaction to plug his cause. But it doesn't matter. I'm dropping my story off to the publisher in the morning. Everything will be out in the open."

"What if he doesn't publish it? Can you live with being the face of segregation, even though the clips were blurry, and no one knows your name —for now?"

She was right. I couldn't allow them to use me as a front for racism. "What if I call the police and tell them I was trying to stop it?"

"The police are probably swamped by women taking credit from both sides of the Civil Rights fence."

"Well then, problem solved. Let someone else pose for the billboards. I'm heading for Jeffers tomorrow for my new assignment. I doubt the story will come out before then."

Glory's voice lowered. "The timing of your article is the least of your problems my dear, naive friend. Your problem is that most of the men in that cafeteria, maybe even Maddox, are likely members of the KKK. They don't much like uppity Yankee women calling them out. They can't be very happy with you—or what you might say to reporters. And if they find out you *are* a reporter it could get really ugly."

A noise from the alley startled me and I stretched the curly phone cord to look out my window at a car cruising slowly along the back of my building, toward the liquor store on the other side of the alley. Then it turned around and came back, stopping below my window. I thought about the beatings in Birmingham, and the students who went missing in Mississippi last month. "You mean…?"

"Yes. If Maddox's hooded buddies think you were spying on them for the newspaper, you won't be safe anywhere in Georgia. Is the article worth it? It's going to be an interesting holiday. Why not visit me for a few days and wait it out?"

She was offering me an excuse to back away, but I couldn't.

"Yes, It's worth it. Those men were waiting for the ministers to come back and planned their attack in advance. In fact, two of Lester's Negro employees told me to be careful, but I didn't know what they meant."

Glory's chuckle carried a sour note. "And of course, you didn't listen to them. So, think about who knew that you were going to the restaurant, who you saw there, and who knows your name. And most important, who knows where you live."

I hugged a pillow against my churning stomach. "Okay, I told Mr. Winkler about the appointment. Big Billy was there with his attorney, but they'll want to keep it quiet."

"*Big* Billy? Big Billy, the Caddy King of South Georgia?"

"How did you know that?"

"Honey, everybody from Georgia knows Big Billy. Be careful, he's got a reputation with the ladies. Now keep going. Who else?"

"Nobody. Winkler told my co-workers I moved back North and when Billy introduced me to Maddox, he just used my first name."

"Very good. Go on."

"Oh, my God!" I moaned, my hopes crashing with one thought. "What if this hits the Boston papers and WHDH-TV? Father watches it every night. What if *he* recognized me?"

It was a reflex reaction. When I left Boston, he as much as told me I was dead to him, but everything I did reflected on the Stainsby reputation. And he did *not* like bad press.

"Take deep breaths, girl," Glory soothed. "*I* know you better than anyone and I didn't recognize you. You're a blonde now and moved around a lot. It's also the last place he'd expect to see you. Who else was there?"

If God was a woman, which I consider a possibility, given the mysterious and whimsical nature of the universe, she'd sound just like Glory. I reluctantly put myself back at the Pickrick. "Billy's cousin Jeremy called me Miss Stainsby when he let me in, but only a mop-boy heard him."

"I think we can rule him out."

"Well, you wanted everybody."

"Right, go on. You're doing great."

"There was the white chef. He pushed me aside when he ran out the door and looked right at me when I was in the window. I don't think I'll ever forget the hatred on his face." I rubbed my throbbing temple. "Really Glory, besides Maddox and a teenager who rushed in when the ministers arrived, I'd only recognize a couple if I saw them again. Nobody could have followed me home because Billy gave me a ride."

I sighed with relief. "They won't find me."

"Not so fast, Chère. Your car was in the film footage, parked up close to the door. It won't take much to blow up the picture and see the Massachusetts license plate that you haven't changed in six months."

"It doesn't expire until December," I defended myself. "And it's expensive."

"Well it could be an expensive mistake. The Klan is everywhere. If they want to find you, they will."

"Shit," I whispered. "Jeremy drove my car here. It wouldn't have been hard to follow. Glory, what am I going to do?"

"Well, you could hide. The Old Fourth Ward is far enough from Midtown. Maybe Edwin will hire you at the dry cleaners, but since you have no labor skills, you'd have to start on the ironer. Oh, and you'd have to stay in the back, because you're white."

"What?" Glory's half-brother ran a dry-cleaning business near Dr. Martin Luther King Jr.'s family home. Her gallows humor brought me out of my pity-party. "Very funny."

"It wasn't meant to be. It would only put Edwin in danger too."

After a moment's thought, she said, "I have two words for you. Leave and town. You're planning on it anyway. If you won't come here, find a motel somewhere and lay low until your trip. But first, turn off your lights and look out the window."

I obeyed without question. The drugstore's neon sign had gone dark hours earlier, leaving the back lot barely illuminated by a half-moon in the clear sky and the blinking streetlight on the corner. The car I'd seen before was parked by the oak tree, facing my apartment. Two heads in the front seat were backlit by the moon. As if they'd seen me with the phone, the engine roared to life. Headlights flashed twice as they drove away. *A warning?*

"This has to be a bad dream."

"Maybe not for too long," Glory said. "President Johnson signed the Act on a holiday weekend for a purpose. People will be preoccupied by bands, beer, and fireworks, at least for a while, but what happened at the Pickrick shows just how badly Southern feathers are ruffled."

For the first time, the usual night sounds of rustling oak leaves, cicadas, and tires thumping on the ragged pavement felt sinister. "And how does that help me?"

"Well, it does, and it doesn't. What might have been dismissed a year ago as a hot-headed restaurant owner chasing off a couple pushy black ministers, is now a battle cry for both sides of the argument. And you, my dear friend, are a puppy in a pool of alligators."

"What do you mean?"

"Well, I've been drinking, but I don't think I'm far off in predicting a feeding frenzy between the TV news and the press. You were the only person besides Maddox, his men, and his help seen inside the restaurant. You're a reporter, what would you do?"

I sighed. "I'd go to Maddox for her name. But he only knows my first name. And Billy was back in the kitchen calling the police. We left right after they came."

"OK. Then the good news is they can't check your plates until Monday. Something else may trump the Pickrick in the news, but if McGill publishes your story, I wouldn't bet on it."

"Okay. I'll be out of here in an hour."

"Hold on!" Glory shouted. "Where are you going?"

"To the only person who has more at stake than me in keeping his presence at the cafeteria a secret. The Caddy King of South Georgia. He gave me a fake ID and a hotel reservation at Ho-Jo's for Sunday night—under the name Sarah Tucker. I'll just show up early."

"In the middle of the night? It's a four-hour drive across the state. How much sleep did you get last night and how much coffee have you had tonight? You should try to sleep at least a few hours before you leave, or you'll end up wrapped around a telephone pole."

She was right. I was almost dead on my feet. "OK. I'll pack now, take a nap, and leave by dawn."

Glory sounded like an anxious mother when she said, "Call me when you get there. Bondye avèk ou."

"What?"

"God be with you," my agnostic friend translated. "Let's hope she isn't busy,"

I breathed easier knowing I had a plan and rationalized that my inebriated friend may have exaggerated my danger. The car in the alley was probably teenagers getting drunk, but the headlight wink still gave me chills.

It was nearly one o'clock, but if I took a three-hour nap, I could still beat the holiday traffic and arrive at a decent hour to check in early. I packed enough clothes for a long weekend, including a wrinkle-free rayon dress and matching pumps for my meeting with Billy.

Dropping the article off at McGill's office in the morning was no longer an option. I didn't have any stamps, so I looked up the publisher's address in the phonebook. It was only ten minutes out of my way. After writing his name on the envelope and underlining, "URGENT" three times, I'd drop it through his mail slot on my way to the new Interstate.

At four o'clock, after a restless, but rejuvenating nap, I stuffed the thermos, Billy's envelope, and the article into the macramé purse slung around my neck. With my suitcase in one hand, a pillowcase stuffed with essentials cradled in a sheet tied around my neck, and my little typewriter in the crook of my other arm, I inched down the creaky wood stairs, hoping I wouldn't wake Mr. Newell, my landlord who lived downstairs. At one time his watchful presence had been a comfort. Now it seemed dangerous. Everything seemed dangerous.

I wondered how Billy would take it when I showed up early—especially if he'd seen the news. My favorite scenario was him welcoming me with open arms—literally. The attraction surprised me. Maybe it was his maturity compared to Ricky and the few college boys I'd dated. I assumed he'd had his share of women, but the thought only made him more attractive.

CHAPTER 5

At half-past eight, I drove by the, "Welcome to Jeffers" sign, touting its status as the County Seat along with the various historic, patriotic and civic groups rooted in its red Georgia clay. The postcard-perfect little town with white-steepled churches and red-brick buildings reminded me of the village in my brother Adam's Lionel train set—and a very disturbing episode of *The Twilight Zone.*

The unsettled feeling dissipated in the five minutes it took to reach the edge of town, where the grass wasn't quite as green, porches sagged, and businesses lured customers with neon signs instead of classic awnings. Neighborhoods had given way to fields of sawgrass before I saw a big blue spire atop the familiar orange roof of *Howard Johnson's Motor Lodge.*

Energized by my upcoming investigation, I rolled down my window and breathed deeply of fresh air and summer flowers. Then I sneezed. Repeatedly. It reminded me that for every flower, there are ten weeds. Ragweed is their king, and like hatred, it thrives everywhere. When I recovered, I walked into the A-frame entry toward a young man behind the desk.

I noted the name embroidered on the pocket of his white shirt and smiled. "Good Morning, Hollis."

He smiled back with slightly buck teeth. "It is that. What can Ah do you for?"

I leaned toward him so he could get a whiff of my Shalimar perfume.

"Well, Hollis, I have a room reserved for tomorrow and would like to check in early."

He shook his head. "Sorry, Ma'am, it's a holiday weekend. We been booked for a month."

Ma'am? I thought I'd have another decade until I qualified for that, but I was too tired to argue. "But I have a reservation. Lau…., I mean Sarah. Sarah Tucker. I had to leave early and have been driving all night. And I'm *utterly* exhausted. Surely there's a room somewhere. It doesn't have to be fancy."

I'd have taken a cot in the kitchen.

He ran a finger down the registry. "Yep. Miss Sarah Tucker. For tomorrow." He looked genuinely disappointed when he repeated, "Sorry, we're full up. Folks is stayin' over for the fireworks an' some for the big debate on Sunday. Won't have a room before your reservation."

"Well, perhaps someone won't keep their reservation," I suggested. "I can wait."

I dabbed a tissue at the corners of my ragweed-irritated eyes to stall for time. Jeremy hadn't provided a background story for Sarah other than the fake ID from Boston and a vague reference for the secretarial job at Patrick O'Grady's plantation. As the waterworks from my allergies ramped up again, I took advantage of the weepy moment.

"My maw-maw just died and I'm here to arrange her burial," I said, pulling a five-dollar bill from my purse. "It's early. There must be someone who hasn't checked in yet. I'll gladly pay double if someone's reservation has been…lost…by mistake."

I realized too late I was flying the family colors, using money to get what I wanted, no matter the inconvenience to someone else. But Hollis didn't take the bait.

"I am so sorry for your loss," he said, looking like he meant it. "She's in the Lord's hands now." Then he shrugged. "Check in lasts to nine o'clock tonight."

I dabbed at real tears this time. If I waited until nine and everyone showed up, I'd have to sleep in my car. The next town was twenty miles up the road, with no guarantee I'd have a better reception there. Looking at Hollis' sad-puppy eyes, I turned to the door. "It's just that I don't know where else to go."

"Well, maybe there is a place," He piped up and scribbled something on a Ho-Jo's note pad, ripping off the page and handing it to me. "The Glass

House is the only other hotel in town. It's a bit pricey and has been booked for weeks too, but sometimes there's a room or two open—for *special* visitors. My brother Leroy works there. Tell him I sent you."

"Thank you so much!" I wanted to hug him, but a line was forming behind me.

He blushed. "My pleasure."

I followed his directions back through town, taking a hard right just before the town circle, onto a cobblestone drive leading to a red-brick, antebellum mansion. With double stained-glass doors and the sign, "Bradley/Glass House, circa 1735," I'd mistaken it for a private home.

The doors opened before I reached the brass handles. "Welcome to The Glass House," came from someone who looked exactly like Hollis. I stopped mid-step and noticed that this Hollis' smile seemed sly, his manner more curious than eager.

"I'm sorry," I answered. "I was at the Motor Lodge and you look so much like Hollis."

"Yeah, I know. I'm his older brother, Leroy." He didn't sound happy about it.

"Oh? I'd have sworn you were twins."

"I'm three minutes older," he said blocking the door like a troll.

"Okay. I see the difference now," acknowledged his seniority and he ushered me into the mansion's foyer.

"Hollis called," Leroy told me. "Drivin' a blue Beetle. Said you needed a room."

I rubbed my arms against the sudden chill in the air-conditioned lobby and nodded.

"You're lucky. Hotels in the whole county are full, including us, 'cept one room that's leased. No sense wastin' it." His wink told me he expected a good tip.

I gave him credit for entrepreneurship, if not his brother's squeaky-clean morals. "It's kind of you both to help me out like this. I really appreciate it."

"That's the plan." His smile was sly as he pocketed my two-dollar tip and stepped behind a podium the size of a pulpit. "That'll be twenty dollars."

I swallowed hard at the price, but it was my fault for arriving early. I handed him the cash, he grabbed a key, and without having me sign the register, led me up the curving staircase. Two rooms from the second-floor landing, he opened the door to what looked like Tara—before the War. It even had fringed velvet draperies, though red, not green.

Speechless, I took the key to the room, handing him the key to my car and another two-dollar tip to bring up my things. Stepping inside, I whispered, "Rhett, honey, Ah'm home."

I was sitting on the edge of the canopied step-bed when Leroy appeared with all my baggage, including the Royal. His disappointment in the quality and quantity of my belongings showed in his frown when he handed me the typewriter and dropped both the suitcase and sheet/bag just inside the threshold.

"I packed in a hurry," I explained unnecessarily. "I'll have to buy some things while I'm here. Do you know of a good department store in town?"

His arms crossed over his chest and his head cocked to the side to test me. "Hollis said your maw-maw was from here. Don't you know?"

He was bright, this one. I'd have to be on my toes with him. "She moved up north when she was young, but she wanted to be buried with her kin. Here."

"And who might they be?"

Damn, he was nosey, but it gave me a chance to test my story. "Tucker," I said, hoping there wasn't a clan of Tuckers in town waiting to claim me as a long-lost relative and grill me about my fictitious grandmother.

"Never heard of 'em."

I tried not to show my relief. "They died out a long time ago."

He still didn't look convinced but seemed happy enough with the twenty-four dollars he'd pocketed in ten minutes. Knowing he'd taken as much risk in renting out a private room as I did for arriving early, I said, "Maybe we can keep my stay in this room between us."

Understanding registered in his narrowed blue eyes under a thatch of thick, dark red hair. Quid pro quo. I'd keep his secret if he kept mine. I was flying the Stainsby family colors again, but unlike them, I'd keep my word.

He nodded and was half-way down the stairs before I closed the door. I left my things in their heap to call Glory. Collect.

Fortunately, she remembered my alias. "Chére, are you all right?"

The connection crackled, either from the hotel operator still on the line or the volume of holiday calls. I kept in character. "I'm fine. Maw-maw Hester died and I'm in Jeffers to meet the funeral director."

"I see."

I let her know where I was staying for the night and gave her the phone number printed on Hollis' note. "I'm going to take a nap and settle in for the fireworks tonight."

"Haven't you had enough fireworks for one weekend?"

She wasn't joking, but I tried to make light of it. "Very funny. You know I love fireworks. And there's a debate tomorrow, kicking off the campaigns. It should be interesting."

The crackling on the line stopped and Glory warned, "Be careful. I know you fancy yourself a chameleon, but don't try to win an Academy Award. If the going gets tough, get going. Understand, Chére?"

"Chère?" I countered. "A few weeks in New Orleans and you're a Creole? Who's the chameleon now?"

"Okay, Okay."

I missed her so much. Besides Rose's funeral, we'd only seen each other one evening in the last two years. On her way to New Orleans, she'd stopped to visit Edwin, who had inherited his father's dry-cleaning business. We met at his apartment behind the storefront rather than risk a segregated restaurant, Negro or White. That was when I realized how dangerous our friendship was in the South. "Is Edwin all right?"

"So far, but I'm concerned."

So was I. Both Edwin and Glory were exceptionally intelligent and outspoken, but while Glory was beautiful, with a café-au-lait complexion, her half-brother was dark-skinned. That and his sharp tongue labeled him an, 'Uppity Nigger'.

The phone clicked again. "We should get together soon," Glory said. "When we can talk more. Call me after you meet with the funeral director."

I unpacked my things and made a few notes for my investigation into the O'Grady family before answering the call of the Scarlett O'Hara bed. My growling stomach woke me at one o'clock.

With plenty of time for a light dinner before getting the lay of the land, I descended the stairs in a fresh pair of Bermuda shorts, a white blouse, and red cardigan sweater to enter a lobby where men wore suits and ladies were in dresses, hats, and gloves for the holiday afternoon. While the dowagers and social climbers frowned, smiles from the men confirmed that maybe gentlemen *did* prefer blondes.

I sat at a small table with a view of Main Street, ordering ham with biscuits and green beans. The delicious food and people-watching consumed my attention until the room was nearly empty and a tall man blocked my view of the window.

"Pardon me. Laura? Is that you?" came from his shadowed face.

The deep voice sounded vaguely familiar and the hint of Boston laced into his pronunciation of 'pardon' didn't surprise me. While the South berated the barbarians to their north, they stumbled over each other to educate their young men at Yale and Harvard. I hid my surprise at hearing my name by taking a sip of water. When I looked up, he'd stepped away from the bright afternoon sunlight and I saw a wide, friendly smile, sea-glass green eyes and a neatly trimmed head of honey-colored hair tinged with silver at the temples.

"I'm sorry, I'm afraid you're mistaken," I answered. "My name is Sarah. Sarah Tucker."

His laugh sounded hollow in the stodgy, late eighteenth-century parlor before he sat opposite me, leaning toward me on the elbows of a fashionably rumpled white linen jacket. "My apologies. Except for your hair, the resemblance to someone I knew, albeit a long time ago, is remarkable. My name is Glass. Ambrose Haliday Bradley-Glass."

A giggle erupted before I could stop it. "Ambrose?"

His smile remained, but his voice was cool. "I encourage people to call me Hal. Please do me the favor."

I wasn't sure that was better. Hal was a name for a plumber, or a real estate agent, and his suit screamed tailor-made. "Of course, Hal." I repeated. Then I got it. "Glass? As in the Bradley-Glass family who have owned this house since 1735?"

His eyes crinkled at the edges when he said, "Guilty. The end of a long line of slavers, scalawags, and pirates generally referred to as the founders of the great state of Georgia." He waved at the opulent room with a wry smile. "But they left me the family home. And as proprietor of this establishment and local attorney, people put up with me."

Proprietor? Crap.

He leaned in, lowering his voice, "So, Miss Tucker, I hope you're comfortable in the Scarlett suite. May I ask what business you have with our *esteemed* car salesman, Billy Berens?"

I'd only been there a few hours and the boss knew what room I was in? I remembered Leroy saying my room was leased for "special" guests. My father had a similar arrangement with the Boston Ritz-Carlton. I must be in

Billy's room. If Billy had wanted me here, he wouldn't have booked me at Ho-Jo's.

Damn, I could not get a break. I already had one strike against me for falling apart at the Pickrick. My talent for undercover reporting notwithstanding, if Billy found out I tried to scam a free night on his dime, he'd likely show me the door the moment I arrived at his dealership.

The lies came a little too easily. "It's personal. I'm here to arrange my maw-maw's funeral. She was an acquaintance of Mr. Berens. He kindly offered me his guest suite."

Instead of a sympathetic Southern smile, Hal's lips pressed into a thin line, making him look older. "Quit while you're ahead, Laura," he said. "While Senator Stainsby excels at lying with a straight face, you were never very good at it."

Something in the tone of his voice seemed familiar, but I couldn't place him. I attributed it to my exhaustion. But I'd learned to never admit a lie, even if called on it. "No, you're mistaken. I'm Sarah Tucker. I'm from Cambridge. Massachusetts."

He folded his hands on the tabletop. Graceful hands with long fingers, a Harvard signet ring on his left ring finger with a jade pinky ring next to it. An Italian gold chain necklace barely showed beneath the open top button of his blue pinstriped shirt. The expensive Rolex watch on his left wrist reminded me of Ricky's fondness for jewelry, but I didn't judge Hal. It was his hotel.

Dishes crashed behind us and he turned to the young, black busboy frantically picking up shards of fine china. "Leave it, Jacob," he ordered kindly, then told the other three busboys, "Take a ten-minute break. It's going to be a busy weekend. We'll use the tourist plates tomorrow."

They scrambled through the kitchen doors like children let out of school early. Hal nodded to Leroy leaning against the bar, and he followed the boys. The owner of the Glass House leaned toward me, tenting his long fingers under his chin. "We don't have time to dance, Laura. You're early. I thought Jeremy booked you at the motor lodge."

Feeling like Alice with the White Rabbit, I looked around the now empty room. "I don't know what you're talking about. The food was wonderful Mr. Glass, but I need to go."

Andy Griffith's Mayberry charm faded with his smile, and his voice deepened. "You can drop the charade, Miss Stainsby. I remember you from the Westmoreland Academy. I also remember your dream of becoming a crusading reporter and I still subscribe to *The Boston Globe.* When Jeremy told me about Billy's plan to destroy Patrick O'Grady, I recalled your work on the illegal adoption ring in Boston. I called Bob Healy and he told me you were at the *Constitution.* I mentioned it to Jeremy and…," He clapped his hands with the flourish of a magician. "…Voilà, here you are."

The Westmoreland Academy! *Mr. Bradley.* Twelve years ago, he taught Renaissance Poetry and was senior advisor on the school newspaper while I was reporter, typesetter, proofer and editor. His thin, angular features had filled out, obscuring the sharp lines of his jaw and high cheekbones. He was probably barely over forty, but he seemed so much older—or was it jaded? I wondered what he thought about the saccharine verses of his Elizabethan poets now.

I tried to sound unfazed. "Okay, you caught me, Mr. *Bradley*, but you should also remember I don't play games. What's your angle?"

He frowned. "Patrick O'Grady is a good man. His family, the Langesfords and O'Gradys, have sacrificed a great deal for this community and state, going back to the first settlement. I want to make sure what's reported about them is the truth—within context. Billy and I don't speak, and he doesn't know that Jeremy and I do. I'm asking you to keep this conversation confidential and inform me before you take anything to Billy. In exchange, I won't tell Patrick your true purpose in town."

More quid pro quo. I was shocked at how small the world really is, but this was not the charming, romantic, high school teacher I remembered. Worse than jaded, he'd become manipulative. Maybe it was the law degree.

The sarcasm in my voice surprised me when I said, "How gallant of you. Loyalty these days is a rare thing. But besides Truth, Justice and the American Way, what do you really want?"

He stared at me like he had when he caught me reading *Lord of the Flies* instead of Christopher Marlowe, and his voice showed the same disappointment. "So, the debutante-turned-bleeding-heart-journalist is now a career-buster for hire," he answered. "Why the masquerade?"

It hurt, but I had nothing to lose. If I couldn't convince him I only wanted to write the truth about both sides of the story, there would *be no story.* I leaned in. "If you remember me at all, you know that for me, being a Boston Stainsby is the masquerade. I'm here to write the truth about

Southern politics in this election and I'm hoping one of the candidates is an honest man."

I stood, looking down at one of the few men I'd ever admired. "But I'm not the only pretender in the room, *Hal.* You don't seem at all fond of Big Billy, yet you do business with him. And while you obviously like O'Grady, you helped Jeremy hire me to investigate him. As someone who's been played most of her life, it looks to me like there's a bigger game afoot. Jeremy seems like a good kid. Who is he to you? And most important, what's in this for you?"

He stood too, looking down his aristocratic nose at me. "You're very perceptive, *Sarah,* but my relationship with Jeremy is private. Just know that I mean no harm to him, you, or Patrick O'Grady."

I noticed he left out Billy, but Leroy interrupted us with my bill before I could ask.

"It's on the House," Hal told him. "Can you mind the desk?"

When the boy was out of earshot, Hal said, "Sadly, you seem to have forgotten the most important thing about being a journalist. A good one doesn't assume *anything* until they have all the facts." Leading me past Leroy, toward the stairs, he said loud enough for the boy to hear, "Stay as long as you like, Miss Tucker. I'll be happy to help you with whatever estate matters you may have for your maw-maw.

He leaned close to me at the foot of the staircase. "You're very clever, Laura, but cleverness won't be enough if you want to survive Billy's Machiavellian schemes. Take it from me, sitting on a fence can be very painful. Sooner or later, you'll have to pick a side."

"What do you mean?"

His eyes, empty of the humor and—innocence—I remembered fondly, narrowed. "You need to understand two things about Jeffers. The first is that there are no secrets."

I doubted that. Between Billy, the O'Gradys, and now Hal, there seemed to be plenty of secrets. "And the second?"

"Billy always gets what he wants—except the one thing he wanted most."

CHAPTER 6

Restless after the big meal and Hal's bombshell, I left the Glass House to explore the town circle and quaint side streets lined with antique stores and gift shops. A few blocks down, I stopped short in front of what looked like a cathedral dominating a neighborhood of stately Victorian homes. I took off my sunglasses to appreciate the Romanesque tower looming above three stories of weathered white limestone and red sandstone.

The carved limestone arch above a double, mullioned oak door read, "Jeffers Municipal Library—1877".

I wondered out loud, "How did a Renaissance Revival building made of New England limestone end up in the heart of Dixie?"

"Yankee money."

I spun around to face a man whose build reminded me of my brother Adam, the youngest of my three older brothers. Like Adam, he was tall and lean, with thick black hair. But this man's haircut was more James Garner's Maverick than Sean Connery's James Bond. And Adam wouldn't be caught dead in a blue linen shirt *without* French cuffs. I glimpsed blue eyes matching the cloudless sky before he shifted his gaze up to the tower.

"Excuse me?" I asked.

"The old library burned during the War," he answered, looking up at the tower.

I didn't have to ask which war. There was only one that mattered in the South. "The War of Northern Aggression".

Still admiring the classic lines of the building, he explained, "During Reconstruction, Yankee moneymen came to buy up plantations for pennies on the dollar. A few eased their guilt by building monuments to themselves."

"You mean this was built by a carpetbagger?"

He turned back to me, his patient smile melting the tension I'd felt since my conversation with Hal. "Nope."

Smile or not, he was beginning to irritate me. "But you just said…"

"That Yankees tried to buy up the South. The Yankee who paid for this architectural anomaly was a Boston doctor who never set foot here. The story is his family amassed a fortune from the slave trade and he wanted to atone by helping rebuild the South. The locals hated him of course, but money is money. His name is on the base of the monument in the park behind the library—in very small print."

The glint of humor in his voice prompted me to ask, "If that's the story, what's the truth?"

His smile faded and he shrugged. "Who knows? And does it matter?"

I was about to say the truth *always* matters when, "Daddy! Daddy!" turned my attention to a little girl about five or six years old. She moved out from behind him to tug his hand. "Hurry, we can't be late for the fireworks."

Black, Shirley Temple-sized ringlets bobbed with each word. Still smiling, he bent toward her. "Hush, Kitten. Don't be rude." Then to me, "She's right. It's a big weekend."

With a nod toward the library, he said, "Yankee money notwithstanding, it's a great building. We keep it and the gift shop open on Saturdays for tourists—unless Christmas falls on a weekend. Ask for Tammy Eldridge. She'll give you a tour."

They walked back toward the circle, his big hand holding Kitten's tiny one while she hopped, skipped, and jumped over cracks in the sidewalk.

There were no cracks in the sidewalks around Stainsby Manor, and the few times my father walked with me, I had to skip to keep up with him. When I fell, he told me to get up on my own, saying, "It'll make you strong."

I watched the man and little girl until they turned the corner, then cleared the *what-if* cobwebs from my mind and stepped toward the library of my dreams. A few steps inside, I stopped in the middle of a mosaic Mariner's

Compass to stare up at sunlight beaming through the glass dome of the circular tower. A few more steps took me to a circulation room the size of a bungalow, where a fireplace dominated a reading area furnished with tiger-oak tables and old-fashioned reading lamps with green glass shades. Rows of bookshelves followed the curved, paneled walls.

I approached the card catalog in the center of it all, breathing in the intoxicating scents of old wood, beeswax polish, and aged leather bindings. *Home at last.*

"Hello there," sounded like an angel calling from heaven.

I turned in a tight circle. "Hello. Where are you?"

A giggle came from the other side of the card catalog, a drawer snapped shut and the sound of rubber-soled shoes on the polished wood flooring came my way.

I heard, "I'm sorry. Sound does strange things in here," as she rounded the corner of the cabinet and I faced the epitome of The-Girl-Next-Door, complete with blue dungarees rolled up to her calf, white bobbysocks, and red Keds on her feet. A tortoise-shell headband held her natural-blonde pageboy in place. She was at least a head taller than me and filled the darts in her blouse better than I could ever hope to. I revised my label to, 'Country Barbie' when she said in a deep Southern accent, "Kin Ah help you?"

"A gentleman outside told me to ask Tammy Eldridge for a tour," I answered.

A young mother with a toddler hanging onto her skirt approached the checkout desk. The girl touched my arm and smiled. "I'm Tammy, hon. Jest 'scuse me a sec."

As a line formed behind the woman and toddler, I strolled around the room, looking for a sign to the genealogy room, where libraries kept copies of old birth records and land deeds. It's what separates the wheat from the chaff in the archival world. While I enjoyed access to libraries in Boston, New York, and Washington, I'd heard of more than a few top-notch ones in towns not much bigger than Jeffers. It was where I planned to begin my research into the nasty feud between the Berens and Langesford/O'Grady clans. With no luck on the sign, I riffled through the card catalogue while Tammy finished up with her customers.

"If you're too busy now," I said. "I'll just wander…" I paused, looking past her at a pen and ink drawing of a Colonial-era neoclassical mansion.

Tammy noticed and smiled. With the enthusiasm of a born docent, she said, "That's the old Jeffers Academy. It was built in 1736, the third home in the county, after Langesford Plantation and the Bradley-Glass house. Some say Washington stayed there. When the Jeffers family died out, it became the first college in Southeast Georgia."

A tanned arm swept to the right and left of us. "This part is built on the old foundation. Additions came later, of course, including the new genealogy wing."

Genealogy *WING?* My pulse quickened, but I knew we'd meet another time. It was past three o'clock. You don't rush an introduction to a whole wing devoted to local genealogy. Besides, I was curious. "What happened to it? The house and the academy, I mean."

She shrugged when a couple grumblers shushed us from tables near the periodicals section, then fake-whispered, "The War, of course."

I glared at the shushers. How often do you find a walking history book that looks like Debbie Reynolds and sounds like Scarlet O'Hara? "You seem to know a lot about the town's history."

Her pageboy bobbed, then fell perfectly back into place. "I'm a history and education major over at Georgia State. I'm going to be Head Librarian here someday."

Her professional aspiration impressed me. While she looked like she could check out books in her sleep, I'd put my time in at the Smith library and didn't have anything to do until the fireworks. I also didn't want to run into either Billy or Hal. "Can I help?"

For an hour, she stamped books in and out while I filed the cards and sorted the book return cart. During a lull, I asked, "So, what's the story about the Glass House?"

"Isn't it wonderful?" she gushed. "The Bradley/Glass home and Langesford House are the only antebellum homes east of Atlanta still occupied by the original families. Langesford is older. Parts of it go back to the original cabin. The Glass House is technically a hotel, but Ambrose lives on the third floor and nobody's ever questioned it. They're both open during the holidays to raise money for our county's poor and orphans. It's God's will you know, to take care of those in need, and we take care of our own."

God's will. Apparently, Lester Maddox had missed that part of his scripture lessons.

"Good for you," I acknowledged.

Her jaw set. "You're not from around here."

Maybe I should have said, 'praise the Lord', instead of 'good for you'.

"No," I admitted. "My name is Sarah Tucker. I'm from Massachusetts."

Like every lie, it came easier every time I said it.

Her narrowed gaze told me she needed more information and I summarized my cover story. "I'm here to arrange my maw-maw's funeral and thought I'd research our family history. She never talked much about her..." what was the word they used in the South? "People."

The smile returned. "Good for you. Our roots grow deep down here. It's hard to leave for long. Ambrose did for a little while. Boston, I think. But he came back. Everybody does—eventually. Where are you staying?"

I dodged the question to ask, "Wasn't this area on Sherman's path to the sea during the Civil, I mean, The War?"

"Yes, the March was a *terrible* time." She lowered her voice as if remembering, rather than recounting the story. "The smoke of burning farms blocked the sun for days. Most of what few animals the Yanks didn't steal, died from poisoned water."

Tammy was a very good storyteller and the fireworks at Courthouse Park didn't begin until dusk. I leaned toward her. "Can you tell me about it?"

With only a few people left in the building, I sat on a three-legged stool and she settled into an old plantation chair. "It was Hell of course," she said. "The blockades nearly starved us out. We had fertile ground, but no seeds. And while ginned cotton rotted in warehouses, we didn't have cloth to make our own clothes. Folks ate roots from the ground when they could find them."

I nodded at the tragedy. "What about the Langesford, and Bradley families? How did they survive?"

She brightened. "Langesford house only escaped the torches because my Great Grandmother, Miss Camilla tricked the soldiers into thinking there was a fever in the house that carried in smoke."

She snorted in a most un-Debbie Reynolds fashion, "Stupid Yankees," and I was surprised to bristle at the insult to *my* ancestors.

When pink and gold tinted the sky above the tower, Tammy said, "C'mon, I gotta put these books back and make sure nobody's hiding in the johns before I leave. I'll give you a quick tour. Truth be told, I'll be glad for the company. It can be creepy this time of day."

I pushed the cart while she barely looked at the spine of each book before finding its exact spot on the shelf.

"And the Glass House?" I asked. "How did that survive?"

"Stupid name, don't you think?"

I shrugged. *What's in a name?*

"Ambrose named it that just to annoy people. The house belonged to his mother's people, the Bradleys, but he said her married name, Glass, 'fit the old crone' better." She turned to me. "*Old Crone!* Can you believe he calls that magnificent—and *irreplaceable*—historical treasure a *crone*? He's an odd duck, that one."

She didn't know the half of it.

She stopped on the Mariner's compass and said, "This was part of the original Jeffers House, and was a hospital for a while." She pointed to the center of the mosaic as if she could see through it to a pine floor stained red with the blood of her ancestors. "It was December of 1864. School desks not needed for operating tables became firewood and the wounded, both blue and gray, lay shoulder to shoulder on the floors of all three stories."

She'd make a marvelous docent in Boston or Washington, I thought, rubbing the goosebumps on my arms. "How awful."

She looked at me, her big blue eyes glittering with pride. "Yes. But we survived."

As if on cue, *Dixie* filled the room through the open front doors, and we watched the Jeffers High School marching band strut down the street under a sky now streaked with more orange than blue. When I turned, Tammy was gone. I followed the sound of her squeaking Keds, calling, "Tammy, where are you?"

"Up here."

Her voice came from the spiral staircase to the tower. "I always check up here at the end of the day. It's a great view. Come on up."

I tested the spiral staircase with both feet on one step before following the light from above to an alcove rimming the dome. Marks on the walls of the hexagon-shaped room hidden from the floor view, testified that shelves had once lined them.

"Kids like to sneak up here and make out," Tammy said from behind me, holding a tattered, leather-bound book.

I cocked my head. "What's that?"

"I'm not sure. It looks like a journal of some sort. We stored old books and some of the Langesford archives up here. It must have fallen behind the shelves when they moved everything down to the new wing."

She opened the priceless example of antique bookmaking and cocked her head. “This is odd. It’s really old and is hand-written in what looks like French, but I’m not sure.”

Without thinking, I said, “I minored in Romance Languages in school. Can I see?”

She handed it to me, and I opened it. My hand trembled at the treasure left casually lying on the marble floor. “This is in Creole French,” I told her. “The pages are dated. It could be a journal. They’re very rare. Most Creole families were big, and the women didn’t have much time to themselves. How do you think it got here?”

I gave it back to Tammy. She shrugged and held it as if it was the Holy Grail. “I wouldn’t know, but there are stories that Miss Camilla’s mama was from New Orleans, way back in the day.” The striking sunset above the dome cast a golden tint to her sun-colored hair as she shook her head and whispered, “I wonder if it’s hers.”

She looked at me with big blue eyes that literally glittered with hope. “Can you translate it?

“Maybe,” I said. “But it could take a while,”

“Would you try? Your roots are here, so I trust you. I just want to make sure it goes to the right place.”

She thrust it at me so fast I had no choice but to accept it. At least that’s what I told myself at the time. The truth was that I loved old books. The smell and feel of leather bindings and ancient paper made from rags and cotton fibers, connected me to the long-dead writers. While I doubted it would have any bearing on my investigation, if it was Tammy’s great-great grandmother’s, it could shed some light on her family history.

“How did you know I love old books?” I asked.

“The way you stopped dead in your tracks on the compass when you came in. When you looked up, it was like you were lookin’ at the Pearly Gates. That’s how I feel every day I’m here. Someday, I’ll write a history of my family, Jeffers, and the South—the way it really was. Maybe then we can move on.”

I followed her down the staircase, my free hand clutching the railing. She set the books on the counter and flipped a card to me from a nearby rack. “Fill this out while I lock up.”

She disappeared down a shadowed hallway while I entered my alias into the Jeffers library system, using the address on my fake ID.

"Why don't you join us under the live oak?" Tammy asked when she returned. "We have plenty of blankets and beer. And you'll love my cousin's daughter. I call her Little Einstein. She's only six and can read like a fourth grader. It's a little scary."

I pictured dark ringlets surrounding a face dominated by big, green eyes. Old souls, my Nanny Irene called them, but as good as a cold Budweiser sounded, I thought of the journal and the old four-poster bed in the Scarlett room. "Thanks, but it was a long drive and I'm exhausted. I think I'll call it an early evening."

"Suit yourself, but we have the best fireworks in three counties. We'll save a seat if you change your mind. Just cut across the circle and up the hill behind the Bradley, I mean Glass, House."

She adjusted her headband, made sure the library doors were safely locked, and bounded down the steps. "You can't miss the oak. It's the best seat in the park."

We separated at the circle by the municipal parking lot and I waited until she disappeared behind the hotel before going upstairs to my room. The old-fashioned push-button light switch summoned the warm glow of a Tiffany-style lamp on the bedside table and I pulled on my muumuu, crawled into bed and caressed the embossed fleur-de-lis pattern on the red-leather cover of the journal.

I'd spent a fair amount of my youth haunting Boston's antique bookstores. I learned that red leather covers were very rare before the twentieth century—and very expensive. Likewise, the hand-sewn saddle-stitching securing expensive linen rag pages imprinted with what looked like a family crest. The end paper on the inside of the cover was nearly pristine, with only the initials "D. T." and the year, 1840, written in fancy script.

Unfortunately, the first five months of entries appeared to have been brutally ripped out, jagged edges of the fine hand-laid paper testifying to the violent act. The first remaining page was dated *Juin 10, 1840* and it was indeed written in Creole French. I called it French with a twist, but no Smith girl graduated without being fluent in the language of romance. As an overachiever with a gift for languages and virtually no social life, I became fluent in both versions.

The historical significance also fascinated me, and the fine lines written with what was likely an expensive crow or owl feather, screamed a female author. Letters and journals from Creole women in the eighteenth and nineteenth centuries were rare, and I saw parallels in their lives to my own. The pampered '*demoiselles*' of Louisiana's ruling class lived a life of luxury that included an education, but no opportunity to use it. And while many of them owned property and ran businesses, their true purpose was to produce the next generation of elitists.

Those few who stole precious moments to write between giving birth, running households and rearing children, hid their thoughts, prayers, and sorrows behind fanciful curlicues and flourishes until the script was nearly as difficult to translate as Hieroglyphics. I was rusty, but after spending six months deciphering Adeline's scrawled handwriting at the *Constitution*, I welcomed the challenge.

At full-dark, I took a break to watch the small town celebrate its independence. A soft breeze carried laughter, music, and happy voices to me like a gift. Sitting on the window seat, my chin resting on my knees, I ignored Frederic Douglass' dire description of Independence Day as, "A day that reveals gross injustice and cruelty…a thin veil to cover up crimes which would disgrace a nation of savages."

To me, this was what America should be—for everyone. Tammy was right about the fireworks. The magnificent bursts of green, gold, and yellow, along with traditional red, white, and blue, rivaled Boston's celebration on the Esplanade along the banks of the Charles River. As a child, I'd clutched the rail of my father's river yacht, pretending the colorful explosions were real bombs bursting in air. I smelled the gunpowder, felt the soul-shattering power of the canons. I cried when the church bells pealed, and I joined Boston to sing the National Anthem. Now, singing along with the people of Jeffers, my eyes misted with pride at living where the simple dream of democracy had changed the world. Where freedom was intended to be more than just a word.

The party ended for me when I turned on the local news at 10:30 and saw a replay of what was being called, "The Pickrick Incident". Glory was right. The cameras jumped around so much I barely recognized my own face in the window.

It offered little comfort, so I snapped off the TV and again picked up D.T.'s journal, wondering what had made her angry enough to rip out the pages. From June 10, 1840, all the pages seemed to be intact. And it started with a bang. The young, pregnant demoiselle's father was forcing her to abandon her lover and marry a stranger in a ceremony that was little more than a business transaction.

Unfortunately, she'd written for her eyes only, referring to her new husband as, "A" and her new home as her, "loathsome exile". There seemed no way to trace the book's journey to the alcove of the Jeffers Library tower. I closed it at the point she bade farewell to her beloved Belle Rivière.

CHAPTER 7

Church bells chiming *Praise God from Whom All Blessings Flow* woke me on Sunday morning. I smiled, thinking some things are unique to America: fireworks in the hot July sky, brass bands playing old patriotic songs, the devout and pretend-devout dressing up on Sundays to sit on hard benches and contemplate a power higher than themselves.

The bells quieted and I realized I had several hours to kill before the candidates' first debate of the campaign. The town circle was nearly deserted, the library and businesses closed as politically disinterested tourists packed up for the trip home. Despite what promised to be a classic, sticky summer day in Georgia, I decided on a run. Running wasn't the most acceptable physical activity for women, yet Smith encouraged athletics. I was too small for basketball and while I never won a race, I found running to be effective at clearing the mind.

After nearly an hour, my head was free of the tragic unfinished journal, but I was hot, thirsty, and starving. Brunch was in full force at the Glass House and I gave Leroy a dollar to bring a quiche up to my room. The quiche and a sweet tea were at my door when I finished my shower. I devoured them both and packed a few things for the afternoon debate between Billy Berens and his opponent, Patrick O'Grady.

I headed out to call Glory from the phone booth outside Hoffman Drugs. She confirmed that my Pickrick story was in the afternoon holiday edition of Saturday's paper. McGill had expanded it to raise the bigger question of potential Federal charges against Lester Maddox for violating the new Civil Rights Act. So far, he'd vowed to shut down his restaurant before he'd integrate. Not a big loss as far as I was concerned.

Glory sounded like the mop-boy and cook at the Pickrick when she warned, "Be careful. Cracker politicians may look all down-home and friendly, but they have teeth like a mama boar and are twice as mean."

I could barely hear her as the marching band again made its way around the circle. They were just warming up, but I didn't want to miss a minute of my first southern political debate. "I can't hear you," interrupted her order for me to call her on a regular basis. "Gotta go," I said. "I need to find a good seat."

I rushed back to my room for my things, taking Tammy's shortcut to the park. It surprised me that more than an hour before the debate, the folding chairs in the 'bowl' were almost filled. Everywhere I looked, families lounged against trees or sat on blankets along the grassy slope, while children chased each other with leftover sparklers.

The fireworks bunker from the night before was replaced by a portable stage with a bright red awning, and two podiums angled toward each other. Folding chairs were lined up behind them. For VIPs and the candidates' families, I assumed. I still didn't know if Billy was married, and while I knew O'Grady was a widower, I figured two men that rich and eligible wouldn't be without lady-friends.

The live oak Tammy mentioned was hard to miss. Atop the slope overlooking the stage, it would take at least four adults to wrap their arms around it. It was already claimed by bright quilts and picnic baskets and I saw Tammy in a poppy-print sundress, her blonde hair nearly platinum under the bright sun. She waved when she saw me, almost clocking the boy next to her. "Hey, Sarah! Come on over."

Grateful for a shaded seat, I joined her, and she hugged me like a long-lost friend. I spread out the afghan from my room and a chirpy brunette asked Tammy, "Ah hear Evelyn got married last month and moved down to St. Marys. Who's watchin' Dani?"

"Me, Mattie, and Ela for now," she answered. "But school starts after Labor Day for me and Ela's heading back to New Mexico in a few weeks. Truth be told, it worries me. With the farm and all the other stuff goin' on, Paddy hasn't been looking very hard for a replacement."

The girl shrugged. "Shouldn't be a problem. He's quite the catch." She nudged the boy next to her. "Too bad I'm taken—and just got a job at the new *Dairy Queen!*"

She squealed the last part, and I joined the little group to applaud and congratulate her.

We fell silent when the marching band took the field playing *The Battle Cry of Freedom.* They never missed a step as they circled the rim of the hill and descended the slope to stand in perfectly straight rows facing the stage. The crowd roared when they finished.

"They played in the Rose Parade last year," Tammy shouted above the cheers and applause. "I played clarinet my senior year. We Wildcats take our band as seriously as our football team—State champions for the last ten years."

I couldn't fault her home-town pride. Boston sports fans were rabid in their loyalty to the Sox and Celtics. "Congratulations."

"Testing, Testing." A middle-aged man with a straw hat and a beer belly tapped the microphone on the stage until it squealed.

"Can y'all hear me?" he shouted, recoiling from the feedback.

"We always hear you Mayor Andy," rang out from a smart-ass in the audience.

The mayor's chest puffed out with self-importance. "Well then let's git this here rally rollin'," he shouted again, a safe distance from the mic this time. "Y'all know why we're here."

Without waiting for an answer, he raised an arm. "We're here to celebrate our great state of Georgia and our God-given rights to Truth, Justice and the American Way."

I stifled a chuckle at the over-used cliché I'd referenced with Hal. Then the band struck up the Civil War anthem dedicated to the fall of Ft. Sumter and the crowd stood to sing *The Bonny Blue Flag.* I felt as if I'd stepped back in time until Mayor Andy again waved his arms for silence, utilizing what I called the 'political three beats'.

One, state the obvious. "Today," he bellowed from the edge of the stage, demonstrating he didn't need a microphone. "Our nation is once again in the throes of change."

Two, pause for a little chatter.

Three, one last statement of the obvious. "And now more than ever, we need strong leadership."

Number three usually led to introductions, but he surprised me by taking off his hat and holding it over his heart. His audience followed suit to bow their heads while he led them in prayer. "Lord, we mourn the loss of one who dedicated his life for our cause and was taken from us too soon. Edward O'Grady and his family have stood with District One since the founding of our country, defending our right to a fair share of our own tax money. Now we pray for guidance in choosing the right man to replace him as our representative in Washington. Amen."

Pause, replace the hat, and strike up the band, I thought. *Dixie*, of course. When it was over, Mayor Andy paced up and down the stage shouting, "It's time for new blood to take us to a new era. And the good Lord has blessed us. Today, two of our own Jeffers boys have stepped up, ready, willin', and able to fill the shoes of our fallen neighbor."

He spread his arms wide and turned to his left with all the gusto of a circus ringmaster. "Ladies and gentlemen let's hear it for the Republican candidate for the US House of Representatives. Our own rags to riches story, Mister William Henry Berens the Thirrrrd."

Billy ran across the stage waving his arms like Moses parting the Red Sea. I suppressed a chuckle as the crowd roared their approval with a chorus of, "Billy, Billy, Billy."

Only those under the live oak and a few clusters of blacks lining the unshaded crest of the hill, maintained a semblance of decorum. Billy sat in one of the folding chairs behind the two podiums, and Mayor Andy's enthusiasm diminished when he announced, "And now for the candidate representing the Democratic party, Patrick Ooooo'Grady, the Second."

The crowd surprised me by being equally enthusiastic about the tall man who slowly approached center stage. Even the ridge-sitters called out their support of the status quo represented by the son of the Favorite Son. My companions jumped to their feet, cupping their hands to their mouths to chant, "Ooo'Grady, Ooo'Grady."

Finally, the mayor stepped aside to afford me a view of both candidates. Billy, in his navy blue and white pinstripe suit, and his opponent—the man I'd met outside the library.

Tammy jabbed me with her elbow. "That's my cousin Paddy."

I couldn't believe I'd met Patrick O'Grady II. From Billy's description, I half expected him to have a handlebar mustache and carry a cat 'o nine tails. I'd *never* have guessed the man with the quiet voice who doted on his little girl was a politician. In my world, children of politicians were props to be trotted onto stages like this one to sit quietly during debates and speeches. No matter how hot it was, how thirsty we were, or if we needed to use the bathroom, we sat still. When it was over, we smiled, waved, and walked out quietly. And when the cameras stopped flashing, we folded up like puppets to go back into our boxes. I hoped O'Grady, a political brat himself, would change that image by shielding his daughter from the limelight.

Winkler had said he was a reluctant candidate, but he looked perfectly comfortable crossing the stage, hand extended toward Billy. Trapped in his chair, unable to rise without pushing O'Grady away, he was forced to accept the gentlemanly offering.

Mayor Andy handed the microphone off to an elderly man with a clerical collar. The minister raised his hands and lowered them slowly, signaling for quiet. Wondering how much church this town needed on a given Sunday, I lowered my head while he asked the Good Lord for protection from the madness in our cities. I hoped he meant the hatred and oppression.

After the mayor droned on about how the debate would be conducted, wiped his brow and left the stage, Billy made a dash for his podium, turning to wait for his opponent to catch up.

O'Grady's steps were precisely measured, his movements fluid, graceful even. When he reached his podium, he removed his panama hat, handing it to a clearly flustered mayor. Then he faced the crowd, rested both hands on the sides of the podium, and nodded.

As if a switch had been pulled, the crowd quieted and took their seats.

Since the meat of any political debate is *always* in the summation, I pulled out my pad and pencil to sketch the candidates before they faced off. Billy gripped his podium like a ship's wheel, gesticulating as he made the standard promises no one could keep; jobs for everyone, two cars in every garage (one of them probably a Cadillac), and of course, peace in our time. He apparently forgot about the Communists spreading over Cambodia, Thailand and Viet Nam. And totally skipped the Civil Rights stink bomb. But this was Jeffers. Home was all that mattered.

The crowd was practically eating out of his hand when he promised to keep the Federal Government from interfering with life in District One. Unfortunately, he didn't say exactly *how* he planned to do anything. But it didn't matter. In the South and most of rural America, political rallies were hoedowns, with lots of noise, kicking, stomping, and waving of arms. His showmanship won the crowd.

I felt sorry for the handsome aristocrat waiting patiently for his turn to speak. Hang it up farmer O'Grady, I thought. Billy Three has them razzle dazzled.

But Patrick O'Grady didn't seem fazed. He focused on the audience, preaching the Four Pillars of Civilization: industry, education, infrastructure, and employment. He set a middle-of-the-road plan for projects that while not shiny, were essential to life as they knew it. Who could argue with the four pillars?

While Billy had leaned into the microphone, amplifying his used-car-salesman voice until it was an assault on the ears, O'Grady recognized the park as a natural amphitheater. He stayed an arm's length away from the mic, his voice carrying naturally, so people leaned in to focus on his words. I gave the late Edward O'Grady points for teaching his son well.

I'd finished sketching O'Grady and started to close the book when Tammy leaned toward me. "No way!" she shrieked. "You didn't tell me you're an artist."

"Well, I'm not really. I just like to draw sometimes. Hey!"

She grabbed the pad. "Dang, if that don't look just like Paddy. Where'd you learn to do that?"

I'd sketched most of my life. It kept me quiet through endless campaigns and debates. My mother was a perfect subject. She could sit stone-still for hours, every hair in place, legs crossed perfectly at the ankles, lips frozen in a Mona Lisa smile. I'd considered art school, but that wouldn't do for a Boston Stainsby.

Tammy gave me the pad back as the debate finally began. When asked about the Civil Rights Act's attack on the Jim Crow Laws, Billy promoted the current, separate-but-equal bullshit without acknowledging that in the South, Negroes were indeed separate, but nowhere close to being equal. And when it came to school desegregation, he preached that school desegregation would upend the natural order of society.

While O'Grady's hand clenched at his side as he waited for his turn, he surprisingly kept his cool to point out the financial benefit of consolidating educational resources to enhance the system. He even cited busing as a safe, convenient way to transport both white and black rural children to their combined schools. When the mostly white audience booed, he pointed to one of the loudest, "Randy Logan, how many kids do you have in school?"

"None," he answered. "Now."

"You own your house?"

"Sure do," Randy responded proudly.

O'Grady nodded, taking a beat to ponder the man's answers. "So, you don't have a dog in the busing fight, but you don't want to save on property taxes by centrally locating schools and improving the quality of education for *other folks'* kids."

While Randy sputtered, O'Grady looked out at the rest of the audience. "I don't like this being forced on us any more than you, but our world is changing. Technology will revolutionize our lives. We need ALL our kids to know it or we'll lose the fight to China, Korea, and Japan—even Russia."

Brilliant, I thought. Introducing an enemy of a different color in the form of international competition. Many of the older men in the crowd had fought in the Pacific and Europe during World War II. Others had sacrificed limbs taking worthless hills in Korea. And two years ago, the threat of Russian missiles only ninety miles from our shoreline, had kept local bomb shelters stocked.

But he wasn't finished. "And if having a good education will keep us in the game…" He dismissed Randy with a disdainful frown. "…we need to create a future that includes EVERYONE!"

I looked toward the ridge. While being thrown into an unfamiliar school with hostile white students had to be frightening, most of them were shouting, whistling, and applauding. I hoped they'd registered to vote. It surprised me that a good share of the Whites supported his logic with civilized, if not enthusiastic, applause.

Billy turned a few shades of red, bordering on purple, and resorted to name-calling. With no facts to back him up, he called his opponent a liar and his family, "An evil nest of carpetbaggers, thieves, and murderers."

The audience took a collective breath, including me.

The sly lift of Billy's mouth showed he'd gotten exactly the reaction he wanted. He'd thrown the proverbial gauntlet. O'Grady had two choices. Both bad. He could sling insults back or take it on the chin. Either way he'd look like a spoiled rich boy running on his daddy's reputation.

Choosing neither option, he let the pause linger while he smiled condescendingly at Billy. "This is 1964, *Billy-Boy*. Every closet in this town has a skeleton or two in it, including more than a few in your own, I'd say."

Billy's face flushed so red I was sure the ridge-sitters could see it. His mouth opened, but anger slowed his tongue, allowing O'Grady time to deliver the death blow.

Unlike Billy, who'd been in constant motion, his unfocused gaze scanning the crowd, O'Grady took his time, standing ramrod straight in his ageless, white planter's suit, shoulders relaxed, hands folded in front of him on the podium. And in solid, down-to-earth terms anyone could understand, he told them how he'd represent his district to the House Appropriations Committee his father once headed.

He concluded by nodding to his neighbors in the bowl and raising a hand to the families along the ridge. Then with the power of a tent preacher, he told them, "It's time to lay the past to rest and build a future for the next generation. As we approach our country's second century, I ask every parent here today, what do you want more? A Cadillac? Or a quality education and safe place for *all* the children of District One to live and work?"

He held out his hand and little Kitten skipped onto the stage to take it. Disappointing, but also genius. He turned to the audience, raising a hand to silence their cheers. Then, holding his daughter's hand, he approached the edge of the stage.

"If it's the latter, send those children on up here, because I'm telling you, *they* are the reason I'm here. *They* are the reason I'll leave Langesford and go to Washington. And *they* are the ones I'll be thinking about when I vote on how Georgia's money is spent."

Chaos erupted as the crowd stood, cheering, whistling, and waving. Children rushed the stage, pushing the childless Billy Berens back to his folding chair. The debate was over.

CHAPTER 8

I left when Tammy ran to congratulate her cousin. Fortunately, I missed Hal, who was waiting for me to agree to share the results of my investigation with him. While I'd once trusted my old teacher, I didn't know if I could trust the man he'd become, and I had to know more about both candidates.

The Patrick I'd seen on stage was certainly not the wicked wastrel Billy and Winkler had described, and Billy's own performance was at odds with his professed dedication to American values. It made me more determined to report on both sides in this election. It would be tricky because I basically had to play both sides of the fence to get the truth about how campaigns are run in the Deep South.

Winkler would be livid that I didn't follow the plan of digging up the dirt on O'Grady and would likely fire me. And McGill might be averse to risking his subscribership with an article critical to their culture. But other papers, including the *Boston Globe* would jump at it—and maybe take me back. With a sad farewell to the Scarlett room, I loaded up my car. And since I hadn't checked in, left without checking out.

Hollis welcomed me at Ho-Jo's with a big smile and gave me a room with a cozy desk by the window. I ate a light supper alone at the buffet and spent the evening typing up my notes and making slow progress on the Creole woman's increasingly scattered journal entries.

I woke early Monday morning and reviewed my sketches. Not bad, I thought, though no one would see them. The charcoal pencil had captured Billy's arrogance and audacity, and some of his naivete of how the game is played

O'Grady's sketch was less clear. I'd accurately depicted his strong jaw and the intensity of his gaze, but he seemed stiff, like an actor playing a role. Winkler said he was a reluctant candidate. I wondered how reluctant.

I turned off the *Today Show* broadcast rehashing Alabama governor George Wallace's 4th of July tirade claiming the Civil Rights Movement was a fraud, a sham and a hoax that threatened individual liberty, free enterprise and property rights. I recognized that Billy's style, and even some of his phrasing at the debate the next day were eerily similar to Wallace's. But the sentiments were common enough in the South.

I dismissed my suspicions that Billy had plagiarized Wallace to carefully apply my new makeup for blondes, put on the wrinkle-free black suit, and slip into matching pumps. Instead of a hat, I opted for a rose-print silk scarf, smiled at Hollis and exited the motel like the WASP princess I was trained to be.

Jeremy met me at the curb in front of the dealership, looking more than a little piqued. "Park by the service door in the back. It's more private," he ordered.

Uh-oh. In politics, the morning after a debate is a bitch for the loser. I wasn't surprised to see him metaphorically walking on eggshells, especially since Billy had owned the crowd until O'Grady used his daughter for a Hail Mary pass.

I parked where I was told and followed Jeremy through a small metal door at the back of the repair shop to meet Billy. He looked like one of his campaign posters in spit-shined wing tip shoes, a pressed khaki suit, light blue shirt and red silk tie. The only thing missing was the big politician grin.

We followed behind Billy to a tiny office with a single fluorescent light hanging from the ceiling. The dingy room smelled like motor oil and paint thinner. It was a far cry from the swanky executive office I'd imagined. Billy crossed his arms and leaned back in an industrial desk chair behind a metal desk. At his nod, Jeremy and I sat in beat up, vinyl chairs.

After a long, uncomfortable minute, Billy growled, "You came a day early. That was a surprise. I don't like surprises,"

I twisted in the uncomfortable chair. "I can explain."

"I hope so." He leaned toward me. "Because I need to know what in God's name you were thinking when you decided to stay in *my* room at the hotel, cozy up with Hal Glass and that magpie Tammy Eldridge—and run all over town in short-shorts, turning heads and making tongues wag."

How could he possibly know all that? I remembered Leroy hovering in the background of the dining room when I told Hal that Billy had 'offered' me his room. Did Leroy carry that lie to Billy in hopes of a reward for turning me in? Perhaps I'd underestimated the boy.

My hands felt like ice, while my dress stuck to the back of the chair. I repeated, "I c…can explain."

"Then do it! Before I send you packing."

Sometimes the truth is the best defense, so I gave it a try. "I came early because I was afraid Maddox would tell my name—and yours—to the press. A strange car flashed its lights at my window after midnight and I was afraid someone had followed Jeremy. So, I left."

He cocked his head, no longer looking like he wanted to murder me and stuff my body in the trunk of his big Caddy, but still not convinced I was telling the truth. I took a chance and leaned toward him. "But it turned out to be a good thing."

He folded his hands on the coffee-stained blotter. "How so?"

"Ho-Jo's was full. They sent me to the Glass House. I didn't know the room was yours until Hal introduced himself to me in the dining room and asked how I knew you. I explained I was here for my grandmother's funeral and you were an old friend—of the family."

His mouth relaxed, but the glare remained. "Hal Glass is a lot of things, but stupid isn't one of them. He's the town historian and knows every family name in Jeffers. He'll know you're lying about the dead maw-maw."

I thought fast. "All you gave me was the ID and a letter of reference. When he confronted me about staying in your room without a reservation, I had to improvise. The story about the grandmother got sympathy from him. He even offered to help me with the arrangements."

His, "I'll bet he did," was sly. "What about Tammy?"

That one was easy. "I met her at the library and didn't know she was O'Grady's cousin until the debate. But I found out he hasn't replaced his nanny yet, so now I have an inside track with him. Isn't that what you wanted?"

I leaned back. "Overall, I think it was a very productive weekend."

He fished a pack of Marlboros from his jacket pocket, lighting one with the engraved Zippo lighter. After only a couple of drags, he crushed it out in a glass, "Big Billy's Cadillacs" ash tray.

"Okay. For now," he exhaled. "No harm done I suppose. And O'Grady likes blondes, though Barbara's was natural. But no more surprises, y'hear?"

"Barbara? You mean his dead wife?"

I remembered Billy had said he picked me for the job after one look. "Why does the color of my hair matter? I'm here to do an investigation, not an impersonation."

"Is that so, *Sarah?*"

"That was your idea, and you know what I mean. I won't be a whore to get a story."

His gold eyes reflected the flash of the blinking fluorescent light. He leaned toward me. "We're all whores, Laura. We sell a piece of ourselves every day. It's called survival."

A chill ran up my spine in the suffocating room. Where was the man with dreams of uniting the country? The man who tried to stop Lester Maddox?

"Is that why you ranted about the collapse of society as we know it if we integrate Southern schools? Do you really believe Negroes don't deserve a decent education? Or did you just say those things to get votes?"

I blinked first under his cold amber stare and he said, "In case you haven't noticed, the purpose of a debate—of a campaign—is to *get votes!* People don't like change. I told them what they wanted to hear, not necessarily what will happen. I still believe what I told you in Atlanta."

Sounding like Winkler, he added, "You're smart, but your tongue's a little too sharp for my taste. Here in the South, we dance before we lay down together."

So, the debate was just a dance to him? He was unlike any politician I'd ever seen. Mercurial didn't begin to describe it. Or naive. In Atlanta, he'd called the police about Maddox attacking the black men in his parking lot; then in his hometown, declared them to be barely human. Which was the real Billy?

"So, you didn't mean the racist things you said yesterday?"

"Racist?" He chuckled. "Honey, I grew up too poor to be racist. The Civil Rights ball is already rolling. Coloreds have their rights on paper.

Whites will find ways around the law, and life won't change that much. I'll go with the flow."

Coloreds? It was another label used to further denigrate all shades of black people. It may have been his Georgia Cracker roots showing, but his amoral approach to justice made me sick. While he wasn't so different from most politicians in 'going with the flow', at least he admitted it. And I had to stay unbiased. It could all come out in my story.

Still, I couldn't let him think I was a pushover. I stood to lean over him, my clammy palms on the gritty desk. "Well I don't dance—or lay down—with my bosses. You said you had information on the O'Gradys going back generations. I've heard about the feud between your families. If I'm going to do what you hired me to do, I need to know all the players, alive *and* dead."

The twitch in his lips told me my power-stance had given him a perfect view down the front of my scooped neckline. I sat down, thinking the only way to get a man's attention in the South seemed be through your cup size.

He finally looked at Jeremy. "Park the Beetle in the number three garage and replace it with something from the used car lot. I think we have a Dart 330 ready to go."

"Wait a minute! You can't take my car."

Mischief now glowed from Billy's eyes. "Didn't you say it was on the news?"

"Well, yes, but I've already been seen in it here. It would look strange if I had a different car after only two days. And I've told people I'm from Boston, so the plate isn't a problem."

I held my breath while he decided the fate of my Pacific Blue baby. He nodded to Jeremy. "Run it through the wash while *Sarah* and I have a little talk."

"Sure thing, Billy. Sir." He stumbled over his chair in his haste to leave.

When the metal door down the hall slammed shut, Billy took the seat next to me. His Jade East cologne filled my senses and my pulse raced when a long, tanned finger touched my cheek. "So, you want to know my family history."

"Well, yes. But only as it applies to the investigation."

"Oh, it's relevant, all right. It's the beginning of the Langesford and O'Grady trail of lies." His face softened the way Tammy's had when she told me about the history of the library. As if the past felt more real than the present.

"In 1732, the first William Berens, a stonemason, was one of the few debtors in London's Newgate Prison to sail with James Oglethorpe's gaggle of fops and second sons of gentry. His wife, for lack of a doctor willing to muddy his shoes at their doorstep, died in childbirth. He was thrown into prison for stealing milk for his motherless child. After the babe died, he was supposed to be grateful for a chance to serve in the galley of the *Anne*."

The posturing car salesman and shouting politician disappeared as Billy recounted his family's legacy. Without the fake hype for TV and radio ads, his deep voice was mesmerizing. If he'd been more like this at the debate, O'Grady would have met his match.

Resisting the urge to touch his hand, I listened to the story of how the founder of his family, a poor and uneducated stonemason, contributed as much to building America as Patrick O'Grady's ancestors—and mine. I realized how often we forget about the men and women who risked their lives for little pay and no recognition to build America's homes, bridges, dams, and roads.

William Henry Berens was one of those men. And his second wife, Elizabeth, who bore seven children in the New World, was one of those women.

"Wow. That's some story," I said when he finished. "But it's ancient history. As unfair as it is, nobody cares about debtor prisons anymore." *Or who founded the great state of Georgia.*

"I disagree," he snapped. "While my family struggled to survive on a few acres of land, James Langesford got rich off the backs of poor Whites."

"And Blacks," I added.

"Yes, the Negroes. Well, that's another story."

"What other story?"

The wicked smile returned. "That's where you come in."

"What do you mean?

We turned when Jeremy knocked on the open door. "The car is ready."

Billy nodded to him and looked at me for a long moment. "In due time, Laura."

I followed them both to my car. When I'd stepped inside and closed the door, Billy leaned on the open window frame to say, "Keep your head low from now on."

I couldn't argue with that. For someone who prided herself on being invisible, I'd made enough mistakes in the last few days. I should have let

Jeremy know I'd arrived early. Leroy at the Glass House was way too curious, and I didn't know if I could trust Hal. But if I'd waited until Sunday morning to leave Atlanta, I'd have missed the debate. For me, it was worth it. I reached for the key in the ignition.

"Hold on," Billy said. He pulled a notepad and pencil out of his breast pocket, jotting something down before ripping off the page and handing it to me. "Directions to my cabin."

"Cabin? What? No!" I tried to give the note back to him. "I'm okay now. I have a room at the Motor Lodge. It's cheap, and close to town for the library. Really, I'm fine."

"I'm the boss, remember? You're too noticeable in town and the motor lodge has housekeepers in and out of the rooms. And you don't need a library. I have everything you need. We'll go over it later."

"But…"

"No buts. Go back to Ho-Jo's and tell that lunkhead Hollis you found a long-lost relative to stay with. Jeremy will pick up supplies and meet you at the light on Route 41 in an hour."

My stomach tightened as I stared at the address. I knew the difference between a street and a road. No matter where you lived, streets were paved, and roads were little more than ruts. And a road named Moccasin Wallow couldn't be good.

"Wait a minute. Where is this? I can't just disappear. Mr. Glass invited me for lunch." It wasn't true, but I didn't like the idea of being in the middle of nowhere with only this unpredictable man and his toady knowing where I was.

The car salesman smile disappeared, and his voice lowered to little more than a growl. "Don't worry about *Mister* Glass."

"But—" Male voices from the morning shift reporting for work cut me off.

Billy flashed the smile I'd seen at the Pickrick and leaned closer. "We'll talk later. The cabin has a generator, running water, and a phone. Trust me, you'll like it."

I didn't hear anything after generator. "Billy, I don't like this. I…"

His lips suddenly covered mine. The gentle pressure and surprise touch of his tongue left me speechless when he pulled back.

"Hey, Billy," came from behind us.

He stepped back with a smug smile, turning toward a man in a blue shop uniform. "Logan" was embroidered on a red and white patch above his breast pocket.

Billy waved. "Hey, Randy," I'm finishing up an emergency battery charge. Give us a minute."

Logan, I remembered. Randy Logan from the debate? The one O'Grady had used as an example of red-neck ignorance?

Billy handed me his business card and said louder than he needed to, "Don't worry, Miss Tucker. We stand behind our service. If you need anything, call—any time."

He turned from me to join Randy and they swaggered back to the garage.

"Good ol' boys," I muttered, spinning gravel when I left the parking lot.

CHAPTER 9

I followed Jeremy for twenty minutes, from the light on Route 41, otherwise known as Negro Island Road, and turned off the pavement at a weathered, hand-painted wood sign saying, "Berens land—keep off". After another five minutes of bouncing between Georgia pines on ruts made for a wider vehicle, like Jeremy's Bonneville, or Billy's Cadillac, I parked next to him at the edge of a clearing.

I stepped out, surprised at how cool it was on the edge of the old pine forest, then looked ahead at Billy's cabin. "What the hell?"

While it technically fit the definition, the one-story Cracker cabin with hand-notched logs had a wide porch atop a fieldstone foundation, and a sloped metal roof. In short, it was every writer's dream. I followed Jeremy up the wide wood steps and while he unlocked the shuttered front doors, I veered left, resting my hands on a varnished pine railing overlooking the gently sloped clearing.

"This is my second favorite version of heaven," I said.

"Heaven and Hell are in the eye of the beholder," he answered from the now-open front doors. "I'll start the generator out back."

He took the steps two at a time and I stepped through pine doors inset with stained-glass panels of calla lilies, into a large, open interior. The great room floorplan had a gourmet kitchen/dining/living area with a breakfast bar and furniture arranged around what looked like an original stone fireplace.

Natural light chased the shadows from what I assumed was the bedroom at the back. A low hum outside told me the generator was working and Jeremy came inside, arms filled with grocery sacks.

"A few supplies?" I laughed. "This could last a month."

"You never know how long something like this will take," he muttered.

"But doesn't Billy live here?"

"No. He has a place above the dealership," he answered, focusing on loading food into the enormous Frigidaire's bins.

I wandered off to peek into the bedroom, again surprised at the tasteful, understated furnishings in the glitzy car dealer's country home. Rustic pine beams lined the ceiling paneled in more Georgia pine above an antique double bed covered by an heirloom, bear's paw quilt. Did Billy know the pattern was a signal for escaping slaves to follow the mountain trails?

I looked around for a bathroom. Billy said there was running water and I saw a modern stainless-steel sink in the kitchen, but the only door in the bedroom led to the great room.

"All set," Jeremy said from behind me, a smile finally lightening his features. "C'mon, I'll show you the outhouse."

"Outhouse?"

"Right. Billy loves anything big and new but holds on to the past with a vengeance. The old house wasn't big enough for a decent bathroom and he was careful to keep the original footprint when he renovated."

"But an *outhouse,"* I whined, ready to run back to my car.

For the second time that day, I heard, "Trust me, you'll like it."

I followed him as he stepped past me to open a floor-to-ceiling armoire and walked through it onto a narrow, Spanish-tiled pathway toward another, smaller building next to the cabin.

"It's a dog trot," he explained. "The house is split in two with a space between. I think they're called breezeways up north."

It wasn't like any breezeway I'd ever seen. Instead of walls, tightly packed, six-foot shrubs beneath a roof/trellis of fragrant, purple wisteria, led to a cedar-frame building almost half the size of the main house. I hoped the half-moon cutout on the door was just for whimsy.

Speechless, I followed him inside to see a full sauna next to an oversized claw-foot tub. On the other side of the sauna, a water closet and separate shower big enough for two faced a cedar-lined walk-in dressing room. It was like walking into a European spa in the middle of a Georgia swamp. I repeated, "What the hell?"

"This is where the old kitchen and woodshed were," he explained. "The water's heated by a hot spring on the other side of the woods, on Langesford land."

"Langesford? How?"

His voice lowered. "It's a long story. But they never complained, especially after they built the dam that floods our land every spring."

For the moment, I didn't care about water rights. I just wanted to try out that claw-foot tub. "This is amazing."

"I suppose so—now," he conceded and turned to leave.

"What do you mean?" I asked and followed him.

Once outside, he took a deep breath and looked toward the forest. "The first house was here, on the original twenty-acre homestead given to Oglethorpe's crew members. The first William chose timberland and watershed, along with good rich soil, while the aristocrats like James Langesford, took the high ground. After the Revolution, Langesford finagled state land grants and bought out the small householders around his land. But we wouldn't sell—then or any other time they offered."

His dark eyes looked sad when he said, "The story goes downhill from there. Billy tells it better than me."

I had to step quick to follow him around the house, past the humming generator and back to the front porch where the two wood rockers begged for someone to sit down—so we did. Our chair runners sounded like synchronized hearts on the weathered plank floor, as we rocked in comfortable silence. We could have been old friends enjoying an afternoon lemonade.

Jeremy broke the silence. "Billy inherited the land from his pa when he was twenty, but my Great-Granddaddy, Cyrus Berens, lived here all his life. Billy inherited it when he was twenty, but never set foot here until after old Cy died. By then, the roof was cavin' in, windows were broken, and the pump barely worked."

The sadness in Jeremy's voice when he mentioned the old man, hinted they'd been close. "How long ago was that?"

He stopped rocking and leaned forward, staring at his hands. "'49. I was almost seven and he was eighty-six. He nodded toward the new spa. "My ma found his body back by the old privy. The path was rough back then. Likely he tripped during the night and hit his head on a stone. But I remember him. He was strong as an ox. While we lived with him, he was more like a daddy to me than a great-granddaddy."

Lived with him? Here? With broken windows and no plumbing? Why? How? But those were questions for later. As a Bostonian, I knew early Eighteenth-Century architecture. There was no way this house had stood for more than two centuries. Not in Georgia, and so close to a river. Floods notwithstanding, the humidity, weeds, and bugs would have consumed it in sixty to eighty years, no matter how well the railings were varnished.

"Are you saying this house has been here since the 1700's?"

"Of course not," sounded sharp. "The flood after Langesford built the dam in 1798 took the first one down the river, along with most of the good topsoil. The second was destroyed by Cherokee, and Sherman burned the third. But a Berens has lived on this land since the first William stepped on it. And every replacement has been built on the original foundation."

He swatted at a fly. "Old Cy was first cousin to Billy's Granddaddy, William II."

"Tell me about Cyrus," I urged.

Maybe it was the fresh air, or the distance from Billy, but he seemed to relax for the first time since we'd met. "He was born in the third cabin, before the War. While it belonged to Billy's side of the family, he helped build the fourth after Sherman burned it. They let Cy and his family live here, even after his son, my grandfather, moved to town."

He gave me a long look before adding, "My ma moved here when—before I was born. We stayed on after Cy passed. When Hal came back to town, he offered Ma a job at the Glass House and a place to stay. Billy started fixing it up about ten years ago."

"But why, if he doesn't live here? Is it for guests?" If so, I wondered why he leased a guest room at the Glass House—especially given his dislike of Hal. *Curiouser and curiouser.*

"The hotel is for business guests, but he brings...other people here now and then. He fixed it up for Barbara."

"Barbara O'Grady?" I choked.

He stared at the field in front of us. "Her name was Kinney back then. She and Billy were close...when they were kids. She dated Patrick in high school, but when he left for Emory, over in Atlanta, she went back to Billy. He was fixing to marry her."

It took only a few seconds to put two and two together before I bolted up from my chair. "So, Billy hired me to get even with the man who married his girlfriend? I'm glad I didn't unpack my car."

Jeremy stood too, his chair joining mine in a manic rocking frenzy. "No! Don't go! You really are here because of the election. It's way past time to put the bad blood 'twixt our families to rest. That's why I took Hal's advice to hire you. I'm not sure why Billy picked now to dig up the old grudges, but he's cutting his nose off to spite his face. Nobody's gonna look good if all the dirty laundry is hung out."

"What do you mean?"

He ran his fingers through an ivy league haircut very similar to Hal's and flopped back into his still-rocking chair. "I don't know a lot, but Cy told me crazy stories about how a Langesford 'debauched' a Berens woman, then kidnapped her baby. He ranted about an O'Grady murdering Billy II, and rumors that a Langesford robbed a Yankee mint during the War. He claimed some of the lost gold was buried on our land. Dug holes all over the woods looking for it."

His smile was a little sad. "I was just a kid and believed every crazy thing he said. The first summer after he died, and we moved to town, I snuck back and poked around some. But all I found was an old washtub partly buried alongside the old privy, near where we…found Cy. The lid was rusted shut, but I opened it enough to see some leather pouches, junk and a couple small bricks inside. Billy caught me and I showed it to him. He said he wouldn't tell my ma if I promised never to come back."

"What about Barbara—and Billy?" I pressed.

He took a deep breath. "After Patrick left for Emory, Billy took a job as a traveling salesman and picked back up with Barbara. Then he started fixing the place up. After a couple years, he bought the Caddy dealership and told everybody they were getting married."

What could have been a laugh sounded more like a snort when he added, "Everybody except Barbara I guess, because two months after Patrick came back, she married him. A year or so later, they had a kid. When she died, Billy accused him of killing her."

I shivered in the warm breeze at learning about Barbara O'Grady's mysterious death. But it only confirmed that Billy hired me out of revenge for losing her. That wasn't the story I came to write. Still, the holes in Jeremy's tale intrigued me.

"Look, I'm sorry about your great-grandfather, and that you had to live like that—here—but I won't be party to Billy's vendetta for being jilted. There must have been something besides papers, bricks, and silverware in that box you found for a small-town mechanic and traveling salesman to buy a car dealership." I waved at the hand-made stained-glass doors. "And renovate this house in just a few years."

He shrugged. "Truth be told, the dealership was all but dead due to old man Tait's gambling problem and fondness for 'brown sugar'.

"Brown sugar?" I asked. "Oh. You mean…"

"Heroin. Yes. There, you have everything I know. If you want more, you can ask Billy. But be careful."

That again. "Why?"

"Because our family's been called thieves and treated little better than niggers for generations. I just wanted you to understand the bad blood between our families—and between Billy and Patrick."

He took a deep breath and stood, tossing me the house key. "It's getting late. I gotta go before the deer come out. My number is on the refrigerator. Call me if the generator stops."

I watched the Bonneville glide over ruts that had nearly swallowed my Beetle. When he turned at the end of the trail, I rubbed my arms at a sudden chill. Winkler had said Billy and Patrick were distant cousins. It must have been from that ancient seduction and baby-napping. And the feud was still going on nearly two hundred years after.

Billy had promised to come 'later', but as dusk settled with no sign of him, I made a grilled cheese sandwich and washed it down with a 1954 Merlot. I put on my muumuu and got comfortable on the couch with the old journal and the rest of the Merlot.

D. T. was not a faithful journal-keeper. After her forced marriage to the '*farmier*' she only seemed to turn to it in times of crisis. I was grateful that over the years, she included more English words into her French, and I couldn't put it down as the entries painted a riveting portrait of the tragic young *demoiselle's* life.

By 1851, she'd given birth to two children, her first the son, "B" she'd hoped for and referred to as '*mon petit chou*'—an eight-pound baby boy born two months early—that she'd apparently had no trouble convincing her besotted husband was his. The daughter who came four years later was another story. Her mother declared the red-haired, "C" a '*diable*'.

I stopped reading after the author ranted about how the rebellious "C" had ridden her brother's spirited stallion through her mother's Renaissance picnic and that the much-maligned husband, "A", had refused to whip the child. I took a deep breath and reached for the wine bottle, pouring what was left into my glass and taking a long sip. I set the half-filled goblet next to the book on the side table before switching off the light to rest my eyes.

The sudden glow of white light through the stained-glass calla lilies startled me awake in the unfamiliar room. Then the light went out. Recalling the flashing headlights outside my apartment, I nearly knocked the lamp over fumbling for the switch.

"Shit," I moaned at seeing both my glass and the book on the Navajo rug, wine already staining the priceless Native American artifact and seeping onto the end pages of D.T.'s journal. I dropped to my knees, picked up the journal and empty glass with one hand, while using the other to sop up the mess with my muumuu.

"Sarah, I'm home," Billy called playfully when he opened the door.

I popped my head up over the back of the couch. With his jacket over his arm, sleeves rolled up and tie loosened, he looked like Cary Grant in *The Man with the Gray Flannel Suit.* The top two buttons of his shirt were open, and a five-o'clock shadow darkened his face, making him look dangerous—and so attractive.

"Laura, are you all right? What happened?" He dropped the jacket, covering the distance between us in two strides to scoop me into his arms and rush toward the bedroom.

I pushed at him with sticky red fingers when I realized he was heading for the antique quilt. "No, wait. I'm fine," I slurred. "It's wine, not blood. Your headlights startled me."

He stopped, and I slid down his body to stand on the cool, polished wood floor. Then I unwrapped my arms from his neck and stepped back, waiting for him to fire me for my fourth strike. After the Pickrick fiasco, arriving early in Jeffers and picking the wrong tree at the rally, now I'd ruined his priceless Navajo rug—and very expensive suit.

He looked from me to his stained clothes and surprised me by laughing. Then I laughed. Still more than a little drunk, I dropped to the floor, laughing and crying at the same time. He sat beside me, pulling me into his lap and holding me until my wine-induced hysteria stopped. I raised my head slowly. Instead of anger or disgust in the self-made man's face, those translucent gold eyes glowed with—understanding?

"You done?" he asked with a Cheshire Cat smile and rose to offer his hand.

I wiped my face with the hem of my muumuu and resisted the absurdly gallant offer to stand on my own, albeit a little shaky. Then I caught my reflection in the cheval mirror.

"Oh my God," I shrieked, covering my face with my hands. How much worse could the evening get? I peeked through my fingers.

He stepped past me in his ruined shirt and tie, then opened the fake armoire to the dog trot, and bowed, "Ladies first. I'll make us something to eat while you clean up."

I couldn't disagree but also couldn't seem to keep my mouth shut. "No, it's okay," I babbled. "I had a grilled cheese after Jeremy left. And I need to clean the wine from the rug before it dries, or it'll never come out."

"No! What you need to do is pull yourself together."

He wasn't smiling anymore, and I knew that voice. My father, my brothers, even Mr. Winkler. But I was in no position to argue. A glance at the Halloween zombie in the mirror told me he was right. And I'd waited all evening to ask my questions about Barbara O'Grady and Jeremy's washtub treasure.

"Right," I answered, still a little tipsy, and turned to rifle through my bag for clean underwear and a change of clothes. When the bedroom door closed behind him, a humiliated moan crept up from my soul.

CHAPTER 10

A half-hour later, wearing fresh jeans and a clean blouse, I followed the aroma of rosemary chicken to the kitchen where I stepped up to sit on a stool and tried to look nonchalant.

"Well, well," Billy said, his gaze assessing me from head to toe. "You clean up good."

His smile again took my breath away, especially knowing how his lips felt. He'd tossed his dress shirt, wearing a sleeveless undershirt tucked into clean, well-fitting jeans. The aroma from the oven made my mouth water—while the play of his muscles through the thin shirt made other parts of me tingle. I shifted on the stool. "Thank you, I think. When do we eat?"

"Don't worry," he said when I looked toward the living room where I'd just ruined an irreplaceable rug, not to mention a historically significant journal. "Club soda takes out almost any stain. I think there was more on you and that old book, than the rug."

I groaned. "The book."

"What's the matter?"

"It's really old and could be valuable. Tammy loaned it to me. She thought it might be part of the Langesford collection, but she was wrong."

"How do you know?" came from inside the refrigerator.

"It's written in French. Creole."

The refrigerator door shut with a solid thud. "Creole?"

He smiled at my nod. "The chicken will be done in a few minutes. Let's sit down and relax before we eat."

He led me back to the couch and the rug I'd defiled. The bottle and glass were gone, and the journal sat alone on the coffee table. Most of the carpet stain was gone. What was left blended with the rug's natural dyes until it was barely noticeable.

I picked up the journal, turning it over in my hand. The leather binding had repelled most of the wine, but the end sheet on the back page was still damp and stained crimson. I checked the pages from the back to the front. D. T. had stopped writing well before the end of the journal. Why?

Billy sat next to me. "Whose is it?"

"I don't know. A young girl in New Orleans who was forced to marry a man she didn't love. It's hard to translate after all this time. Creole penmanship was very individualized, and the writing was fragmented, to say the least."

His right eyebrow rose. "I thought I saw initials on the inside cover."

"Yes. 'D.T'. She wrote that her new husband was from what she called, the wilderness of Georgia. Perhaps it was around here—not that Jeffers is... was...wilderness."

"No offense taken." He lifted a glass of what smelled like fine scotch. "The description probably fit the whole state at one time. Do you know when it was written? Who she married?"

His interest in a long-dead French woman's diary didn't fit with the macho image he favored. I suddenly felt uncomfortable sharing D.T.'s private thoughts and set the journal back on the table, out of his reach. "The entries are scattered from the 1840s to the '60's. I felt like a voyeur and just skimmed it."

That was a lie. She'd become real to me. I'd felt her heart break when her new husband's carriage pulled away from her beloved Belle Rivière. And I felt it turn to stone when she vowed to see her father dead.

"Voyeur?" Billy chuckled. "You do realize she's long dead." He touched my cheek. "I know people in New Orleans. If there's a name in there, I can have them check it out."

"No!" I said a little too harshly, touching his arm when he reached for the journal. "I mean, she only used initials. It's very valuable, historically speaking, and I've already nearly ruined it. It needs to dry out and we have other things to talk about."

He stood and gave the journal a narrow look, sounding testy when he said, "We can talk business after we eat. I'll check on the chicken."

The meal included more wine. White this time. While it doesn't knock me for a loop like red, it still loosens my tongue. I droned on about my life in boarding schools, excluding the night Ricky and I consummated our—friendship—after an Amherst frat party. But when I questioned Billy, he reciprocated with what sounded like a well-rehearsed story about a hard-scrabble childhood and boring bachelor life, omitting his courtship of Barbara Kinney.

It was well past midnight when we finished the dishes. He grabbed another bottle of wine, a Castellani Chianti this time, and we returned to the couch. I smiled at his choice. "You saved the best for last."

"Not even close." He looped his arm through mine as we sipped together.

He put a record on, and Aretha Franklin sang the blues while the ceiling fan distributed night breezes from the surrounding forest. The air smelled of fresh, damp earth, old leaves and green grasses, sweetened by the clean scent of pine. I was barefoot, the top two buttons of my sleeveless blouse open, while Billy seemed more than comfortable in his undershirt and jeans. He pulled me close and I leaned into him, my cheek resting on his bare shoulder.

"Tell me about Barbara," I whispered.

He stood so quickly my head bounced off the back of the couch. Aretha began, *Won't be Long*, and Billy held out his hand.

"Let's dance."

I smiled, remembering his comment that in the South people danced before they laid down together. It didn't matter. I set aside politics and slid into his arms to dance through *Running out of Fools.* And when Aretha began. *It's in His Kiss,* we did.

It was slow, hot, and lasted so long I felt dizzy. Or was it the red wine followed by white wine, followed by Chianti? This time I didn't protest when he picked me up and headed for the bedroom.

I knew from the way he undressed me that he'd had practice in seducing women—and I didn't care. Standing close to me, he slowly opened each button on my blouse, his lips and tongue tasting the skin along my throat, my chest, and belly until I writhed against the constraints of my jeans.

"Please," I moaned, "Now."

Instead, he pulled away and the Rock Hudson smile melted my insides. "Patience, Laura," he whispered in my ear. And as if he knew about my regrettable marriage and otherwise clumsy experiences with men, said, "Let me show you how a Southern Republican treats a lady."

Still standing, he reached through my open blouse to unhook my bra. I arched against him as he slid it and the blouse down my arms, then paused to admire his handiwork.

Suddenly embarrassed, I moved to cover myself, but he redirected my hands beneath his undershirt and raised his arms. I followed his lead to take things slow, despite the heat building inside me. I pushed the shirt up and he shrugged it off. My fingers and lips traced a path down the dark hair on his chest, reading the hard lines of his body that included old scars.

From his rough upbringing, I assumed, then unzipped his jeans and slid them down over strong, lean hips to discover he wasn't wearing boxers—or briefs. When I looked up, I recognized the heat of real passion in a man's gaze for the first time.

The dark centers of his eyes were rimmed by gold flecks, like the shimmering halo of an eclipse behind the shadowed moon. He stepped out of his jeans and I leaned closer to him, moaning as he slid mine, along with my panties, down to my ankles. I shook them off and wrapped my legs around him. His hands firm and warm under my hips, he turned to the bed. My breasts came alive when they touched his chest and we fell onto the priceless, antique quilt.

He leaned in to kiss me, then reversed our positions.

"We'll get dizzy," I laughed, stretching out on top of him.

His tongue tickled my ear. "This is only the beginning."

"You promise?"

I gasped when his hand cupped me...there...and his thumb touched the spot Ricky never quite discovered. It throbbed against his massaging fingertips until he flipped me and something else hard and warm touched me.

"Now, Laura," he said with as much urgency as I felt, and we both pushed at the same time. A collision? An explosion? The meeting of two irresistible forces? I was a writer and had no words for the pleasure my body felt when we both hit our climax that continued even after he gave, and I received.

Even in the throes of my first orgasm, my mind registered the difference between a full-grown man's passion and a virgin, adolescent boy's clumsy attempt at making love.

Then I forgot all about Ricky Hamilton and, "Oh my God, Billy," escaped my lips.

Instinct kicked in after that. Or carnal desires. Or just plain lust. Whatever it was, I knew love had nothing to do with us, at that moment, or the rest of the night. There were no tender words, no soft, gentle caresses. Our coupling came from a greater need than love, or even affection. It was about proving something—for both of us.

Afterward, we lay entwined in a tangle of rumpled sheets, both of us moist and breathless, the musky smell of sex mixing with the scent of jasmine and pine outside the open window. I blew an unfamiliar wisp of blonde hair from my face, finally able to define an orgasm.

"Wow."

He leaned on his elbow. "Wow yourself. You're one bright student."

So, my inexperience in the sack showed. I pulled the sheet up. "What do you mean?"

He pushed it back down and began that thing with his thumb and forefinger around my nipple until it begged for his tongue.

"I mean I know people in Hollywood," he mumbled against my neck. "I've even seen some of Dirk Sullivan's movies. Or should I say Richard Hamilton's? You're a very passionate woman—for a Boston Yankee. Marrying him was a terrible waste. Why did you do it."

So, he knew about my failed marriage. I damned Winkler's big mouth. But I didn't like his reference to either Ricky's secret life or my Boston background, and suddenly remembered my purpose. For the time being, anyway, I was Billy's employee.

Sober now, I grabbed another lump of sheet and rolled over. "I'm tired."

A few minutes later I heard the snore of a satisfied man lying next to me. At least Ricky went to his own room after sex.

I slipped out of bed, wrapped myself in the top sheet, and walked out to the shower. When I returned, Billy was still sleeping but his snores had diminished. I put on fresh panties and his discarded undershirt, then crawled back into bed as far away from him as possible.

It seemed I'd only closed my eyes when bright sunlight woke me, along with—birds?

"Wake up sleepy-head," was followed by a chaste kiss from lips tasting of coffee and something new. A slightly nutty flavor.

One eye opened, then the other and I beheld a bare-chested Billy, his hair still wet from the shower. Wearing plaid boxer shorts, he stood in a halo of sunlight with two steaming cups of that wonderful brew. I sat up to take one, and he stretched out next to me, on top of the sheet.

I held the cup with both hands, trying to look and sound nonchalant. "This coffee is wonderful. What's that other taste?"

"Chicory root. So, what do you think last night was about?"

I stared into my black coffee. "Temporary insanity."

His belly-laugh far exceeded the humor of my comment—which wasn't intended to be funny. "Temporary insanity is just an excuse for letting go of stick-in-the-ass inhibitions."

He gave me a hard look. "You should try it more often."

"What?"

"It's not your fault. You were raised that way, but when you let go, you're amazing. Admit it, at the Pickrick, when you were scared shitless, did you ever feel so alive? And last night, when you let yourself go, have you ever experienced that kind of freedom?"

I couldn't disagree with either point. I'd felt like another person when I was pounding on the window at the Pickrick. Brave. Willing to fight for what was right and suffer the consequences. It wasn't until it was over that I crumbled like a stale cookie.

He was also right about last night. It was a new experience for me. It brought out something I'd been hiding—or protecting—far too long. But while both events were terrifying and intoxicating, I couldn't afford to lose my head. I'd come to write the truth about Southern politics, and so far, Billy seemed more a mystery than the man he hired me to investigate.

He nudged me. "I didn't think so. Jeremy should be here soon. Time to go to work."

The mention of work roused me. Where I was from, work always came first and I didn't want Jeremy to see me like this. I gathered my clothes. The jeans would work another day, but the blouse was a mess. So was the dress from the day before. And the muumuu.

I ransacked my bag for one more blouse, then realized Billy was still on the bed, half naked. "Shouldn't you be getting decent too?"

He winked. "Oh Sugar, I'm more than decent, no matter what I wear. Or don't wear." After pulling a short-sleeved shirt over his bare chest, he stepped into a pair of linen trousers from the bureau.

All I could find at the bottom of my bag was a red-checked halter top. *How did that get in there?* Oh yes, it was next to the peasant blouse I'd planned to pack.

"Shit," I muttered when someone knocked on the front door. *Jeremy.* Grateful he'd knocked rather than using his key, I looked at the mess around us. "He's early!"

"Take it easy, girl. I'll handle Jeremy," Billy said. "Get dressed and clean up this mess. Meet us on the porch in ten minutes."

Ten minutes? He had to be kidding, but I accepted the challenge.

"I just got here myself," I heard him tell Jeremy at the door. "Woke her up." He chuckled. "Let's give her some time to put her face on."

Put my face on? That, along with being called sugar and girl, annoyed me, but I *was* wearing nothing but my Tuesday panties and his undershirt. It was time to clean up my *own* mess.

I ran to the bathroom to freshen up and put on the Daisy Mae outfit. Exactly ten minutes later, the bed made, the scent of gardenias outside the open window masking our night together, I put on my Boston dinner party smile and stepped onto the porch.

"You're early," I told them both.

Jeremy stood while his boss remained seated. "I'm so sorry. I figured you'd be up."

"Yes, *Sarah.*" Billy smiled, tilting back in the rocker. "We rise with the sun 'round here. I expect you'll get used to it."

You expect too much, I thought. One roll between the sheets did not make me his sugar, or his girl. I may have lost my mind to his amazing body once, but it wouldn't happen again. Somehow, I had to avoid his purely animal attraction and maintain my objectivity. Step one, stay away from wine.

"Still, you look well-rested," he added. "Fresh air and exercise suit you."

"Thanks." I sat on the top step, my back against the post.

"I'm so sorry," Jeremy apologized again and pointed to his rocker. "Take my chair, please."

Billy stood too, but not to offer me a seat. "We're not here to sit around and gab. Jeremy, take the evidence inside. "Laura, I mean Sarah, and I have business to discuss. I'll meet you back at the office later."

"Sure thing." Jeremy rushed past me to unload his car.

I glared at Billy. "Very funny. You should talk to him."

"Don't worry. The kid doesn't know a thing. The bloodline thinned out by the time it got to him. If you ask me, he's a little fey."

"A little what?" I knew what it meant, but all I saw in Jeremy was sincerity, loyalty, and an eagerness to please.

"A little on the girly side," he explained while lighting a Marlboro. "His pa left before he was born, and his ma raised him with her granddaddy. But he's under my wing now. I'll make a man out of him, one way or another. Let's get started."

He walked ahead of me into the cabin. Leaving the door open, he grabbed the briefcase he'd dropped by the threshold the night before.

It's better this way, I thought. We'd dealt with the animal lust thing. Once and done, for both of us. Now we were sober and could take care of business. He set the briefcase on the coffee table while Jeremy lumbered through the door balancing old banker's boxes and overstuffed leather pouches.

I caught a box just before it fell and said, "We can put these in the bedroom."

We stacked them by the bureau near the door, but he frowned when he looked at the bed. I hadn't covered our tracks as well as I thought and had made the bed hastily. There were more wrinkles than one person sleeping alone would cause. Frankly, it would never be the same.

His jaw set in disapproval and I finally saw the family resemblance, though not to Billy. Jeremy wasn't much younger than Hal had been at Westmoreland. And I'd seen the same clenched jaw and icy glare when I tried to slip anonymous essays into the Westmoreland Herald.

"Well that's all of it," he said, loud enough for Billy to hear, then surprised me by pressing his business card into my hand. "Call if you need me. Any time."

"Don't get too cozy in there," Billy called from the living room.

"Yes sir, I mean no sir," Jeremy called back with a mock salute only I could see. I slid the card into my pocket and followed him to the front door.

CHAPTER 11

When the Bonneville was out of sight, I met Billy's narrowed gaze. "I'm starving," he said. "Be a good girl and scramble up some eggs and bacon. And the left-over potatoes. We don't waste a thing in the South. And turnabout is fair play."

It rankled, but he'd made me dinner the night before.

I was in no mood to eat—maybe ever, so I threw all the leftovers into a frying pan. Twenty minutes later, I set a plate on top of his briefcase.

His lips dipped into a frown. "What did you do?"

"You said to scramble eggs, bacon, and potatoes and that's what I did." I sat beside him. "Do I get a tip?"

He took a bite and surprised me with a bacon-egg-and-potato-flavored kiss. "Name your price. I could get used to this."

I bet you could. "Okay, tell me about Barbara O'Grady. Who was she to you? And how did she die?"

His face froze, then he smiled slyly and opened the case just enough for me to see it was packed with my favorite kind of documents. Old ones.

"You sure you don't want to see what's in here first?"

Deflection. Perhaps the best tool in a politician's bag of tricks. I shook my head. "Nope. If I'm going after O'Grady, I need to know the background, especially if it's connected to you. I understand you and O'Grady are distant cousins and you dated Barbara before she married him."

His tanned complexion darkened and lines I hadn't noticed in the throes of passion, deepened along the sides of his mouth. His gold eyes reminded me of the wolf in *Little Red Riding Hood.*

"Jeremy has a big mouth."

"Questions are part of my job."

He considered it a moment. "Okay, I'll tell you the background, but she's off-limits. Never speak her name in front of me again."

His feral glare told me it wasn't a request. It was an order, maybe even a threat. I tried to lighten the mood by holding up my little finger. "Okay, I pinky-swear."

"You know I'll have to cut it off if you break your promise."

"I'm willing to take the risk," I answered, and he wrapped his matching finger around mine, pulling hard enough to make me flinch.

"Pour me a scotch," he said after nearly pulling my little finger out of its joint.

I wondered where the tenderness he'd shown me the night before had gone. Oh, right, he'd gotten what he wanted, and didn't need to be courteous. *Chauvinist pig.* Furious with him and even more with myself, I opened the antique radio/liquor cabinet and did as he ordered—without asking for another tip.

He downed it in one long gulp, then lit a cigarette. The smoke hovered between us like a tiny storm cloud, despite the ceiling fan circling above us. When the cigarette was down to the filter, he stubbed it out in the scraps on his plate, took a deep breath, and let it out slowly.

"The Kinney farm was on the other side of the woods from ours. It was an old sharecropper plot, ten acres of played-out dirt and weeds. I fell in love with Barbara when she was seven years old and punched me in the stomach for taking her lollypop."

His gaze fixed on the open window as if it was a portal through time. "Her ma died when she was four, trying to birth a son, who died too. At six, Barbara was doing double-duty as the woman of the house and farmhand."

He paused, a tiny smile flirting with the corners of his lips. "But now and then, we went skinny-dipping in the river—until her pa caught us. She was eight and I was eleven. Her pa beat the shit out of me." He scowled, handing me the glass to refill and draining it again before skipping ahead. "When she was fifteen, he died from work, worry, and whiskey. I started school late and was only two years ahead of her. We both hated it. The hillbilly, cracker jokes, and bullying never ended. I could fight back, and she knew how to throw a punch, but girls wound with their tongues, not their fists."

He could have set the house on fire with the hatred burning in his eyes when he finished, "Then Patrick O'Grady left his fancy private school and came to Jeffers High. The girls fluttered around him like flies to honey, but Barbara kept her distance. Maybe that's why the bastard took to her. Forbidden fruit."

The glass he'd been twirling in the morning sunbeam banged the table and I wondered if I was forbidden fruit to Billy. A rich, Yankee socialite to conquer and then humiliate. How sad. He had no idea I'd already been demoralized by the biggest of the Big Bullies—my own father.

I pictured Barbara, a tattered little moth in second-hand clothes hovering at the edge of the light shining on the resident rich boy, Patrick O'Grady. Billy was right about girls destroying their victims with acid tongues and dirty looks. Even money didn't protect you if you were different. I'd endured the whispers, giggles, sneers, even accusations of being a lesbian, for wanting to learn instead of flirting my way through school.

I also understood why Barbara dumped her poor buddy Billy for O'Grady. It was the '50's. A poor-but-pretty natural-blonde didn't have a lot of options besides snagging a rich husband. And a little town like Jeffers wouldn't have a lot of choices.

"Why did she and O'Grady break up?" What I really wanted to know was why she went back to Billy.

"Patience is a virtue." He handed me the empty glass. "I'll take another."

Wow, three straight-up scotches. At this rate he'd be smashed before noon. I hoped he wasn't a mean drunk. But I really didn't know Billy at all—yet.

He answered, "After graduation, O'Grady went off to stuck-up, stick-in-the-ass Emory and dumped Barbara cold. She fell apart. Couldn't sleep, wouldn't eat. Cried all the time."

His fist slammed the coffee table. "But I was there for her, Goddammit!"

I jumped, surprised to see tears in his eyes before he blinked and looked up at the ceiling fan. "Anyway, we got back together. I was her first—you know, before O'Grady. She always belonged to me."

Belonged? "What happened?"

After a long, uncomfortable silence, he said, "I worked at Smitty's Garage, takin' night classes from Middle Georgia Tech. while Barbara worked at Woolworth's, downtown. Then O'Grady graduated from college and came back." He raised his glass and glared at me. "An' that was the end of Barbara and me. So, there's your *tip*. Happy now?"

Not at all. The story was so cliché I didn't want to believe it. But the crack in his deep voice when he admitted Barbara jilted him, wasn't faked. I also knew he'd left a whole lot out. Men like Billy didn't give up that easily.

I blinked away my sympathy to say, "I'm so sorry you lost your love and understand why you would hate O'Grady." It may have been cruel, but I had to ask, "But did you hire me to ruin him because he gave Barbara Kinney the life you couldn't?"

If looks could really kill, I'd have been a pile of ashes, but his voice was steady when he opened the briefcase. "No, *this* is the reason I hate all the O'Gradys—and all the Langesfords before them."

He pulled out a pile of musty-smelling documents and files. "This, and the boxes in the bedroom have everything you need to tell the *real* story about exactly what kind of people have been running Georgia for the last two centuries."

He stood, as steady as if he'd been drinking lemonade. "I need to get back to the shop. A load of new convertibles is coming in. If it's up to Jeremy to unload, they'll be junk before they hit the lot. I'll be back tonight with the pièce de résistance,"

"What's that?"

He ran his thumb over my lips. "Patience, Laura. It's all in the documents. Thanks to that crazy old coot Cyrus, I can finally bury the O'Gradys for good."

Grabbing the now-empty briefcase, he set his hat at a cocky angle and headed to the door. "Leave the light on, honey. I may be late, but I'll make it worth your while."

Hal's warning that Billy always won, except for the one thing he wanted most, reminded me of the proverb, "Revenge is a confession of pain." Billy's pain had to be excruciating if he couldn't bear to hear Barbara's name. Would destroying her husband ease it?

I shivered in the warm room. Nanny Irene insisted sudden chills on a warm day were a warning from beyond the grave. I rubbed my arms and thought about quitting, but I'd dreamed of being a crusading reporter all my life. What Billy was planning to do was wrong, and it was past time for me to stand for something.

A cursory look through the boxes in the bedroom revealed maps and crumbling documents going back ten generations. If authentic, they'd be priceless, despite their terrible condition. I wanted to dive in, but it was too hot for rubber gloves and I'd need a mask against mold spores and rat droppings.

I moved to the couch to separate Billy's documents by family, type and year. Fortunately, someone (Jeremy?) had included a simple family tree for both clans, so I could follow the soap opera without wanting to shoot myself.

Grainy copies of original maps supported assertions of greed by the Langesfords, as successive plat maps incorporated smaller farms from the early settlement into Langesford plantation, along with a huge Georgia State land grant after the Revolution. But the first William Berens wasn't an easy mark. He chose the lowland for more than the fertile soil. I found a water lease agreement signed by Langesford in 1784, with terms that increased two percent every ten years—until 1900. Those types of forward-thinking terms were unheard of back then. I wondered if it had something to do with the allegedly kidnapped Berens child.

Obituaries, short newspaper notices and letters more than a century old chronicled the Berens' other unverified accusations against the Langesfords, including a pre-Civil War letter accusing Anthony Langesford's wife of murdering Nathan Berens, a groom at Langesford. An 1892 newspaper article accused Sean O'Grady, Patrick's great-uncle, of murdering Billy's grandfather, William Berens II. I leaned back on the couch and breathed easier. If this was Billy's 'evidence', against the Langesford/O'Grady legacy, I doubted it would influence voters—or a judge—in 1964.

After a break for left-over rosemary chicken and a Coke, I noticed Confederate enlistment papers dated July, 1863, listing a Samuel Berens, and a Brent Langesford as comrades in arms. It was followed by an old Daguerreotype photo of two Confederate soldiers with "S & B, 1863", scrawled on the back.

The dueling cousins stood shoulder-to-shoulder in their Confederate uniforms, bayonets polished, ready to march off to a war only one of them had a stake in—and that only marginally. By the start of the war, few plantations in Georgia held more than fifty slaves.

I paused to check Jeremy's family tree. Samuel was Billy's great-grandfather—father of William Berens II, the man Sean O'Grady allegedly killed. Samuel's likeness to Billy was amazing, with the same dark hair, square jaw and cocky half-smile. If not for the thin mustache, Billy could have posed for it. But it was Samuel's eyes that confirmed the relationship. Light-colored, they seemed to look right through the camera lens, daring anyone, or anything, to get in his way.

Lieutenant Langesford's thick dark hair was long for the day, curling at his neck, a stray wave falling over his forehead. Like Samuel, his eyes were light, but his lips curled into a sly smile on his clean-shaven face, as if amused by the whole thing.

Samuel Berens' obituary indicated he'd returned from the War and died of influenza in 1882. Poor thing, I thought, but what happened to Brent?"

Digging into the Langesford file, I found that Brent died a hero at the Battle of Chickamauga only months after he enlisted. The rest was obliterated by a dark ink stain on the back of the paper that had bled through. I turned it over to see crude, block lettering forming the word, 'TRAITOR'.

A year later, in 1864, the death notice of New Orleans-born Danielle Trémon-Langesford, listed Brent as her previously deceased son, her husband, Anthony Langesford, and daughter Camilla as her surviving family. Again, much of the memorial was obscured by ink from the other side. I turned it over and found, 'NIGGER'. written in the same hand as on Brent's death notice.

"Whoa, Nelly," I whispered. Was that the O'Grady secret? The one that Billy said would be their political ruin? My Yankee mind told me it was too long ago to matter, but my months in the South reminded me it was possible. Post-Revolution anti-miscegenation laws were still in effect throughout the South—and still enforced more than half-way through the 20th century. The revelation could bring into question O'Grady's rights to Langesford Plantation. No wonder Jeremy insisted on hiring someone to verify the accusation.

If this was in the washtub Jeremy found as a child, I wondered why Billy had waited so long to pursue it. It pissed me off that Jeremy was holding back. Why?

I looked up at the mantle clock. Seven-thirty? How did that happen?

While I didn't know Billy's definition of late, I scrambled to the kitchen to whip up my only specialty besides grilled cheese. Meatloaf. Then back to the obits. I bumped the side table, again sending the beleaguered red leather journal onto the carpet.

It opened at the back cover. The wine-soaked end sheet had peeled away as it dried, revealing two tissue-thin papers folded behind it. My heart raced and my head throbbed. Why hide something in the back of your own diary?

I picked it up gently, hoping against hope, that the initials, D.T. on the journal did *not* stand for Danielle Trémon. The wife of the owner of the great Langesford Plantation—and the woman accused of murdering Nathan Berens in 1851.

I stared at the journal as the mantel clock ticked away the minutes. No, it couldn't be that easy. Another sudden chill told me it was.

While sympathetic with the writer's plight at first, I'd stopped feeling sorry for her as she continued to worship her unnamed lover and denigrate her hard-working husband, "A". And after the diabolical daughter vs. angelic son parts, I really had no interest in taking it back up. Now, the note hidden behind the stained end page dared me to open it.

I pried it loose with my fingernail file and pulled the expensive hand-laid paper with an elaborate 'T' watermark, from its hiding place. The wine had only tinted the outside edges, leaving the rest remarkably well-preserved. It was dated 1851.

He rode a pale horse. After eleven years, I knew him the moment he raised his head to me. My beloved, my one true love! He dismounted, giving his horse to that sniveling Berens boy, Nathan, who lingered overlong. I chased him off and ran to my love. At last! He'd found me.

But he asked after my husband instead. Husband? My dearest Delmont will always be my husband. My first, my always. He had no worries. My jailer lived with his precious horses. We strolled to the shadowed arbor, hope filling my heart. Was Papa finally dead?

We were startled by my darling Brent and I pulled him to my side, introducing Delmont to his son. My heart leaped for joy when he recognized his own tousled black curls and high forehead. A moment later he dismissed our child and told me my Papa has been dead five years. It was greed that spurred my love to come to me. Greed that has turned him into a cruel monster.

Still clinging to the hope of our reunion, I asked about my inheritance, only to be told that after banishing me, Papa succumbed to the sins of the flesh. Belle Rivière went to the tax collector, and he took a room in the Quarter, dying a pauper in a pool of his own filth.

But Delmont's father was a wealthy attorney. Surely it would only be a matter of time before the Marchaud holdings passed to him. I offered to sell my mother's jewels to join him in New Orleans. His laugh sent starlings to flight and my world crashing around me. He said our love was an abomination, our child a monster. I write his words here because I cannot bear to say them aloud:

"Fate gave you Philippe Trémon's fair hair and skin, but from your stature to your bearing, you favor your real mother, the slave named Flora DeBoucher. You are a nigger, he spat. "And so is your high-yellow son."

I demanded to know why he said these cruel lies, but my love was gone. Hatred glowing from his dark eyes, he pulled out a copy of a page from his father's journal, written the night I was born. Choking on my tears, I listened to the violent tale of my birth from a woman of color, while my father's wife died in childbirth, taking their son with her to heaven.

Flora, my nursemaid, my slave, is my mother! But the Devil wasn't finished with me. Another page confessed that my marriage was arranged to keep Delmont from marrying a Negress! My whole life is a lie! A cruel joke by an unjust god. Yet I continued to draw breath. For Brent. I tore the hellish papers from him and ripped them, tossing the pieces into the shrubbery. Then I asked what price his silence commanded.

My mother's jewels. Or rather, the jewels belonging to my father's wife. I hid my joy at his paltry request. They mean nothing to me now. My heart is hollow. I close this journal now to await the reckoning. Until then, I live only for my son!

CHAPTER 12

Negro blood, I thought. The antiquated, "One Drop Rule" still in effect in most of the Southern states, declared that no matter how slight, evidence of a Negro ancestor legally defined you as one. Despite President Johnson's good intentions with the Civil Rights Act, anti-miscegenation laws declared inter-racial marriages illegal—thus denying the offspring of mixed-race relationships their rights of inheritance. The laws were still enforced in Georgia and as Billy had pointed out, the War had never ended for the South. I had no doubt this was the 'crime' Billy hired me to confirm, and if what I'd just read was true, Patrick O'Grady's political career could be in deep, deep trouble.

My hand shook with the realization that Tammy Eldridge had handed me a secret her family had successfully hidden for generations. A secret that could change history. Forgetting I professed to be an agnostic, I crossed myself like the nuns at St. Vincent's school had taught me.

But you can't put a genie back in the bottle, un-say a word once it's spoken, or un-know a certainty because you don't *want* to know it. I jumped as headlights again announced Billy's arrival. My head buzzing with the implications of my discovery, a meatloaf still in the oven, and Billy about to turn the key in the lock, I stuffed the obituaries back into the pile of papers and returned Danielle's confession to its pocket in the back of the journal, tucking it under a sofa cushion.

I breathed deeply to fight the panic gripping my stomach. Billy had seen the journal, and I'd blathered about when it was written and that it was in Creole French. It was probably too much to hope that he hadn't connected it to Danielle Langesford. But how much *did* he know?

Enough, I thought, based on the scribbling on the back of her obit, to accuse the O'Grady family of living a lie for over a century. But not enough to prove it—without authenticating the journal. Of course, I could destroy it, but it was a valuable historical artifact. And it didn't belong to me.

I shivered in the warm evening air. Would Billy really play the race card with just the journal? It wouldn't likely work in court, but the accusation alone would be headline news and potentially win him Edward O'Grady's seat in Congress. Patrick's slander lawsuit would be buried on page ten, if it was mentioned at all—and could take years to resolve.

Billy opened the door quietly this time, telling me he couldn't stay long. He had an early meeting with a campaign backer from Atlanta the next day. No doubt the wealthy donor would drive back in a nice new Caddy—at cost.

He also didn't bother to hide his disgust at my attempt to cook, offering to bring takeout from Dexter's Steak House next time. I didn't tell him there wouldn't be a next time, or that I planned to go back to the motor lodge in the morning.

"Suit yourself," I answered, my fork hovering in the air. "What did you bring for dessert?" reminded him of his 'piece de resistance,' though nothing could top what I'd already discovered.

He tossed his napkin on top of the food he'd barely touched. "What, no foreplay? You disappoint, Laura. What do you think of my evidence?"

I slowly folded my napkin on top of my own leftovers and told him what he wanted to hear. That I was shocked at the things the O'Gradys had gotten away with for generations, including the deaths of two family members—three if you counted Alice Berens/Langesford's death during childbirth. Then I leaned in, elbows on either side of my plate. "There was something unusual in the obits," I fished. "Traitor was written across Brent Langesford's and Nigger on the back of his mother's. What's that about?"

His lips twitched, and I knew I was right. He'd hired me to confirm the allegation.

He pushed his chair back and stood, smiling down at me. "I think it's time for dessert."

I followed him back to the couch, sitting on the cushion above the journal and refusing a scotch. Billy poured a double for himself and sat next to me to take a sip, light a cigarette and open his briefcase, in that order. It was empty except for two laminated sheets of plastic holding the tattered shreds of old-fashioned stationery.

My stomach lurched. They had to be the notes Danielle tore up and threw into the shrubbery. Someone had put the jigsaw puzzle of mangled shreds together. I doubted it was Billy, considering he'd stuffed priceless historical documents into bankers' boxes.

He handed it to me. "This is what killed Nathan Berens, my great-great-grandfather. And it's only one of the crimes the O'Gradys have been hiding for generations."

Now I wanted a drink. But I knew my hand would shake if I tried to pour one. And I was afraid to leave the cushion hiding the journal. "But this is in French."

"Yes, Einstein, just like that little journal Tammy gave you."

I looked at him. The real him. Not the charming salesman, crusading politician, or practiced lover. Rather, a jealous, vindictive man driven by his own interests.

"What does it say?"

His impatience showed in his lowered voice. "I had enough French in high school to make *some* sense of it. You're the expert from fancy Smith College. Read it yourself. Out loud," he snarled. "Exactly as they're written! *In English.*"

Apparently, this wasn't his first drink of the evening.

"Okay, okay." I picked it up and looked at him. "It's in bad shape."

"Stop stalling!"

I jumped and read slowly, as if struggling to translate, the precise penmanship of the attorney named Marchaud.

"August 12, 1826: This night, Young Otis from Belle Rivière arrived during a raging summer storm. All Hell was breaking loose he said. Philippe Trémon had sent him for me. As his friend, attorney, and comrade in arms at the Battle of New Orleans, I rushed to help him defend his home from all enemies, no matter how fierce.

My friend greeted me, his face gray, cheeks greasy with sweat. I recoiled from his blood-covered hands. Then he led me upstairs. The sight of his beautiful wife

Elouisa, dead on a bloodstained sheet, a scream of unbearable agony etched on her young face, will haunt my nightmares forever. Next to her in the bloody sheet, lay the still form of a dead man-child, the life cord tightly wrapped around his throat.

Elouisa, still two months before her time, had collapsed in a gush of blood from her loins. But as stubbornly as the child fought to be born, her body held it back. Still, I wondered why he summoned me instead of the priest—then he led me to a servant's room."

I stopped reading. "Look, this is very personal. It doesn't have any political..."

"They're all dead. Finish it." Billy's eyes glowed in the last rays of the sun, sending shivers down my spine.

"It's getting dark and it's hard to read."

He reached over me to turn on the light.

"Give me a minute to find the important points," I stalled. "I'll summarize."

"No! I want to *hear* every single word."

I inched away from him, closer to the light.

"In the soft yellow glow of a lantern, I felt serenity amidst insanity. A woman with doe-colored skin cradled a newborn infant with soft, downy blonde hair, to her breast. Philippe had taken his placée from the Vieux Carré into his home as she approached her time. And on the same night his wife and son died, she gave him a healthy, golden-haired daughter.

What cruel ironies life plays on us! That the girl-child with no name should come into the world healthy, while the man-child with the noble birthright is strangled in his mother's womb. But it was not just irony that would be heaped upon us for the rest of our days. It was sacrilege!

As the heavens fought to strike us down, we buried the unbaptized soul of a white boy in an unmarked grave, while the bastard girl with tainted blood sleeps in his cradle. And in the stead of a doctor, I falsified a certificate saying Elouisa gave birth to a healthy infant girl. It is beyond me how Philippe will live in sin every day with the Negro woman who pretends to be her bastard daughter's nursemaid. For this, we three are doomed to eternal torment.

I choked back tears, but Billy grinned and handed me the second sheet.

"Now this one." He inched closer, blocking my way off the couch. "Word for word."

"But I have to go to the bathroom." My car keys were in the bedroom and I was willing to make a run through the dog trot.

"Hold it."

The plastic shook in my hand because I knew what it would say.

26, May 1840. My old friend has approached me to add more lies to the web of deceit woven so many years ago. My son is enamored of Philippe's daughter. Fearful that our house of cards will come crashing down upon us, and out of love for my son, we have added another crime to our list of unforgivable sins.

A young man visiting from Georgia seeking an investor for his horse breeding business is smitten with the beautiful and dangerous Danielle. To keep my son from illegally marrying the daughter of a Negress, and to keep my vow to my friend, I have completed a marriage contract before young Langesford comes to his senses. I pity him, for Danielle Trémon's soul is as tainted as her blood.

From my own family's lamentable history as slavers, I was well-informed about the nuances of the slaving industry and aware that many African tribes had light skin. They claimed high prices in islands like Haiti. In the revolution of the early-to-mid nineteenth century, many of them escaped to Louisiana to live among the more open-minded Creoles. Flora, her mother, or both, may have been among them.

I took a deep breath. It could be years before the state anti-miscegenation laws followed the way of the Jim Crow laws. Until then, these two documents, when/if validated for authenticity, supported by Danielle's journal, could destroy the reputation of one of Georgia's founding families—and question their legal ownership of Langesford Plantation.

My heart fell for another reason. This job had nothing to do with politics. It took everything I had to keep my hands steady, my voice calm and my backside on top of the journal when I gave him back the papers and played dumb. "What is this?"

Ecstatic, Billy held my hands and I fought the urge to pull away. "Proof," he shouted. "Patrick O'Grady is a direct descendent of a Negress—and a murderess."

"What do you mean?"

His eyes narrowed and his jaw set as if I was dense. "Stop playing dumb. Did you even *read* the documents?"

I tried to sound contrite. "Well some, but I was tired, and they were a little 'dry' you know. I may have fallen asleep"

Stupid bitch was written all over his face, but he held it back to say, "Maybe it's for the best. I want you to understand your purpose here...perfectly."

Then he explained much of what I already knew. "My Great-great-grandfather, Nathan Berens, was a groom at Langesford in 1851. He overheard an argument between Langesford's wife and a visitor over a letter. They spoke in French but, *nigger* is *nigger* in any language. She ripped up the letter and Nathan picked up the pieces." He pointed to the laminated sheets, "*These* are the letters.

He poured another drink, holding it up in toast.

"Nathan, the poor bastard, couldn't read any language, so he took the pieces to his cousin's wife, who was a Creole. She glued them together with candle wax and translated what she could. Days later, Nathan was trampled in a stall—by Danielle Langesford's Andalusian mare."

I wondered how much more Billy could drink without falling on his ass, let alone drive a car. He had to stay sober, so he could leave. "Do you really think the Mistress of Langesford would care enough about Nathan to murder him? He was an illiterate nobody to her, and Andalusians are very high-strung. Accidents happen."

"Do you even understand what 'dirt-poor' means?" Billy growled.

"Of course, I do."

"No, you don't!" his reply thundered through the cabin. His eyes were dilated when he leaned close and breathed scotch into my face. "You think it means livin' with dirt-floors, but it's more'n that. It's 'eat-dirt-and-grass' poor. After the bitch murdered Nathan, his family—*my* family—was tossed out of their cabin by the quarters. The only one of his five children to survive was my Great-grandfather, Samuel. He moved into the old homestead with a cousin an' grew up workin' the Langesford cotton fields like a slave—'til the War."

I winced when he slammed his drink on the table, golden liquid sloshing over the rim of the glass. "The papers got lost, an' nobody could prove it, but the story was passed down the generations. When Jeremy found an old washtub buried by the privy, they were rolled up inside a whiskey bottle sealed with wax."

"Don't," I said when he reached for the bottle of scotch. "You have to drive back, and we need to talk."

He eyed the bottle, lighting a cigarette instead. "Okay, so talk."

"I think I know where you're going with this, but I advise you against it. You can't prove anything. Think about it. Those notes were hand-written more than a century ago. You don't even know who wrote it. And you have no proof *any* of it's true."

His breath hot against my neck, he said, "Finding proof is *your* job."

He put the laminated sheets back in his briefcase, handing me photocopies. "Keep those with the other papers. Maybe git your high-yellow friend in New Orleans to check around some. I'll be campaigning, but there's another debate with O'Grady here, on Labor Day. Get my proof ten days before then—or you'll be lucky to write obits for a weekly rag in Dog Patch."

I could hardly breathe. How did he know about Glory? "What do you mean?"

His scowl made him look older. Meaner. "I told you I had friends in New Orleans. Friends who also have friends, especially in the Quarter. I did a little research on you before we met. I almost cancelled when I found out you were roommates with a colored, girl-lawyer but figured she could be useful."

He grabbed my wrist when I raised my hand to slap him, squeezing it painfully. "Don't call me," he said. "Keep in touch with Jeremy. We'll meet here ten days before the debate."

I already had Billy's irrefutable proof. Danielle's admission of her bloodline, written in her own hand—though it was based on someone else's confession.

"You don't need to do this, Billy. What about your belief in what's right? About making a difference. It happened so long ago. Does it really matter?"

"Murder matters!" he shouted. "They killed three of my kin. They stole our water. They *lied* about their race. When Anthony Langesford died, his daughter had no right to inherit that land. As the nearest *White* relation, Langesford should have gone to my Great-grandpappy Samuel. *I* should have inherited that plantation, not a run-down shack in the woods. Langesford is rightfully mine!"

Eyes shining with anger and hate, he ground out, "Prove it, Laura, or there'll be hell to pay. I have friends everywhere, even in Boston."

He grabbed his hat and briefcase and stormed out of his own cabin. When I heard him spin gravel on his way down the rough path, I wrapped my arms around my churning stomach, moaning. Were there no honest men in politics? In business? In my life? Did Patrick O'Grady even know about his Negro blood? And how far would Billy go to get what he wanted?

I barely made it through the dogtrot to the fancy French toilet in the outhouse. After I expelled the meatloaf and what was left of the leftover rosemary chicken, I sat on the Italian marble floor and wondered how it could be that the only man I'd slept with besides Ricky, was a racist monster.

At least I didn't have to worry about being pregnant. After Rose's difficult birth, the doctor said I wouldn't likely have another child. My breath caught at the realization that with Rose…gone, I'd never have a family of my own. Maybe it was for the best. Maybe if I'd stayed home from work that day, Rose would still be alive. I couldn't dwell on it. Right now, I needed to warn Glory. But not from Billy's phone.

CHAPTER 13

"Laura," she shrieked when I again called her collect, this time from the payphone outside the Shell station on Highway 41. "How is the Caddy King? Is he as big as they say?"

It irked me that she'd guessed I'd slept with him, but as usual, she was right. "I made a big mistake and need your advice."

"What happened? Did he hurt you? Do I need to come?"

"No, no, I'm okay. Well, not really." I took a deep breath and filled her in on the blood feud between the Berens and O'Grady families, including the personal angle with Barbara.

"Billy's obsessed with revenge because she married O'Grady and blames him for her death. And he...Billy...has something on the O'Grady family. Something really bad."

"Take a breath." Her voice lowered with concern. "Just tell me what it is."

Straight to the point. That's my Glory, but it settled me down. Pausing now and then amid the noise of trucks and cars coming and going from the busy pumps, I rushed, "It's a long story, but Billy has evidence of Negro blood in the O'Grady family going back to Patrick's great-great-grandmother in New Orleans. His proof is sketchy from an old journal, but he plans to invoke the One Drop Rule to dispute O'Grady's legal ownership of his plantation."

A double gravel hauler grumbled past the phone booth, spitting tiny stones at me like a machine gun. "The One Drop Rule," Glory shouted over the noise. "It still gets a headline now and then, but I don't recall any recent cases going back that far. And an old journal entry isn't much proof. Is it true?"

"It could be. Well, I'm pretty sure it is. But Billy doesn't care. I have until the week before Labor Day to verify it. And if I can't *disprove* it, he'll make it public—true or not."

"How can I help?"

"I was hoping you'd say that. I don't trust the mail from here. Do you have a pencil?"

"Of course. Spit it out, girl."

I rattled off, "O'Grady's great-great-grandmother's name was Danielle Trémon, her Creole father was Philippe Trémon from Belle Rivière Plantation, outside New Orleans. Her real mother was Flora DeBoucher, Philippe's placée, in the Vieux Carré, sometime in the 1820s. The lawyer who wrote the journal was Marchaud. He had a son named Delmont. That's all I know."

"Good details," Glory acknowledged. "But it's a long-shot. People were racially mis-identified all the time back then. A claim that old will be next to impossible to prove."

"In politics you don't need to *prove* allegations," I reminded her. "You need to *disprove* them before they become an issue. Marchaud signed the birth certificate saying Danielle was white. Whether it's true or not, we need that certificate. Can you take me on as a client? I'll copy everything and mail it to you from Omer, it's a small burg a few miles out of town."

"Girl," she answered. "That is one twisted tale. Why is it so important to Billy?"

"He and Patrick are distant cousins. If the bloodline was known Billy's great-grandfather would have inherited the plantation."

"Ki kaka sa!"

I knew 'shit' when I heard it, even in Creole.

I jumped when a man in an Ace Trucking jacket knocked on the smudgy, bug spotted glass door of the phonebooth. I opened it a crack. "I'll just be a minute."

He slapped his hat on this thigh. "I got a schedule lady. Make it snappy."

"You could be over-reacting," Glory said. "Journals are hard to prove in court, even if you can verify the handwriting. Billy-Boy needs more than that to disprove O'Grady's right to ownership. Even in a White Southern court."

I lowered my voice, hoping she could hear me. "Yes, but O'Grady is land-rich, which means he's likely cash-poor. We both know it costs more to defend a suit than file one. It could bankrupt him. Either way, Billy wins. Please tell me I'm wrong."

"Shit," she said in English this time.

"Stop saying that! What can we do to head this off?"

"Does O'Grady know?"

"I don't know. Billy just hit me with it last night."

"Well, you're right that hearsay can be deadlier than the truth in politics. What do you know about Billy's past? I think they call that counter-intelligence in the spy trade."

In other words, blackmail. Why hadn't I thought of that? I'd already had doubts about Jeremy's version of Billy's rags to riches story. "I'll see what I can find," I told her and yelled, "In a minute!" to the impatient trucker.

"Well, Creoles keep meticulous records," she told me. "And I met somebody who may be of help. Vernon Thomas. He's with the FBI. When you send me what you have, fill me in on Billy too. Nobody's self-made. He's got to have his own secrets,"

We disconnected and I took my time straightening my skirt and gathering my purse before exiting the phone booth. The trucker and I exchanged annoyed nods and I went back to the cabin to pack up the documents I wanted to copy. With rubber gloves and a dish towel dust-mask, I sorted through Billy's mildewed boxes, finding no more references to Danielle or Sean O'Grady. That was curious. The case against him had to have been resolved in some form. I'd check the newspaper archives at the library.

On Thursday afternoon, I went back to the "castle" hoping Tammy had time for my tour of the genealogy wing and would let me use the copy machine. Her face lit up when she saw me, as I suspected it did for everyone,

"Hey Sarah. How you bin?" she asked. "That rally was really somethin' right? Our Paddy sure knows how to kick up a crowd."

"He sure does." *But could he keep it going?*

She giggled. "An' Billy's gonna get some ribbing about selling cars to flyin' purple people eaters. You here for that tour?"

Grateful I didn't have to bring it up, I answered, "Yes, if you're not too busy. And I think I'd like to stay a while and take some notes—for a history of my family."

"Oh, are you a writer?"

"No!" I answered too quickly. "I mean I can write, but mostly I've been…a secretary. My boss didn't like me taking time off, so I thought I'd look for something around here—while I do my research. Do you have time to show me around?"

"Sure thing. This is the slow time o' day."

She bounced from her chair, put the 'I'll be back' sign on the counter and led the way to the Jeffers County Genealogy archives.

My breath caught when she opened a heavy, black-walnut door and flipped on modern, low-glare lights. It was like expecting a grass shack and getting a castle. State-of-the-art fixtures and storage equipment blended into the elegant design of the historic building.

I ran my fingers over rows of flat file drawers holding maps encased in protective lamination and cellophane, thinking of Billy's rotting treasure-trove at the cabin. "Amazing doesn't begin to describe this, Tammy."

Neatly labeled plat books, census records, and blueprints for long demolished or renovated antebellum homes were stacked on stainless steel shelves supported by arching, solid oak timbers. Green felt tabletops and fluorescent ceiling lights invited researchers to explore the historical tapestry of their county and state. But it was the sturdy bookcases in the center of the room that captured my attention.

All sizes of thick tomes, with family names stamped in gold foil on worn bindings, stood side by side, in alphabetical order. I read the names of Jeffers' elite. "Abercrombe, Allenton, Barclay, Berens," while Tammy filled me in on each family's status as in, died-out, going-strong or hanging-on.

The books ended well short of the end of the shelf, at "Kelly" and I wondered if it was because the Berens and Langesford histories couldn't be trusted on the same shelf. "Wow."

She grinned. "I knew you'd get it. It's like they're alive, just waiting to tell their stories."

We laughed, two history lovers on the same page, and moved to the next shelf where the section began with Lewis. "What's your family name again?" Tammy asked.

"Tucker. They were sharecroppers in Tennessee, burned out during the… War. They came here for a new start." The lies came easier as the fictitious

Tucker family began to take shape in my imagination. I could almost picture my dear, recently deceased maw-maw rocking on the porch of a cabin much like Billy's.

Tammy patted me on the shoulder. "Well, I never heard of 'em, but I'll check to make sure. Smaller files are in the reference desk."

I drifted alone to a section with a brass plaque labeled, "Founders," featuring the half-dozen English families who sailed with Oglethorpe and slept in cabins rather than on the deck or in tiny canvas slings below deck. I recognized the names of local buildings, businesses, and streets, impressed that so many families had survived and stayed in the area for so long.

Looking at the pitifully small Bradley/Glass section, I thought that after Hal passed without an heir—unless he acknowledged Jeremy—they'd be relegated to Tammy's died-out category. The Berens family too, unless Jeremy had children. I doubted Billy would. Some people only love once in their lives. Trying again isn't worth the effort.

While Tammy looked for my fictitious family, I found the floor-to-ceiling, Langesford section. "Are all these books about your family?" I asked.

"Yep," she answered from across the room. "But the O'Gradys are there too. When the original name changes due to marriage, we combine them."

Not surprisingly, she returned to me emptyhanded. "I know it looks like we're hoggin' the room, but we been packrats for generations. Thanks to Miss Camilla saving the house from the Yankees, we have nearly every important document signed by them since James Langesford stepped off the *Anne.*"

Camilla. The red-haired devil Danielle's journal called, "C"? The courageous woman who at eighteen, ran the plantation when her brother died, and her father accepted a commission in the Confederate army. And the cunning trickster who talked the Yankees out of burning the plantation. What would have happened to her if the truth about her mother was known back then?

Tammy rambled, "Her son Clay, Paddy and my grandfather, was the family historian. Lordy, he was a packrat. The ballroom on the third floor was stacked with Langesford and O'Grady stuff, and then he added Great-maw-maw Fairchild's family records from Rosewood Plantation. When Aunt Thelma wanted to update the ballroom for parties and fundraisers, Uncle Edward sent most of the old stuff over here."

She nodded toward a shelf filled with well-preserved revolution-era books. "Those are from when our family served in the Georgia legislature after the Revolution. We'll send them over to the State Capitol eventually. When I'm finished sorting the ones from the first Patrick's tenure in Congress, those will go to Washington."

While it didn't compare with the Stainsby Room in the Boston Library, the number of volumes was impressive. "That's a lot of books," I said.

"Yes, I think Uncle Edward felt guilty for taking over the tower room while they were renovating the ballroom at Langesford, so he and Aunt Thelma had a big gala last year at the Elks Club, for donations to build this room. He had the plans and contractors all lined up.

Tears suddenly filled her eyes. "It was the night of the accident. I wish he'd got to see this finished."

Raised to be stoic, I didn't handle others' emotions well. "You certainly did a great job here."

Her face brightened when she smiled. "Well, just because I'm neat doesn't mean I'm done," she said on our way back to the miscellaneous file. "I'm sorry I couldn't find anything about the Tuckers. You should check the Court House."

Thank goodness! "Yes, I'll do that as soon as I can. So, you have more things from your family that aren't out?"

"Oh, my Lord. Tons! Mostly covering the first Patrick from when he went into politics in the 1880's."

She looked around as if the walls had ears. "He was an Irishman from Boston, but we don't know much about him before he became partners with my Great-great-granddaddy, Anthony Langesford. It was just after the War."

Boston? Back then, the Irish were treated little better than slaves. But instead of debasing auctions, the desperate Irish sold themselves and their children through indenture contracts they could never hope to repay. I remembered the picture I'd found in our attic of a maid and her baby. Mary was written on the back. I wondered if she and her child survived, though the odds were against it.

The modern room suddenly felt oppressive with the weight of the past. "Well, thanks for the tour, and for looking for my family's file."

Tammy smiled. "No trouble, sweetie—I should get back to the desk. We can be dead all day, and the moment I leave, people come in."

"There may be something in the old newspapers about the Tuckers. Obits, maybe. You can look at the microfiche if you want. An' if you want to make a copy, go ahead. A nickel each. Put the money in the jar on the reference desk."

Copies? How had I forgotten? Since it was her idea, I didn't mention that my oversized bag was stuffed with things to, well, copy. "Newspapers," I answered. "My favorite. Thanks."

I spent two hours straining my eyes at the microfiche machine, and soiling the library's white linen gloves with newsprint, trying to find a reference to Sean O'Grady after his sudden disappearance with his Apache woman accomplice. Other than the wanted poster I already had, I came up empty and finally copied what I'd brought with me, dropping two dollars into the jar.

Not ready to go back to the isolated cabin, I took up the stool next to Tammy again, sorting returns, chatting about her family and town gossip. We both jumped when the six-o'clock town siren blew.

"Thanks for helping," Tammy said. "You saved me hours of setting things straight for Merrilee tomorrow."

"Merrilee?"

"The head librarian. She works mornings with her friend Cindy, when *no one* is around. I get the afternoon, before-dinner, and weekend rushes —alone."

"That doesn't sound fair."

Her sigh sounded tired. "It's just for the summer. I can use the money."

"Really?" It surprised me that a member of one of the premier families in the state had to earn her own spending money.

"I'm an Eldridge. My mother inherited Rosewood Plantation from her grandmother, Louise Fairchild-O'Grady, while Uncle Edward inherited Langesford. We're comfortable enough, mind you, but Pa's only willing to pay for college if I earn enough for everything else. I've been helping Patrick with Dani and his office since Evelyn got married."

Another Southern stereotype shattered with the revelation that Tammy was nanny to her cousin's child. "I'm surprised Pat…your cousin, doesn't have help for his daughter."

The ever-present smile faded. "You mean a colored 'mammy' to raise Dani, polish the silver, and clean bathrooms she ain't allowed to use?"

That was exactly what I meant, but I had no idea why it irked her. Except for the word, 'colored', it described Nanny Irene perfectly.

"Well, I guess," I stammered. "I just assumed."

"Well you assumed wrong," she huffed. "Paddy's wife Barbara grew up without a mama, and since she came from the wrong side of the hollow so to speak, she didn't want what she called, 'Uppity House Nigras' judging her while she learned the ways of the gentry."

Her eyes misted at the memory of her cousin's young wife. "But she needn't have worried. The O'Grady's ain't hired by color in generations."

"I see," I said and changed the subject. "Well, it looks like you have a full schedule."

"You don't know the half of it." She grabbed the book cart. "My boyfriend is well, busy too. We don't have much time together, if you know what I mean."

I didn't, really. I barely dated in college and after one night with Ricky, ended up pregnant. Though Tammy couldn't have been more dissimilar in appearance and background, she reminded me of Glory, who had worked two part-time jobs while taking a full course load through Smith and Columbia—and never complained. She just did what needed to be done.

I had no doubt Tammy would get that degree, replace Merrilee as Head Librarian, and write a blockbuster history of Jeffers County. "You've really made me feel welcome," I said. "Let me know if there's anything I can help you with while I'm here." *Until Billy destroys your family.*

Tammy put a book away, making sure it was perfectly aligned with the end of the shelf, and looked at me a long moment, arms crossed over her chest. "How are you with kids?"

"Kids? What? I mean, I like kids." I blinked away the emotions that followed any thought of Rose. "But I haven't been around them much —lately."

Was never allowed to even be one.

"I see," she said. "Well, with the election coming up and me heading back to school, Paddy needs somebody to organize his affairs. And I need a break from dusty old books. You said you were a secretary, and practically drooled when I told you about all that old stuff at Langesford. If you could use some extra cash, I can put a good word in for you with Paddy. Pay's not bad either. And if you can handle Princess Danielle, I bet I can get him to pay twice minimum wage. Interested?"

Princess Danielle? I wondered if Patrick and Barbara knew what they signed on for when they named their daughter after her great-great-great-grandmother. Was I interested? Hell yes, but not for the reasons Tammy thought—or what Billy would think.

Somehow, I didn't know exactly how, I'd stop Billy from winning this election at the cost of another man's family legacy. And $2.50 an hour would keep my emergency fund alive, especially after I gave up Billy's free room and board.

I tried to sound uncommitted. "Sure, why not?"

"Great." She grinned. "I'll set it up and call you. Where you staying?"

I couldn't tell her I was at Billy's cabin. "I'm between places right now but will be meeting with Hal about my maw-maw in the next few days. I suppose you could leave a note with him."

She patted my shoulder this time. "Don't you worry, we'll find you a decent place."

Did I look that pitiful? *Oh God, she probably thinks I'm sleeping in my car!*

"Thanks," was all I could muster before she gave me a sympathetic hug and dashed off to lock up before telling her boyfriend the good news that she was getting her life back.

I went directly from the library to the J. W. Ippel Department Store for sensible shoes and dresses that covered my knees.

CHAPTER 14

Billy was traveling, and I didn't expect to hear from Tammy over the weekend. Even Jeremy left me alone in my woodsy retreat. I'd spent my life surrounded by the noise of airplanes going in and out of Logan Airport, traffic, and trains, as well as the chaos of boarding school dormitories that proved no woman is an island. So, if asked about spending a weekend without human contact, I'd have said I'd go crazy.

Instead, I went un-crazy. My mind cleared, my hearing sharpened, and I focused on how to rescue my mission, which was *not* supporting a personal vendetta and racist witch-hunt. I clung to the hope that I could write an objective article about Southern politics facing a new social paradigm, but what was going on in District One had little to do with politics or paradigms, Southern or otherwise.

I was stuck between the proverbial rock and a hard place. But before I decided whether to switch sides or hang it up, I had to know if Patrick O'Grady was worth the price. The only way to do that was to get to know the man, though not in the way I'd known Billy. Remembering O'Grady's smile by the library when he took his daughter's hand, I told myself *that* couldn't happen again.

Late Sunday afternoon, I recognized Jeremy's Bonneville through the dust cloud as he drove up the rutted trail. After nearly three days of solitude,

I admitted I was ready for some company and trotted out to meet him, leaning in when he rolled his window down.

"Hey Jeremy. What's up? Checking to see if I burned the house down trying to cook?"

I stepped back, and he stepped out, wearing jeans and a tie-dyed T-shirt. He had a nice smile when he wasn't with Billy. "Great look," I said. "You're practically a Beatle."

He cocked his head at my cutoff jeans and halter top. "Very funny. Just come from an audition for *The Beverly Hillbillies*?"

"Touché!"

He reached for a six pack of Carling's Black Label on the passenger seat. I may have grown up with champagne on ice and aged wine in the cellar, but I became quite good at smuggling cheap Ballentine into dorm rooms at the Westmoreland Academy.

"You sure know how to please a girl," I quipped when he pulled a bottle out, twisted the cap, and handed it to me.

I took a deep swallow. It was still cold, but I knew he wasn't on a beer run. "What's up?"

He opened his bottle and headed to the porch, dropping into a rocker. "I bring news."

Ah, the messenger. With news from the king? Both Billy and O'Grady came to mind. Two favorite sons dueling over the tiny kingdom of District One. I swatted a pre-dusk mosquito before sitting in the other rocker.

"So, what's the news?" I asked after an unladylike burp that tasted of hops.

He did the same, only with more gusto, and handed me a note. "I saw Tammy after church. She asked me to give this to Hal—to give to you."

"Already?" I unfolded it. Sure enough, Tammy had landed me a ten o'clock job interview with Patrick O'Grady at Langesford Plantation the next morning.

"Did you read it?" I asked Jeremy.

"Didn't have to. She told me." He set his bottle down a little harder than necessary. "You're really going through with it?"

"With what?"

He stood suddenly, the runners on his chair beating franticly against the pine floor while he paced the length of the porch, fists clenched. He was an entirely different man than the one I'd met at the Pickrick. Why?

He stopped pacing to glare at me. "When I talked Billy into hiring you, I thought you were professional enough to keep him from going off half-cocked. And as a recent divorcée, I'd hoped you could resist his so-called charms. Then he got you in the sack.

"That was a mistake. I was drunk and…"

"I know, Billy's very convincing. That's what they all say—after he hurts them."

He pointed to the note sticking out of my pocket. "And now you're using Tammy to get close to Patrick."

I wondered whose side he was on and stood too, poking a finger into the bullseye on his multi-colored shirt. "As I recall, *you* offered to pay *me* to expose the many sins of the family who *allegedly* stole your precious ancestral land—and women…well, Billy's woman. And *you* gave me the fake letter of recommendation to O'Grady. Why are you so upset that I'm doing what you hired me to do?"

His face blanched. "He told you about Barbara?"

"A little. Mostly what you told me."

Thinking of the tragic lives of both Barbara Kinney-O'Grady and Danielle Trémon, I held up my beer. "Cherchez la femme. Whenever things between two men get this fucked up, there's usually a woman involved."

"Amen to that." He tapped his longneck against mine. The truce called, we finished our beers as the sun dipped behind the trees and voracious mosquitoes banded together to feast on my thick, Northern blood.

"Let's go inside," I said.

He set the half-empty six-pack on the floor by the couch, and sat propping his feet on the table, next to the stack of priceless historical documents. I took off my sandals, moved a few maps, and planted my pink-painted toes next to his leather boots.

"What's really bothering you? Do you want me to do this job or not?"

"What do you think?"

I wasn't surprised the recent law-school graduate could answer questions with questions, but I could play that game all day long.

"Well, I *thought* you and Billy wanted me to uncover the O'Gradys' heinous crimes and make Billy a hero so he can win the election. How can I do that without talking to them?"

"Not by using Tammy. She's never said or done an unkind thing in her life and doesn't deserve to be used. She's off limits." The accusation in his eyes again reminded me of Hal.

I wasn't surprised that, family feud notwithstanding, Jeremy knew Tammy. They were close in age and likely attended school together, but the threat in his voice told me they were more than childhood friends—or distant cousins. "You're Tammy's boyfriend, aren't you?"

His blush confirmed it.

"Does Billy know?"

He shook his head. "Tammy and I got together at Emory two years ago. She transferred from Jeffers Community College and I was accepted early into law school. We've been seeing each other since then, but not…in town."

I touched his arm. "I like Tammy, too. I'd never do anything to hurt her."

Hypocrite! I'd found information about her family and kept it from her. I used her to get a good seat at the debate and, albeit unintentionally, manipulated her into setting up an interview with her cousin. When she offered trust and friendship, I grabbed it because it served my purpose.

"I'm so sorry," I said. "But it's not what you think. *I'm* not what you think." But I was. A reporter out for a story about ruthless, Southern politicians.

He stood. "Then what are you?"

"Please, sit down."

"I'll stand."

I sighed. "Okay, I know I agreed to investigate the O'Gradys, but despite our *one* time together, I'm not going to help Billy get revenge for Barbara choosing Patrick over him."

He crossed his arms and even in the ridiculous T-shirt, I saw the lawyer Jeremy *could* be.

"Cut the crap," he said. "Hal and Tammy seem to trust you, but I know you're ambitious. After seeing you with Billy, I have my doubts."

He checked his watch. "I need to go."

I lunged for his arm. "Don't! Please, just hear me out. You approached me, remember. You're playing on both teams too. How do *you* sleep at night?"

He dropped onto the couch, running his fingers through hair that fell perfectly back into place. "You're right," he said. "The guilt is killing me. You have five minutes before I walk out of here and call Tammy with the truth about her new best friend. And about Billy's plan. And my part in it."

Thinking of Winkler's sixty seconds, I said, "I'll take it. I came here to cover crooked Southern politics, but now I don't know who to trust. Billy's vendetta muddies the water, I still think I can turn it around into something worthwhile, but I need to know both candidates better."

A desperate hope lit his eyes. "How?"

"Don't interrupt," I chided. "Every time you do, I'll tack on another five minutes. Just bear with me."

"Go on."

I crossed my legs on the couch, facing him. "There's no way I'll help Billy ruin what everyone tells me is District One's Holy Family—unless they've committed *real* crimes in *this* century. But even if I walk away, we both know Billy will go ahead with the smear campaign. What does he really have on the O'Gradys?"

"This is your five minutes," he countered. "You tell me."

"No. If I'm going to switch sides, I need to hear it from you."

He thought for a long moment. "Billy caused a scene after Barbara's funeral. He said a lot of crazy things about Patrick. Accused him of killing her. Called him a…Nigger. Said Barbara was leaving Patrick and going back to him—and that Dani wasn't Patrick's daughter.

"Patrick beat Billy almost to a pulp before Sheriff Coulter hauled him off. I took Billy home. That's when he showed me an obituary with *Nigger* scrawled over it and an old note written in French that he said proved Patrick's great-great-grandmother was a Negro."

He took a deep breath. "Billy didn't make a lot o' sense, but what he meant was clear enough. Someday, he'd throw that obituary in Patrick's face. I tried to take it from him, and it ripped. He never mentioned it again, until Congressman O'Grady and his wife died—and Patrick agreed to run for the office."

I touched his hand, but he wasn't finished.

"That's when Billy decided to run. He called Winkler at *The Atlanta Constitution*, but he wouldn't publish the story without proof. Then Billy wanted me to call radio stations and billboard companies and do it himself. I went to Hal for help and he gave me the Wash-Mart article, along with your name."

"How does Billy know Winkler?"

"He backed Billy's petition campaign for the nomination. I used your article to convince Billy that a story from a real investigative reporter with credentials, especially a Yankee, would be more believable than from one of Winkler's hacks, or some country radio DJ.

"So now that you know Billy's motives, why stay?" he asked. "This isn't the kind of story you write. Why don't you just quit? Why worm your way into the O'Grady family? You don't seem the motherly type?"

Though unintentional, the judgement hurt—a lot. I snapped, "You don't know me at all."

And I didn't know him…really. Jeremy was more complicated than I'd thought, and as a Berens, he'd benefit from a case against O'Grady almost as much as Billy. I couldn't trust him—yet. "*If* the accusations in the French letter are true, do you realize the ramifications?"

He snapped back, "I may be young, but I *am* a lawyer. *If* it's true, it could nullify old Anthony Langesford's marriage to Danielle Trémon, negating Patrick and Tammy's parents' rights to both Langesford and Rosewood plantations. It could take years and cost a fortune to sort it out through the legal system."

He sounded a little like Glory. It was humbling. "Okay," I conceded. "What's the worst that could happen?"

He paced to the window, looking over what was left of his own family's legacy and confirmed my fears. "Under the Intestacy laws, When Anthony Langesford died, the oldest living white descendent through Alice Berens-Langesford, Samuel Berens, was the legal heir. Since Billy is Samuel's great-grandson, he could petition for ownership."

"Wouldn't you also be in line for it?" I speculated.

"You think I want any part of this?

"If not, why are you still working for him?"

"We're family." He sighed. "All that's left of the Berens clan. I just don't want to see anyone get hurt."

Then he turned the tables. "And I'm assuming this story could make your career."

"Perhaps," I admitted. "But I want it to be about the important issues in this election, not a mud-fight prompted by revenge and greed. So far Billy doesn't have any more proof than he did when you found the washtub. What alternatives are there for Patrick?"

"Under adverse possession rules, even if Langesford's marriage was invalid, twenty years of his family's occupancy would have put ownership in their hands. But only if they filed a claim."

"And since they didn't know about it, they didn't file," I pointed out the obvious.

"Right," he said. "Ownership would still be in dispute."

His responses explained why he'd graduated from law school so early. "Can you talk to your father about what counter measures O'Grady can take?"

I smiled when his jaw dropped and he said, "What do you mean?"

"Look, if we're going to work together, we have to trust each other with everything. I was one of Hal's students—in Boston. Except for the eyes, you're the spitting image of him back then. Does Billy know? Don't lie because I'll know."

His head lowered. "He hates Hal enough, so he may know. But we don't talk about Hal—or my ma—now she's passed. But after her funeral, Hal told me about being with her in high school, before his folks sent him up north to college. But when he came home, they got together…sometimes. We keep it private."

He even sounded like Hal. "Good. Then you'll ask him about those counter measures?"

His eyes narrowed to put *me* on the stand. "You found it didn't you? The proof. Lying about race is a mortal sin in the South. Patrick and Tammy's families could lose everything! I recommended you because I thought you'd be able to disprove it—before it all came out. Truth be told, I never believed it."

My mind raced to form a plan. "We could show O'Grady what Billy has," I ventured. "If he withdraws from the election, maybe Billy will let it go."

"That's a big maybe." He turned toward the door and I followed him to the Bonneville.

"What aren't you telling me?" I pressed.

Dropping into the seat, he slammed the door and poked his head out the window. "I'll trust you with two words that could get us both killed. Barbara's Bungalows."

CHAPTER 15

I left the cabin for good the next day to air-mail Glory copies of both journal entries, along with the family trees and important obits. Depending how the interview with Patrick went, I'd either go back to Ho-Jo's with a job in the O'Grady household, or to Atlanta to tell Winkler I wouldn't report on an unprovable century-old, racial vendetta. The proverbial coin of fate was in the air. Heads meant the chance to warn Patrick. Tails meant leaving him at the mercy of rumor-loving voters.

Wrapping the rose-print scarf around my head, I headed north with the top down and the radio up. I drove fast, waving my arms and singing, *You've Lost that Lovin' Feelin',* with the Righteous Brothers—until a pothole brought me to my senses. The paved road narrowed to a sand and gravel track winding through rows of hundred-foot-tall Georgia pines dripping with Spanish moss. A mile or so of driving through what was left of an ancient forest, I pulled off at the crest of a hill, next to an abandoned green pickup truck, to check my map.

It was beautiful there. Quiet, with a fresh, pine-scented breeze. I nudged the door open with my foot and stepped out, focused on opening the map. The heel of my pump turned on a stone and my arms flew up, sending the map flying and me face-down on the stony ground. I pulled myself up using the open door as leverage and swearing, "Goddammittohell."

Fortunately, my polyester skirt protected my knees and the dry soil brushed off easily. But my white blouse wasn't so forgiving. And the breeze had blown the map into the brush along the slope. My left ankle barely held my weight as I limped toward the map, looking for a stick to reach it. When I found one and raised my head, I saw one of those images you carry with you to the grave.

Below me, surrounded by a natural clearing, a three and a half-story antebellum mansion shone bright white in the summer sun, a vision of elegance, and tranquility. Windowpanes in the main floor rooms reflected sunlight like mirrors on a disco ball. Two sets of French doors opened onto a veranda with steps that widened like outstretched arms toward a curving, magnolia-lined drive. The second story balconies were bordered by ornate wrought iron balustrades, and shuttered dormers dotted the third floor on either side of a Palladian window.

"Oh, my god," I said out loud.

"It's an illusion," startled me.

My twisted ankle buckled, and I teetered on the edge of the ravine, clawing the air for something to keep me from toppling over. An arm wrapped around my waist from behind, pulling me back against a chest that felt hard as a tree. Though I'd been saved from falling, I fought like a badger against the man whose voice had caused me to lose my balance and—*almost die,* goddammit.

"Let me go," I screamed as he dragged me backward toward the pickup truck.

"Stop fighting," he growled into my ear.

It only made me fight harder. "Then let me go, you son of a bitch."

My good foot kicked his shin and when one arm loosened, I bit his other one.

"Jesus H. Christ," he snarled, scattering the few birds and animals that weren't already scared away by my howling. He dropped me like a stone onto the gravel in front of my Beetle. Tasting blood, I wiped my mouth on the ripped sleeve of my blouse and gripped the bumper to slowly stand.

"You bit me," the man said, from inside the car.

I leaned on the fender to hop toward the open door. "And you tried to drag me into your truck."

My assailant sat in the driver's seat, his booted feet on the ground, wrapping a red handkerchief over an oozing wound on one arm. *Oh my God!* The blood I'd tasted was the crazed redneck's, not mine! My stomach lurched.

His preoccupation with his wound was my chance to get away, but behind me was a rocky fall. In front, a deserted road, with dense undergrowth on both sides. I was willing to try for the road, but my ankle refused to cooperate. I addressed his hat. "Look, you can have my car. And whatever's in my purse. Just let me go. I won't tell anyone about this."

Finally finished with the makeshift bandage, he took the keys from the ignition and unfolded his tall frame to stand on the other side of the open door. The low brim of his hat still shadowed his features while his broad chest under a Western-style cowboy shirt, rose and fell slowly, as if he'd just stepped across the street instead of dragging me around like a sack of fertilizer. Pointy-toed boots gave the front tire of my pride and joy a disrespectful kick.

"Why on God's green earth, would I want this little toy? Where's the wind-up key?"

My response to the insult froze in my throat when he lifted the brim of his hat and I recognized Patrick O'Grady II.

He stepped to the side, holding out the keys. "You can go any time you want, Miss…?"

"Tucker," came out almost naturally. "Sarah Tucker." I grabbed the keys and hopped my way around the door. But when I put my weight on my left leg to slide inside, it caved. I dropped the keys and flopped onto the seat like a fish into a bucket.

I rested my head on the steering wheel, blinking away tears of pain and frustration. He'd never believe a clumsy Yankee—*who bit him.*

"Well, Miss Tucker," he said and retrieved the keys. "I'm afraid we got off on the wrong foot, so to speak. I'm Patrick O'Grady and I live in that house down the hill."

I looked up. His crooked smile and attempt at a joke were charming, but the pain in my ankle killed my sense of humor. Then I realized this was probably the bluff where his parents died. Was that why he was here? Was he still mourning?

I rested my forehead on the steering wheel and shuddered.

He pulled my sweater from the back seat, laying it over my shoulders.

"Don't go into shock on me. Your ankle could be broken. We're a long way from a hospital. Let me check it."

Break or sprain, it didn't matter. My foot was already swelling out of my shoe. I'd have a hell of a time driving a stick shift back to Jeffers. And I couldn't leave a job half-done. But today obviously wasn't the day.

"No," I jerked my foot away. "I'm fine. I was on my way to meet you, for an interview. At ten o'clock," I said and noted his blank stare. I wanted to disappear. Did Tammy forget to tell him? Was it too much to hope for even one thing to go according to plan?

"She gave me a note. It's in my purse."

His shoulders sagged and the grim set of his lips softened. "I'm so sorry," he said. "Tammy did tell me about it. But I've been a bit pre-occupied lately and completely forgot. And then for this to happen. Let me help you. I've had a good deal of experience with sprains."

I didn't resist this time when he cupped my foot in one palm, gentle fingers touching throbbing skin that felt like it was on fire. "I don't feel a break or dislocation," he said. "But you should have an X-ray to know for sure. We're closer to Langesford than Jeffers for the call."

He scooped his unbandaged arm under my knees and the other one around my back to pick me up, heading for the truck. I twisted, pushing against his shoulder. "Wait a minute! Where are you going? I can't leave my car. Put me down."

"Nuts," he said as if he hadn't heard me. "There isn't room to prop up your foot. You'll have to ride in the back with Clarence."

In the back? With Clarence? I craned my neck toward the truck bed to see a big lump of fur napping in the sunshine. "No, no, really, Mr. O'Grady. I feel better now. I'm sure it's just a sprain. We can reschedule the interview." I pointed to my car. "Put me back. Please."

Instead, he turned toward the truck's tailgate. I kicked in his arms and my injured ankle hit the truck's side panel. Hard. The blue sky turned red, then white, then black.

~

I dreamed I was rocking in a hammock on the porch of my parents' summer house in the Hamptons, the rhythmic hum of distant waves a gentle lullaby. But I was late for work. When I tried to move my leg, pain shot through my entire body. It all came back to me. The near fall. The sprain. Patrick O'Grady and the pickup. I raised to my elbows to see that I was on top of a blanket spread over a bale of hay—or maybe it was straw—sandwiched between several others. Above me, pines dripped Spanish Moss under a cloudless, blue sky. Then the face of a dog of unknown breed appeared above me and *licked my face!*

Feeling like a wine bottle in a shipping box, I took a deep breath to raise my head. The head of the beast now lay on my stomach, soulful brown eyes staring at me. "Clarence, I presume."

He blinked, and a bushy tail brushed my good leg. The gentle animal allowed me to use his big skull to push myself up until my shoulders rested against the bale behind me. Moments later, we hit a pothole, the bale under my foot shifted and I closed my eyes to the shooting pain, counting, one breath at a time. I was at sixty 'Mississippis' when we stopped.

A door opened and Patrick O'Grady's deep voice said, "Welcome to Langesford, Miss Tucker." He unhooked the tailgate and smiled at me as if he were opening the door to a limousine. "I'm afraid I had to improvise, so we'll take it easy."

The dog jumped down but when I tried to follow, his master ordered, "Don't move. I splinted your leg with a crowbar and tire iron, along with a blanket and a little baling wire. Stay put 'til we get you out of here."

He turned to his left. "Henry, have Ela call Doc Hill. Then get a stretcher. And Alvarez."

Tire iron? Bailing wire? I looked down and sure enough, wire was wrapped around a thick blanket wrapped around my leg. Moments later, the candidate for Congress re-appeared with wire cutters to set me free.

A young black man I presumed to be Henry, jumped into the truck bed with a stretcher that smelled like a barn. I pushed it away. "No! I don't need that. I can stand on my good foot."

O'Grady nodded for him to back off and pulled the bale I was on to the end of the tailgate. Then he let me calculate the odds of landing on the right foot. Angry tears at being helpless flooded my eyes before I nodded, "Okay. Do what you must."

He freed my leg and I wrapped an arm around his neck for him to carry me up the shell drive, and the steps of the verandah, and through the mansion's double doors. "No!" I shrieked as he prepared to drop me onto a red-velvet settee in an authentic-looking Victorian parlor. "You'll ruin it."

He finally seemed to notice the pieces of straw sticking to my clothes, the dust from both the fall and the drive, his blood, and Clarence's drool on my blouse. "My office then," he said.

It was a magnificent example of Reconstruction-era carpentry intended to blend with late-Eighteenth Century master-craftsmanship. I gaped at an original Adam fireplace, silver-oak parquet flooring, and three solid walls of floor-to-ceiling bookshelves. He laid me gently on a leather couch, propping my foot on a pillow.

"Check on Doc and Alvarez," he told Henry. Then to me, "Comfortable, Miss Tucker?"

The spark of humor in his eyes, along with the half-smile I'd seen in front of the library, puzzled me. Did nothing faze this man? I picked straw from my hair. "You mean other than an ankle the size of a softball and smelling like a stable?"

My outrage melted when I saw his arm, still wrapped in a bloodstained bandana. "I'm so sorry I bit you, Mr. O'Grady, and thank you for the ride, but I'll be fine. I understand if you've changed your mind about the interview." So, it's tails, I thought. He's on his own.

He sat on the coffee table made from a single slab of wood mounted on a polished granite base. "Please, call me Patrick. And *I* apologize for forgetting your interview, scaring you, and dragging you here in the back of my truck."

He looked like he meant it. "It wasn't your fault," I admitted. "I overreacted."

His smile made me forget the disgusting, disheveled mess I'd become. He said, "We can waste the whole day arguing about who's to blame, but what happened, happened. I know it isn't a good time for you, but Tammy spoke well of you, and I'm in a bit of a bind. If you're still interested and up for it, we can talk after the doctor comes."

"Doc's busy," came from Henry, again standing on the other side of the threshold. "Car accident North o' here on Simpson Road."

Simpson Road was the one I'd turned off to stop at the bluff. If I hadn't stopped, I may have witnessed the accident—or been part of it. I felt a chill at how a split-second decision can alter fate—or determine it. Like when I agreed to help Ricky prove his masculinity by having sex. It was the first time for both of us. Who knew I'd get pregnant from one roll on the sheets?

"Where on Simpson?" Patrick asked Henry.

"North o' the overlook, outside Briarwood. A T-bone at the crossing."

"They need help?"

"Naw, Sally said the ambulance was there. Doc could take a while though."

"Okay, then ask Ela to make an ice pack." Patrick nodded toward me and told him, "My key is still in the truck and hers are on the seat. You and Joey go up to the lookout and bring her car here. Be careful. It's a little bit of a thing. Foreign."

Two dark fingers touched the tip of Henry's cap before he turned.

"And where is Alvarez?" the plantation master shouted after him.

"Right here," accompanied the sound of bootheels on the entry's slate floor. "I was up to my elbows in a heifer's hind quarters, turning her calf around. Figured I'd wash up first."

Like Henry, he stopped at the threshold, as if awaiting permission to enter. When he saw me, he took off his battered Stetson hat. "Sorry for the language, ma'am," he said in a softer tone with a hint of a Southwest accent. When his gaze caught the throbbing monster my foot had become, the hat flew toward a Queen Anne chair by the fireplace and he crossed the room in a few strides. He bent on one knee and whistled low.

"I'm fine," I snapped. *Or at least I was until I bounced around in the back of a truck with one of the hounds of the Baskervilles drooling on me.* A low whine from under the table told me Clarence might be able to read minds. "I am very grateful for your concern," I told them, "but I've had sprains before. I just need ice."

Alvarez shook his head. "Won't know if it's broke 'til the swellin' goes down."

A young woman slid through the doorway without an invitation, saying, "Henry told me someone's been hurt. I brought ice."

She was gorgeous. Petite, with a strong body, a clear, naturally tanned complexion and straight, shoulder-length black hair. That, and the concern in her black-opal eyes suggested she was related to Alvarez.

The pride in his voice confirmed it when he stepped aside. "What do you think, Ela girl?"

I braced for the cold, hard icepack, but Ela set it on the rug to kneel next to me, her hand hovering just above my injury. I barely felt it when she gently placed her fingertip above the lump obscuring my ankle.

"It helps if you close your eyes and breathe deeply," she said. "Raise your hand if there's a sharp pain." Her fingers felt cool and light against my skin as she applied pressure to the spots just above and below my ankle, while gently rotating it.

I never raised my hand and the throbbing eased until I was able to wriggle a swollen toe without wanting to scream. Even her smile seemed to lessen my pain. "It's not broken."

The icepack replaced her warm hand against my skin. "What did you do?" I asked.

"Reflexology,"

"Reflex...what?"

"Ology'. An ancient Chinese technique for pain relief and healing. It can work miracles without surgery—or drugs. Of course, Gringo doctors think it's Voodoo." She winked. "So, let's not tell Doc Hill anything about this, Okay?"

Chinese medicine from a woman with a Southwest accent who didn't look much older than Tammy? I asked, " Are you a nurse?"

She cast a wary glance at Alvarez, adjusted the icepack, then stood and turned to him. "In a way. I want to be a doctor and am one of two Apache accepted for the first class at the University of New Mexico's new School of Medicine."

While Alvarez gaped in what looked like shock, Patrick's face split into a grin. He stepped around me to pull her into his arms saying, "That's my girl. Finally, a doctor in the family!"

Family? Ela stiffened. Alvarez cocked his head toward me, and Patrick frowned. "You must be so proud."

I ended the awkward moment with, "Congratulations. When do you start?"

"Late August," she answered. "I'm waiting for Patrick to replace Evelyn."

"Did someone call for a doctor?" came from the doorway. The tired-looking older man with thin gray hair looked more like a grocer than a doctor, but Patrick rushed to take his bag.

"The accident, Doc?"

"Kids. Joy ridin' with the top down in Hollis Robertson's '32 roadster. Cops said the signal was out, an' it caught the tail end of a pickup crossin' the road. The jalopy rolled over and slid into the gully. I was on my way back from deliverin' twins at the Simpson's farm. Wasn't nothing I could do but pronounce Toby Coulter and Hollis dead. His brother Leroy, and the oldest Whitfield boy walked away, but they ain't talking. Sheriff Coulter's a mess."

Ela moaned and rushed to her father's arms, sobbing.

The doctor's shoulders slumped, and he brushed a hand over his balding head before looking at Patrick. "I was comin' back when Sally called my radio with your emergency."

"Hollis, who works at the motor lodge?" I broke in. "And Leroy from the Glass House?"

The doctor nodded and tears filled my eyes when I remembered Hollis' smile, his hand offering me a tissue, the eagerness in his voice when he gave me Leroy's name. It couldn't be. "I met them when I came to town last weekend. They helped me…find a…place to stay."

"And the truck?" Patrick interrupted, reminding me that it wasn't about me.

The doctor brightened just enough to look alive. "It spun out and hit a tree, but Charlie Green and his daughter are okay. She's with her uncle."

"Thank God," Patrick sighed. "Em is only four."

The doctor nodded. "A miracle, as much as I kin see. Can't for the life of me figure where those kids were rushing to—or from—at eight-thirty in the morning."

I did. They were coming back from an all-nighter and Hollis was likely late for work.

Patrick voiced my thoughts. "Were they drinking?"

He shrugged. "Broken beer bottles all over, but don't know where they came from. Deputies were still sweeping up the mess when I left. An autopsy would tell for sure, but I don' think the parents'll go for that. Sheriff Coulter's already hauled Charlie to jail. Thought you'd want to know, since he works for you. Hal Glass was at the scene before me. He may know more."

Patrick gave a worried look to Alvarez, still holding Ela in his arms. Then the physician who'd likely seen more than his share of miracles and tragedies, set his bag on the table and looked at me. He fished into his jacket, and pinched little Ben Franklin glasses onto his nose before lifting my leg. "So what have we here?"

"I tripped," I said.

"That so?" he answered. "Swelling's not too bad." He squinted at Ela. "You have a hand in this?"

She nodded, wiping a sleeve across the tears dripping down her cheeks.

A hint of a smile softened the doctor's life-worn features. "Never thought I'd say this, but if you was a boy, you'd make a damn good doctor. Any Injun Reservation should feel lucky to have you as a midwife."

His touch was rougher than Ela's when he bent my foot up and down and back and forth. "And you're a lucky little lady. A bad twist. Some say it hurts more'n a break. You got some bruisin' coming up. Don't put weight on it for at least a week. He looked at my naked left hand, raising a bushy white eyebrow. "You got help?"

Help? Oh, he meant a husband. His assumption of both Ela's career prospects, and my marital status irritated me, but he'd been through a lot, and it was only ten o'clock.

"I'll be fine."

I looked at the soon-to-be-slandered candidate for Congress. "I'm sorry about the confusion over the interview, but it doesn't look like I'll be able to help you out, after all."

Wishing Patrick O'Grady luck, I said, "As soon as my car gets back, I'll be on my way."

"Oh, no you won't," came from the doctor. "I just told you, young lady, no weight on that foot for at least a week. That includes driving a car."

Patrick added, "I caused the injury. I shouldn't have come up to you from behind like that. And you were on your way here for an interview I'd forgotten. Tammy said you were new in town, with no family. You're welcome here for as long as you need—to recover."

I should have been thrilled that the proverbial coin of fate had flipped yet again, affording me one last chance to prove Billy wrong, but I hated using my sprained ankle to get close to these kind and generous people and probe their darkest secrets—even if it was the only way I could keep Billy from destroying their lives.

In case Patrick's invitation was just to be polite, I gave him an out. "I couldn't possibly. It's just a sprain. All I need is a ride back to town."

"If you're worried about how it'll look, don't bother," Patrick interrupted. "I'm leaving tomorrow afternoon for town hall meetings in Brunswick and the Sea Islands. I won't be back until Sunday. If you're up to it, we can do your interview tomorrow morning before I leave, and we can see how you feel when I come back."

My ankle throbbed at full force after Doc Hill's prodding and twisting, and the strangling ace bandage he'd applied like a tourniquet. Ela stared at me, something, a light in her eyes urging me to stay. Clarence rolled onto my good foot, and the doctor was holding out two cute little pink pills. I accepted both the invitation and the pills.

CHAPTER 16

Something poked my arm and blew warm, moist air into my ear. "Wake up!"

I sensed panic in the little voice but couldn't move. There was a heavy weight on my chest and my limbs felt like rubber. It took all my strength to raise my eyelids, one at a time. Metal blades churned the air above me, their constant rotation making me queasy until I shifted my gaze to the open window across the room. I stared at white, puffy clouds, until my insides calmed, and I remembered where I was. *Langesford.*

My memory came back in disjointed spurts. The Righteous Brothers on the radio, a beautiful plantation house, someone died. Wire cutters. I closed my eyes again as the events of the day fell into place. I had a badly sprained ankle. Hollis and the sheriff's son were dead.

"Are you awake?" followed another poke in the arm.

I'd heard that childish voice before and turned my head to meet bright green eyes in a tiny, freckled face surrounded by wild black curls. *Kitten?*

Patrick's daughter leaned over me her lips pressed in a concerned frown. "I thought you were dead."

What an odd greeting. I again thought of old souls, concluding that Kitten must have picked a wise one on her way into the world.

"No, I'm not dead," I assured her and nudged Clarence's head off my stomach to push myself up against the headboard of an antique four-poster bed.

I looked at what could have been a nineteenth-century, New Orleans brothel. "Oh my."

The little girl climbed onto the foot of the bed. "I saw you before. At the library."

"Yes, you're Kitten."

She was on her knees, perilously close to my elevated foot. "Only Daddy calls me that. My *real* name is Danielle, but I don't like it. It sounds mean. I like Dani better."

Good choice. "Then I'll call you Dani. My name is…Sarah."

"Sarah," rolled off her tongue. Her lips puckered as if tasting something bad.

"I don't like it!" Princess Dani pronounced. "But it's okay until I think of something better."

We both turned at the light knock on the door followed by Ela stepping inside. Dani put a finger to her lips, making a shushing sound. "I'm going to think of a new name for Sarah," the child told her. "But it'll be a secret."

Ela's bottomless dark eyes sparkled with love and humor as she wagged a finger. "Secrets can hurt people, *niñita*." She tapped the finger on the center of Dani's forehead. "Be careful that what you keep hidden in here…" then tapped Dani's chest above her heart, "is only to protect those you keep in here."

Ela's composure surprised me. She'd just lost someone she obviously cared about, though I didn't know if it was Hollis or the sheriff's son. And less than two weeks ago, even a college degree and acceptance into medical school wouldn't get her into Malloy's Cafeteria in Jeffers. I wondered how she could be so calm in the face of such tragedy and injustice.

Dani put her hand over her heart and with an innocence only a child can manage, she promised, "I will only keep the secrets that will hurt the people I love. That's why I never tell anyone you're my cousin."

Ela's gaze shot toward me and her body stiffened, waiting for my reaction.

It explained Patrick's enthusiasm at her good news about Medical School. "Your secret is safe with me too," I assured her, though I had no idea how I'd keep Billy Berens from hurting everyone she loved.

"Your name is beautiful, Ela," I changed the subject. "I've never heard it before."

Dani blurted, "It's Apache and means Unity. I don't know what *that* means, but I like how it sounds."

Ela tickled the little girl into a fit of laughter that shook the bed. "Unity means being together," she explained. "In mind and spirit. When that happens, so can miracles."

If only it were that easy.

"Can unity bring my mama back?" Dani asked.

It surprised me. She couldn't have been more than three when Barbara died. I wondered how much she remembered of her mother. More than I thought, judging from the sadness on her expressive face.

I still felt the crushing pain of losing my child. The feeling that a part of me would always be missing. Was it the same for children who lost a parent?

"There's no need, *querida*," Ela answered. "She is always with you, in your heart."

The dog whined and Ela said, "I think Clarence needs a walk, and you need to change your clothes to help Mattie set the table."

"Can I wear my Sunday dress, since we have company?"

Ela's glance was cautious. "I don't know. Miss Sarah may not be ready for the stairs."

"Please?" Dani urged me. "After, we can play games. Chinese checkers. Or puzzles."

She reminded me of Glory, never taking no for an answer. Was Glory like that as a child, I wondered? Always busy, always questioning, analyzing, *thinking*. They'd have been a great pair. The ankle still hurt like hell, and I had no idea how I'd make it downstairs, but I said, "I'd love to come down. If I'm not intruding."

"Of course not," Ela and Dani said together.

I asked Ela, "Is my car back? I had a bag in there." I couldn't find a clock amid the clutter of antique French porcelain. "And do I have time to wash and change?"

Ela checked her turquoise-inlaid watch. "It's half-past six. Supper is at seven-thirty, after the news, and your car is parked in one of the garages. Your things are in the armoire. I brought them up."

Fortunately, she didn't ask why I brought virtually all my personal belongings to a job interview. With a glance at Dani and Clarence finally leaving the room, she sat at the foot of the bed. "But let's see how your foot looks before you take on the stairs."

Those magical fingers again gently pressed my ankle, slowly rotating and massaging it at the same time. "Swelling's down. Doc was right. Nothing's broken. I think he has X-ray vision."

"Maybe so," I agreed less enthusiastically. "But he doesn't have your bedside manner."

Her smile was kind. "You caught him on a bad day. He can diagnose people before city doctors put on their white coats. And I've seen him bring peace to people who lost limbs or loved ones in horrible ways."

She fell silent and I knew we were both thinking about what the good doctor had faced back at the mortuary—while I was sleeping off my Percocet.

I touched her hand. "Was it Hollis or Toby?"

She cleared her throat. "You are very perceptive."

"I'm a writer," slipped out. I held my breath as her bottomless eyes seemed to see into my very soul.

"Hollis," she answered, then pointed to a corner by the door and changed the subject. "I thought you'd want to be up and around, so I brought crutches while you were sleeping. Be *very* careful on your way downstairs—and up too, I suppose. Patrick will give you a hand," she added with a weak smile.

"Patrick? No," I started. "I mean, he's helped me enough for one day. "I'll be fine. I broke my leg skiing once and got around pretty well on crutches." *When I was twelve.*

I looked down at my blouse with Patrick O'Grady's blood still on the sleeve, and wet spots from Clarence's fresh drool. I picked a piece of straw from a buttonhole. "Can you point me to the bathroom? I need to clean up."

She nodded at a door to what was probably once a maid's room and explained, "When Patrick's parents updated the house, they added bathrooms for guests." A new kind of sadness shone from her ravaged eyes. "But Patrick doesn't entertain much anymore."

It never occurred to me that this room could be occupied by anyone—alive. "I hope I'm not taking your room."

A very unladylike snort came before a nervous giggle. "Me? Stay in Miss Danielle's room? Not even if I was white."

It reminded me that in most of the country, American Indians were treated like blacks, both legally and socially.

"Miss Danielle? Do you mean Dani?"

"No, no. This room belonged to the queen of the Langesfords. Patrick's great-great-grandmother. Stories say after her son was killed in the War, she never left it, and hung herself from this very bed—out of grief."

We both looked up at the sagging mahogany canopy frame.

"I'm sorry if I shocked you," Ela said. "But if you're here more than a day, you'll learn all about it. No one has seen her ghost, but if it worries you, we can find another room."

"I grew up in a Pre-Revolutionary mansion," I answered. "You can't do that and not believe in ghosts—or let them bother you."

I was eight years old the first and last time I looked for a ghost. I snuck up the steep, narrow stairs to the old third floor servants' quarters, where I found the old photo of Mary in a carpet bag beneath a loose floorboard. I moved to the window, using my poodle skirt to wipe a clean spot on the wavy glass. A sudden gust of chilly air in the stuffy, closed-up room scared me and I took the picture back to my room, tucking it behind the velvet backing of my ballerina jewelry box.

My grandmother had given me the box that played *The Tennessee Waltz.* A loose piece of velvet lining the top of the music box was the door to my secret place. Photos, feathers, small stones. It didn't hold much, but they were my treasures. When I felt lonely, I'd wind up the music, pull out the photo, and talk to Mary as if she was a long-lost ancestor. I guess out of habit, I'd stuffed the now silent jewelry box into the pillowcase when I left Atlanta.

Lost in the memory, I jumped at Ela's gentle voice when she asked, "Are you sure?"

"About what?" I let her think I was still hazy from the Percocet, which may have been true. I hadn't thought about that picture in ages but remembered it twice in a few days.

"Oh, ghosts," I said. Reaching back to my Freshman anthropology class, I knew most American Indian tribes believed that dead ancestors play a part in the lives of their descendants. Christians too, for that matter, with their saints and personal communications with a silent, invisible deity. "The dead can't hurt us," I said, perhaps a little too sharply

"Perhaps." She sighed. "I'll let you change for supper. Nothing fancy. Patrick has asked my father and me to join you."

I chose jeans over the cut-offs or the little black number I'd worn to Billy's meeting. Despite my bragging, I was rusty with the crutches, and nearly fell trying to answer a knock on my door. "Come in," I said.

Patrick O'Grady stepped inside wearing a clean blue cotton shirt and khakis. "I thought maybe you could use some help."

"It isn't necessary," I lied—again. "I have crutches." When his smile faded at my rejection of his Southern gallantry, I recanted, "But they seem a little tall. I might be better off sliding down the banister. Assuming I land on the right foot, of course."

"I've tried it. It's trickier than it looks." He stepped toward me. "I have a better idea."

I held the crutch out defensively. "No! You don't have to—"

"Don't worry, I know you don't like being carried."

He handed me an antique, black maple walking stick with a carnival glass crystal top. "It was my great-grandmother's. Camilla was a lot like you. Highly independent. Fearless. She had this made after falling from a horse when she was seventy-five. She died in her nineties, but we keep it around for emergencies."

I held the antique crystal knob up to the light from the window, enjoying the colorful kaleidoscope reflecting from the diamond-cut facets. "It's beautiful. And priceless. I don't want to break it."

"No worries, you can practice up here in the hall. Just remember, walking with a cane is different than crutches. You hold the cane on your good side." He demonstrated by holding out a pretend-bad left leg and putting his weight on the stick on his right side. "Think of it as a third leg."

"Something tells me you've had experience."

"I raise horses."

So, the crutches were his. No wonder they were too tall. I gave the walking stick a try and found it more natural, though my ankle reminded me when I forgot and tried to step on it.

His approving smile took my breath away. "You're a natural," he said. "Ready to go down?"

I held my breath at the top of the stairs. The flat, level surface of the hall was one thing. A curving, carpeted staircase was something else entirely. But there was no going back. Patrick stayed close to me while I clumped down the seemingly endless staircase, one jarring step at a time. Fortunately, he only had to wrap an arm around my waist a couple times before we reached the bottom.

After a heavy sigh of relief, I raised my head to see Alvarez, Ela, Dani, and a tall, austere looking black woman in a gray uniform and starched white apron, staring at us. Mattie, I assumed. They applauded, and I made a clumsy curtsy before limping into the dining room.

Supper was chicken and sausage gumbo, flavored with a Creole seasoning Mattie said she found in the recipes from a long-passed servant named Flora. I choked at the name, knowing she was literally her daughter's slave.

I soon learned that Mattie's austere demeanor was at odds with her generous spirit. At least when it came to Patrick, Ela, Dani, and to a lesser degree, Alvarez. But the Yankee twang in my voice seemed to hit a raw nerve. I won her over when I asked for a second helping.

Ela said little and ate less. Greif, I thought. Poor Hollis. Only the good died young.

I waited in vain for Patrick to talk about his victory at the debate, or the election just a few months away. At the Stainsby table, politics and news always led the dinner discussions, except for occasional kudos to my brothers, or rebukes to me for overstepping my feminine boundaries. I gave Patrick points for shielding his young daughter from the ugly and dangerous events happening across the country.

After we devoured the best peach cobbler I'd ever tasted. Ela rose and took Dani's hand. "Say goodnight to your daddy, *chica*. And to Miss Sarah. You have a big day tomorrow."

I expected a battle like I'd so often pitched at being sent to my room while other kids were still playing in the shadows of Historic Boston's ancient oak trees. Instead, she jumped up, announcing, "Yes! Medallion's foal! Wake me up early, I don't want to miss when it's born."

I was shocked that a six-year-old would be allowed to watch a horse give birth. *I* didn't want to watch a horse give birth.

Ela smiled. "You won't. But you must stay back. The mama horse needs room to breathe, you know."

Dani's curls bounced in agreement before changing the subject. "Will you read that book about the wooden horse with soldiers inside? How did they fit? Why were they there?"

Her questions faded as they made their way upstairs. I looked at Patrick. "*The Iliad*? To a six-year old?"

He shrugged. "She likes the action. She'll understand more when she's older."

I looked at Alvarez. "And birthing horses?"

His grin took years off his rugged features. "The circle of life," he said. "It is better to focus on the beginning than the end."

I couldn't fault either man's logic and cautioned myself against getting too involved. I was there to keep Billy from destroying the family reputation, not tell Patrick O'Grady how to raise his child. I'd already stepped over professional bounds by becoming physically involved with Billy. I couldn't become emotionally attached to the extended O'Grady family.

I licked cobbler crumbs from my fork. "I see."

Alvarez stood, nodding respectfully. "I need to check on Medallion."

With just the two of us at the table, Patrick leaned toward me. "I know it's late Sarah, but if you're up to it, we could have our interview now."

Interview? Now? After I *bit* him, got doped up on Percocet, and napped in the bed his great-great-grandmother hung herself from?

"But aren't you traveling tomorrow? Don't you have things to prepare?"

A speech? A campaign? Didn't he understand how dangerous Billy was? Winkler had said Edward O'Grady attracted money like flowers did bees, but so far, his son didn't seem to have a clue about pressing the flesh for currency. Billy had already beaten him to Brunswick, picking the pockets of Barry Goldwater's former Southern Democratic Party supporters.

"I'm as prepared as I'll ever be. My daughter and Langesford come first. But it's been a terrible day for you. I understand if you'd rather wait 'til I come back."

A spark of mischief lit his sky-blue eyes. "Or, I suppose we could do the interview at the stable in the morning, between contractions."

Was he testing me? Nanny Irene's, "Don't put off until tomorrow what you can do today," flashed through my mind. "No! I'm fine now. As you know, I had a rather long nap."

I glanced at the stairs. "But my letter of reference is upstairs."

"Don't bother. We can just talk. Tammy spoke well of you and I can see how much Ela and Dani already like you. Has my daughter given you another name yet?"

He chuckled at my confusion when I answered, "She's thinking about it. Why?"

"She only does that for people she likes. Are you up to talking in the office?"

I pushed my chair back with one leg and reached for my walking stick. "Of course."

I hobbled close behind him to his office and again breathed deeply of the smell of wood, leather, and old books; this time without the haze of pain and confusion—or horror over Hollis' unnecessary death because of a faulty traffic light.

This time, Patrick sat behind the enormous partner's desk placed kitty-corner to the old fireplace. At his direction, I sat in the chair opposite him, stretching my bad leg into the desk's kneehole and resting the walking stick against the chair's tufted, cowhide arms.

"How's your arm?" I asked. "Human bites are toxic. Did the doctor look at it?" Way to go, I thought. Remind your future employer about how you bit him like a little dog while he was only trying to help you.

He rolled up the creased sleeve of his shirt to show me his wound. Or rather, his band aid. "Right as rain." He smiled. "It appears your bark is worse than your bite."

I wanted to laugh but didn't know if he'd meant it as a joke. "I'm so sorry."

A shrug. "It's nothing."

I broke the awkward silence with, "Dani is a real gem. She seems more mature than most children her age. And Tammy mentioned helping you with your record-keeping and correspondence. I've had some writing classes, and other clerical experience in Cambridge. Massachusetts."

He leaned toward me. "I'm familiar with the city, and the accent. We've met. I remember you now."

I held my breath. Our families were both Democrats, though Southern and Northern ones were often at odds. But if he knew my father, he may have seen me, or God forbid, been among the political cadre invited to my ill-fated wedding.

"On the Fourth of July, by the library. How was Tammy's tour?"

I exhaled. "Wonderful. She's an amazing docent, as well as the most efficient librarian I've ever met. And the genealogy addition is out of this world." It felt good to tell the truth.

"Yes, she said you were looking into your family. Any luck?"

"No. She suggested I try the Court House."

His gazed softened. "I'm sorry to hear that. Family and good honest work are the only important things in life."

His scarred, working man's hands folded on the desktop. "So, fill me in on your experience—and how you ended up here—not that I don't have faith in my cousin's instincts."

I leaned toward him within the muted glow of a refitted Tiffany lamp and tried to keep my lies to a minimum. "Most recently, I worked as a stenographer. I had to quit for...personal reasons, as you know, from Tammy. But even though I haven't found what I expected, I really like this town. I'd like to stay here longer...to do more family research. And I'm grateful to Tammy for this interview."

At least the last part was true.

"Yes, she's a gem," he agreed. The big grandfather clock chimed nine o'clock, and he checked it against his Timex watch. "So, what should I know about you?"

Omitting my degrees, I told him, "I type sixty words a minute without errors and keep a balanced checkbook. I'm good with tight schedules, and my organizational skills rival a Swiss clock. I also love children."

One child. For too short a time.

After a long look at me, he stood. "Well I'm in a bit of a bind with both Tammy and Ela heading back to school. And I'll admit that with the campaign, I may have taken advantage of them both. I'll need you to manage my office as well as watch over Dani. Since its two jobs, will twice minimum wage, including room and board, work? We can re-evaluate the responsibilities and pay after the election. Mattie and the others will be able to fill you in on the schedule and duties and help with Dani as needed. Any questions?"

"Only one," I said. "On the overlook, you said, 'It's just an illusion'. What did you mean?"

His jaw set. "Peace."

CHAPTER 17

I slept surprisingly well on the ancient feather-tick mattress in the "French Room" even after flushing the rest of the Percocet down the toilet. The ankle still throbbed like a son of a gun, but Aspirin would have to do. At five-thirty in the morning, Dani woke me to again invite me to the impending birth.

"It's a tradition," she explained. "Everyone goes to Morning Bird Stables, so the baby horse feels welcome."

Until it's sold, I thought, and used my ankle as an excuse.

The precocious child's frown showed her disappointment, but she accepted my logic. "I'll tell you all about it when we get back."

I hopped downstairs at seven o'clock to call Glory from Patrick's office before she left for work. I was distracted by the scent of fresh blueberry muffins and followed it to the empty kitchen. Grabbing a muffin from the plate on the table, I was surprised to see a second phone by the refrigerator when only a quarter of all homes in Georgia had even one.

I stretched the cord to the counter, where I could watch the door, and dialed Glory's number, reversing the charges, as always.

"Hey girl," she breezed. "Did you mail those copies?

"Yesterday. You should have it today or tomorrow. I don't have much time but wanted you to know I have a job at Patrick O'Grady's plantation, as secretary and nanny."

"Nanny!" screeched into the phone. "How in God's name did you manage that?"

I kept the details to a minimum in case the family came back early, finishing with, "He's leaving today for Brunswick. Call me when you get my envelope. The area code is 912 and the number is 792-1094. And remember to ask for Sarah."

A truck door slammed, and a rumble of voices approached the kitchen. "I gotta go. The horse must have been born."

"What?"

"It's a long story," I said and hung up.

I was leaning against the butcher block table with a half-eaten muffin when Dani yanked the old screen door open and ran in, red stains all over her white pinafore.

"Dani!" I lunged for her, forgetting the walking stick.

"It's the birth stuff from Star!" she shrieked while I checked her for injuries.

My heart still racing, I used the countertop to pull myself back up to my good foot and assumed Star was the name of the newborn horse, or pony, or colt, while Dani explained the equine birthing process. "She just popped out. Like a pea from a pod. All wrinkled and messy." "And when the mama feeds the baby, it grows stronger. She raised her arm to show me a tiny bicep. "Like me."

Ela followed Alvarez inside and took Dani's stained hand with her own red-tinted one. "C'mon little one, we need to clean up."

Patrick came in last, the sleeves of his stained blue work shirt rolled up, showing tanned forearms, one of them sporting a fresh band aid. He smiled as if he'd just come home from the office, and asked, "Feeling better?"

"What?" I looked down at my now-throbbing bandaged foot. "Yes, thanks. I made it downstairs—with the help of my trusty scepter/walking stick." *That was now across the room, on the floor, by the phone.* "I don't think I'll need it much longer."

"Take all the time you need."

"Thanks." I shuffled aside for him to pass me in the narrow space between the table and countertop, but he didn't move.

"It looks like I have some time before I head out to Brunswick," he said. "Let me change my shirt. We can review the things I've let go, and I can give you a tour of Langesford, if you're up to it."

Up to it? Hell no, but I wouldn't miss it for the world. "Of course. I'm curious about the new, uh—"

"Foal."

"Right, I knew that." I hoped it would be cleaned up by the time we got there.

Fifteen minutes later, we faced each other again across the expansive desk. He emptied the contents of two drawers, making it clear that Evelyn's priority was planning her wedding, while Tammy's was the magnificent library.

He frowned at the mess. "I'm a bit disorganized and keeping things in order can be time consuming. Some of these are my father's papers that I still haven't gotten to."

"Didn't he have a secretary?" I asked, hoping to put a timeline to the disarray.

"My mother."

Wishing I could click my heels and disappear, I offered the standard, "I'm so sorry."

I wanted to comfort him by sharing my own sense of loss for the woman who'd held my father's career—and our family—together. Since her death, Father had never had the same connection to his constituents. Even his campaign manager, Abe Liebowitz, seemed confused about reading the winds of change. My brothers disappeared into their own lives, and I was, well, just plain lost.

"Thank you," Patrick said. "My mother was an amazing woman. Most O'Grady women are."

His eyes glazed for a moment, no doubt thinking of Barbara, the woman who gave him that amazing daughter—and died too soon. As if eager to leave the room," he added, "I'd like this sorted and filed. Anything older than ten years can be packed away in the old summer kitchen downstairs.

I raised an eyebrow at storing family archives in a basement kitchen and he added, "Musty old receipts for the most part. My father unloaded the most important documents onto the library, but it only created a small hole in our mountain of memorabilia."

He nodded at the desk. "A hole that seems to fill up rapidly."

Morning sunbeams streamed into the comfortable old room and I noticed worn spots in the oriental rug, fade marks on the Queen Anne chairs, and a crack now and then in the old leaded-glass windows. Was the antebellum décor due to preference or necessity? I wondered. Necessity lent credence to my land-rich and cash-poor theory. I answered, "Waste not, want not."

He nodded. "Exactly, but there need to be limits. If you have the time and the inclination, feel free to apply your Swiss-watch organization skills to any processes you deem necessary. Tammy can help. By adding Dani to the mix, the job may require more than forty hours a week, I'll pay overtime and you can make your own schedule—within limits of course."

I concluded he had to be the most sought-after employer in the district and hoped his largess would help him on election night. Which brought me to the question I'd been dying to ask. "Where are your campaign materials? Buttons, flyers, posters, signs? I've had some experience with promotion."

Some? I could do it in my sleep.

I added, "I know I've only been here a short time, but other than at the debate, where you were great by the way, I haven't heard anything about your platform. What *is* the direction you plan to take if—when—you're elected. People will want to know."

His lips set into a thin line. I'd gone too far—again. His family had been in politics nearly as long as mine. Like me, he'd probably been trotted out on the campaign trail most of his life, and to him, I was just a nanny/file clerk.

"If you mean where do I stand on Civil Rights, I stand where my family has always stood, during the Revolution, the War, and now. We've always abhorred slavery as a system and an ideology, reluctantly accepting it as a necessary evil to do business. Before Sumter, my great-grandfather, Anthony Langesford, recognized its inevitable demise due to automation and the drain of the Underground Railroad.

"When he joined the Army of Northern Virginia, he freed his slaves and granted rent-free, century-long leases to any family that stayed and worked the land. When those leases matured the remaining families received deeds. Fortunately for me, they've resisted selling out to investors looking to build mini-malls and drive-in movies."

I flinched at the unintentional reference to Billy's plan and leaned on the walking stick's crystal bulb to follow him to the window, where we watched the people who kept a family business alive. "That is my platform," he said. "I'm a Democrat and a Southerner, so I'm labeled a Southern Democrat. But I'm an American first. I believe in freedom. Civil Rights is *not* an issue for me personally. Our Declaration of Independence and Constitution are very clear about the rights of *every* citizen. I also believe a good education is a right, not a privilege, and no one should be denied a seat on a bus, a drink at a lunch counter, or a place to relieve themselves."

A corner of his mouth lifted when he turned to me. "I also believe the founding fathers intended the word, 'men' to include women. But while most anyone will agree with what I just said in theory, I can't say it in a Georgia town hall meeting and expect to win an election."

I couldn't disagree.

On our way back to his desk, he explained, "I haven't published my platform because it's not very popular right now and may never be. I don't lie well, so I cloud it behind a milk-toast position of common sense and compromise. It's a very painful fence to sit on."

I drank in his kind blue eyes, bright with sincerity and conviction. While I'd fallen in lust with Billy's impassioned speech in the car outside my Atlanta apartment, I fell in love with Patrick O'Grady's honesty and humanity, doomed as they may be.

"And you think dancing around the issues will get you elected?"

"At one time, maybe. But things have changed. Now, I'm not so sure, but I'll try my damnedest and push as hard as I can." He touched my arm. "C'mon, let me show you my world."

He helped me into the front seat of his twenty-year-old truck. Despite being a working vehicle, it was washed, polished, and without a dent.

He noticed my assessment and said, "It was my first. Love at first sight."

I wondered if he and Barbara had sat together in this truck, planning their future. A sudden chill made me scoot to the end of the worn leather bench seat, closer to the window. "It's very nice."

Thoughts of Barbara Kinney-O'Grady faded as we put the house and magnolia-lined drive behind us, coating the truck's finish with a layer of fine red Georgia dust. As we drove past the skeleton of an old gin house he said, "My great-grandmother, Camilla shot and killed a KKK member here," as if it happened last month, and not a century ago. "They tried to burn it down because her father's Yankee partner—the first Patrick O'Grady, built it."

Then came the old slave quarters. Renovated to resemble a little village, it now housed full-time employees and migrant families at the now-diversified farm complex. There was also a bunk house for single ranch hands and men with long commutes who stayed during the week. All the buildings were well-kept, some with little gardens and flowerbeds.

"A great tax write-off," I observed, calculating the depreciation and maintenance credits.

He hit the brakes in front of a field of sweet potatoes. "Langesford doesn't do things for people in order to get tax breaks," he said sharply. "They deserve decent housing, even if it's temporary. That's why I never have trouble hiring good help, and have an experienced, reliable pool of seasonal employees. Some have fine homes in Texas, New Mexico or Arizona. They come back every year to earn college money for their kids and teach them the value of honest work."

"I'm sorry," I answered. "But you could claim it."

He put me in my place with, "I have degrees in both economics and agriculture. I know I can, but I won't use people that way."

He punched the old V-8 engine and we turned back onto the dirt and gravel road. His mood seemed to brighten as we followed split rail fencing to a rustic arch made of tree limbs. A hand-painted sign welcomed visitors to Morning Bird Stables. His other love, I thought. And from the delighted, little boy smile on his face, his passion. I gaped at horses of all breeds, colors and sizes grazing and running together as if in the wild.

Alvarez met us inside the gate where more exotic horses pranced in the exercise yard. A half-dozen men wearing chaps and leather vests looked like they'd just stepped out of *Bonanza*. Fortunately, they were unarmed. One black cowboy tapped a finger to his hat before taking the lead of a huge, white stallion.

"Andalusian," Patrick said. "Anthony Langesford started breeding them before the War. He brought his first stud from New Orleans. The first Patrick O'Grady brought the mustangs and pintos from out West after the War. He named the stable after…a Comanche friend. Now, we breed mustangs for their agility and stamina, walkers, quarter horses, Morgans and a few racing breeds."

Even with the walking stick, I was grateful for his supporting hand on my elbow to steady me on the uneven ground as we approached a small, gray and brown spotted mare standing with a spindly-legged *foal* suckling her. The mother moved as we came closer, dislodging the baby. The newborn turned a head way too big for its body toward us and I noticed a white, star-shaped blaze on its—nose?

"Is that—"

"Star. She's a paint. Some say pinto. They're smart, gentle and loyal." He glanced at Clarence, sleeping in the shade under a nearby tree. "Like big, leggy dogs, only more useful. Dani's ridden double since she could walk, and this year, she rode alone on an experienced mount. In two years, when Star is ready and Dani's more skilled, they'll pair up."

The mare shook her head and approached us. I stepped back on the wrong foot, but the walking stick kept me from falling onto the muddied yard.

"You all right?" Patrick asked.

"Me? Sure," I huffed. "I love horses. Ride 'em all the time. All over the place."

His smile was patient. "I see. Would you like to see more of the stable? Maybe pick out a nice gentle mare and take a ride? After your foot heals of course."

"Sure, that would be nice. Some other time. Down the road."

Despite my wariness of horses after a bad fall during an event at Boston's elite, Meadowlark Equestrian Academy, I was a little disappointed that I wouldn't be around long enough to try it. Checking my watch like a good secretary, I was surprised that it was almost noon. "Shouldn't we get back?"

"There's time. I'll still beat the traffic if I leave right after dinner. And I can say goodbye to Dani."

An hour later, tired from the ride and the fresh air, and badly in need of more aspirin, I propped my aching foot across my good knee in the truck, leaning my head against the half-closed window. I bumped my head when we hit the hole in the road by the turn-off to the house. "Why don't you fill that?"

"There's a story to it."

Everything at Langesford—and in the South—seemed to have a story.

The front door was open when we pulled up. Mattie and Dani both stood with legs apart, arms folded across their chests. Patrick helped me out as Mattie scolded, "Nearly missed dinner. Terrible waste o' food. You jest in time afore I throw it to the hogs."

Dani rushed to his arms, tears in her eyes. "I thought you left without saying good-bye."

Her fear of losing another parent constricted my heart. I was an adult when my mother suffered through surgery and months of chemotherapy before finally giving up. We'd had ample warning of her impending death, but a little piece of me died with her last breath.

I couldn't imagine how terrifying it must have been for Dani to learn the finality of death at only three years old. The thought of her living with the fear of losing her other parent, brought tears to my eyes. I blinked them away as Patrick set her down and stooped to her level.

"You know I won't ever leave without your permission, sweet pea. I'll only be gone a little while."

His voice carried an emotion I'd never heard from my own father. Pure unconditional, eternal, and undemanding love. He stood, putting Dani's hand in mine. "You have a new friend to keep you company while Ela and Tammy get ready to go back to college."

She squeezed my hand and I thought of Rose and what might have been, even if the marriage to Ricky was doomed from the start. With Dani on my walking stick side, Patrick wrapped his arm around my waist to guide us both up the steps.

An hour later, he was gone. Dani and I stood on the veranda, watching him drive away in an almost-new, white Ford Mustang. The anti-Cadillac.

Ela was tending a hand who'd fallen off a tractor. Mattie was in the kitchen cleaning up and getting ready for supper. It was time to go to work. Clarence followed close behind us, hanging his head as if already missing his master.

I was pleasantly surprised when Mattie served supper before the news—cut up hot dogs in spaghetti. Nanny Irene made that when my parents were out, and Cook had the night off. It was one of my favorites, second only to Kraft macaroni & cheese. It was good to see that some things hadn't changed. Dani chattered about the foal and convinced me her daddy let her watch the news.

I doubted it, but it was only six o'clock, and despite rising before the sun, she balked at going to bed early. Since I had a mountain of work to do in the office and hadn't seen the news in days, I let her join me, planning to switch stations if it turned ugly.

The Pickrick was old news, with only a footnote about Maddox's charges for contempt of court. Except for a brief mention that the students who disappeared in Mississippi weeks ago were still missing, the upcoming Republican National Convention in California monopolized the commentary.

I seethed at clips of the Republican nominees' posturing and ultra-conservative rhetoric. Of the nine candidates, only Nelson Rockefeller and

Barry Goldwater stood a chance. A rich, New York aristocrat vs. a hot-headed cowboy. Goldwater opposed the use of legislation to achieve Civil Rights. The liberal Rockefeller seemed open to it, but I figured if the Republicans wanted that, they'd be Democrats. I turned off the TV.

While Dani had insisted on watching the news, she paid more attention to coloring, putting a puzzle together, or playing with a doll. Now, she looked up, her big green eyes glassy with fatigue. "Why did you do that?"

"Because I didn't like what I was hearing," I said. Burying my head in the sand, perhaps, but I'd had a good day and didn't want to spoil it.

"Me either. Why do they all scream so much?"

The little minx! I thought she was totally immersed in her new Barbie dreamhouse.

"Because they think whoever talks the loudest will win."

"Does it work?"

"Only for men, it seems." While I doubted Patrick O'Grady was the kind of man to scream himself into office, I had no doubt Billy could bluster his way through a tornado. The weight of my real purpose for being there suddenly exhausted me.

"C'mon," I said, tickling her bare toes. "Time for you to go to bed."

Her face screwed up in protest, but I appealed to her generous nature. "You don't want me to get in trouble my first day on the job, do you? Besides, I think I have some Lily of the Valley bubble bath. I'll share it with you—just for tonight. To celebrate Star's birth."

Pleased with the bargain, she bounced up to gather her toys for the trip upstairs. Bath time went fast, considering it was her second of the day, and she leaped into bed pointing to a huge tome that must have come from the library downstairs.

"My book is over there."

I pulled it down, wondering how long it would take before she gave up on *The Iliad* and begged for, *The Cat in a Hat.* She was sound asleep after ten pages, looking innocent and fragile, even after watching a horse deliver a foal.

I wondered if she had any friends her own age. It was doubtful, given their remote, self-sufficient setting. She'd start full-time school in six weeks. I hoped her generous and loving spirit wouldn't become tainted by racism. But I'd probably be gone by then. Best not get attached. I turned on her Donald

Duck nightlight and tried not to thump my walking stick as I limped out of her room.

I sat on Patrick's side of the old partner's desk and turned on the Tiffany lamp to scoop all the invoices, bills, and letters together. Mostly bills, I noticed, though only a few were past due.

Mattie left at seven, to the remodeled laundry building she shared with her grandson, Henry Hawkins. Dani and I were alone in the big old house, but I only felt the presence of Clarence snoring next to my feet. I took comfort from the sounds of the old house, still settling after more than two hundred years. The lack of family portraits was a welcome change from Stainsby Manor, where every wall was filled with portraits of long-dead relatives, their pale eyes judging from every angle.

I'd seen only one at Langesford. In the office, above the fireplace. A young woman with russet hair in a blue day dress, circa 1860s, standing by a pool of blue water. It was surprising to see a woman in a portrait from that era in a dress without a hoop. Her bright green eyes matched Dani's, but the adult woman's life reflected from those eyes, the set of her lips and jaw, and I saw sadness, loss, strength and wisdom. A slight woman compared to her natural surroundings, her back was straight and proud. The tiny brass tag on the frame said, "Camilla Langesford O'Grady 1846 – 1942."

So, this was the red-haired devil Danielle had described so cruelly in her journal. The woman Tammy said lied to Yankee soldiers to save her home. And who still rode at nearly eighty years old. I smiled and held up her walking stick. "Hello, Mrs. O'Grady. Thank you for the loan of your stick."

No answer of course, but the evening shadows gave the portrait an illusion of a nod. Perhaps it was time for a break, I pulled one of the Queen Anne chairs closer, facing her. "We have a little problem here, Miss Camilla," I said. "It seems a descendant of someone you knew, William Berens II, wants to destroy your legacy. I'd appreciate your help in stopping him."

A cloud floated across the moon, deepening the shadows in the room. Clarence growled in his sleep and I jumped at the loud thwack of the walking stick falling to the wood floor. Thankfully, the crystal top withstood the impact. When I looked up, the pensive young woman in the portrait seemed angry. I rubbed my tired eyes and looked again. Nope, no change.

The grandfather clock in the hall chimed eleven. I returned to the desk, checked my piles of documents, then opened the other drawers to make sure

I hadn't missed anything. The bottom left drawer stuck, but a good tug freed it.

"What the hell?" I whispered. Atop yet another pile of papers, lay an old key ring.

I smiled at the portrait and resisted the urge to blow out the candle-shaped bulb in the converted Tiffany. Turning the switch, I retrieved my stick, nodded to the O'Grady matriarch, and walked with Clarence toward the light at the top of the stairs.

CHAPTER 18

Patrick came back on Saturday evening, just in time to kiss Dani goodnight. I expected him to brief me on the trip and check my progress on the filing and correspondence, but after confirming I was almost fit to walk on two legs instead of three, he left to meet Alvarez.

At breakfast, Dani wouldn't allow him a moment that didn't include her. They spent the day at the stable with Star and I sat in his chair at the desk, facing a pile of newspapers on the floor. The July 9th edition of the *Atlanta Constitution* was on top. It looked like it had been read.

Midway down the front page, I saw, "Maddox answers for 'Pickrick Drumsticks', referring to the restaurant's famous chicken dish and the ax handles. The story reported that NAACP Legal Defense and Educational Fund attorney, Constance Baker Motley, had credited an eye-witness account for their swift action to investigate and prosecute. I turned to page three and saw a reprint of my article. The byline said, "L. Stainsby, Staff writer".

Staff writer! McGill had not only published it *with* a byline, he'd sent it to the top female Negro Civil Rights attorney in the country! I had to get back to Atlanta and thank Mr. McGill. Then I thought of Billy. Patrick had no idea what he was facing. I couldn't leave yet.

"Terrible mess, that Pickrick Incident, don't you think?" Patrick startled me from the doorway.

I rose for him to sit behind his desk, but he chose the seat opposite me, hands folded in his lap. He looked relaxed, but his gaze was cold, as if waiting for my answer. Was he testing my politics? "Yes, it was—I mean—it sounds, horrible."

"You've made quite an impression here over the last week." He'd changed the subject, but not his sour expression. "Kitten tells me you're her best friend, though she still hasn't settled on a new name for you."

"Well, there aren't a lot of children around here," I offered. "And she's very special."

"Yes, she is. I'll do anything to see she isn't hurt." His voice sounded tight.

I didn't like the way his eyes narrowed, as if studying me. "Are you concerned about Dani's safety? I heard that people aren't happy about your offer to bail out Charlie Green. Do you expect trouble?"

Finally, my patience snapped at his obstinate silence. "I may be a Yankee, but I'm not stupid."

"I'm sure you're not, *Miss Stainsby*." His voice was low, almost threatening. "And I may be a Georgia Cracker, but neither am I."

My brain was too shocked to tell my lungs to breathe. My career could be over before it took off if Patrick sued for ethics violations. I hadn't written anything, but I did use false pretenses to gain access to his home and files, intending to publish what I found. How could my pitiful little past catch up to me twice—in Podunk Georgia?

I looked at Camilla's portrait, straightened my spine and took the high road. "How did you know?"

"We've met. Before the library."

The idea floored me. He was eight years older than me and admittedly a homebody who even went to a Southern college. And if we'd met, I'd have remembered him. "That's not possible."

"Yes, it is."

"When? Where? How?"

"1954 Boston," he answered, his voice thick with inexplicable anger. "My mother was ill, so I went to the Stainsby Christmas Ball with my father. You danced very well by the way, despite the heels."

I remembered that ball. My first. I was fourteen. Gangly, defiant, and totally pissed off at the pink ballerina gown with a "V" neckline I didn't come close to filling out. But I'd loved the high heels, thinking tall meant attractive. Too bad I could barely walk in them and basically stumbled around the dance floor with pimply-faced boys and doddering old men.

Then I remembered. My mother had dragged a young man over to dance with me, introducing him only as, the son of a Georgia congressman. If she'd mentioned the name, I ignored it. He was my brother Adam's age and twenty-two was old to me back then. I was repulsed at how the sorority daughters of the old guard drooled over him.

I barely looked at him as we danced, and never spoke. When the music stopped, and he re-joined the frat-boys by the bar, I ran upstairs, stuffing the expensive gown behind a loose wallboard in my closet. It was probably still there.

I looked at him closely now. He'd filled out. There were lines in his forehead, and his skin had darkened from working in the sun. Tiny creases spread out from the corners of his eyes. "*The Tennessee Waltz,*" I said. "But I was just a kid. How did you remember?"

"I didn't, right away. You seemed familiar when we met at the library, and again at the overlook. There was something about how you carried yourself, the tilt of your head, that seemed familiar, but I couldn't place you."

He nodded to the papers on the floor. "I picked up some back issues in Brunswick and saw your byline. I see Adam now and then at Ag conferences and called him. He confirmed you were working at the *Constitution.* And this morning, when I heard you laughing with Kitten, I finally placed you.

"You had brown hair back then, pulled back in a ridiculous ballerina bun, I recall. You were with a skinny boy on the terrace, mimicking the conversations going on inside. It was quite hilarious. I was about to applaud when your mother found us both and threw us onto the dance floor. You just went through the motions. I apologize for my lack of charm."

He didn't look apologetic, and his frown told me the stroll down memory lane was over.

"Why are you here Laura?"

"My editor sent me here to cover the campaign," I hedged.

"That's not what I meant. Why are you *here.* In Georgia. Adam told me about the divorce, but said you were doing great work at the *Globe.* What happened?"

Apparently, Adam didn't go into the gory details of my drunk husband running over his own child in the driveway, then passing out without calling for help. I couldn't tell him—or anyone—about that, so I pointed at the editorial. "I came here to report on the Civil Rights Movement. I was the woman in the window at the Pickrick."

"I see. And the alias?"

I went cold inside. What did I have to lose at this point? The assignment? I'd already burned that bridge. My career. What career? I said, "As you know, my last name is well known in political circles."

"But why here? Why Jeffers? Why Langesford? What *story* is so important you'd use my cousin—and my daughter—to gain access to my home?"

He nodded toward my ankle. "Did you plan your 'injury' to get my sympathy?"

How could he think that? "Of course not!" Then my blood ran cold and the dam broke. "Okay but be careful what you ask for. Billy told my editor he had proof of allegations of corruption and crimes committed by your family. He assigned me to research the evidence.

"And exactly what corruption and crimes are you investigating?" His voice sounded like thunder in the closed room. But he didn't seem shocked about the so-called allegations. "The Berens clan has accused my family of imaginary crimes for generations. Jeremy's the only one worth a dime, and that's because...well, never mind. What witch-hunt is Billy on now?"

I raised a hand. "Please, just listen. I stopped working for Billy when I discovered his real motive." *But not until after I slept with him. And he doesn't know I quit.*

Patrick stood, stuffed his hands in his pockets, and walked to the window. I followed him, drawing strength from Camilla's walking stick. "He says your family is hiding a Negro bloodline. He plans to bring it up during the campaign and contest your ownership rights to Langesford."

His snort surprised me. "That's his plan? It's hard to throw a stone at a white crowd in the South and not hit someone with a slave in the family tree. He'll be laughed off the stage."

So, it was true. His cavalier attitude annoyed me. I knew first-hand that careers had been destroyed by lies supported with less than what Billy had.

"Perhaps. For someone with a little pink house by the railroad tracks. But your family is White Southern royalty. And Langesford is valuable in more ways than you may think. What if Billy is already working on plans to challenge your ownership rights? Can you afford the fight?"

He turned from the window glaring at me from a face that could have been carved from stone. The rest of his body was just as rigid. I sensed the rage that had driven him to beat Billy after Barbara's funeral, but stood my ground. "I came here—to Langesford—to see if you were worth risking my career to stop him."

But the man from the library, the man who brought me to his home to recover from my own clumsiness and offered me a job with no references was a stranger now. His sarcastic, "How kind of you," chilled me to my bones. "But I really don't think I need *your* kind of help."

I could hear the damn coin of fate flip back to tails. I'd warned him. It was all I could do. The story I'd come to write was dead, and I should go back to Atlanta. "I'll get my things and leave now," I said. "Please give Dani my love."

I meant it. I fell in love with her the moment I saw her bright green eyes and watched her jumping over cracks in the sidewalk. My hope that he'd call me back withered with every slow step toward the stairs, every limp up them, and down the hall to Danielle Trémon-Langesford's room. Dani was sitting with Clarence in the middle of the vintage quilt on the bed. Her grin changed to panic when she saw me. Sensing my upset, she cried, "What's wrong?" and ran to throw her arms around my waist asking, "Why are you sad?"

Such an extraordinary child. Like Ela, just her touch seemed to start the healing process. I stooped to her level, colliding with Clarence's generous tongue. How I'd miss them both. And how was that possible after knowing them such a short time?

I hoped her old soul would understand when I said, "It's nothing, sweetie. I'm so sorry, but something has changed, and I have to go—home."

"Where's that?"

A simple enough question. I couldn't go back to Boston and I couldn't work for Winkler again, even with Mr. McGill's support. And as much as Glory pressed, I'd never be comfortable in New Orleans. Too late, I realized I *was* home—in Jeffers.

I'd never felt so comfortable as in the park, the library, even the Glass House. And especially Langesford Plantation. I also knew I couldn't leave knowing Billy's plan to ruin this loving and generous family. Even without Hollis' smile to greet me, I'd go back to the motor lodge and find a way to protect them.

"I'm sorry, Honey," I whispered. "I…" I turned at a soft knock on the open door. Patrick's eyes were still the color of a dark blue Boston-winter sky, but his jaw had softened, his shoulders relaxed.

"Please," I started.

"Stay," he finished.

Dani squealed, hugging me, her father, and Clarence before running out to announce to the world that I was staying.

I stepped aside to let him in. "Why the change of heart?"

He sat at the foot of the bed and I sat in the first Danielle Langesford's dainty, gilt-edged vanity chair. How small she must have been, I thought. And how sad. Young and pregnant, she'd been forced to marry a man she didn't love, was reviled by the one she loved with all her being, then realized her entire life was a lie. And finally, she lost the son she loved more than life itself.

I could relate to at least some of that and looked up at the sagging canopy bedframe, wondering if she simply got tired of secrets.

"It appears I'm facing an ugly, personally vindictive campaign—" he said, sounding very tired. "You seem to be unemployed at the moment, and Dani adores you…."

"There's one more thing I have to tell you," cut him off.

"What else could you possibly have to tell me?"

My finger toyed with a scrolled "D" etched on the top of a silver hairbrush. "Billy also says he has evidence of crimes committed by your family that will ruin your legacy."

He flushed, seeming more concerned about losing the legacy than his land. "What crimes?"

I looked up at the sagging canopy beam and felt a chill. *Be careful.*

"Murder. He says Sean O'Grady murdered his great-grandfather, and before that, Danielle Langesford killed another member of his family, Nathan Berens."

"That old bone?" He exhaled loudly and leaned forward, folding his hands between his knees and addressed the first allegation. "The infamous, alleged, 'murder' of the second Billy Berens. My Great-uncle Sean caught the bastard trying to rape a young Apache woman staying with the family. The real murderer was a fly-by-night gambler who disappeared out West. Sean ended up marrying the girl. They're Alvarez' grandparents."

I wasn't shocked at the revelation of Patrick's relationship with Alvarez—hence his joy at Ela's acceptance into medical school. Jeremy's family tree hadn't shown a date for Sean O'Grady's death. Did he become a fugitive and disappear out West after William II's 'murder'? It looked like another interracial relationship had been kept quiet, at least in Georgia.

Patrick rubbed his hands together. "Every wild accusation Berens has is based on jealousy and a refusal to face the truth that his family caused their own problems. It's ancient history based on gossip and legend. For instance, Samuel Berens, father of Billy's rapist great-grandfather, Billy II, went off to War with my great-great uncle Brent. Brent died a hero at Chickamauga, while Samuel came back, calling him a traitor and ranting about a secret mission to rob the Denver Mint. Old Sam spent the rest of his life chasing kids off his land and died a penniless, drunken joke. Sadly, his son Cyrus fell for the story and spent his life digging for a treasure that never existed.

He reached toward my hand but pulled back. "Those stories are old news, Laura. Billy may want to make this election personal, but I won't let him. It's about moving the South forward, not backward. I have nothing to hide."

I believed him, but Billy's hatred went deep, and he believed his own lies. That made him the most dangerous enemy of all. I again beat myself up for jumping into this assignment without doing my homework. But according to Nanny Irene, everything happened for a reason—and all things worked for the good. It was telling the difference that made it hard.

"It may be old news in Jeffers, but not to the rest of District One. Billy hates you for marrying Barbara and blames you for her death. He wants Langesford Plantation and he'll do anything to get it."

He jumped to his feet. "Barbara has nothing to do with this!"

I stood too, facing him. "Billy loved her, and you married her. She has *everything* to do with this. It's time you accept that."

His, "Keep Barbara out of this," wasn't negotiable as he stalked to the door, then turned back to me. "And if you want to stay, you won't have any further contact with Billy. Understood?"

I nodded, promising myself it would be my last lie.

His mention of the Denver Mint robbery piqued my curiosity. A History minor at Smith, I knew it was true. A rogue, Confederate 'suicide squad' was rumored to be the culprit, but no sign of them or the gold ever surfaced. A century later, people were still searching the caves of the Sierra Madre Mountains for the legendary, "Rebel Gold."

Jeremy said the box he found by the privy held small, heavy, black-painted bricks. Shortly after Jeremey turned it over, Billy bought the floundering Caddy dealership. Then he remodeled the house.

Like Hal, I could add two and two. And my calculation added up to black-market gold. It was too soon after the War for old Samuel to spend his ill-gotten gains, so he likely hid what he had. Then he died and Cyrus spent a lifetime looking for it. But by the time he found it, private ownership of gold bullion was illegal. If Billy used it to buy his business, he could go to jail. Turnabout is fair play, he liked to say. Perhaps that could be my leverage.

Even if I couldn't prove it, threatening him with the Feds might be enough to put the brakes on his vendetta and at least save the O'Grady family reputation. But how? I'd have to think about it. It had been a long day, and I had a funeral to attend in the morning.

CHAPTER 19

"Why not leave Dani here?" I suggested to Patrick after a tense breakfast. "She's so young. I'll stay with her."

As if sensing my crippling aversion to the customs surrounding death, he frowned and stood, tossing his napkin over his empty plate. "Death is part of life and funerals are about the living, not the dead. Dani knows that better than most. Make sure you're both ready on time."

Ela and I rode with Alvarez, arriving behind Patrick and Dani. I took Ela's hand to follow them inside, but she held back, her eyes flooded with tears. "I can't."

I was about to ask why when I remembered she wasn't white. Though her parents were born in New Mexico, her mother's parents were Mexican, and Alvarez was one-quarter Apache. Both were considered colored in the South.

I looked at the church. There was no "Whites Only" sign and I considered God to be colorblind. "You don't mean—?"

"It's hot," she said. "They'll keep the doors open. I'll listen from here, with the others."

The 'others' were lining up behind us. I recognized a few of the kitchen boys from the Glass House, some hands from Morning Bird Stables, and a few whites with Howard Johnson's name tags—apparently not acceptable enough to face the altar.

Most of the "qualified" mourners made a point of ignoring us as they entered the church. Then Tammy came with her parents. Her father, Frank Eldridge, was a cotton and grain farmer who looked uncomfortable in his suit. Her mother, Edward O'Grady's surviving sister, Linda, stopped to hug Ela and introduce herself to me before joining Patrick and Dani in the Langesford box. Jeremy came alone, and other than a brief nod to Tammy, ignored us.

Billy showed up, his red Caddy taking up two spaces in what was becoming a very long funeral procession. He snubbed the outsiders, many of whom were too young to vote, and raised an approving eyebrow at my little black dress. Then he noisily entered the house of God, tapping registered voters on the backs, waving and nodding as he looked for a vacant seat closer to the Founders' boxes.

Hollis and Toby were from old Jeffers families, hard-working, middle-class whites. Hollis' father was Head Custodian at Jeffers High and Toby came from a long line of county sheriffs. I believed Mattie's prediction that the church would be filled, "cheek-to-jowl"

"The Langesford box is at the front," Ela whispered. "Next to the Bradley box."

The grieving families of both dead boys entered after Hal, bound for the front pew below the pulpit. Moments later, the deep chords of a pipe organ began, *Amazing Grace*. In the shade of an old oak, we sang along with the white Southern Christians inside the building.

I wasn't aware of Ela squeezing my hand, or that both our faces were crusted with tears, until the service was over. Similar tracks on the others' faces, testified that the music and loving words about two local boys taken too soon, had the same effect on them. After the caskets were taken out, hanky-wielding church-people exited with heads bowed. I wondered if the turnout would have been the same for Charlie Green and his daughter Em. *Em. Not Emily, or even Emmy. Just Em.*

The procession to the cemetery at the edge of town followed the same protocol as the church. Prominent Whites led the way through a manicured lawn dotted with monoliths, angels, and unreadable ancient stones, to sit in a circle of folding chairs around Hollis' newly dug grave. Less prominent Whites stood behind them. Ela and I joined the others in the outermost circle. Somber, respectful and separate—equal only in our ultimate destiny.

After the ritual was repeated to lay Toby to rest, Patrick and Dani walked toward the older, wooded section of graves.

"Barbara," Ela said. "She didn't feel right about being buried on Langesford land, and asked to be in her family plot, next to her mother."

Before turning to wait by the cars, I caught a glimpse of Hal talking with Toby's father. Sheriff Coulter waved his arms angrily, jabbing a finger into Hal's chest. His face was flushed from grief and the mid-day sun and he swayed on his feet, swatting at Hal's offer of a steadying hand.

I nudged Ela. "What do you think that's about?"

Her face darkened with a rare frown. "The families want to charge Charlie with two counts of murder. Hal Glass is defending him."

"Murder? How can that be? It was an accident."

Patrick interrupted to drop Dani off with us while he visited both homes, offering condolences, sharing memories, and eating food prepared by caring neighbors. I doubted anyone in either family would eat much, but it was symbolic, I supposed. Defying death by the simple act of devouring life-sustaining food—though at my mother's memorial, I'd heaved what little I'd eaten before dessert.

Patrick came home late and announced another trip. He'd be gone a week this time, up the middle of the district, to the western border near Valdosta. He told me, "It Looks like Charlie Green will be in jail a while."

I kept Ela's confidence to ask, "Why?"

He rubbed his temple. Migraine? God knew he had enough stress.

"The families are pressing separate charges of second-degree murder for driving impaired. The other two boys say they didn't have any beer. It's Charlie's word against theirs."

Superficially contrived as it was, it didn't look good for Charlie. "What about his daughter?" I asked. "I heard she's with his brother."

Patrick sighed. "With emotions running so high, it's better if he keeps his head low."

"What do you mean?"

"That I'll be adding another child to your care—for a while."

My heart broke for little Em, her father, and his brother. While I couldn't refuse, I wondered how I was going to help Patrick while watching two kids. "Of course," I answered, "But we should plan your strategy against Billy before you leave. You need a solid platform."

He took too long to consider it, but finally nodded at the wisdom of my plan.

At dusk, we met Charlie Green's brother George on the verandah. He carried little Em up the steps and declined my invitation to come in. His black eyes in a face as dark as a maple tree after a rain, held little Em's attention—and mine—when he told her, "Be brave little one. Don' mess wit' nobody, no matter what they say. And keep your eyes down, so they don' know what you think." He kissed her cheek. "And don' sass, y'hear?"

At a nod from Patrick, he handed her to me. She felt light in my arms, wearing a clean cotton nightgown and smelling like ivory soap. *Like Rose did after a bath.*

The confused little girl nodded to her uncle, rubbed her eyes, and laid her head on my shoulder. My tears mixed with hers when George Green started his ancient truck and turned north at the end of the drive. I knew I'd never forget that moment, just like I'd never forget Dani holding her daddy's hand while jumping over cracks in the sidewalk.

"Where is he going?" I asked Patrick.

"Michigan. A friend of mine manages a Buick assembly plant in Flint. He needs good men. And if things go badly here, Em can join him there."

I thought of George, who had likely never set foot out of Jeffers County. He'd worked his whole life outside in fields and in open barns while working his way up to head mechanic at Langesford. According to Henry, George could fix anything. Now, he'd spend ten to twelve hours a day inside a sunless factory, assembling cars he'd never be able to afford.

I rocked Em in my arms, my hips swaying to the universal rhythm of life. "I need to put her to bed. Will you still be up?"

"I'll take her," Ela said. "I'm sure Dani's still awake. They can sleep together until we set up a bed tomorrow."

Em's little hand clung to my hair at being handed off yet again, but Ela murmured something in her native tongue, and sleep again shielded the child from harsh reality.

"So, he's not coming back," I said while Patrick poured two straight-up Kentucky Bourbons in his office.

"No. He's a good man. I'll miss him."

We faced each other across the desk, and he raised his glass. "Mair an saol."

"Live life," I repeated. It was Nanny Irene's favorite Gaelic saying. We both downed the liquor in one gulp.

He set his glass down and slumped in his chair, running his fingers through his hair.

"What's wrong?" I asked, when the better question would have been, 'What's right'?

"Everything."

I refilled both our glasses. "Tell me."

He leaned toward me, his eyes glassy with weariness, rather than the bourbon. "You were right. Billy's campaign is ugly. Unlike anything I've ever seen."

A fist punched the air. "He's all over the map when it comes to issues, policy, even existing law. His response to anything the least progressive is reactionary to the point of inciting the crowd against each other. They either love him or hate him."

"Yes, people love to hate." My second glass of bourbon went down easier than the first.

I put my hand over my empty glass while he poured himself another drink. "We were at a town hall meeting in Marshall. When I questioned or refuted his bizarre claims, he jumped somewhere else, presenting twisted facts and unrelated generalizations. It was like trying to fight an octopus. When I cut one arm off, another one came out of nowhere."

Downing the third drink, he said, "The bastard actually said there was *scientific proof* that Negroes are less intelligent than Whites because the *pigment* in their skin slows the blood flow to their brains."

I'd heard worse. "Did they believe him?"

Dropping his head into his open palms, he moaned, "Some. With a standing ovation. But worse, he's been accusing Charlie of being drunk in a bar, telling folks he wanted to take some white boys down a peg. He's pushing for Charlie to be prosecuted, 'to the fullest extent of the law'. Do you know what that is?"

"The death penalty," I whispered in the darkened room.

He nodded, his eyes glittering with emotion. "Even in his own home, no black man in his right mind would threaten a white man out loud, let alone in a bar. Even a Negro one. And Charlie never went to bars. He bought a six-pack of Black Label after work on Friday and drank one before bed every night except Sunday, to dull his arthritis pain. The accident was on a Monday. If there was anything but empty bottles in his truck, somebody put them there."

He emptied the bottle of Bourbon into his glass. "But people believe Billy. Because they *want* to believe him. They want to blame someone else for their troubles. To find excuses for not giving Negroes the rights they deserve."

I hated to play devil's advocate, but if I didn't, a prosecuting attorney would. "What about his brother George? Could he have bought the beer without Charlie knowing?"

"He doesn't drink," came slow, as if the effort of talking had sapped his strength. "Charlie raised George after their parents died and George helped when Em's mother was killed in a hit and run six months ago. She was walking to church and they left her lying on the side of the road like a possum. She bled to death in the sawgrass."

He swallowed hard and I blinked back tears at how horrible humans can be to each other.

"George and Em are Charlie's whole life," he said. "If he thinks they're in danger, he'll confess to starting World War II. So, with George gone and Em with us, we've convinced him they're safe—for now."

He reached for my hand. "You were right *and* wrong, Laura. It *is* personal. Billy blames me for everything he didn't have, should have had, and tried to have. Barbara is only a small part of it. No one can steal something from you that you never had. She was his childhood friend. Nothing more. But he took advantage of her. And she never told anyone."

"What do you mean?" *Say it isn't so.*

"Billy missed a lot of school. When he was gone, I watched over Barbara and we got to know each other. When I graduated, we were in love, but I was accepted at Emory and she couldn't wait four years for a wedding."

I didn't try to explain that four years is a *very* long time to a beautiful-but-poor blonde, especially if her boyfriend is the pick of the county. But he wasn't finished.

"She turned to Billy then. He'd managed to graduate and was working at Smitty's Garage. I'd heard rumors he hit her, but she'd never admit it. Then, just before her graduation, she got pregnant and came to me for help."

"What? Why you?"

"Because I loved her. She needed help finding a place where she could have her baby and adopt it out. She wanted to leave Billy, but he'd never let her go if he knew about the pregnancy."

I thought of Dani, but there was no way that smart, loving, generous child was Billy's, and the timing was wrong.

Patrick studied me a moment, as if gauging whether he could trust me before answering my unspoken question. "I offered to quit school and marry her, but she said no. I found a place in Atlanta for her to go, but we'd waited too long. Billy found her packing and accused her of being with me. He beat her, and she miscarried. And he blamed me."

I demanded, "Why didn't he go to jail?"

"She wouldn't press charges, but I made it clear to him that if he ever came near her again, I'd kill him. I may have even mentioned some creative ways I'd accomplish it. Anyway, Billy held to the bargain and Barbara and I got married after I graduated."

I was still recovering from the nightmare of thinking Dani was Billy's child when Patrick said, "Sometime between high school and our wedding, Billy came into money. He bought Smitty's Garage, started to rebuild that old wreck of a cabin, and crowned himself the Caddy King of South Georgia.

"But I was too busy with a new wife and the responsibility for Langesford while my parents spent more time in Washington. It was a rough time. Barbara's next pregnancy was difficult and after Dani was born, a lot of things went wrong on the property. Broken equipment, downed fences, random fires and such. I was too busy to think they were anything but accidents and coincidences. Then Barbara got cancer."

There were no words to console him, so I went right to the point. "What happened between you and Billy after her funeral?"

His eyes narrowed, but he didn't ask how I knew. He waved at empty air. "I beat Billy to a pulp ten-feet from my wife's open grave. It was the talk of the town for weeks. Billy backed off, but I underestimated him. The bastard is both patient and lucky. My father was too powerful for him to take on, but with him gone, if Billy wins this election, a lot of innocent people will pay for my lack of judgement."

CHAPTER 20

Patrick barely spoke to me in the morning except to announce he'd decided to stay a few more days and leave on Friday. He spent Tuesday with Alvarez and Wednesday with Hal, coming home in time to see Dani and Em to bed. On Thursday morning, I cornered him on his way out of his office

"Did you decide what to do about Billy's claim?"

"Which one? That I'm the spawn of the devil, or an ignorant rodeo cowboy?" His smile faded at my scowl. "Oh, you mean the One Drop Rule. Anyone can accuse anyone of anything. I can't see how he can prove it."

Still no denial.

"He's very confident," I said without revealing Billy's deadline for my non-existent proof. "Have you talked to Hal about a strategy?"

"Hal has enough on his plate with Charlie's case. Billy's rich, but he doesn't have the time or resources to pursue that kind of legal wild-goose chase before the election."

An angry flush brought perspiration to my forehead. I paced a small circle to calm down before stepping up close to him. "He doesn't have to! Timing is everything. If Billy makes the allegation *before* the election and you can't squash it before the vote, the innuendo alone could sway voters against you. And if he wins, he'll have all the time, money, *and* political clout he'll need to take it through the courts."

I still couldn't take the chance of revealing Barbara's Bungalows, not because I believed Billy would kill Jeremy, but the fear that Patrick would kill Billy. I asked, "How much do you know about your great-great-grandmother from New Orleans?"

His eyes glinted with humor, his smile condescending. "Is that where Billy's rumor comes from? Come with me. Maybe then you'll realize how ridiculous his allegation is."

He took the old key ring from the desk drawer and stepped over to a bookshelf, pulling down *Gulliver's Travels.* He inserted a key into a hidden lock, turned it and stepped back. A narrow section of the bookcase the size of a door, swung open, revealing a stone staircase. He pulled a string on a lone lightbulb above the opening and I followed him down. At the bottom, he used another key to open an ancient solid pine door and we stepped inside.

A flip of a switch showed that the cavernous old basement room had been updated for electricity and had a new concrete floor. Fieldstone walls at one end were lined with shelving stacked neatly with canned and dry goods, as well as first aid items and a cot with blankets.

A tornado shelter, I assumed. The remains of a huge fireplace and oven niche set into the fieldstones confirmed it had once been a summer kitchen, built into the hill to keep the heat away from the main house.

He led me to a wall stacked with gilt and tortoise-shell picture frames holding portraits of long-dead Langesfords, and a few O'Gradys. Two matching gilded frames stood next to each other at the end of the wall. One was a much younger version of Camilla O'Grady in a white, hooped gown with a pink sash. She did not look happy. Even her chestnut hair seemed to rebel against its stylish chignon prison.

He drew my attention to the other portrait. "This is my great-great grandmother, Danielle Trémon-Langesford, in 1862."

My assumption of a dark-haired, olive-skinned, French Creole was replaced by a fair, almost platinum-blonde beauty with blue eyes very much like Patrick's. Based on the portrait, the odds of her having any mix of Negro blood were slim to none; yet I had it straight from the man who saw her with her real mother just after her birth.

My hopes rose that Flora DeBoucher's bloodline was thin, but the gene pool is a mysterious thing. While other states set a measurement of up to $1/16^{th}$ ancestry, Georgia held that *any* Negro ancestor fit the rule. Danielle's marriage to Anthony Langesford could be ruled illegal—her descendants ineligible to inherit. I needed more proof than a portrait that couldn't be verified.

"I see," answered the victory in Patrick's eyes. Too bad he didn't.

"So, you'll let this go?"

"I'm not the one you have to worry about letting go," I muttered, turning from Danielle's coy smile. "Are we done here?"

"I am if you are." He checked his watch. "I need to get going."

We were on the other side of the bookcase when I mentioned driving back to Atlanta for the weekend. To collect my things from my apartment, I told him. "Ela's still here, and Mattie said she'd work the weekend if needed. And Henry and Alvarez are never far away. I'll be back before you are."

"Of course."

His smile said I'd over-presented my case and I looked forward to seeing if Glory could get away for the weekend in Atlanta. Maybe even meet up with Edwin.

After Patrick's usual promise to return and parting hugs to both Dani and Em, he drove a 1958, maroon Chevrolet Impala down the drive to visit the more rural areas of his district. As usual, we watched until he turned off the drive.

The girls followed Mattie to the kitchen to make cookies and I headed for the office to call my landlord. My rent wasn't due until the end of the month, but I wanted to let him know I was okay.

"Don't bother comin' back. Ain't nothin' left," Mr. Newell shouted.

"What do you mean?"

"I mean you damn near burned my store down the night you left. I shoulda knew better than to rent to you. Cars comin' and goin'. People runnin' up and down the steps in the wee hours of the morning. Had to close for a week."

So, the car with the headlights *was* a threat.

"But I left about four in the morning, for a trip. Everything was fine then. What happened?"

Both his volume and tone softened when he realized I didn't start the fire. "'I woke up 'round then with somebody making a racket on the stairs. You, I guess. 'Round four-thirty, cars started pullin' in. It was quite a party up there. They only skedaddled when I threatened to call the police. Then I smelled smoke."

"Oh, my God, Mr. Newell!" I cried. "Are you OK?" And finally, "Is there anything left in the apartment?"

"Fire Department aimed at savin' the store. It's a waste of your time to come back. An' you *ain't* getting your deposit back."

"I understand." I hung up, shaking from the close call. What if I'd stayed? He was right. It wasn't worth the drive. I'd taken my important things with me: the typewriter, clothes, notes, and for some odd reason, the old jewelry/music box.

The thought of returning to Atlanta to meet with Glory and Edwin now filled me with dread. I wasn't worried about the Klan for myself anymore but couldn't place my two dearest friends in danger. I called Glory to thank her for convincing me to leave Atlanta quickly—and check on her progress.

"My friend Vernon at the FBI pulled some strings with the curator of the archives at the St. Louis Cathedral," she said. "Flora DeBoucher's mother was a full-blooded free black woman from Saint Domingue. She died in 1820. After her death, the rent on her home in the View Carré was paid by a Creole named, "Philippe Trémon—until 1822."

"The year Danielle was born," we said together.

"What about Trémon's wife?"

"I knew you'd ask," she answered. "Elouisa Dumont Trémon died in, you guessed it, 1822. In childbirth. The same day Danielle was born. Her death certificate was indeed signed by Trémon's attorney, Renée Marchaud, attesting she died giving birth to a healthy girl."

"Danielle was also baptized at the Cathedral and registered as White. I had certified copies of both documents made, as well as the Negro registry for the same time. I sent them to you at Langesford—registered mail."

Tears filled my eyes. Certified copies of fake information signed by a Bishop of the Catholic Church trumped a torn up, anonymous, unverified, journal entry. "You're a godsend," I gushed. "I'll never be able to repay you." My hopes dimmed when I realized copies could be forged, and sometimes looked better than the originals. How hard would it be for Billy to have a fake one made with the correct information?

"I'm sorry," I said. "But I have one more favor to ask. Billy isn't above making up his own proof. You were right about having something on him for leverage. I think I have something, but I need help."

I shared Jeremy's story about the buried washtub, and Billy suddenly coming into money. Glory confirmed that the penalties for owning and selling gold bullion doubled for Federally minted gold—like the gold from the Denver mint. It could send Billy away for a long time.

But the few gold bars were a longshot. To turn a failing luxury car business into such a success in only five years, didn't sound right. Glory agreed to see if Vernon could look into the dealership's financials. She also volunteered her half-brother, Edwin, a Civil War buff, to check Samuel Berens' assertion about the Denver Mint robbery.

I hung up, and like Scarlett O'Hara in *Gone with the Wind,* vowed that with God as my witness, Patrick O'Grady would *not* lose his plantation, and Em Green would *not* grow up without her father. I just didn't know how to accomplish it.

With Patrick gone and my trip cancelled, I put on a new J.C. Penney mail-order sundress and visited my old teacher, Hal Bradley-Glass, Esquire, to discuss the One Drop Rule and Charlie Green. I was surprised to see Leroy standing at the hotel door so soon after his brother's funeral. His black eye was fading, but there were still bandages over nasty cuts on one side of his face. I'd given him my condolences at the funeral and there seemed little else to say.

"Is Hal in his office?" I asked.

His glare told me I was persona non-grata.

"Okay, I'll just keep knocking on doors until I find him."

He nodded toward the stairs. "Third floor. But you'll have to get through Sadie."

I smiled. Neither Leroy nor Sadie had seen a Stainsby in action. I ascended the curving staircase and found a woman in her mid-to-late fifties sitting behind a black-cherry desk on the third-floor landing. She smiled at me. "How may I help you Miss…?"

"Tucker," I answered. "Sarah Tucker. Mr. Glass is my attorney…Sadie."

Apparently pleased I knew her name, she held out her hand. "Ah yes, Mr. O'Grady's assistant. We haven't officially met. I saw you with that Indian girl at the funeral." Leaning forward as if someone on the empty floor would hear, she said, "I think she and Hollis were, well…close, if you get my drift. That sort of thing is frowned upon, but it was kind of you to stand with her."

Despite Sadie's friendly smile, the hint that Ela wasn't good enough for Hollis rankled. I summoned my imperious voice. "It wasn't kindness. We're friends and she shouldn't have had to stand outside. Is Hal available? I need to see him immediately."

She summoned her guardian-of-the-gate voice. "I'm afraid he cannot be disturbed when his door is closed." She held a freshly sharpened pencil over a blank calendar. "I'll make an appointment for you. Maybe next week."

"It's not necessary. Call him. He'll see me."

Her lips compressed, highlighting the lines around her mouth when she pressed a button on her phone and spoke into the console. "Mr. Glass, a Miss Tucker is here. She says she's a client." With a mean look at me, she added. "Shall I make an appointment?"

"No!" blasted through the speaker.

The door opened, and Hal stepped out, hand outstretched. "Miss Tucker, thank you for accepting my offer of service for your family estate. Follow me please."

Fluorescent lights set in grids above a suspended ceiling reflected off white walls decorated with expensive, original modern-art. And instead of the Brobdingnagian desk I'd expected, an oval, white-oak table sat in front of the Palladian window overlooking the street.

I turned a slow circle in the astonishingly transformed antebellum room, taking in the chrome beverage cart and *orange* tulip chairs in front of the desk. A few feet away a comfortable-looking white, Naugahyde couch, matching side chair, and glass-topped table filled the center of the room.

"What the hell?" I laughed, kicking off my pumps to shuffle through the pale blue shag carpet and drop onto the couch.

Hal grinned. "I hate antiques." He turned to the refreshment cart to pour two scotches into silver-rimmed glasses etched with a gothic, "G".

I accepted both the short response and the scotch, determined to decline a refill. Gesturing to the room, I asked, "Who did this?"

"Someone…special. Not local."

I understood why Hal and Billy didn't get along. They couldn't be more dissimilar, both in taste and temperament. But it didn't explain Hal's friendship with Patrick. Compared to this, Langesford was an eclectic mess of worn Victorian flourishes rubbing elbows with Western Rustic.

Thinking of Jeremy, and Hal's non-local friend, I raised the glass. "To secrets."

He put his barely tasted drink on a sterling silver coaster, and I did the same. "We may have to ditch the Tucker thing," I confessed. "As they say in the movies, my cover has been blown. It seems Patrick and I met at my father's Christmas ball in '54."

"Ah, the best laid plans," he said, and we both finished the Robert Burns quote in its original Scottish, "Gang aft Agley."

Unfortunately, a lot here has gone astray lately," I said. "I need to officially engage your services, which I assume will include attorney-client privilege."

"Consider it done. Is it related to that exposé of Southern politics you mentioned?"

"Don't be coy. Nothing that's happening here is about politics. Billy wanted to use me as a Barbara look-alike to get inside Langesford and verify his accusations about the O'Grady family's racial background. But you knew that didn't you?"

"Is that reporter-speak for digging up the dirt in the O'Grady garden and giving it to Billy to spread like fertilizer?"

"Not funny."

"No, not funny at all," he agreed. "Berens has as many, or more, skeletons in his closet—most of them of his own making. He should be afraid the mud he slings will stick to him."

"I don't think Billy's afraid of anything when it comes to destroying Patrick, but in the interest of saving time, what if Billy's accusation about Negro blood is true?"

He flushed and walked to the window.

"Give it up," I said. "Jeremy spilled the beans to me. All the beans. You know about—well, everything.

He turned to me. "How do you know if it's true?"

"I think it goes back to Patrick's great-great-grandmother." I moved to one of the tulip chairs and faced him for my third legal opinion on the matter. "So, can an inter-racial marriage, five generations ago really threaten current property ownership?"

I felt sick when he echoed Glory. "It hasn't been tested at the Federal level and it's a can of worms not likely to be opened any time soon. But from what I've read, Georgia courts have supported it."

"Is that why you recommended me? To disprove it? You could have told me up front, especially since it's true."

"I recommended you because I knew you'd expose Billy for what he really is, even if it brought Patrick's bloodline into the open. You told me as much in the dining room. I also know you well enough to know you had to find out on your own."

"I suppose so," I conceded. "But the bloodline isn't our only problem."

He groaned and sat down at the desk while I scooted my chair closer, resting my forearms in front of his clenched hands. "I think the race claim is just a smokescreen. And while Billy wants Langesford, I don't even think it's about turning it into a development. He wants to obliterate the Langesford-O'Grady legacy until Patrick is living in a shack on a played-out dirt farm—like the Berens family."

An eyebrow raised. "So, you're a shrink now, and you came to all these conclusions in three weeks?"

"I pay attention. But Patrick has another, more politically dangerous problem than ancient history. His support of Charlie Green. I understand you were at the scene before the doctor."

"To answer your first point. Yes, Patrick's support could be disastrous for the election, but there's no way he'll let Charlie go down for the accident, which he shouldn't, because Charlie is innocent. And yes, I heard the call on my CB radio and got there quickly."

I didn't take Hal for an ambulance chaser, but Jeffers was a small town. Tourism aside, I doubted the Glass House did much more than break even. And based on his office decor, He had a lifestyle to support.

"I got there before the ambulance, and before things got moved around," he continued.

"What do you mean, moved around?"

He brushed a hand through his hair. "When bodies are involved, things get crazy. Hollis' hotrod was on its side. Leroy and the Whitfield boy, Evan, were sitting in the grass by the ditch, nursing their wounds. Charlie was pinned in his truck against a tree that likely stopped him from going head-first into the Chatauqua River. He was out cold, but his little girl was crying up a storm on the floor. She was covered with a big teddy bear that had protected her from flying glass. I called for help, but the cops were busy trying to get to the boys."

My, "How awful," didn't come close to describing the helplessness Hal must have felt. "Who called it in?"

He moved to the tulip next to me, looking oddly misplaced in the delicate chair. "Evan. He and Leroy were thrown clear. Leroy was cut up badly. Evan ran to the gas station a quarter mile up the road. He's on the track team. It didn't take him long."

"What do you think really happened?"

"There's some disagreement on that, and as my client, Charlie's story is confidential. But it was clear to me at the time that he was headed south on Simpson Road, taking Em to her babysitter before work. Fresh tracks from the marsh matching the roadster's old tires were headed north. It looked like the roadster made a U turn. The road was wet that morning and it's likely the hotrod spun out, hit the truck, then flipped on its side and skidded off the road, stopping half in the ditch.

"You mean Hollis turned the car around to follow Charlie?"

No. Not Hollis. Not the boy Ela loved.

"No. Toby Coulter was trapped behind the wheel. Coulter is saying he wasn't driving, but I'm fairly certain I saw Hollis crushed on the passenger side. When things like that happen, cars don't always end up in the direction they were going, and bodies get moved. It's true the new light was out again, but those tracks didn't lie. It wasn't a T-bone."

"Did you get pictures?"

He hung his head. "I carry a Polaroid but didn't have a chance to use it. Coulter showed up while I was looking after Em. The minute he saw the tracks, he hopped back in his car and drove over them—several times. He wouldn't let me near the car and ran me off before Doc got there."

"Shouldn't you be telling the State Police this?" I felt terrible trying to blame the two young boys who died but felt worse for the innocent man with a little girl.

He shook his head. "I'm Charlie's attorney, and I didn't see it happen."

"What about the broken beer bottles on the road? Were they Charlie's?"

"Maybe. There was a lot of glass, but his tailgate was up, and I was worried about Em."

"So, Sheriff Coulter lied about how the accident happened. And about who was driving."

Hal's hand covered mine. "You may think you know a lot after a couple weeks in town, my naive little Yankee friend, but you have no idea how fast a lie becomes the truth in a small town. Especially when two white boys died, and two Negroes lived. I'm working on it."

Hal agreed to take on Patrick's defamation suit against Billy if he played the race card before the election. But Charlie Green's plight seemed far more dangerous—and pressing. I wondered what little Em remembered about the accident, but it wouldn't matter in court. Em was only four. She also hadn't spoken a word since the night she arrived.

Dani and Em were napping in their room after chasing Clarence around the yard most of the morning. I asked Ela to come to my room and she sat at the foot of the bed while I again took the vanity seat. "Don't ask me how I know, but Toby was driving the car that morning. Why would Hollis let him drive, especially if they'd been drinking?"

She squeezed my hand until my fingers hurt. "Toby was a monster. Everyone feared his temper. If he wanted to drive, he would drive. Hollis thought he could help Toby change, but I knew it could never be. Someone like Toby only feels alive when he sees fear—or pain—in someone else's eyes." She broke into sobs, repeating, "I warned Hollis not to go with him. He had to work in the morning, but Toby wanted to chase jack-o-lanterns in the marsh."

"Jack-o-lanterns?"

"Negro boys," she whispered. "They fish the marshes at night for crabs, and sometimes reds, to sell to the stores and restaurants in town. They use lanterns to find their way in the dark. The town boys call them jack-o-lanterns."

My heart sank, but I had to ask. "You mean, Hollis?"

"No, not for a long time. He went to make sure no one got hurt."

"Are you sure?"

"Yes, I know it." She raised a hand to her heart. "In here. He was going to tell Toby he was going to New Mexico with me."

I wanted to believe that her love had shown Hollis the error of his ways, so much so that he'd leave his white family to move across the country and live in sin on a reservation, but I couldn't. Had he seduced her, then bragged to his drunken friends about having sex with an Indian? I held her while she mourned a love that I feared she only imagined.

"Ela," I asked. "Did the boys drink when they went to the marshes?" *Did fish swim?*

She pulled away. "Why?"

"Because Charlie could go to jail for drunk driving—or worse."

She sniffled. "Only beer. They didn't have enough money for the hard stuff, and even Toby knew 'shine could kill them."

"What kind of beer?

"Black Label. But sometimes homebrew in old Black Label bottles."

I pictured the scene. The night was hot and still. A good night for fishing—and hunting—and like wolves, bullies hunted in packs.

"Were they meeting anyone else that night?"

"A couple older boys who work in Billy's garage. I saw Toby Coulter with them once in the Sears store. He stared at me like I was naked and touched his pants...you know where...then licked his fingers."

She blushed, focusing on her boots. "I was with Pa, but he didn't see. I was too ashamed to tell him."

I remembered Randy Logan's smirk at the dealership the morning after the debate. He'd made me feel more like a juicy hamburger than a woman. And at the debate, when Patrick asked him if he had kids in school, he'd answered 'not anymore'. I wondered if he had a son.

"How often did they go there?"

"Every Sunday night if the moon is out. Hollis didn't always go."

I patted her hand. "I'm so sorry for putting you through this, but with Toby driving, and knowing they drank, your information could help Charlie."

I'd pass it on to Hal, though I worried about Charlie in jail. Protesters had been jailed for months without bail, sharing cells with criminals who beat them. I hated to think what could happen to an innocent black man being railroaded for the deaths of two drunk white boys on a joyride. Or maybe only one was drunk. Leroy and Evan insisted they were all sober, but without the lab tests, we'd never know.

CHAPTER 21

Word that Patrick had hired Hal to defend Charlie spread fast in the small town, and from there through the district and state-wide grapevines. He received a half-dozen death threats against both him and Charlie—all typed on the same ball typewriter with a clogged letter 'a'. Patrick pressed to have him transferred to the Brunswick County Detention Center for protection.

After the funeral, Patrick and I transformed his liberal platform into something less threatening to both Democrats and Republicans. He tested it the next week on small day trips to the surrounding towns and I barely saw him.

I'd confessed my identity and *some* of the reasons for the sham to Tammy, convincing her of my commitment to help the cousin she adored. While I ordered new campaign material, she organized groups of students to run door-to-door campaigns. Everyone loved Tammy and she talked businesses into putting signs in their storefronts, and neighborhoods to post signs in their yards, including those where weeds replaced potted plants and streetlights didn't always work.

Thanks to Glory, the Student Nonviolent Coordinating Committee sent volunteers to help and encourage Negroes to register to vote. The committee would be back at election time to get them to the polls. Watching it all come together, I felt some of the enthusiasm my mother must have known in promoting Father's career. The irony didn't escape me, but I reminded myself it was only temporary.

I met Patrick in the office after I put Dani and Em to bed the night before he left for the Sea Islands and a side-trip to Brunswick to visit Charlie. The Tiffany lamp on this desk glowed soft and yellow. He was on the couch instead of behind the desk, a pile of papers stacked on the table. "Give Charlie Em's love when you see him tomorrow," I said. "Any news?"

Looking like he hadn't slept in days, he answered. "Nothing good. Coulter's still pushing for double-vehicular murder. Even if it's bargained down to involuntary manslaughter, it'll put him away for five-to-twenty years —for each death—if he lasts that long. His only chance is an innocent verdict."

He leaned forward, cupping his face in his hands. "And he doesn't have a snowball's chance in Hell of that unless we get the truth out of Leroy and Evan. With Coulter and Billy stirring the pot, there's a lot of pressure on Judge Harrison. He won't wait much longer."

"Do you really think a jury will believe a man on his way to work, with his daughter in the truck, was drunk before nine in the morning? That he'd put her in danger by chasing some dumb kids who yelled at him, or that the boys were fishing—without equipment or catch to support it?

I paced, waving my arms to punctuate my words. "Those are the facts, Patrick. How can *anyone* ignore them?"

But I knew how. Grief, hatred, and fear. Toby Coulter had been a troublemaker most of his life, but he was the sheriff's son. Charlie was black. A nobody who kept to himself. People were calling him a loner now, whispering the words, 'sullen' and 'sneaky' to describe his quiet manner.

I flopped onto the couch next to Patrick. His shadowed face in the semi-darkness looked tired. "Juries are just people, Laura," he said. "They believe what they want to believe. There were enough broken Black Label bottles to build a case for them being Charlie's. He took four empty six-packs to the landfill the second Monday of every month. They were all broken, so there's no way to know if there were more than his."

Black Label. Poor Charlie simply couldn't get a break. And Patrick was right. Things were getting uglier every day the trial was delayed. I'd felt it only a week ago, when I went to town with Dani and Em.

People stopped talking when we approached, then whispered when we'd passed. Faces that once grinned at Dani, frowned at Em's dark hand in hers, frightening the child who no longer laughed or spoke. Now, it broke my heart when Em shook her head and hid behind Mattie when I mentioned going into town again.

Something was brewing. While there wasn't much worse than extending racial hatred to children, the issue seemed to be dividing the town, if not the district. Those who knew about Toby Coulter's bullying and Sunday night 'hunts', weren't surprised at his end. And to those who didn't know him, putting Charlie in jail meant one less 'uppity nigra' on the street.

"There has to be a way to save both Charlie and the campaign," I said, though for the life of me, I couldn't think of it.

He stood and walked to the fireplace, looking up at the portrait. "There's still time—for both," he said. "Not everybody is lost in the fog. And that's what this is, a smokescreen. Charlie is innocent. Hal is the best lawyer I know. And I won't stop doing what I feel is right."

He turned from the sound of insects and the gentle rustle of rose bushes outside the window to come back to the couch. "I never wanted to run for office, but I'm in this now. I have good ideas for bringing in new business and improving our schools, but it takes time to convince people that not all change is bad."

Patience is a virtue I'd always lacked. Shortly after the funerals, when Ela and I were shopping at Ippel's Department Store, Hollis' mother stomped up to us, calling Ela a filthy Indian whore. Ela stared and I called Mrs. Robertson a white-trash-bitch. It didn't endear me to the store management, and we did the rest of Ela's college shopping via mail order catalogs.

The memory of that day made me realize that by avoiding confrontation, the O'Grady family was pulling away from the town their ancestors founded. Under the circumstances, it was a natural defensive measure—and exactly what Billy wanted.

I touched Patrick's shoulder. "You need to go into town more. You're doing nothing wrong by insisting Charlie get a fair trial outside Jeffers. Or by caring for the traumatized daughter of an employee. You stood by Barbara when she was pregnant with another man's child, and you were there for her when she was sick. That's what good men—good people—do. You can't avoid town when people turn against you for being good. You need to look them in the eye and show them what you stand for."

He turned then and kissed me. We didn't drink, and we didn't dance, but my arms wrapped around his neck and our bodies pressed against each other.

His kisses were slow, so deep all thoughts drifted away except the touch of his lips on mine, his fingers running through my hair, caressing my cheeks, my throat.

With Ricky as my first experience with intercourse, and Billy with lust, this was my introduction to making love. My skin warmed to his touch, but instead of a rush of hormones when we embraced, I felt his warmth, his strength. It was like coming home. I wondered if that was what people who really cared for each other felt. As if they were being reunited with their other half. Completed. Was that how love felt?

I knew it couldn't be love for us, after knowing each other such a short time, but it was…something…more than I'd ever felt before.

"I've thought about this since the day we met," Patrick whispered against my ear.

"You mean the day you kidnapped me," I answered, my skin warming along the path of his fingers.

I regretted it when he lifted his head. But blue eyes that had been dulled by work and worry for too long, glittered with humor. "I prefer to think it was the day I rescued you from certain death."

"My hero." I smiled, and he kissed me again. Warm. Hard. Impossible to resist. But neither one of us was in a hurry. Our bodies pressed together, my arms around his neck, his big hands covering my breasts.

"Babs," he whispered into my hair.

I pulled away, "What did you say?"

He shook his head as if waking up from a dream and sat up. "I can't," he said.

I'd been close enough to him to know perfectly well that he could, but it woke me up to the insanity I'd been so close to repeating. "You're, right," I said. "This was a mistake."

I smoothed my skirt and stood.

"Don't," he said, catching my hand when I turned toward the door. "You're beautiful, brilliant…and well, wonderful, but..."

But I wasn't Barbara. And I'd be leaving soon. "It's okay, I understand."

"No, you don't."

He took my hand, pulling me back to the couch. Our knees touching, he brushed back his hair and rubbed the stubble along his cheek and chin. "I'm sorry. I was out of line. I didn't mean to…compromise you. I really don't know what to say."

Not saying his dead wife's name while holding me would have been a good thing. I picked up a couch pillow, hugging it to my chest, and answered more sharply than I meant, "Then don't say anything. It's been an emotional roller coaster ride. You're exhausted. And I'm…" *Stupid.*

I started picking up the papers. "It's okay. We don't have to mention it again."

He bent to help me. "I leave for St. Mary's tomorrow."

The damn clock chimed midnight, and he corrected himself. "Today. I should be back by the end of the week."

"But Dani was planning on spending the day with you."

"I'll say goodbye before I leave. The drive will give me time to think." He took the papers from me. "You must be tired. Go on to bed. I can take care of this mess by myself."

It felt like a slap in the face. Yes, he could pick up the papers by himself. He could run Langesford and raise his daughter himself. But if he wanted to save his plantation and be a positive force for the future of Georgia, he needed *me*, not Barbara.

I blinked away angry tears. "I see—Mr. O'Grady."

CHAPTER 22

I stayed in my room after getting Em and Dani up and sending them down to breakfast. When I heard the roar of the Mustang's engine heading down the drive, I checked on the girls and sorted through correspondence, speaking invitations, news clippings, and drafts of his speeches scheduled for Madison and Evansville.

I was still shaken by what had happened in his office. Not the attraction. I realized I'd been attracted to him the moment I saw him at the library. And again, when I heard him at the debate. But last night had revealed to me the emotional side of making love. That it could be more than a duty or a recreational diversion. But his sudden mood change said he was still in love with Barbara. And she'd been dead three years.

While the rejection stung, I tried to think of *his* feelings. Something I wasn't used to doing. He'd married his first love, knowing she had carried another man's child. And according to Mattie, he was devoted to her through her ordeal with breast cancer. After her death, he threw himself into Langesford and Dani.

"He ain't even looked at another woman, since she passed," Mattie said. "But it ain't stopped the ladies from tryin'."

Barbara must have been some woman to win the undying love of two men as disparate as Patrick and Billy. I'd been told she was beautiful but hadn't seen even one photo of her in the house. I asked about it while helping Mattie with the dishes.

"Grievin' is a strange and personal thing," she said, elbow-deep in soapsuds. "Some folks want to remember. They gather friends, family, and things around, telling tales and enjoying the memories. Some talk to the dead like they's still in the room and never change the curtains or pack the clothes away, because the scent lingers. Others can't bear the memory and think they can lock it away, outa sight. Mr. Patrick's one of them."

While I dried and stacked the antique English bone china, now chipped and cracked with regular use, she said, "After Miss Barbara's funeral, when he and that alligator with arms, Billy Berens, had words, Mr. Patrick was in a horrible state. He come home, took down all her pictures and locked 'em up in her room. Then he threw himself into the business... even more'n before."

"But what about Dani?" I asked. "Does she remember her mother? There must be photos of birthdays, holidays, her parents' wedding. It seems cruel to deny her those milestones, even if they were just pictures and stories. What was Barbara like?"

I'd gone too far. Mattie frowned at me and removed a stock pot from the soapy water. "Don't judge," she said, pulling the rubber plug from the sink and reaching for a towel. "We all got our demons. Mr. Patrick, he got more'n his share. You too, I 'spect. If you got more questions, best be askin' him."

"Yes, ma'am," I groveled. "Thank you. I understand his relationship with Dani better now."

As if summoned, the little girl screeched from the doorway, "Laura!"

I'd suggested she call me Laura instead of Sarah after Patrick discovered my ruse. But before agreeing to it, she walked up and down the hall singing Shirley Ellis' *The Name Game.*

After three choruses of, "Laura! Laura, bo-laur-a. Bo-na-na fanna, fo-faur-a, Fee fi mo-maur-a, Laura!" she announced, "Yes, I like that."

Now, she judged me from mischievous green eyes, head cocked, hands in the pockets of her pinafore, weight balanced on the outside edges of her shoes. As usual, Em stood behind her like a shadow, mimicking her pose.

"You missed Daddy," she accused. "He said you were tired, and I shouldn't bother you. But he said to tell you thank you. What did you do?"

Thank you? He told his daughter to thank me for—almost sex? "Just my job, sweetie, I dodged. "And stand up straight, both of you. You could sprain an ankle standing like that."

I wondered when I'd become Nanny Irene and squatted to receive both girls into my arms. How good they felt. Two little heads of black hair, one wiry-nap and one silk curls, both smelling of lemon soap and sunshine. "I'm sorry I missed breakfast. Let me make it up to you both. I'm going to work in the office today. You can play in there by me."

Two sets of eyes grew big. Other than when I'd let Dani watch the news, the office was off-limits. It was a place of business, commerce, politics. And Patrick's refuge. It reflected far more of him than his sterile closet/bedroom upstairs. I also suspected he spent more nights on that couch than next to the locked master bedroom.

"Can I look at the books?" Dani yelled, though I was right in front of her.

"Yes, but you have to ask me first. Go upstairs and pick a game. One Em can play too."

Em surprised me by shaking her head.

Her hair is getting out of control, I thought. "Why don't you want to play a game, sweetie?" I asked, hoping she'd speak.

As usual, Dani spoke for her. "Alvarez is taking her to see her daddy today."

"What?" I looked at Mattie, who suddenly had to check something in the cupboard.

The back door opened, and Alvarez wiped his Mexican boots on the woven rag rug. I faced him with my hands on my hips. "You're taking Em to a jail?"

He took off his hat, turning it in his hands. "Nope. The Brunswick District Court House."

Though he only spoke when spoken to, and answered only what was asked, I'd grown to like and trust Patrick's taciturn cousin. The Court House could only mean that Charlie Green was finally being arraigned. The good news was that it wasn't a local judge. So was the bad news.

A local judge might have known Charlie as a good and gentle man. A stranger would only see a lanky, uneducated Negro who did manual labor and lived on a tiny patch of land provided by his employer.

"Why are you taking Em?" I grilled him, then remembered the girls were watching, eyes wide with interest. I smiled at them. "Dani, you go on up to your room and pick out your game. And Em, you find a coloring book for the ride."

Both girls skipped toward the stairs and I closed the swinging door to the kitchen to hiss, "What is Patrick *thinking*? She's *four!* She can't watch her father be accused of murder! And Patrick never said anything last night."

A thick black eyebrow raised.

"When we were *working*."

Alvarez looked at his silver-tipped boots. "Got the call this mornin'. He didn't want to...concern you." He looked up then, his black gaze shining with emotion. "Dani isn't your responsibility."

"They are both my responsibility. How could it not concern me!"

The tough horse wrangler stepped back at my explosion.

"I fell in love with Em the moment I saw her. She's so frightened she can't speak, for God's sake. And she turns to *me,* not Ela, not Patrick, not Mattie, when she has nightmares about the accident. So, you wait right here while I change. If Em goes, I go."

"No. You can't—shouldn't."

I looked down at the strong, dark hand circling my forearm. "Why?"

He let go and lowered his voice. "You're a Yankee. Courtrooms are for Southern Whites. I know things are changing, but for now we have to play by their rules."

We? I'd forgotten. If you weren't born in the South, you were forever a foreigner. Alvarez had come to Langesford when his wife died, and Ela was Dani's age, but he was still considered an outsider—and colored.

He exchanged a glance with Mattie and led me out to the rarely used parlor. I sat on the old settee and he stood over me.

"Patrick moved Heaven and Earth to get this arraignment," he said. "It's Charlie's only chance to—you know."

Live, I suspected and nodded.

"He cancelled his last trip to Savannah to go up to Washington and talk with the Attorney General, Robert Kennedy, himself. He has Kennedy's support, but it has to go according to Georgia State Law."

I felt light-headed. "Robert Kennedy? Why?"

Having already said more to me than he had since we'd met, Alvarez answered, "To understand the process and make a plan. The arraignment is the first step."

"I know how the criminal prosecution process works. And even if Patrick didn't tell me, I'm glad he did it. But Em will be terrified. She needs to know I'm there." I crossed my arms, Nanny Irene-style. "I'll sit in the back."

"You're a Yankee," he repeated. "If a white, Yankee woman shows up coddling a black child, Charlie's case goes from a hot-rod/truck accident, to Civil Rights."

It *is* about Civil Rights, I wanted to shout. "But—"

"No buts. They see a Yankee do-gooder and they'll send him to jail quicker'n you can swat a mosquito. And it won't be no county jail. It'll be the State Pen—for life."

Turning his hat in his hand, he added a polite, "Miss."

I was horrified, but he was right. I fought my tears to moan, "But who will hold Em?" Then I brightened. "Ela? Em likes her and she's not white—or a Yankee."

My heart broke when he shook his head.

"You don't mean Child Services? No! I know they mean well, but they're strangers. She may never recover her speech." I touched his arm. "Please let it be someone else—from here."

"It is," came from behind me.

I turned to meet Mattie wearing a fresh gray uniform with a crisp white apron tied around her generous waist. Tears filled her eyes when she said, "Me." Then her voice softened to explain, "You see, black women can take care of white chillin' and black chillin', but Whites can only take care of white chillin, except teachers, who don' have no choice. You ain't no teacher an' I helped birth little Em. She loves you, but she knows I'll keep her safe."

Mattie's expressive dark eyes told me she'd do it or die trying. Then she nodded to her grandson in the kitchen doorway. "An' don't worry. Henry'll keep an eye on things around here for you and Dani."

Alvarez added, "Mr. Glass had Doc Hill do an alcohol test when he checked Charlie over at the jail after his arrest. It shows he wasn't drinking that morning, or anytime near it. Glass thinks if the judge knows that and sees Em, he may doubt what the boys say."

Doubt. A lawyer's favorite word. But was it enough?

"Will that get him off, you think?"

He shrugged. "I ain't a lawyer." He sounded like Hal when he added, "But two white boys is dead. Somebody's got to pay for that. Glass says it may get the charges down so Patrick can take him under house arrest until trial."

But Charlie could still face ten to twenty years in prison—if he survived that long. Em would be grown. They'd be strangers. I muttered, "So, it's the Devil or the deep blue sea,"

Mattie tried to be hopeful. "With the Lord's will on our side, it won't be that. An' Mr. Patrick will see Em has a home here, long as she needs one."

I heard the doubt in Alvarez's voice when he answered, "You keep saying your prayers, Mattie, because we'll need 'em."

Then to me, "Berens is making this election about Charlie. Patrick's trying to cut him off in Savannah and the western counties. I'll be back with Mattie an' Em before bedtime and he'll be back when he can."

The situation notwithstanding, it rankled that Alvarez knew more about Patrick's strategy and calendar than I did. *That* would have to change.

Mattie mistook my frown for concern and patted my arm. "You got a big heart girl, though a little worse for wear, I think. But where there's hope, there's God. I'll see to Missy Em, and you pray for us all."

"Pray," I repeated. I hadn't prayed in years. Not since I became an embarrassment to the family and was banned from the, 'Stainsby Sunday Showcase' at Boston's King's Chapel. But what could it hurt? "Okay. I'll stay here with Dani—and pray. But first, I'll get Em ready."

I glared at Patrick's co-conspirators. "I wish I'd known sooner she was going to be on display. She has to look perfect for the show, and I know just what to do."

Twenty minutes later, after digging through Dani's cedar chest of outgrown clothes, I found the perfect white dress with puffy sleeves and a collar embroidered with tiny pink flowers. A pair of matching embroidered anklets and not-too-scuffed black patent-leather shoes completed the costume. No one would think Charlie could afford an outfit like that, even second-hand, but I hoped Patrick's generosity would tug at the judicial heartstrings—if such a thing existed.

So, we had the costume, and her satin-smooth dark-chocolate colored baby-skin needed no enhancement. But her hair. Even after years of twisting, teasing, and pinning teenage mops into masterpieces of hair engineering, I had no idea how to shape the unkempt tangle twice the size of her face, into something manageable. Mattie would have helped, but she'd have done braids or pigtails. Em needed to look—angelic.

"Get me a brush," I ordered Dani, who'd been uncharacteristically quiet throughout the process. Did she understand the importance of Em's mission? I remembered her dancing onto the stage at the debate. Perhaps.

Em seemed to grasp the importance of the trip too and stood silently in front of the mirror while I pulled and pushed hair away from her proud little forehead to draw attention to her mesmerizing black eyes. But when I let it go, it sprang back into a wild, curly mop.

"Try this," made me turn. Ela stood behind me with an exquisitely woven white feather headband laced through her fingers. Together, we secured the band at her hairline and I stepped aside for Ela to take over. She rubbed her fingers into a jar of something that smelled wonderful. "Aloe," she said with a smile. "The Apache cure-all."

With just a little on her fingertips, she smoothed Em's unruly fuzz into a halo of neat curls that kissed the angelic feathers framing her forehead. "Aaah," was the first sound Em had uttered since the day her uncle left her in my arms. Her smile took my breath away and tears filled my eyes.

Ela took Dani's hand. "Come, *Chica*. Let's go find some trouble."

Alone with me in Dani's room, Em's joy at her transformation turned to fear. She trembled from the effort to hold back tears, and I pulled her close.

"Be brave, little one," I whispered into her ear. "Do that for your daddy. When they ask you a question, answer it the way you remember. If you don't know, just say so."

I kissed the tears dripping down her cheeks and wiped my own on my sleeve. "But you must speak, baby. Your daddy needs you."

It surprised me when she pulled away, her eyes clear and her hand squeezing mine with surprising strength. "But that boy, the yellow-haired one with black eyes," she whispered. "He said they'd kill me if I said a word. I want to see Mama in heaven, but I don't want to leave Daddy alone."

Evan Whitfield had dark eyes and sun-bleached blond hair. So that was why she hadn't spoken. I pulled her close, kissed her cheeks, her nose, her forehead. "He's a mean boy, but he can't hurt you. Mattie, Alvarez, Mr. Patrick, and Mr. Glass will be there. And the judge will protect you."

She stiffened at the mention of the judge and I forced a smile. "Don't be frightened of his black robe. He just wears it to cover the soup stains on his shirt."

Her lips lifted a little at the image and her tiny voice asked, "Why aren't you coming?"

I saw her courage falter when I shook my head. "I can't. They don't like Yankees in that court, and I don't want to make trouble."

Her smile was weak, but I took it as a victory. I couldn't promise everything would be fine, so I gave her one more hug and held her hand as we walked down the stairs to the approving grins of Alvarez, Mattie, Ela, Dani, and even Henry. I nodded to Mattie. "She's ready for her close-up."

Dani and I watched from the office window as Alvarez drove Patrick's station wagon down the tree-lined drive. Though I hoped for better results from it, my first prayer since my mother was diagnosed with cancer, was to protect Em and her father.

When they were out of sight, Dani and I sighed. The worry in her ancient eyes mirrored mine when she asked, "Will they hang Charlie?"

By now I'd learned to expect the unexpected when it came to her insights. Like a moth to a flame, she hovered on the fringes of adult groups, silent and mostly unseen. When they noticed her, she'd turn her head, pretending to focus on the nearest butterfly, or horse, or plant. I'd seen her mood change more than once when someone mentioned the arrests or called someone, 'Nigger' or 'White Trash'.

"Where did you hear that?" I asked.

I led her to the couch, but she just shrugged. "Around." Then she changed the subject. "Let's sit on the floor, like Ela does when she prays. We can pray to God, and Ela's spirits, to not let them hang Charlie."

No more TV news for Dani, I thought, but agreed that a little "meditation" couldn't hurt. We sat facing each other cross-legged on the old rug in front of the fireplace hearth, beneath the portrait of Camilla Langesford-O'Grady. We were silent for a long time, hands clasped, eyes closed in prayer.

At least hers were. I couldn't close mine without seeing pictures of the Alabama and Mississippi lynchings. But mostly I thought of Patrick—who didn't trust me enough to share his plan to defend Charlie—or that he'd traveled to Washington.

I knew Bobby Kennedy. I could have helped, goddammit! I told myself he thought he was protecting us, but after last night, it hurt—a lot. I finally closed my eyes and took a deep breath to compose my second prayer.

Moments later, I opened them to a bright green gaze so much like the woman in old portrait above us. "What are you doing?"

"Watching you breathe," Dani answered as if it was the most natural thing to do. "When Mama closed her eyes, I left her, and she went to heaven. I wasn't there to wake her up. I didn't want to leave you."

Was Dani the last person to see Barbara alive? Was that why no one mentioned her name? I knew from grim personal experience that silence is no solution for grief, so I rose to my knees and took her hand. "Tell me about your mama."

As expected from a toddler of three at the time, Dani remembered sensory things. "She smelled good. Like roses. I think she loved roses."

I wondered if her mother had planted the rose bushes around the house.

"She liked to sing, too," Dani announced and sang all the verses of *What do you do with a Drunken Sailor*, complete with lop-sided staggers and stumbles. Then she flopped back on the rug next to me. "She stopped singing when she got sick."

I couldn't stress her any more to satisfy my curiosity. "Well, I don't sing very well, but I bet your Daddy has some records. Let's look for them and we can dance."

She shook her head. "No, all the records are in Mama's room. It's locked now, and I can't find the key." Then her face brightened. "But I know another place we can play. Follow me."

She scampered to the partners' desk and yanked open the bottom drawer, where I heard the clank of the old key ring. "Wait a minute," I ordered, standing with hands on my hips. "How did you know those were there? And do you have permission to use them?"

Any other child would have cowered under my Nanny Irene stare, but she saw through me. Curls bounced with her nod. Her arms spread wide, the key ring dangling from her wrist, she whispered, "They're skeleken keys. They open all the doors in the house except Mama's. Even the Treasure Room." Her little jaw set just like her father's. "Mama and I played there when Daddy was gone."

CHAPTER 23

Treasure Room? The one with the portraits? The sterile room stacked with supplies, sheet-covered furniture, and creepy portraits didn't seem like the ideal child's playroom. But I was too anxious about the hearing to sort receipts and bills. A little play would pass the time.

I'd learned enough history about the family from everyone *but* Patrick, to know Camilla Langesford's father, Col. Anthony Langesford, was an expert strategist and close friend to Robert E. Lee. By the end of the War, the South was bankrupt, it's money worthless. Did Anthony mastermind a robbery of the Denver Mint and send a squad of men, including his son Brent and Samuel Berens, on a secret mission to fund the Confederacy?

If so, only Samuel returned. And if those bricks in Jeremy's washtub were part of the robbery, what happened to the rest of it? My gut told me the answers were here, in Langesford house, but *where*? The office had been remodeled by the first Patrick O'Grady during Reconstruction. Besides the basement summer kitchen, could there be other hidden rooms behind the bookshelves?

The thought was barely complete when Dani climbed onto the library ladder and reached for a ragged copy of a *McGuffey Reader,* saying, "Better step back."

Like the summer kitchen door, a narrow section of shelving opened revealing a door. She climbed down the ladder and moved toward it.

"No!" I shouted.

"It's okay, Mama let me play in there. Don't you want to see?" the little vixen dared me.

Yes! Who wouldn't? I took the key from her. "Well, just this once, but I won't let you in until I know it's safe. Go sit in the chair."

In a rare fit of temper, she crossed her arms and flounced to one of the Queen Anne chairs. "It's safe. Mama played with me in there. She liked the big old pictures with lines all over them. And the trunks and pictures of old-fashioned people."

Her mercurial face suddenly turned sad. "We had fun, but when I found the stone, Mama made me put it back. And we never played there again."

"What stone?"

"A funny-colored stone. Mama said it was dirty. She didn't like dirt, but she liked the other stuff. Old clothes, hats, and big wide skirts with petticoats. She put them on, and we played, *Alice in Wonderland.* I was Alice. Mama was a Queen, and sometimes a scary rabbit."

The clarity of her memories intrigued me. I'd read that even before they start speaking, infants and toddlers understand some verbal language. Some children retain it and remember things from their toddler days until they're seven or eight. Still, I wanted to be sure she wasn't making it up.

"You were only three back then. How do you remember so much?"

She shrugged. "I just do. I remember my bunny mobile and Mama telling me stories about mountains that glowed red at sunset and were filled with gold. And I remember how sad Daddy was when Mama went to heaven."

Dani's memories showed me a different picture of both Patrick and the beautiful, mysterious Barbara Kinney-O'Grady. A native of Jeffers, she'd probably heard stories about Samuel Berens' gold bars. The papers with lines on them were likely maps. Was Barbara looking for a map to the treasure? Settle down, I told myself. It's just a blocked off storage room filled with dusty old clothes—and apparently dirty stones.

As if sensing my doubt, Dani said, "And there's books, and letters with teeny-tiny writing, and pictures made of metal. Mama made up the best stories about them. I used to tell them to my dollies." She frowned. "I can't remember them much now."

Books? Letters? Daguerreotype photos? It was like offering candy to a child. Poor Dani looked so sad. And she was worried about her friend. How could I say no to that face? I looked at my watch. “Well, we have some time until dinner.” And since cooking wasn’t my strong suit, I bargained. “If you’re good, and stop when I say, I’ll take you to the new McDonald’s on the highway.”

“I love French fries!”

“Who doesn’t?” Looking forward to a thick, cold, chocolate milkshake, I slid the key into the lock and turned it, letting her put her hand on the crystal knob and shout, “Open says me!”

It opened at the turn of her tiny hand and she looked up at me with a triumphant smile. “Please pick me up so I can turn the light on.”

I could easily reach the cord, but this was her adventure. I picked her up and she shouted, “Let there be light!”

After a little tug on the string, the light went on at her command, circling our heads with a dusty yellow halo in what was a long, narrow room. Probably an old storage room for linens and china, I thought, but a house as old as this would have had several remodels. Being so close to the summer kitchen, it could have been a connecting passage between it and the original cabin.

Dani smiled and took my hand. “Welcome to The Treasure Room. This is what didn’t fit in the summer kitchen.” Her eyes glowed with happiness and mischief. “The really good stuff.”

Who could argue with the ‘really good stuff’? “Okay, show me the treasure.”

She pulled me along a narrow path, like a proud March Hare in Alice’s Wonderland, pointing out petticoats and vintage hats, some small enough to fit her tiny head. There was another lightbulb at the end of the room with a longer cord within her reach, and she again commanded light. With her hands on her hips, she proudly surveyed her little kingdom.

I began to see a pattern. This wasn’t a basement storage room like the summer kitchen. Rather it was a tiny museum. Had Barbara done this? Aside from the clothing, I recognized eighteenth-century furniture likely brought over on the *Anne*. I opened a stunning French Rosewood armoire, surprised to find museum-quality Pre-Civil-War gowns looking fresh enough to wear. It puzzled me. After four years of blockades, Southern women were so adept at cannibalizing their pre-war wardrobes that few examples existed. Dani modeled a suede riding hat with a tattered veil, and I felt a chill. I asked, “So where are these trunks of books, letters and photos you promised?”

She set the hat and veil down with great reverence, leading me to several vintage steamer trunks lining the wall. Sounding like Tammy, she said, "This is the O'Grady corner. The rest is Langesford."

"How do you know all this?" I asked my little docent.

"Tammy told me."

While the Langesford legacy seemed to be well-documented, the first Patrick O'Grady was still a mystery. There was nothing on file in the library about him before he became partners with Anthony Langesford during Reconstruction. As much as I ached to open every trunk and read every letter, Dani didn't have a lengthy attention span. I'd come back after she went to bed.

Thanks to…somebody…the O'Grady corner of the room was arranged by generation, beginning with an old steamer trunk with, "P. O." stenciled on one side, and a well-used saddle branded, "U S". A few feet away, a larger, metal trunk from the twenties was labeled, "C.O.". *Camilla O'Grady? Or her youngest son Clay?*

There was a cleared-out corner that I assumed was reserved for my project, Edward O'Grady's personal papers. I had six bankers' boxes ready to store, with only the last box of receipts and personal documents left to be reviewed. Tomorrow, I promised the space, and joined Dani in front of the steamer trunk with, "C.O." painted on the side.

I asked the curator of the Treasure Room, "Who's is that?"

She counted on her fingers. "My great-great-great-grandmother," she announced proudly. "She had green eyes, like me."

I opened the heavy domed lid, propping it up with a riding crop and an umbrella on each end. It was filled with old photos and a few pieces of clothing. Dani pulled out an exquisite vintage fringed, black-silk shawl, hand-embroidered with tiny, multi-colored birds and flowers. I guessed it was worth a small fortune and held my breath as she put it over her shoulders to twirl in the cluttered room.

It was nearly noon. Alvarez, Em and Mattie should be in court by now, I thought. "Where did you put the stone that you found?"

"In the saddlebag. But Mama told me not to touch it again."

"Well then, you look at the pictures, and I'll check out the bag." Wishing I'd brought a flashlight, I dragged it closer to the light above Dani's trunk.

Still wrapped in the shawl, she sat cross-legged in front of it, sorting pictures. "Boys go there," she indicated to her left. "And girls go here," on her right side.

"Why are you sorting them like that?"

"Because except for Daddy, and at Langesford, boys hurt girls, and girls should stay away from them."

I counted to three before asking, "Why do you think that? Did someone hurt you?" *Please God, no. Besides her trauma, Patrick would kill them.*

"No, but a boy hurt Mama and she told me to stay away." She picked up a photo from the girl pile. "This one looks sad, like Mama did sometimes."

I reached for it and the saddlebag pouch tipped over onto her lap.

"Yuck," she said and dropped the shawl, shaking grit off her hands and dark blue pinafore.

I looked closely at the photo of a girl holding a baby wrapped in a moth-eaten, woolen shawl. *Mary?* The picture was in much better condition than the one I'd found in our attic, but there was no mistaking the grim set of my Mary's lips in a delicate, heart-shaped face—or those haunting, light colored eyes. My hand shook as I again felt her sorrow. I turned it over and whispered, "Who are you?"

"Mary O'Grady," came from Dani.

"Miss Laura! Miss Dani." We both jumped at Henry's voice.

"On our way," I called, slipping the picture into my pocket. It was one-thirty, still plenty of time to clean up, go to McDonalds, and be back before Alvarez and the others returned. I sent Dani to the kitchen to wash up and met Henry at the office doorway.

"Mr. Patrick called," he said. "The others is on their way back."

Thank goodness Henry had caught the call. "So soon? Did he say anything else?"

"No. Jest for ya'll to stay close to the house."

"Why?"

His shrug didn't surprise me. Patrick would only tell him what he needed to know, but he warned us to stay close. If he was worried, what did that mean about the verdict?

While I was surprised the arraignment ended so quickly, I couldn't get my hopes up. No matter the outcome, people would still be unhappy about Patrick's support for Charlie, which no doubt concerned him.

"Thanks for taking the message," I said, and Henry rushed off to notify the farm and stable crews that they'd be bunking in for a couple nights. McDonald's would have to wait.

I'd just turned to check on Dani when I heard her shriek, "Lauuura," from the kitchen.

She stood on a stool staring into the chipped white porcelain sink. I thanked God her little hand was dripping water, not blood, and took a deep breath. "What's wrong?"

Her head bobbed toward the sink. "Look, it sparkles."

"What?" Sure enough, tiny yellow specs dotted the dirty water in the stoppered sink. I held my hanky over the drain when I pulled the stopper. The water drained slowly, but the shiny little specs clung to the tightly woven linen.

Dani peered down from her stool. "What is it?"

Gold.

"Glitter, honey. Some other little girl must have played with that saddle bag. Let's get you out of this dress so I can wash it. I pulled it over her head, leaving her in her little cotton slip. "You run upstairs and change."

I rolled both the handkerchief and the dress into a dry dishtowel and took it to my room.

After a dinner of Kraft macaroni and cheese, Dani set up her dollhouse in the office while I sorted through the last of Edward O'Grady's scattered notes and receipts from the weeks prior to his death. A crumpled yellow receipt from Randy's Garage & Service Center was dated the day before Edward and Thelma died, and signed by Randy Logan.

I checked it. The fifty-dollar repair bill included brake fluid, oil, spark plugs, tire rotation, a tune up, and a valve adjustment. Standard periodic repairs to keep a luxury car humming, especially if there was a deadly curve and drop off on your way home. I thought of Randy Logan, wondering why, if he owned his own body shop, he was wearing a Caddy King uniform at Billy's dealership.

Clarence heard the approaching vehicle before we did. His grizzled head rose above Barbie's second-floor bedroom, listening. He whined, the tip of his fuzzy tail flapping slowly back and forth. When the sound of car tires grinding on the shell drive stopped, so did the whining. The tail-flapping became tail-thumping. When a door slammed, Clarence jumped over both Barbie's house and Dani's head to beat us to the door.

"Hold on there, buddy boy," Henry cautioned, and Clarence skidded to a stop, sitting between Dani and me when Henry opened the door.

"Laura," Em called and ran to me. Thrilled to hear her speak my name, I picked her up, and twirled, laughing and crying at the same time.

"We need a minute," Alvarez said to me and Mattie took the girls upstairs.

"She's one brave little girl," he said when we were alone in the office. Judges normally don't hear evidence at an arraignment, and Em can't testify at the trial, but Mr. Glass is very convincing. The judge allowed it."

He held up a hand when I opened my mouth. "I'm not finished."

My stomach turned at the possibility of bad news, but he grinned. "The judge also let Mr. Glass tell his own tale 'bout how things looked when he got to the scene. It didn't get Charlie off, but it was enough to put him in Patrick's custody 'til the trial."

"When will that be?" I asked.

"Maybe two, three months or more down the road because the jail's overflowing and the court's backed up with protesters."

It was a long conversation for him, and I was over the moon with joy. Maybe prayers worked after all. "Will Charlie be with Patrick when he gets home tomorrow? Where will he and Em stay?"

"We got the bunkhouse for Charlie. Em can stay at the house 'til things settle down."

"What do you mean? Is Patrick expecting trouble?" My throat tightened. How could he *not* expect trouble? Sheriff Coulter would be incensed that Charlie wouldn't wait out the time to his trial—or his funeral—in the Jeffers County Jail. Alvarez looked worried and I understood. Once word got out, if it hadn't already, the Klan wouldn't take it lightly.

"Will Patrick cancel the town hall in Savannah?"

He sighed. "Can't. Berens is preaching that Paddy's defense of colored folks is going to end the world an' that the O'Gradys have 'bad' blood, whatever that means."

I gasped. It was still two weeks from Billy's deadline for proof, but he was already tossing allegations. Testing the waters of public opinion, I assumed.

Alvarez misread my concern and patted me on the back. "Don't worry. Berens is making a fool of himself. The only bad blood is in the Berens' clan. And by bad, I mean evil. The youngest one, Jeremy, is the only good one in the lot."

Patrick had said the same thing, but I hadn't heard from Jeremy since the day before my interview at Langesford. "If you say so. How long will Patrick be home?"

"Not long."

"Why? Where's he going?" *Why was I always the last to know?*

"Boston."

"What? Boston? Why?"

"Crazy or not," Alvarez said. "Berens is kicking Patrick's butt right now, and Uncle Edward was close with a powerful Senator up there. Patrick's hoping for some strategy."

I groaned. "What Senator?"

'Stainsby," he said. "It's on the marker by the library."

Yankee money, I remembered from my conversation with Patrick on the 4th of July. He said the name of the donor was carved 'in really small letters' on the plaque in the park behind the library. If I'd looked at the marker, would I have seen my own name? What was the connection? And how did a picture of someone named Mary O'Grady end up in my attic in Boston?

There was no time to confront Patrick with my questions when he arrived the next day with Charlie Green. Men working near the house met them with joy, laughter, and a lot of back-slapping until Patrick brought Charlie inside. Dressed in the suit Hal had provided for the hearing, the tall, lean man stood in the foyer, turning an old fedora hat in his hands. He was very dark, like his brother, but instead of black, his eyes were an intriguing shade of hazel/green that held you in their spell—when he let you meet them.

They lit up when Em threw herself into his arms with a joyful squeal.

It would make Mattie's God smile—if he, or she, had a face, I thought.

Charlie's grin showed gaps of missing teeth that I suspected went along with the swollen lips and bruises on his face. So much for the protection of the Brunswick Detention Center. But this was a time for joy, not pity.

Though Patrick beamed at the happy outcome of the arraignment, worry tightened his smile. Charlie still faced a jury trial and Patrick had been on the road for weeks, with only short periods at home to tend his business. I wondered how he'd managed a trip to Boston, followed by a five-city whistle-stop tour of town hall meetings—while being dogged by Billy's smear campaign.

Then there was my concern over his meeting with my father. Did father tell Patrick I was here? About Ricky—and Rose? We needed to talk. I nodded to Charlie. "You need some rest. Why don't you go into the office? Mattie can bring in sandwiches and lemon-tea."

Charlie froze, those mysterious eyes glazed by...*fear?* I'd again forgotten that even liberal white people didn't entertain black farm hands in their homes.

Patrick's, "If only we could," saved the uncomfortable moment. "We need to get him settled in the bunkhouse and put up a guard schedule."

Bunkhouse. Guard schedule? I understood Charlie was legally under arrest, but he was home. His daughter was less than a mile away. "Is that really necessary?"

"Yes, it is," he said, reminding me that he didn't have to ask my permission for, well anything.

Charlie reluctantly set Em on her feet. Still wearing the feathered headband, she glowed with joy, looking more like an angel than ever. A tear followed the tired, weathered lines of her father's cheeks. "You go on with Miz Laura," he told her. "Mistah Patrick an' me, we got work to do."

His voice reminded me of Dr. Martin Luther King Jr.'s. Low enough to make you want to hear. Slow enough to make you listen. Clear enough for you to understand.

While Dani would have pressed for more time, using all manner of arguments, negotiations, even tears to get her way, Em understood that work meant food on your table and a roof over your head. Though disappointed, she nodded. "Will you be here at supper?"

Charlie's scarred hand caressed his daughter's cheek. "No, Sweet Pea. I'm gon' get settled in my new place. And when I can, I'll make the best chicken gumbo we ever had—fer jest us two." He looked at Mattie. "That's if Miz Mattie has some spare fixins."

Tears fell from Em's eyes as she nodded and he gave her one more hug, as if it might be his last.

"Don't wait supper," Patrick told Mattie. And to me, "Don't wait up."

CHAPTER 24

Mattie made the usual breakfast of bacon, fried eggs, and volcano of grits overflowing with butter and honey lava for the girls, but Patrick was nowhere to be seen.

"Where is he?" I asked Mattie.

She shrugged. "Left early for God only knows where. Place is falling apart with him gone all the time."

So, he was already on his way to Boston. I'd waited up—in the office—but fell asleep sometime after 3:00am. I'd have heard him if he came in, even from the kitchen, but he must have stayed with Charlie or in one of the nearby cabins. I'd missed my chance to talk with him—again.

It was clear from the papers and local news that Billy's personal attacks were eroding voters' confidence in the young, inexperienced heir to the O'Grady dynasty. Billy presented himself as a rebel hero defending the status quo, and Patrick as the villain sellout to liberal Yankee reform. It was the mid-point of the campaign, with the Labor Day town hall looming. I'd begun to worry that Billy, madness notwithstanding, could win the election. Patrick needed to pull on the boxing gloves or step out of the ring.

Dani announced she was going to the cabins on her new two-wheel bike, and Em asked to visit her father who was working in the maintenance barn.

"No!" Mattie barked and we all stepped back.

She looked at Dani. "You jes' got the trainin' wheels off that bike and ain't yet made it down the lane without falling off. Lookit those band aids on your legs." And to Em's frightened eyes, "Your daddy needs to work. He don't need no little ones messin' with his tools."

Mattie sighed heavily and turned to the window, craning her neck toward the cloudless sky, "Looks like rain. Best y'all stay inside today." Then she smiled and uncovered a fresh peach pie. "See what I made for after supper?"

Diversion. Rule number one for magicians, mothers and politicians. Em was easy to distract with an offer to teach her how to make buttermilk biscuits, but Dani frowned at being denied her bike ride.

"If you help me in the office today, maybe Mattie will give you an extra piece of that pie at dinner instead of supper," I bargained with her.

The peach pie ploy worked on both disappointed girls, and I couldn't argue with Mattie's logic. A storm was indeed brewing, but not in the sky. The South was turning into a war zone now that the bodies of three missing civil rights workers had been found in Mississippi after nearly two months. Their murders had been tied to the White Knights of the Ku Klux Klan. The FBI presence in the South wouldn't be leaving any time soon.

I wondered how bad it would get as Federal and State elections drew near. And how long before the Feds stepped in to punish law enforcement officials like Birmingham's Police Commissioner, for encouraging local Klan members to beat peaceful Freedom Riders.

But why keep the girls inside today? I wondered. What did Mattie know? I whispered in Dani's ear, "Could you help me carry my filing boxes into the Treasure Room? And I think we left a mess in there last time."

Her face lit up. "Can I play with the pictures? And can I make up new stories?"

What an odd child, wanting to make up stories about long-dead people in grainy old photos. But her mama had done it too. Perhaps the stories filled the void of loneliness and loss. I thought of Mary O'Grady in the old photos. Was her child Patrick I? It was a long shot, given the common Irish name and the high rate of infant mortality among Irish immigrants. But it was my only explanation as to how the picture could be in both Boston and here.

Dani poked my elbow. "Well can I?"

"Of course, sweetie," I answered, planning to dig deeper into the trunk and saddlebags. "But we must put everything away when we're done."

"Of course, Laura," she answered in her unnervingly adult way.

While I rooted around in the saddlebag, she arranged the photos along the baseboards, like sentinels along a castle wall, introducing them to each other and telling their stories. A half-hour later, she was bored, and I'd come up with nothing but broken fingernails and dirty hands.

"What's all this?" a low, male voice came from the open door.

"Daddy!" Dani screamed and ran to Patrick. "How did you know about the Treasure Room?"

He stooped to pick up his daughter. "I know about all the rooms in this house."

The smile faded when he saw me. "I'm sorry I keep missing you. I've been, well, busy."

I was tired of begging for his time. "No problem, we kept busy too."

"I see that." He looked at the ravaged saddlebag. "Find anything interesting?"

"Just dirt and sand," I answered a little too quickly. *That glitters like gold.*

I directed his attention toward the old pictures. "But Dani found some new playmates."

He frowned at the line of long-dead ancestors and strangers. "Well, Dani girl, Miss Laura and I have things to discuss. Go wash up. It's nearly dinner time and Mattie can use some help."

I closed the trunk and turned the lights out behind us. He closed the door, locked it and returned the *McGuffey Reader* to its proper position. The phone rang just as we'd taken our seats, ending our conversation before it started.

At supper, I found a note on my plate. Wrinkled and hastily written it said, "Sorry to miss you again. Emergency at the stables." He didn't say when he'd be back, and I refused to be put off again. He had to come home sometime, and I knew the first place he'd go. I again curled up on the couch, wrapped in the antique shawl, and let the night breezes lull me to sleep.

The soft whoosh of the pocket doors sliding open woke me. Patrick's silhouette filled the small opening, but instead of turning on the light, he followed the moonlight to his desk. Hearing the drawer open and the clink of glass against glass, I sat up. "You're late."

"Jesus H. Christ," he swore, sloshing most of his bourbon onto the blotter. "What the hell are you doing here?"

I stood, untangling myself from the shawl and straightening my skirt. "I could say the same for you. We're way overdue for a meeting."

"Not now." He ran his hand over the late-night shadow of a beard.

"No, I think now is exactly the right time." I avoided the temptation to pour myself a drink and sat opposite him, leaning into the desk lamp's tiny circle of yellow light. "What was the *emergency* at the stable—this time?"

I regretted my cocky attitude when he buried his face in his hands. I went to him, kneeling at his side. "What happened?"

He slowly raised his head. Sadness—no—grief shone from his red-rimmed eyes. My heart raced. The Klan seemed to be getting stronger and more violent every day, their crimes inching toward peaceful little Jeffers.

"Is it Charlie?" I whispered.

He shook his head and drank what was left of the bourbon in his glass before standing. "Not this time. But you, Dani, Ela, and Em," he said so slowly I felt his pain with each word. "You need to leave as soon as possible."

"Why?"

He stepped from behind his desk to face the portrait of his courageous ancestor. "This morning, one of my hands checked on the ponies in the East pasture, where they graze at night in the summer."

He didn't bother to wipe his tears when he turned to me. "Last night two of them were butchered. "Two-year-olds. Nearly old enough to start training."

"Who would do such a thing?" My stomach lurched at the scene I could only imagine, and I ached to put my arms around him, but he wasn't finished.

"Their heads were mounted on the fence posts. 'An eye for an eye, Nigger lover' was painted on a bedsheet with their blood."

I couldn't fight the nausea and reached the wastebasket just in time, staying there on my knees, sobbing. I knew people were angry about Charlie's house arrest, but the slaughter of innocent animals sent an even more savage message than I could imagine. I wondered how much Billy paid them to do it.

Patrick helped me up and we clung to each other.

"It was a warning," he said, his breath warm against my neck. "I was a fool to think his hatred wouldn't reach me here. A fool to think I could ignore him."

Him? Did he mean Billy?

"Did you call the police?" His scowl and knitted eyebrows told me it was a stupid question. Sheriff Coulter likely still had blood on his hands.

"I spent hours at the Sheriff's office, waiting for Coulter to show up. When he did, he blamed it on rowdy colored boys. In other words, he was his usual cocky-asshole-son-of-a-bitch self."

He grabbed the bottle of bourbon and left me for the couch. "Sorry for the profanity."

I joined him. "No offense taken. Who can you go to now? The State Police? The Governor? The FBI? He can't get away with this. We must protect Charlie and Em."

When he looked at me, I saw a new light in his eyes. Anger? Hatred? Vengeance? Perhaps all of them, but also a determination I hadn't seen before. It both thrilled and frightened me.

I again heard, "That's where you come in." Only this time it was from the other side of the political fence. I shivered in the warm room. Another warning from beyond the grave?

"Me?"

Holding my hands in his firm, calloused grip, he said, "When I accused Coulter of being part of it, his smile told me I was right. But he wasn't so cocky when I said I could prove it."

"Can you—prove it?"

He left me to pace. "Of course not. But it may settle him down for a while. We don't have much time. I cancelled my trip to Boston. Ela's leaving Sunday morning for New Mexico and we need to get Dani and Em out too. I have a safe place arranged for you to take them right after Ela leaves."

"No!" I shouted and he turned to me. "Laura, you have to understand."

"Oh, I understand," I said, lowering my voice so it wouldn't carry up the heating grate to Dani and Em's room. "This is not a Western where it's time to get the womenfolk out of town." I stepped up close, so he could see I meant it when I said, "I won't go."

"But—"

"Don't! We both know Billy's fanning this fire. And I feel responsible for not stopping him in time. Tammy doesn't start school until after Labor Day. Send her with the girls to this safe place, but I'm here. And I'm staying, no matter what."

A corner of his mouth lifted for an instant, then fell back into a grim, thin line. His hands gripped my shoulders. "This isn't your fight."

"Why? Because I'm a Yankee?"

"No."

"A woman?"

"Well..."

"Wrong answer!" I stepped close to him. "I came here...to Georgia, and to Jeffers...to finally stand up for something. So far, I've just watched things happen and whined about it. It's past time for me to take a stand."

His powerful hands fell away from my shoulders, and his voice went flat. "And to write about it for the *Atlanta Constitution.*"

It threw me off. His eyes looked dark in the dim light. Angry.

"I'm no fool, Laura. Think of the headlines. "*Scion of White Aristocracy Harbors Negro Murderer.*" The story could make that career you want so much."

I felt as if I'd been slapped but didn't want him to see how much it hurt. I turned to the fireplace and looked up at Camilla. "How can you believe that? Haven't you noticed how much I love...Dani and Em? It's like they're my own—"

I stopped short of saying daughters, though I knew it was true, even after this short time. I turned to him, not bothering to hide my tears. "Nothing can happen to them. I won't leave." *Again.* "What's your plan?"

I didn't see him move until his lips met mine. They tasted like tears. *Mine or his?* His fingers caressed my cheeks, my eyelids, my throat, as if committing the shape and texture to memory, before pulling away.

"Coulter wants an eye for an eye, but Charlie can't run. If he does, he'll either be killed, or spend a lifetime as a fugitive. Either way, he loses his daughter. We're moving him to a safe place."

"No," I disagreed. "We both know it's Billy who is pulling the strings in this puppet show."

"It doesn't matter." He cleared his throat and stepped away to stand in front of a glass curio shelf behind his desk. "What do you know about guns?"

He lifted a ceramic horsehead and another hidden panel opened, revealing eight rifles standing at attention, including three Winchester pump-action shotguns and two Sharps carbine rifles. The others were game rifles.

I smiled. "Enough to win first place at the 1956 Falmouth Skeet Club Women's Classic. My brothers called me Skeet-eye for weeks."

He opened a wall safe below the rifles, handing me a Colt .38 Special revolver with a two-inch barrel. Then he tossed me a box of bullets. For all my big talk, the gun and ammunition trembled in my hands. While I'd shot clay targets in prep-school, these guns were meant for shooting people. I doubted I could point one at a person, let alone pull the trigger.

"Isn't this a police gun?" I said. "Where did you get it?"

He winked. "You pick up things over the years." Then he looked at my trembling hands. "Think of Em, Dani, Ela, or yourself," he said. "Try loading it."

The worn wood grip fit the curve of my palm. The small barrel felt light enough to carry in a pocket—or a purse. I blinked away tears. "Is this really necessary?"

"Yes, keep it with you at all times. Here or in town."

He took the gun back and loaded it for me. Then he emptied it, handing it and the bullets back to me. "Now you."

My shaking hand loaded the bullets into their chambers, then took them out again. After doing it correctly three times, I wiped my forehead with the back of my hand. "I pray I never have to use this."

"Me too," he said, closing the cabinet door and replacing the horse head before walking me out.

I answered a soft knock on my door a couple hours later, surprised to see him.

He looked at my new muumuu. "Did I wake you?"

"No. I couldn't stop thinking about those horses. Why Patrick? Why the horses?"

He sat on the mattress, near the foot of the bed and I joined him.

"It's symbolic," he said. "Twenty years ago, there was a sect of Revivalists in the area that used the Book of Revelation as their gospel. In it, horses symbolize war and the number two represents the ultimate death—in a lake of fire. Before burning a so-called sinner's house, they'd post two severed pony heads on their fence. It was their signature. My father helped Sheriff Coulter's father run them off."

Even empty, my stomach churned at what people do in the name of their misguided beliefs. "Who were they?"

"Like most cowards they used masks. But after Billy's father left town, there weren't any more fires. This wasn't planned by a bunch of hot-headed rednecks. It's hard to catch two ponies at night in an open field and kill them —that way. This warning was very well planned and executed, by multiple people."

"Billy," I confirmed. My mind raced. His hatred had to go beyond

Barbara's love for Patrick to master-mind this atrocity. "What's between you two—besides ancient grudges and Barbara?"

"Nothing *but* Barbara." His eyes glistened with emotion. "Billy killed her. And he knows I can prove it. To spare Dani, I haven't done anything about it —yet."

I couldn't wrap my mind around that. "But the obit. You, Billy, and people close to both of you, told me she died of breast cancer."

His flush of anger faded to the pallor of grief. "No, she survived breast cancer with a mastectomy. She died of a drug overdose. Drugs she got from Billy. Only Doc Hill and I know."

I remembered Ricky's dependence on Librium, both before and after Rose's death. Initially for anxiety and migraines, then just to get through the day. The nausea and tremors, memory loss, and confusion were worth it to him for the brief high. Fortunately, we could afford the Hazelden center in Boston to help him beat the physical addiction—and then Hollywood accepted him for who he really was.

"I'm so sorry," I choked. Then it hit me. "You mean Billy was a drug dealer?"

His hand squeezed mine until it hurt. "Since the ninth grade. If you wanted a little something to keep you up before exams or make all the bad things in your life go away, even for a little while, Billy was the one to see. After our wedding, Barbara and I told everyone we went to a spa in Upstate New York for our honeymoon, but it was a drug center. She was clean for a year when she got pregnant with Dani."

He took a deep breath, but his voice still broke. "We were happy, for a while. After she'd finished nursing Dani, she felt lumps in both breasts, but because of her mother, she didn't trust doctors. She delayed having it checked out until she needed a double radical mastectomy. The pain and disfiguration were more than she could bear. I was busy with the business, and Doc Hill prescribed antidepressants. We didn't know she was getting Quaaludes from Billy. Dani was three and a half when she went into Barbara's room. She thought her mother was playing Sleeping Beauty. But no matter how many times Dani kissed her she wouldn't wake up."

He shuddered, ran his fingers through his hair, and rubbed the stubble on his chin. "I found Billy's blue ludes at the bottom of her cigarette case in the nightstand. That's what our fight after the funeral was about."

"But if Billy caused her death, why does he hate you so much?"

"He's always hated me. And he never takes the blame for hurting things. Mrs. Robertson's dog deserved to have his ear cut off for barking at him. Joey Baer deserved to be pushed in front of a car for cutting in line at the movies. He blamed Barbara for the miscarriage that killed his baby, so I owe him mine."

Dani! I couldn't breathe. "He can't *do* that! She's *your* dau…"

Tears in his eyes told me there was more.

"What? You mean? No. It can't be."

His eyes fixed on the floor, but I knew he was somewhere else. In the past.

"I was gone a lot on business after our honeymoon. Barbara was a free spirit, coming and going as she pleased. And Billy could charm the Devil if he tried hard enough."

"No! Dani is yours in every sense of the word. From your great-grandmother's eyes to your strong chin. And she's kind and generous. There is *nothing* of Billy in her."

I hoped I was right. Billy was guilty of so many things, yet he prospered. People bought cars from him, cheered at his rallies. I'd never seen such madness. Yet I'd fallen into his trap. It appeared that Barbara had never really stepped out of it. I felt sick—again.

I swallowed hard and touched Patrick's cheek. "You're not thinking straight. Lay down and get some rest."

He cocked his head. "You sure?"

"As sure as I am that the sun will rise tomorrow. After all, 'tomorrah is anothah day'," I said in my best Scarlett O'Hara voice.

Without a word, he kicked off his shoes and stretched out on top of the old quilt. I took a deep breath and lay down beside him.

CHAPTER 25

I woke to the sound of soft snoring and the comfortable warmth of someone next to me. I checked my watch on the table. Six o'clock. Mattie and the crews started at six-thirty. Dani would soon hear the clatter in the yard and charge into my room calling me Lazybones. She couldn't find her father in my bed, or rather, on top of my bed.

I nudged him, whisper-screaming, "Wake up. Its six o'clock!"

He opened one stunning blue eye at a time. Lips framed by two-days' growth of dark bristles smiled before he rose on one elbow and looked at me. It's when I realized I not only loved his daughter, I loved him.

"Good mornin', Scarlett," he drawled and made me want to kiss him, beard and bourbon-breath notwithstanding. But would he still smile if he knew I'd slept with Billy?

I couldn't worry about that now. Still floored by his revelation that Billy was a drug dealer and had caused Barbara's death, I thought, *Que Sera.* Like the song said, whatever would be, would be. And whatever I wanted didn't matter. Billy was a murderer. I had to keep him from destroying one of the few truly good men left in the world.

We entered the dining room separately, Patrick first. Neither of us had time for more than a quick shower, and while he wore a fresh pair of jeans and clean shirt, he hadn't shaved. I was surprised to see Tammy's father,

Frank Eldridge, sitting with Alvarez at the table, both diving into plates heaped with country ham, red-eye gravy, and grits.

Frank looked both irritated by Patrick's tardiness, and surprised by my presence.

"I'll just take a coffee," I told Mattie. "The girls will be up soon. If I'm not there, they'll run around the house in their nighties." She nodded with a wink and handed me an already-poured mug.

I'd turned to go back upstairs when Patrick said, "Please stay." Then to the men, "She's one of us."

Not exactly sure what that meant, I sipped my black coffee and nibbled a warm cream cheese cinnamon roll, while they talked about the weather, crops, horses and cattle. I noted that while Tammy Eldridge was congenial to a fault, her father didn't bother to hide his disapproval that a Yankee had insinuated herself into the O'Grady family council.

Their plates finally empty, Patrick stood. "Let's take this to the office."

Finally! Their chatter about mundane issues while we were metaphorically sitting on a powder keg was maddening. We followed him to his office single file; Alvarez, Frank, and me. Hal Glass was already there.

Like a commander gathering his officers, Patrick stood behind the partners' desk. Hal sat in the chair opposite him, with Frank and Alvarez positioning their chairs to flank the ends of the desk. Feeling out of place, I took the Queen Anne at the rear.

We all agreed Billy had engineered the horse killings, with Sheriff Coulter and his friends executing the plan. We also agreed we couldn't prove it. He was Big Billy now. He had people to do his dirty work—and take the fall for him. What better dupe than a grieving sheriff bent on avenging the death of his son, no matter that he died terrorizing an innocent man and his daughter? But then, Charlie was only a Negro to them. Being hazed by white boys with a sense of entitlement was par for the course—especially for Toby Coulter.

Unfortunately, none of the recent accidents, fires, and mechanical malfunctions at both Rosewood and Langesford plantations could be tied back to Billy, or Coulter. But putting water in gas tanks and cutting fences was a whole different ballgame from killing horses. It seemed all we could do was watch and wait until the next thing happened—which could be murder.

Without mentioning I'd seen books on mythology in Billy's cabin, I ventured, "Patrick said that Billy's father had been involved in this type of cult activity. But what if it has a different meaning for Billy? In nearly all cultures horses symbolize freedom and power. Life itself, if you will. In battle, killing a man's horse meant not only defeat, it meant death. While it seems obvious that the 'eye for an eye' threat was for Charlie, I think it was really from Billy to Patrick because of...personal reasons."

Thinking of the murdered students, I added, "It might be time to call the Feds."

Hal shook his head. "It won't do any good without proof. Since the Klan is a secret organization, it's impossible to know how many god-fearing men in church pews on Sunday sacrificed their sheets for the sign on the fence."

We all nodded. Too many.

Alvarez' voice was thick with emotion when he reported, "The bodies are taken care of. And the fence replaced. All animals that can be, are stabled or fenced in. Guards are posted. Buildings are secure and guarded, but I don't know how long we can keep it up. The summer workers will be leaving soon."

"I have forty employees this time of year, including seasonal and migrant workers," he told Hal and me. "I've given them all a chance to stay or move on until we catch the men who butchered the horses. Only the three with families left."

It didn't surprise me. Langesford was home to many of them, and Charlie and Em were family. And the stable hands had a personal interest in catching the men who did this. But Alvarez was right. It was impossible for less than forty men to work while guarding a rambling, 2,000-plus acre plantation for what could be months, until Charlie's trial.

"I have twenty men ready for your call," Frank volunteered. "That'll leave me ten for Rosewood, but my harvest is mostly done, and it's smaller than Langesford. They can handle any trouble that comes our way."

Patrick nodded. "Thanks. I hope it doesn't come to that."

I commended their initiative, but it was all defensive, and in sports and politics, a good offense is always the best defense. I said, "Only cowards fight at night. They're biggest fear is being identified, and they follow Billy because he makes them feel safe. It's time to take charge. Let them think they're winning, then unmask them."

"Are you suggesting we use Charlie as bait to draw them out?" Patrick snapped.

Frank stood, glaring down at me. "The purpose of bringing him here was to protect him."

Alvarez nodded to me. "Not bait. Ambush," he said, and I wondered if he'd read *The Iliad.*

Without acknowledging it was my idea, Hal agreed with Alvarez. "Killing horses in a remote field at night is one thing but confronting a man on the steps of his own home is another. I doubt even Billy could get anyone from town to set a match to Langesford House without a gun to their head."

It seemed like a big 'if' to me, but Langesford was a cultural icon, surviving the Cherokee Wars, the Revolution, the Civil War and the Great Depression. It was as much a symbol of the South as cotton, Spanish Moss, and magnolias. It wasn't my call, so I looked up at Camilla's portrait. She'd used a bluff to save Langesford from a Yankee torch. Could her great-grandson do the same with his own neighbors?

Frank surprised me by offering to hide Charlie at Rosewood, in case the Klan forced their way into Langesford.

"No!" Patrick shouted. "I won't let you risk Rosewood. It's me—and Langesford—Billy wants. And I'm the one who took Charlie in. If there's a showdown, it'll be here."

Alvarez nodded. "This place is in my blood too. I stand with Patrick."

Frank conceded, confirming he'd still send men to help protect his wife's family home.

Hal nodded to Patrick and glanced at me. "Whatever you say, boss. And as they say in the movies, we're burnin' daylight. We better decide where to safely hide Charlie—fast. If not Rosewood or the bunkhouse, where?"

I pointed at *Gulliver's Travels.* "What about the old summer kitchen. Tammy told me it fooled the Cherokee and the…Yankees…as a hiding place and escape route, even before the bookcase. It should be good enough to fool a pack of bedsheet-wearing farmers and shopkeepers. I can take him his meals."

All eyes looked at Patrick. He'd be putting everything, and everyone he cared about in the one place Billy wanted to destroy. His weary nod acknowledged it made sense. "I'll talk to Charlie. Alvarez, you set up the guards in case we get a visit tonight."

"I'll get supplies," Frank offered, following Alvarez.

"I need to have a few words with Leroy," Hal said before he too, left the room.

Patrick took the few steps toward me. "I know you and Mattie won't go," he said. "But hate can turn even upright Christian citizens into a crazy mob. The girls need to be safe."

I couldn't argue. Last years' bombing at the 16th St. Baptist Church in Birmingham made it clear that children weren't exempt from racial hatred. "But for how long? Dani starts school in a couple weeks."

"I doubt it'll be that long."

"But if you send them away, Coulter and the others may catch on. It could make them more aggressive."

"I have a plan," finished the discussion.

She's one of us, I remembered him saying. My voice lowered. "You're sending them to Boston, aren't you?"

I didn't know whether to be relieved or worried at his nod. "My family trafficked in slaves. There are places in that house, tunnels leading to Boston Harbor. Cells. The energy, it lingers. It won't be good for Em."

His hands wrapped around mine. "Those tunnels were closed when the slave trade was abolished in 1808."

I stepped back. "How did you know that?"

"I've been in them. My great-grandfather Patrick was born there. His mother was an indentured servant who died when he was a child. He explored every inch of that house, including what was left of the slave tunnels before he ran away. After the War, he went back and confronted his father, securing the old man's promise to fund 'benevolent' projects in Jeffers during Reconstruction."

My mind raced in different directions. I was right. Dani's Mary O'Grady and my Mary were the same woman. And it explained the Stainsby name on the library monument, but he wasn't finished. "Our families have had a conciliatory, if not familial, relationship ever since."

I suddenly found it hard to breathe. Too much had happened in too short a time. And now this revelation that Patrick and I were distant *half-cousins*. "So, my father—and my brothers know?"

"Yes."

"But it wasn't necessary for *me* to know."

I fell back in the Queen Anne and he knelt beside it. "Can we talk about this later? We're in the middle of a crisis here."

It may have been ancient history to him, but for me it was a matter of trust. I didn't know who I was more upset with, my father, my brothers, or

Patrick. If I'd known, I could have warned Patrick. *None of this would be happening!*

"If 'if onlies' came true, the world would be a different place," Nanny Irene preached. And Patrick was right. We were indeed dealing with a crisis here.

"Does my father know you're harboring Charlie and the potential for violence?"

"I've talked with him about the possibility."

Of course, you did. But *I* could be kept in the dark until the last minute. He was too close to me. His hope that we could get past the secret he'd kept from me was too painful. Without considering the big one I kept from him, I stood and crossed the room to the window.

"Does Father know I'm here?"

"No, he still thinks you're in Atlanta, ignoring him. But we discussed the political ramifications of helping Charlie and he's willing to assist me. Privately of course. It's a very strange climate in Washington. Southern and Northern Democrats are gnawing on each other, with the Goldwater Republicans egging them on toward a complete split. If it works, they'll control both houses of Congress. It's not something we can afford right now."

I felt him behind me, close enough to touch, but not daring to. "I need your help, Laura, if just until this is over."

I couldn't argue. The girls needed to be safe and Stainsby Manor was like a medieval castle. I'd walk through fire if it meant Em's father would escape a lynching, and his daughter an orphanage. I nodded and stepped around him to leave the room.

By evening, Dani and Em were happily packing for their first trip out of the state. Tammy would drive them. I thought Mattie would insist on staying, but she wouldn't abide anyone else watching over her 'babies'.

With no offense to Tammy, Mattie complained, "She'll be taken' 'em to that new, McDonald's! Lord only knows what's in that food."

Nobody knew better than the Lord, so she was added to the little troupe.

Reasoning that family men wouldn't likely attack a house occupied by white women and children, we planned to use the confusion around church letting out, and Ela's departure on Sunday to spirit the children away. Once the girls were gone, we'd have time to prepare for whatever event followed the dead horses.

By full dark, Charlie was safe in the summer kitchen, the girls were tucked in their beds early, Tammy watching the road below their window. Lights glowed in the bunkhouse, barns, and house, but twenty-five men were posted in the shadows of all the barns and buildings, at each corner of the house, and in the trees above any road leading to Langesford. And this was only a rehearsal.

~

The next day, Tammy finished overseeing the packing while I went to town with Ela for last-minute items and gifts for her family in Taos, New Mexico. I refused Patrick's offer to send Alvarez with us, reminding him about the .38 Special he'd forced on me.

"We have to act like we don't suspect anything," I said. "Ela isn't afraid, and neither am I. They need to know that. I promise we'll stay downtown, near the Glass House, and be back by two o'clock."

That gave us three hours, including travel and lunch time. We parked my car in the lot by the hotel and set out for Herman's Drug store for makeup, shampoo, and school supplies that would be more expensive in a university town.

The chill we felt inside the store had little to do with the humming ceiling fans. The moment they saw us, women left the checkout counter to stalk out of the store. The poor girl at the cosmetic counter couldn't ring up our sales fast enough.

"Petty bitches," I told Ela. "Jealous of your flawless complexion."

It prompted a wan smile. "I'll believe that—today."

We left from the back entrance, heading for Ippel's Department Store.

"How dare you show your face in town, you murderin' Indian bitch," a low, male voice came from the entrance to the alley between stores.

"Leroy, what's wrong with you?" I shouted, hoping someone would hear. "You know she didn't have anything to do with what happened."

"Shut up!" he told me and pointed to Ela, weaving a little on his feet. "It's her fault Hollis is dead."

"You're drunk," I said. "Stop this now, before you get in trouble."

But he was still sober enough to move fast. He stepped behind Ela and pulled a knife, pressing it against her back. "Into the alley," he ordered. "Quietly." Then to me, "You first."

I obeyed, and with Ela between us, I fished the .38 out of my macramé purse. Near the end of the alley, I turned, hiding the gun in the pleats of my skirt, hoping to talk him out of the stupid stunt before somebody really got hurt. "What are you doing, Leroy? Why is it her fault?"

"The Mexican Nigger-bitch bewitched him to run off with her. Me an' the boys, we talked him outa it. He was comin' back to tell her when that Nigger got in the way."

He poked the knife at her side enough to prove his point. Ela winced but didn't cry out. My heart melted at her grief and pain, as well as the courage in her dark eyes. "Don't believe him," I told her. "He lied at the hearing, and he's lying now. You know in your heart that Hollis loved you. Don't ever doubt that."

"I won't," she shouted and stomped on his foot hard enough to make him stumble. Quick as a cat, she turned and kicked him in the crotch. He dropped the knife to double over, swearing and groaning in pain. I side-stepped him and pressed the gun against his side.

"Ela, go find Hal," I said. Then to Leroy, with more bravado than I felt, "Straighten up before I shoot you for threatening Em Green. If anyone asks, I'll tell them you attacked me with that knife and dragged me into the alley."

He rose slowly from his painful crouch, sweat and tears dripping from his face. "No! I didn't threaten the kid in the truck. That was Evan. I was just along for the ride, but Toby was still mad at Hollis for plannin' to run' off with the greaser. When we passed the Nigger, Toby turned around, but he lost control and hit the truck, then we flipped. Evan and I crawled out the back window to get help. I didn't do nothin' wrong."

"He collapsed to his knees, sobbing, "Please don't shoot me."

So, it was just as we thought. The boys had turned around to harass Charlie. I wondered what else Leroy had lied about.

"You know that's not true," I said, my voice softer but the gun still pressing hard against his spine. "You lied to the police and let an innocent man go to jail. You pulled a knife on a white woman. With my testimony, not even Sheriff Coulter will get you off. Do you have any idea how much inmates love pretty young boys like you?"

Terror glazed his eyes.

"Well, you don't want to," I bluffed. "Now sit down over there, against the wall. I think you have some information you want to share."

As Leroy's shock faded, so did his fear. He refused to move, snarling,

"You ain't gonna shoot me. The Klan boys'll hang you, white woman or not. And nobody'll ever find your body. Jest like they won't Charlie's when they get ahold of him."

"Sit!" I ordered again, nudging him with the gun.

"What if I don't?" he challenged me.

"I could trip and accidentally pull the trigger." Thinking of Em, Dani, and Ela, helped me steady the gun with both hands. "There's a train due any minute. No one will hear the shot—or find your body until we're long gone —unless, you tell me what really happened the morning of the accident."

The approaching train whistle punctuated my words. Then "Laura?" came from the street. *Hal!*

Leroy shrieked, "Help! She has a gun. She tried to kill me,"

"And he tried to knife Ela," I shouted back, lowering the gun and pointing to the knife on the ground. Hal approached us both cautiously and I gave him the weapon with shaking hands. "Patrick gave it to me. For personal protection."

He checked the chamber and smiled when he found it empty. "Remind me not to play poker with you."

"He just confessed to me," I stretched the truth. "The boys turned to run Charlie off the road but ended up in the ditch instead."

Hal ordered Leroy, "Come with me. Taking someone at knifepoint is a felony. And you're eighteen. You can be tried as an adult for this stunt, but this is your lucky day. Give me a witness statement about the accident and agree to testify at Charlie's trial and I may convince these two nice ladies not to press charges."

Leroy hesitated, and Hal confirmed my threat, "How long you think someone like you will last in jail?"

"But they'll kill me if I tell."

Hal pulled him up, answering the questioning gaze of a passerby, "Drunk. Kids today."

The man sniffed, making a disgusted snort before moving on, and Hal turned back to Leroy, his voice softer. "I can keep you safe, but you have to tell the truth."

An hour later, Patrick met us at the Langesford verandah, immediately sensing something was wrong. But even after I explained that Hal would get Leroy to testify on Charlie's behalf, he headed for his truck to give the boy the beating of his life.

Alvarez stepped in front of him. "Ela's *my* daughter. If anybody beats him, it's me. But Ela is safe, thanks to Laura, and Charlie needs him in one piece to testify."

Patrick voiced my own fear. "How can you be sure? Ela's traveling by train alone tomorrow. They could follow her."

"No," her father answered. "I'm going with her. I'll come back after I drop her off with my brother. Raphael and Rosalita will watch over her 'til school starts."

Alvarez was Patrick's right-hand-man. Blood relationship aside, a partner in the true sense of the word. With the threat of the Klan, his absence was a loss Patrick couldn't afford, but Ela's safety was more important.

Patrick nodded and shook his cousin's hand. "It's settled then, *mi primo*."

CHAPTER 26

Alvarez and Ela drove to Jeffers early the next morning, for him to purchase his train ticket. The Eldridge family picked me up for church, and Patrick left with Dani a little while later. Frank let me off a block from the church to walk the rest of the way and I slipped into a back pew, watching surprised heads snap to attention as the extended O'Grady family settled into the Langesford box.

It was cooler than the day of the boys' funerals but sweat rolled down Reverend Baker's cheeks and faces flushed when Patrick nodded to them. Shock or shame, I wondered? Doubting the latter, I smiled at the congregation's weak rendition of *How Great Thou Art.* And during the sermon about Jesus feeding the poor, I guessed which men would soon be wearing hoods, and which women had sacrificed their sheets for robes.

Patrick excelled at heeding my advice to kill them all with kindness. After the service, he lingered over every blue-haired dowager, complimenting them on their dresses, the flowers in their hats, even the accomplishments of their mediocre grandchildren destined to spend their lives at Woolworth's or the new Tasty Freeze.

Men winced as Patrick squeezed their hands, wishing them well. When he let go, most of them pulled out a handkerchief to wipe their sweaty palms and foreheads. Based on nervous tics and a reluctance to make eye-contact, I had a dozen names for my Klan list, and a good guess about the pony-killers.

Word travels quickly in a small town. Especially when it comes to murdered livestock, and Patrick wasn't without allies. After the service, more than a few neighboring planters offered support. The Guilford, Chisholm, and Tildon families were the three most prominent to offer extra security.

Arlen Guilford, a close friend of Edward O'Grady, returned Patrick's handshake, saying, "The pledge my grandfather made to Patrick and Camilla still holds."

August Chisolm nodded in agreement, as did John Tildon.

The town clock chimed the hour and Patrick picked up Dani.

"Understood," he told his father's friends. With a glance at Sheriff Coulter's retreating back, he added, "Stop by later this evening. We can play poker and catch up on old times."

They nodded to him and then to me. "A pleasure to meet you Miss Tucker," Chisolm acknowledged. "Until this evening."

All three older men touched their fingers to their hats, reminding me of the Three Musketeers.

We stepped lively to the busy train station where the red Santa Fe Chief engine rested in the bright sun, nearly ready to board passengers. Alvarez stood next to his daughter's small mountain of suitcases with a saddlebag slung over his shoulder.

We all hugged Ela, and Dani hugged everyone around her until the diesel engine's whistle blew and the conductor called, "All aboard!"

Patrick and Alvarez stepped aside for a private word and I whispered to Ela, "Be safe. I'm told time heals all wounds."

Her smile broke my heart. "It is also my wish for you. And that when you find your true path in life, your spirit will find happiness."

What an odd thing to say, but her eyes looked so old, so wise—and so sad—I couldn't ask.

She turned to join her father, shoulders back, her black hair stirring in the light breeze. Another image I knew I'd never forget.

The bittersweet parting over, I thought about Ela's dream of advancing the use of natural medical treatments, and wondered when it would be safe for her, a young woman of color, to travel alone in the South.

While the others indulged in last-minute hugs, I scanned the depot for anyone who looked threatening. Two stood out. Randy from Billy's garage and a younger version of him.

They didn't look happy about the protective group surrounding Ela, or to see her board with her father. Grumbling as the doors closed, they turned away. I wondered if they had unused tickets in their pockets.

Patrick, Dani, and I left town separately from Tammy and her parents, but instead of taking the highway home, we met them at the county line, where Henry, Mattie, and Em waited in Henry's old truck to transfer the girls and Mattie to Frank Eldridge's roomy Chevrolet Impala.

Tammy would drive them as far as the Holiday Inn in Richmond, where they'd spend the night before descending upon poor Nanny Irene Monday afternoon. I wished I could be a fly on the wall when they burst in on her. I hoped Father had let her know they were coming.

Tammy's parents rode back with us after our goodbyes. The silence fairly hummed with unsaid words, unexpressed emotions, doubts, fears—and for me, questions. We were almost to the bluff that killed Edward and Thelma O'Grady when I asked Patrick, "What did Mr. Guilford mean when he said the pledge his grandfather made to Patrick and Camilla still held?"

"Tell her," his Aunt Linda told him after an awkward pause.

He pulled off the road at the now-fenced off outcropping overlooking his house and turned off the engine. I couldn't imagine the emotions they felt, reliving the horror of that winter night. Patrick finally took a deep breath. "After the War, the Klan was mostly small groups of former Confederates who targeted plantations run by Yankees. They wore black hoods and capes over their Confederate uniforms. A Guilford was one of them. Along with a Chisolm, a Tildon, and a few others."

He looked at me. "The first Patrick had just finished rebuilding the gin house the Yankees burned. Camilla was helping him protect it. She killed the leader, an old family friend before the War. Of the six men with him, three stayed behind to help them. They made a pledge that night to end the violence, binding their descendants to it."

"What's the pledge?" I asked.

He, Linda, and Frank recited, "I pledge with my blood and the blood of my descendants that Jeffers County will be a safe place to live—no matter the color of a person's skin or their place of birth."

Patrick turned to me. "They were Guilford's words, but all five bound themselves and their families to it. When one of us turns eighteen, male or female, we also take the Pledge."

Linda added, "And our spouses. No one has declined, and it's rarely acknowledged. It's just how we raise our families."

The Pledge answered so many questions. The O'Grady family's commitment to local, state and federal government. How Jeffers had remained a peaceful oasis in an embattled South for nearly a century. And why most of the business owners, while observing the Jim Crow Laws, didn't protest when the new Act forced them to open their businesses to black clientele. For a century, it had been a place free of masked madmen bent on resurrecting a long-dead way of life—until now.

Before re-starting the engine, Patrick stared a long moment at the new concrete rail fence across the hilltop, deep in his own thoughts. Did he think history was repeating itself? Was it up to his family and their allies to again protect Jeffers from hatred and violence? Was he up to it?

Hal joined us for supper. Four pickup trucks with twelve men and six women showed up shortly after, parking inside the nearby powerhouse and storage barn. Helen Guilford and her daughters-in-law brought enough to feed an army through an entire campaign. Even Patrick seemed surprised at the turnout.

"It's tonight," Guilford told him. "When you showed up in church, thumbing your nose at their warning, and they saw you send off the Injun and his girl…" He raised his hands. "Coulter's words, not mine. They figured they better act fast."

Patrick cocked his head. "How do you know what Coulter said?"

His friend's craggy face split into a smile. "My grandson Dwight earns college money by cleaning the Sheriff's office on weekends. Seems they forgot to tell him there was a special meeting after church. He was cleaning the john when they came in and he knew enough to stay there. The boy took the oath a couple years ago and when he heard enough, he climbed out the window."

Patrick nodded at the risk young Dwight had taken. "If they find his cleaning things in there, they'll come after him—and you."

Guilford shrugged. "I'm not worried. His folks either, but if you got a place for the boy 'til this gets sorted out, I'd appreciate it."

"Done."

One more outsider granted sanctuary, I thought. Yes, Patrick O'Grady II, could handle this situation. But would there be casualties?

He turned to Henry. "Send out the alert to defend, but not attack. Understand?"

Henry snapped to attention, nodded and left the parlor to notify the men guarding more than three square miles of property, from the house to Morning Bird Stables.

Patrick and Guilford planned where the additional men—and women, of the three families would be posted as lookouts closer to the house.

"When they find Charlie's cabin empty," Patrick said. "They'll come right for the house, but we'll be prepared."

Hiding in plain sight, I thought. It was my idea, but it suddenly worried me. Coulter wasn't stupid. And he was a cop. He'd have the full protection of the law to search Langesford if he suspected Charlie had escaped. But Patrick had the full protection of the law to house Charlie wherever he felt was the safest place on his own property.

Except Patrick was no longer simply protecting Charlie. He was daring the sheriff, the Klan—and Billy—to come after him, risking his home, his business, and his future.

I touched his shoulder. "Are you sure?"

"Trust me." He smiled before dispatching the larger portion of volunteers to their posts.

"Don't anyone try to be a hero," he cautioned while passing out flares. "If you get in trouble, light the flare and get the hell out. We'll be on top of them before they figure out the bright light in the sky isn't the second coming of Jesus. Do *not* engage them. Understood?"

All heads nodded and then he passed out bird call whistles to the sentinels posted between the road and the house. "When they pass you, signal, then follow them quietly. Let them set up their cross. While they're busy getting their little bonfire ready, get in close and surround them. But do *not* make your presence known."

"If you can't do that, please leave now," he told the room full of unarmed men and women. No one left.

Hal brought in a large box, pulling out a dozen sheets and pointed hoods with holes for eyes. All eyes turned to him.

He shrugged. "I have a hotel with lots of sheets. And the hoods are from an old case."

To the few chuckles, mumbles and snickers, he warned. "These won't work for long but should buy some time before they figure there's more men than they came with."

The little group took the sheets without protest, but no one tried the hoods on for size.

"Listen closely and try to identify as many as you can by their voices," Patrick added before sending them to their stations.

As the evening progressed, the light in Dani's room went out at her normal bedtime, followed by the kitchen light when Mattie would leave for the day. Henry wore her raincoat to impersonate her walk to her remodeled home in the old laundry house. Finally, only the tiny lamp in the corner of Patrick's office remained, a dressmaker's dummy with a wig standing in for him behind the desk. Out of deference to the open windows and how sound carries in the darkness, silence reigned.

Just before midnight, Patrick heard Henry's screech owl from the south. A few minutes later, another owl, a little closer. A third came from the turn onto the Langesford drive.

"The bastards skipped the bunkhouse and are coming right up the drive," Patrick swore.

Like Paul Revere, I rushed from one end of the house to the other, carrying the message, "From the drive."

We huddled by the front, back and side windows, until Sally Chisolm's nightingale call told us the lookouts were on their way. From in front and behind the marauders, we watched a dozen men work in well-orchestrated silence, building a brush pile big enough to support a crude pine cross.

Even with a hood, I recognized the jerky movements of the owner of Dash's Grocery's crippled right arm. I put a check next to his name on the list I'd made at church. *One.*

Sheriff Coulter was the easiest to recognize, his arm and hand signals testifying to his training as a traffic cop. *Two.*

Thick necks and musclebound bodies gave Randy Logan and his son away. *Three and four.*

I felt the restlessness in the room as the pyre outside rose above the veranda's top step.

"It's too close," Guilford whispered to Patrick. "You can't let them light it."

He nodded and stood, handing his gun and a flare to his friend. "I'm going out," he said. "If that pile is lit, send this up for all hands to come in, and call the fire department—if they're not already here."

Out? Alone? Unarmed? My mind screamed. Why wasn't anyone stopping him? "They'll shoot you in your own front yard, like Medgar Evers," I hissed.

"Not right away," he whispered back. "Billy may want me, but they want Charlie."

"So, have him escape into the woods from the back door of the summer kitchen."

"Already done." Guilford said, his big hand on my shoulder.

"When?"

"At the first signal. Now, sit tight and let your man talk them down."

My man!? Talk them down? Building a pyre that big on the front doorstep of one of the most prominent homes in Georgia did *not* indicate they could be talked down easily. I stepped away from his hand and followed Patrick through the open front door.

I nearly plowed into him as he stopped suddenly, then stood, legs planted firmly on the wide plank flooring, facing a dozen men with lit torches.

"It's not too late to call this off, Coulter," he shouted directly at the former traffic cop.

A few people murmured, and Coulter hissed, "He's guessing."

"I know all of you." Patrick's deep voice quieted them as he recited the names of the participants without the help of my list.

"Alan Johnson. I see you every Friday at the bank. How is Betty? Did she like the pecan pie Mattie made for her when she was sick last month?"

Then to the grocer. "David. How's that new vegetable cart my carpenter made for you working out?"

He pointed at a man in the back. "And Mr. Beadle," he addressed the principal of Jeffers High School. "Is this how you teach the spirit of democracy to the next generation of Americans we trust you to educate?"

A wave of rumblings traveled through the group. But he wasn't finished. He slowly descended the steps to pause in front of Billy's mechanic-and-son, pulling off the elder Randy's hood, then his son's.

"Randy, how much did Berens pay you to slice the brake line on my father's car? Aren't two O'Grady murders enough for you?" He punched Randy square in the face and the mechanic fell to the ground, choking on blood flowing from his nose and mouth.

A few members of the crowd stepped toward Patrick.

"Stay where you are," came from behind us and every pointed hood turned toward the verandah, where Hal Glass and the heads of the Guilford, Chisholm, and Tilden families stood, rifles trained on them.

Without turning, Patrick stared at Randy's son for a long moment, fists clenched. "You're a bully, just like your father. Do you want to follow him to prison?"

The boy stared, wide-eyed and terrified in front of a Patrick I had no idea existed. Flickering torches highlighted the shadows of his handsome face, now contorted by grief and rage as he fought with his own humanity.

"Patrick," I shouted, but he didn't hear me—or couldn't hear me—I thought, over the thunder of fury coursing through his veins. He pulled a knife from his belt, placing the point against young Randy's throat. "What were you going to do to Ela on that train?"

I screamed, "Think of Dani!"

Sheriff Coulter's, "She don't matter, you little Yankee bitch," sent bats to flight. He'd taken off his hood and raised his torch above the kerosene-soaked pile of kindling. "None o' you move. It's time to end the almighty O'Gradys, once and for all."

"You gonna kill us all?" Hal's voice thundered from the porch as he raised a hand. The lookouts, in from their posts, took off their hoods. Those guarding the house from the shadows stepped forward, rifles raised, circling the little group of confused men.

Frightened murmurs snaked through the crowd of Jeffers' upstanding citizens. The ones who tried to run either tripped over their own robes or were caught by Hal's men in sheets.

"Damn you all," Coulter swore, and threw the torch onto the kindling.

As quickly as it flared, it was extinguished by Chisolm's son, a forest ranger who had "borrowed" a gas-powered extinguisher from the DNR and hid it in the shadows along the side of the veranda. In the distance, sirens told us fire trucks were on their way. One by one, the torches were snuffed out in additional buckets of water rimming the house.

Patrick's men tied the ten raiders, including Randy, still bleeding from his broken nose and missing teeth, to each other using their own ropes stained with the blood of the dead horses. I expected pleading, bribes, even denials, but the scene played out in eerie silence.

It was nearly dawn by the time the State Police arrived and loaded them up to be taken the fifteen miles to the police station in Barnsworth. We were still waiting for the FBI.

With no one dead, and no property significantly damaged, I imagined most of the good citizens of Jeffers would plead coercion from Sheriff Coulter and get away with a fine and a slap on the wrist. But not Coulter.

CHAPTER 27

When the last of the families left for home, I asked Patrick, "How do you know Randy Logan sabotaged your father's car?"

He shook his head as if to clear the memory that he threatened to kill someone in cold blood in front of two dozen witnesses.

"I didn't. I found the bill with the papers in my desk drawer. It was dated the day before the accident. Three days later, the transformer in Randy's garage blew up, burning everything inside to a crisp. He went to work for Billy the next day. And the look on Randy's face when I accused him told me it was true. You were right. What's happening goes beyond Billy's jealousy over Barbara. He's behind my parents' deaths and I'm going to prove it...somehow."

We both looked like hell after only a couple hours' sleep, but there was no time to talk as Patrick oversaw the cleanup, filed his complaint with the State Police, and left to meet with the FBI in Atlanta. Tammy, Mattie, and the girls arrived safely in Boston and would stay a few more days until we knew they'd be safe. Charlie returned from his hiding place in the woods to move into the basement again. And as expected, Randy denied Patrick's charge of sabotage.

The irony that I was sitting on the story of a lifetime, but was too close to write it, did not escape me. I acknowledged I'd committed every journalistic sin in the book by going undercover without researching all parties involved, staying too long after discovering Billy's motive, and the BIG SIN of becoming personally involved with both subjects of my investigation. Rookie mistakes. *Unforgivable.*

Bob Healy had warned me in Boston against becoming a crusader. "You're a reporter, Laura," he said. "You don't make the news. You report the facts behind the news."

I'd managed to walk that fine line in Boston, but somewhere along the way, I'd lost my objectivity. The fake adoption ring assignment had given me a taste of working undercover, and the Wash-Mart article only increased my hunger to expose crime from the inside. Now, after nearly a year in Georgia, in the middle of the social movement of the century, I was sitting on a bombshell, but my credibility was shot. Perhaps it was time to take Ela's advice and 'find my life'.

I spent two days dodging calls from my old colleagues at *The Atlanta Constitution* and *The Boston Globe.* It was the best thing that could happen for Patrick's campaign. Now, instead of being a victim, he was something of a folk hero. But unlike the Pickrick Incident, it was best told by a local.

Dwight Guilford, the young man who warned us about the Klan visit, was a journalism major at Georgia State. I helped him write an eye-witness account that made what happened at the Pickrick look like a tea party. Patrick approved it before I wired it to Mr. McGill, and he promised Dwight an interview after graduation.

I stopped answering the phone at six o'clock, when my stomach announced I hadn't eaten anything since a bowl of Cheerios at breakfast. I had no idea if Charlie had eaten at all and made two grilled cheese sandwiches on Mattie's homemade bread. I took them and what was left of Mrs. Guilford's baked ziti and pork sausage down to the summer kitchen.

Charlie was exhausted and still crippled by the fear of being lynched. I resisted the urge to interview him, choosing to take the time to win his trust. We ate in silence, and a half-hour later, I gathered the dishes, offering hopeful words neither of us believed. He nodded without meeting my gaze and opened a worn Bible.

Leaving the bookcase door open, I thought of the skeleton keys and the funny-colored stone Dani and I had found in the Treasure Room. I grabbed a flashlight from the kitchen and tugged the *McGuffey Reader* to move the bookcase. I opened the Treasure Room door and it was just as we'd left it a week ago, trunk open, pictures lined along the baseboard, the saddle bag on top of a little pile of sparkling sand. Without disturbing the dust, I shined my light into the other side of the bag, finding museum-quality Western gear, including a tin of matches, bullets, and a leather bag of petrified crumbs that may have once been corncake. Digging deeper, I found the sleeve of a cotton shirt stiffened with a dark stain. Blood?

I dropped it, rubbing my hand on my jeans before dumping the entire bag. Empty now, except for more dust, more crumbs, and a thumb-sized stone. I rubbed it against my jeans. Crusty dirt and sand fell off, revealing a rounded edge of—what? Unusually heavy, about a half-inch thick, with a triangular shape, it wasn't a natural stone, rather, it was likely broken off something larger. A copper/green color, it was obviously not the glittering gold bar I'd hoped for.

I ran it under water in the library bathroom, scraping the crust off with a nail file until a tiny spot at the corner glowed under the fluorescent light. "Holy Shit!"

The phone rang. Thinking it might be Patrick, I closed the door to the Treasure Room dropping the stone into my pocket.

It was Jeremy—finally. "Billy wants to see you."

Billy was the last person I wanted to see, but it had to happen sometime. "Why? I still have two weeks before his deadline. And where have you been?"

"I think you know why, and Billy doesn't care about deadlines." He sounded a little too much like his cousin for my comfort, but I let it go. A month of Billy's ranting and off-the-wall speeches had to have driven the lawyer in him nuts.

Billy was also drawing flak from both the press and the Republican party, but it didn't seem to bother him. The masses were fired up and angry—at everyone but him—while he preached to registered white voters that he, and only he, could bring back the good old days.

"I still have two weeks," I insisted. "It's not easy wheedling yourself into the good graces of a dynasty, you know. And Pat…O'Grady's on the road as much as Billy. Cut me some slack."

"Sorry, I know it's been rough," he conceded, finally sounding like himself. "Especially last night."

"Rougher on Billy I bet, since it blew up in his face."

"Don't poke the bear. When Billy latched onto the Charlie Green case, I thought he'd let the race thing with Patrick drop. But after last night, even

Klan-lovers will think what happened was over the top. And since O'Grady stepped up, fence-sitters may think he has what it takes."

"Yes, very bad news for Billy," I gloated, but Jeremy was right. Billy was a bear and one didn't taunt an angry bear.

I lowered my voice. "What will he do next?"

"So far, he's satisfied with Coulter taking the heat. He'll spin it to his advantage, blaming the old guard—meaning Edward O'Grady—for letting Coulter stay in office. But he won't wait long before striking again. The debate's getting close. Did you come up with anything?"

"A certified birth certificate and registry confirming Danielle Langesford was white."

"What about her mother?"

"Nothing. She must have been born somewhere else." It wasn't exactly a lie. "But it doesn't really matter, does it? If Billy's desperate enough, he'll bring it up, with or without proof, unless we find something worse to use against him."

"Like what?" he asked.

"Like Barbara O'Grady didn't die from Cancer. She overdosed on drugs that came from Billy."

"What?"

Did Jeremy not have a clue that his cousin was a drug dealer? I found it hard to believe.

"Okay, I'll spell it out for you. I think those bricks in the tub buried by your privy were part of the Civil War gold Billy's great-grandfather, Samuel ranted about. And since owning gold bullion has been illegal since FDR was president, Billy went underground, using it to expand his drug dealing connections."

"Hold on!" Jeremy shouted. "I didn't see any gold in that tub. And Billy only sold a little weed back in high school."

So, he wasn't completely in the dark about his cousin's drug dealing.

"No, not *only* weed, Jeremy. Quaaludes and who knows what else. He killed Barbara O'Grady."

"Now you're talking crazy," he said, but I could hear the doubt in his voice.

"Jesus H. Christ Jeremy, face the facts. Billy may have been small-time before he found those bricks in the tub, but after he laundered it, he hit the big-time. And he was still in the game when Barbara overdosed. Could still be, through those fancy out-of-town customers he entertains at the cabin."

"You'll never be able to prove her pills came from him," he snarled, showing he was still defensive, but finally coming around. "And you have no idea how dangerous Billy is. You'll get us both killed."

"Everyone dies," I responded with ridiculous bravado. "He's a bully, a thug, and a lot worse, but if you don't believe me," I bluffed, "I'll take my evidence to the Feds."

Silence.

"Jeremy, do you really want to be on his side when I prove it? Do you understand the damage it could do to your career—and freedom—if they suspect you're an accomplice?

"What do you want me to do?" he asked. His voice was weak, but it showed a seed of decency still in the Berens genes.

"Do you have access to his books going back to when he bought Smitty's? And check into his foreign customers—particularly from Mexico, Guatemala, or Columbia."

"Billy keeps all his old records, including the ones he showed you, in a locked shed at the Cabin. He doesn't know I have a key. And he's meeting with a big customer from Guatemala in New York. He left today. Won't be back until Friday night. I'll dig."

We met on Thursday at the Rebel Diner, where I'd stopped for coffee on my way to Jeffers what seemed a lifetime ago. We both ordered black coffees and Jeremy handed me an envelope with Billy's private bank statements.

Even while working as a mechanic at Smitty's, his monthly deposits exceeded his gross pay. By 1950, he had more than twenty-five thousand dollars in the bank.

I leaned toward Jeremy to whisper, "What happened in 1950?"

He shrugged. "Nothing. Ma and I had moved out. It was the year after I found the tub."

Based on my ex-husband's expenses for what he called his 'nerve medicine', I calculated that even adding uppers to his weed wouldn't generate that kind of cash. Billy had to have been either laundering money from something else or dealing the hard stuff.

I also knew from Ricky that the drug trade routes using old prohibition trails from Southeast Georgia through the Okefenokee Swamp to New Orleans and Texas, had confounded the FEDs and local police for decades.

Ruthless dealers and Cartels from South America and Mexico owned the routes. Could Billy have used the gold to buy into a drug cartel and used the dealership to launder his revenue? The answer was an obvious yes, but it would be hard to prove.

I tucked the files into a shopping tote. "What about Randy Logan?"

He shrugged. "All I know is he took over Smitty's after Billy opened the dealership. When his shop blew up, Billy gave him a job."

Jeremy reminded me of Hal when he leaned toward me, jaw set, fingers tented. "I know Randy was at Langesford with the Klan, and Patrick accused him of messing with his father's brakes. Does he have proof?"

I finished my lukewarm coffee and evaded the question. "I think I'm ready to meet Billy, but not until my deadline on the 27th."

He left me to use the payphone outside the diner and came back a few minutes later as I was digging into a double fudge Sunday. "At the cabin," he said. "Ten o'clock."

"No!" I snapped. "I'm not stupid enough to meet Billy alone, in the middle of nowhere, call him a murderer and drug dealer and expect to leave in one piece."

"But that's what he wants."

What did Tammy see in him? "What is wrong with you?" I hissed. "It's time Billy stopped getting his way. Why won't you stand up to him?"

After a long silence, he cleared his throat. "Because he's blood and I owe him."

"Owe him how?"

"He paid for Ma's funeral and my education."

"No, he didn't."

"What do you mean?"

I was again surprised at how little Jeremy really knew about Billy. "Patrick told me Hal paid for the funeral and he was the one who set up your scholarship, not Billy."

He blanched as if a sudden crack had opened in the middle of his world. "No, Billy said…but it doesn't matter." He let out a long breath. "Blood is blood. Loyalty is all that's kept our family alive so far. Billy and I are the last of the line."

I pointed my chocolate-covered spoon at him. "No, *you* are the last of the line. How do you want to be remembered? As Billy's toady and accomplice, or someone who stood up for what's right?"

I could feel the crack widening and wouldn't let go. "Tell me if I'm wrong. Billy ignored you and your mother until you led him to a fortune. Then he threw you out of your home. And when you won a full scholarship from an anonymous organization and graduated from law school, he took credit for it, guilting you into taking the job as his flunky."

His silence told me I'd again created more than a shadow of a doubt.

"He uses people, Jeremy. Your mother, Barbara, Randy Logan, and most of all, you. Think about it, he kept the gold for himself and became Big Billy while your mother washed bedsheets at the Glass House. It was Hal who both gave her a job and found her a better one. I wonder why. Perhaps it's time you had a good talk with him."

I licked the spoon and put it down. "I won't meet Billy alone, so call me when you decide what side you're on."

"I'll be there," he said, sounding like a new, more determined Jeremy.

I arrived a few minutes early, intending to meet them on the porch and avoid going inside. Mine was the only car, but Billy opened the cabin door and motioned for me to come in.

"Where's Jeremy?" I answered shielded by the car door.

"Inside. Now."

To refuse would alarm him. I approached the cabin slowly, stopping outside the Calla Lilly doors to call, "Jeremy?"

When there was no response. I stepped back, but Billy caught my arm, pulling me inside. "He had better things to do."

I flinched when he leaned down to kiss my cheek. "Look at you, all crisp and buttoned up. I prefer the little black dress." He touched my hair, frowning. "Your roots are showing."

Hiding my fear, I responded with the same appraising look. "And you look well, except for the new crop of gray hair. Tough campaign?"

He touched his temple. "Makes me look distinguished. But enough about me. Recently, a cold-blooded killer of two white boys was released into private custody at Langesford Plantation. And a group of my constituents were wrongfully arrested for exercising their rights of free speech. Both miscarriages of justice greatly displease me."

I couldn't control my angry flush, but I could control my tongue. "Our opinions differ on all three points, but I'll leave that up to the judge. Let's get this over with."

I opened a manila envelope and showed him Glory's certified photocopy of the birth certificate and registry. "These are copies of the originals on register at St. Louis Cathedral in New Orleans. They certify Danielle Langesford was White. There's nothing to confirm your tattered little note about O'Grady's bloodline. And there's no record at all for the birth, or death, of Flora DeBoucher.

Looking into eyes as cold as one of those old blocks of gold, I couldn't let him see how frightened I was. "It's over. I quit." I turned and he caught my arm, pulling me to my feet.

His smile turned sinister. "I want to see the originals."

"You of all people should know you can't always get what you want. The Cathedral won't release them. You have no proof—of anything. Your smear campaign is over."

He pulled me close. His free hand squeezed my jaw, his eyes reflecting his pleasure at causing me pain when he pushed me back onto the couch.

He let me go then, to pace the narrow space between me and the table. "People don't quit Big Billy. I refuse to accept your resignation and your so-called proof. Your job was to verify *my* information."

"But it's not true!" I shouted, believing my own lie.

"Make it true!" thundered in my eardrum, then he pulled away. "Or your little colored friend in New Orleans will pay the price."

My gut twisted. "She didn't find anything!"

"Liar!" he screamed, insanity making his once-handsome face grotesque. Then he turned coy, patting a manicured index finger against his pursed lips. "I bet if she tried harder, she could come up with something. And someone with a little talent could produce a copy of one of those certificates with the *right* information on it. Perhaps I'll send a message to encourage her. I believe she recently moved into a little efficiency at 212 Bourbon Street."

"Don't you dare hurt Glory!" I was shaking too much to even move.

"Then do your job. Get my proof—before Labor Day."

"Two can play the blackmail game, Billy," came from someplace inside me that I didn't know existed. I stood, facing him, toe to toe.

It gave him pause, but not enough to call it a draw. His finger slid down my cheek. "And what Laura, do you have that could possibly hurt me?"

Where was Jeremy? It didn't matter. My emotions called the shots as I backed toward the door. “You’re a monster. A drug dealer. And a murderer. You beat Barbara Kinney until she lost your baby. And when she got cancer, you fed her barbiturates and God knows what, until she could barely function. Until she died, you bastard!”

I finally had his attention. If I’d kept my mouth shut, I may have gotten out. Instead, I pointed a finger at his arrogant nose.

“And I can prove it. You mention one thing about the One Drop Rule with O’Grady, and your entire sordid life story as a bully, drug dealer, and murderer, among other things, will come out in the next edition of *The Atlanta Constitution.*”

Panic lit his eyes for an instant, before they turned cunning. “And where is your proof of that?”

“Barbara kept a diary,” I lied and stepped around him toward the door. “I found it in her room at Langesford. It’s in a safe place and someone else knows where it is. If I don’t come back, they’ll send it to the FBI.”

His sharp intake of breath behind me told me it was true. He’d given Barbara the drugs that killed her. Then he laughed. Loud and victorious before he lunged, pinning me against the calla lily door.

I turned and his hand squeezed my throat while he growled, “You don’t have a thing you little bitch. Try a stunt like this again, and you’ll end up gator food on Negro Island, along with your new boyfriend, Patrick O’Grady. But don’t worry about Dani. I’ll take care of her.”

His body pressed against me and I felt his erection as his hand squeezed my throat tighter. My eyes watered, and my lungs burned. His face faded in front of me until a knock sounded on the glass door panel behind my head.

“Laura? Is that you? Open up.”

Jeremy! Billy’s grip loosened but not enough for me to call out.

“Say a word and I’ll kill you,” he ground out. “You won’t be the first body buried in these woods.” As quickly as he’d grabbed me, he shoved me aside and straightened his tie to open the door.

Jeremy stepped in, looked at me, then Billy. “I got stuck behind a hay wagon. Is something wrong?”

“No,” Billy answered. “We just finished our update.” He looked at his watch. “Laura has more research to do for the debate. She was just leaving.”

My throat was a raw wound and I nodded before stepping around them both. I took a painful deep breath on the porch and heard Jeremy ask Billy, “What did you do to her? And where’s your car?”

"Women," Billy answered. "Who knows? I'm parked out back and have an appointment. Lock up after me."

I ran to my car and bounced down the rutted track. On the road, Billy's powerful V-8 engine caught up quickly, pulling up close, then backing away, terrorizing me all the way to the light at Highway 41. Then he roared past me, grinning from behind the wheel.

Somehow, I made it to the overlook before breaking down.

CHAPTER 28

I called Glory as soon as I returned to Langesford and left a warning message, eventually filling her new answering machine over the weekend. Her lack of response worried me, but she'd been traveling a lot, sending me postcards from New York and Washington DC. On Sunday, I put my worry on the back burner to welcome Tammy, Mattie, and the girls, home.

"Nanny Irene took us to the zoo," Dani raved, "The giraffes are so tall they can see everything. I felt sorry for the lion, because he just walked back and forth, looking sad."

"And what did you like about the zoo, little one?" I asked Em.

Her big brown eyes stared up at me. Old eyes, in another old soul—perhaps as old as Dani's—but so very different. "The animals were all so big and scary," she said. "But I liked the bunnies. They taste good in a stew."

"Oh." I understood. Em had little experience with animals that didn't serve a practical purpose—excluding Clarence—who could still be counted on for a good run at a roaming fox, or a menacing growl at an intruder. He'd done his job well the night of the Klan visit, keeping more than one of them from getting away.

Patrick was optimistic about his campaign's recovery after my father offered to gather the support of Edward O'Grady's Northern congressional colleagues. I didn't understand why Patrick hadn't asked for it himself, then realized that he didn't like to ask for help—and he wasn't a politician.

After the chaos of unpacking the girls, Mattie ranting over the condition of her kitchen, and updates from the ranch foreman filling in for Alvarez, Patrick and I met in the office. He again poured a generous bourbon for himself, and a smaller one for me. We clicked glasses.

"In for a penny, in for a pound," he said in toast. "My father's favorite."

"Start what you can finish, and finish what you start. Nanny Irene," I responded, thinking, 'better late than never'. Neither of us laughed at the worn, old homilies as we downed our drinks. Then we sat on the couch.

"I have to win this," he stated the obvious, but his voice lacked enthusiasm.

"Agreed. Are you prepared for the Town Hall? It's only a week away."

"I know when it is," sounded testy, but I breathed easier when he added, "Yes, I think I'm ready. I spent time on the phone with your father's campaign manager, Abe Liebowitz. He laid out almost any question that could come at me, from school funding to unemployment and reapportionment."

"What about Civil Rights? And Billy's going to attack your liberal employment practices." *Among other things.*

"I don't need to be coached on race relations," he snapped. "It's well known the O'Grady's hire based on skills, and retain employees based on effort and quality of work, not color. Nothing's changed on that in eighty years."

"If you think that's true, then Boston was a waste of time," I snapped back and stood, looking down at him. "*Everything* changed, Patrick, when people started getting hung for wanting to vote, or beaten for sitting at a lunch counter. This is *not* your great-grandfather's, or even your father's kind of election. The sooner you accept that, the better."

His face closed, but I wouldn't quit. "Okay, what about Charlie and the Klan? Did Abe help you with those questions?"

"He told me not to comment on an ongoing investigation."

Ah, the ever-useful cop-out.

I countered, "Abe's an expert in generalizations, hyperbole and obfuscation. In other words, a great dancer, but that's not what you are. You're an honest man. That makes you the sweetest meat of all to a predator like Billy."

I watched it dawn on him. Abe's advice would work in Savannah and Brunswick, and maybe the western counties. But in his hometown, he needed to be Patrick O'Grady; neighbor, partner, friend—and protector. It didn't matter that they were afraid of competition for education and jobs. What mattered was that Patrick O'Grady would help them through it.

"Did Abe tell you that when you run for public office, you give up your personal perspective? With television news coverage, the truth can be edited, slanted, and mixed up six ways to Sunday. You'll have to choose your words very carefully."

I finally had his attention. "What will you do when someone asks you—and they will—why you harbored Charlie, put ten upstanding citizens in jail, however briefly—including the sheriff your father endorsed in his last election? What will you say when they ask why you took in Em, when you could have—should have—legally, turned her over to the Methodist Children's Home?"

His face fell when I hit him with, "What about inter-racial marriages and the One Drop Rule? What if Billy accuses you of harboring Charlie because of your family's mixed blood? The One Drop Rule may not have been important in your father's elections, but it will be now."

His mouth opened but nothing came out. "I know it's true, so don't try to side-step it again with the portrait. You need to face the fact that Billy *will* bring it up with, or without proof."

He stood to pour another drink, downing it in one pull and sat behind his desk. "What's Billy's proof?"

I moved to sit below the shadowed gaze of Patrick's great-grandmother, reminding him that this election had consequences beyond Billy developing Langesford into another cluster of identical houses called Barbara's Bungalows. Then the strip malls would come, and the drive-in theaters. If elected, Billy would side with big-money lobbyists to undermine everything that made Jeffers the epitome of small-town America.

I left him to think about it while I brought down my copies of Billy's files. I watched Patrick's reaction to the defaced obituaries, news articles, and letters. Then I told him about the gold bricks Jeremy found, and translated both Danielle's last journal entry and the note glued together with candle wax. But I didn't—couldn't—tell him I'd slept with Billy.

He paled as the implications of Billy's so-called evidence sunk in and handed me the file. His jaw was tense, but his voice was even when he said, "This is impressive. But it doesn't prove anything except how far Billy will go to fabricate a story."

"True," I answered. "But while people are supposedly innocent until proven guilty in a court of law, the opposite is true with the public. Especially during an election. The story is old, but it's a very titillating one. Face it, you and Billy are both newcomers to politics and your strongest asset is your family's reputation. If Billy can kill it with this story, he'll even the odds. His biggest asset is money. Negative press about you and empty promises are powerful weapons. He can afford to use TV, radio, and billboards to plaster his message across the district."

I let it sink in a moment then confessed, "I warned you about this, but you didn't believe me. Hal said that except for Barbara, Billy always gets what he wants. I've got until the debate to either disprove the truth or come up with something worse on Billy. The best I have is the birth certificate signed by the man who allegedly claimed it was false. Other than handwriting analysis, which would be sketchy at best, given the age of the documents, there's no definitive proof either way.

Then I changed the subject. "Dani told me she and Barbara spent a great deal of time in the Treasure Room, looking through old letters, maps and papers." Do you know why she was so interested in your background?"

My heart raced when I saw the dawn of understanding in Patrick's eyes. Then his mouth softened. "I thought I was protecting Barbara by treating her like a precious doll. But it wasn't enough. Nothing would have been enough. I know she loved me, but Billy had a power over her I can't explain."

He pounded a fist on the desk. "He uses everybody. I can't let him win. Not this time."

He walked to the window. Was he looking for Dani? It was almost time for her to burst in after her riding lesson, wearing that ridiculous hat from the Treasure Room. If Billy won, her world would be turned upside down.

Turning back to me, Patrick said, "Hal told me both your publishers praised your instincts, your talent for seeing through the masks people wear to find what makes them tick. They also praised your tenacity, which I've seen first-hand. I'll need your help if I'm going to beat Billy at his own game, but we have to play by my rules—and Dani comes first."

"Okay, but—"

"No buts! Before you do anything related to the campaign, you run it by me. And one more thing."

"What?"

"I'll answer allegations about my bloodline honestly."

"You can't do that. It's what Billy wants. He'll sue for legal ownership in a heartbeat. There's no time limit under the law, especially if a *legal* heir exists. Ask Hal."

"You talked with Hal?"

"I hired him. For advice. Our advantage is that while *we* know it's true, Billy doesn't have anything official to refute the birth certificates—yet. If you admit it, you may as well hand over the keys to Langesford."

The dark blue lake his eyes so often resembled, again froze and my skin responded to the chill. "At least make him work for it. I may have something on him that will blow his accusation out of the water. I just need time."

"What do you have?"

"I think old Samuel Berens' rants about the secret mission he went on with Brent Langesford were true. The Denver Mint was really robbed in 1862. And when Jeremy was a kid, he found an old washtub buried by Billy's cabin. Among other things, he saw two small black-painted bricks. A year later, Billy's drug dealing went beyond selling joints and uppers to high school kids. We just need to prove it."

"How do you know so much about drugs?"

"My ex-husband tried them all. It's a long story. Suffice it to say, the drug trade can mean big money to someone with no morals. Someone like Billy."

~

Dani and Em took up the rest of my afternoon getting ready for their first day of school. Danny chattered happily about being a "big" girl and taking her first sack lunch, while Em looked forward to again seeing her friends at the Baptist Day school. I tucked them both in at eight o'clock and went down to the office where Alvarez, who had just returned, sat by the fireplace, carefully rolling tobacco into a Bugler cigarette paper.

Patrick told him, "The campaign's getting ugly and I'll need to spend more time on the road. My absences have already caused confusion over who's in charge, so I've authorized your signature on the bank accounts for both the plantation and Morning Bird Stables."

Alvarez nearly lost his grip on the thin tobacco paper between his thumb and forefinger, but Patrick continued. "I know it's a lot more to take on, but there's no one else. You're family, and from now on you're my partner. We'll announce it tomorrow morning."

He looked at me as I stood in the doorway. "I believe people are more good than bad. We have to have faith they'll do the right thing at election time."

We all knew it wouldn't be easy. Alvarez was Patrick's second cousin and had been a Georgia resident for nearly twenty years, but with his Apache and Mexican bloodlines I wondered if he'd been allowed to register to vote.

"Do you accept?" Patrick asked him.

Alvarez closed his fist and touched his chest. "I'm honored, *Jefe.* I accept."

CHAPTER 29

Still unable to reach Glory, I called Edwin the next day. He told me she was at a conference in New York for the week. I breathed easier. She was safe.

"Did you find anything about Brent Langesford at Chickamauga?" I asked.

"Nothing. He was on the roster but wasn't listed as a fatality or a survivor. There were five other discrepancies. Could have been deserters, I suppose."

"Was one named Samuel Berens?"

"How did you know?"

"Lucky hunch. Who were the other men?"

Edwin riffled some papers. "One was Tildon, another Chisolm, and one Eldridge."

It was enough for me. "Look, I really need to talk to Glory. If you hear from her, please have her call me—ASAP. And be safe."

"Sho' 'nuff, Missy Laura," he joked. "You too."

Em left for the Baptist Day School and Patrick moved Charlie back to his cabin in the old quarters. This would be the first night he and Em spent together since his return. Clarence would accompany them for comfort and security.

I spent the day alone in the study, reviewing the major issues facing District One. Desegregation was being fought on Federal levels, but in a district highly dependent on seasonal and agricultural industries, employment was a hot-button, along with Billy's favorite—property values. But everything that affected the constituency, from traffic lights to red-light districts, was fair game at a town hall meeting. I'd also roamed the plantation and stables, grilling Patrick's employees about what they felt were major issues.

When we met after dinner, his eyebrows raised at the list of potential questions I'd put together based on their responses. He turned to me, a crooked smile on his lips. "You did this in two days?"

"I'm told I'm tenacious."

He picked up the files and motioned toward the couch. "Well, it looks like it may be a long evening. We may as well get comfortable."

"What's the matter?" he said when I didn't join him.

"What isn't the matter? I agreed to help you win the election, but I learn about key decisions after you announce them, and most of the time I have no idea where you are. If this is going to work, you have to agree to some of *my* terms."

"What do you mean?"

I stood over him, hands on my hips. "One false move at the podium. One ad lib, quip or snide remark, and voters can be lost. To avoid that, a good politician does what his campaign manager tells him. And like it or not, that's what I am to you—until the election.

"After my mother, my father owes his success to Abe Liebowitz's solid, if archaic, advice. Father doesn't make campaign decisions, have meetings, or sign agreements without Abe's take on how it will affect his position as Senator. If you really want to win this election, our relationship has to be like that."

I sat on the wood top of the coffee table. "Do you understand the terms?"

He stared at me, as if weighing the option of potentially losing everything he loved to Billy or trusting me. I hoped he didn't consider me the lesser of two evils. He surprised me by taking both my hands in his.

"I do—understand the terms, I mean."

With one break for him to kiss Dani goodnight, we reviewed the questions. I played Billy, while Patrick was, well—him. I calculated Billy's responses to be mostly ignorant, but always cunning, and phrased in ways that would reflect badly on Patrick.

It didn't take long for him to grow frustrated at my gifted imitation of Billy's browbeating tactics, until I reminded him of the power of rebuttal. Without rebuttal, town hall meetings could get out of hand quickly and Billy was as good at working a crowd into a frenzy as any revival preacher.

Charlie's preliminary hearing had been moved up to September 4th, the Friday before Labor Day. The town hall meeting was on the holiday and could be a lit match in the room. We had to find a way to blow it out.

Abe's recommended, 'I can't respond to questions regarding an ongoing legal investigation,' seemed the best response, but I doubted Billy, or the hometown crowd would sit still for it.

If not, Patrick would take the stance that he was protecting his property —not the legally incarcerated person inside. It would be hard, but he'd acknowledge that the men involved had been duped and claim he held no grudge toward them for exercising their right to free speech. Only how they went about it.

We assumed Billy would wait to see if things were going his way before dropping his bombshell of unprovable allegations against Patrick's legal right to own Langesford. I clung to the hope that in their hometown, Billy's claims would be old news.

"Don't admit or deny anything," I reminded Patrick. "Remember the three beats. Look him the eye and smile. Repeat the question as if you can't believe what you just heard, then answer it with another question."

He knew that of course, and like me, had sat through enough debates to recognize the old bob and weave tactic. But recognizing it and doing it were two different things. We rehearsed to an audience of Dani's dolls on the couch.

When I—as Billy, thought they were bored or Patrick was winning, I played the race card. It made me sick, but he had to hear it. I puffed out my 'Billy' chest, pretending to hold the lapels of my $500 suit while I strutted across the room, claiming, "The Langesfords and O'Gradys have committed murder and treason, my friends. And their very blood is *tainted*."

My stomach hurt when I turned toward a horrified Patrick, to point and charge, "For two centuries, *his* family has lied, cheated, and stolen land from hard-working, *honest* people. And they have lied about their *Negro* bloodline, prospering on land rightfully belonging to the Berens family."

Patrick flushed, and his fists balled, but he waited for the accusation to sink into his plastic neighbors' minds and settle in the place in their hearts that defined a person's worth. Then I leaned toward them and fake-shouted, "They have broken the law of the land. The law limiting ownership to legal, White descendants."

I pointed at Barbie, then Ken, and finally, Tiny Tears. "They lied to you all, while making laws that affect your family's future." My stomach lurched when I said what would surely be Billy's summation, "It's time for an honest, true son of the South to represent you in Washington."

Pretending even a small portion of Billy's hatred toward Patrick was exhausting. Though I wanted to vomit, I stayed in character to smile smugly, then stepped away. Finally, after shaking off the evil alter-ego, I said, "Now you."

I saw that Patrick had visibly suffered from the wounds I'd inflicted with surgical precision and worried I'd done my job a little too well. He seemed to finally understand that one deception, however well-intended, personal, or old, could bring down the wall of integrity the names Langesford and O'Grady symbolized.

Before responding, he looked up at the painting, repeating Danielle Trémon-Langesford's words, "The sins of our fathers."

"You've always known, haven't you?" I said.

He nodded. "We all do, including Alvarez, Ela, and my cousins who also have the Apache burden. But we're not ashamed. It reminds us of our responsibility to protect others with—diverse lineage."

"Did Barbara know?" She didn't seem like a reliable confidante.

His jaw set. "She was part Cherokee, but because she was blonde, no one suspected. Not even Billy."

"Samuel Berens was right. According to my Granddaddy Clay, Brent Langesford wasn't at Chickamauga. He died somewhere out West on a secret mission for the Confederacy. And though Great-Uncle Sean didn't kill Billy's great granddaddy, he'll paint them as criminals. It's impossible—no, stupid —to have to defend any of them after all this time. After all my family has done for the South."

Pacing like one of the poor lions Dani saw at the Boston Zoo, he said, "I don't care if Billy convinces them I'm the spawn of Satan. He'll *never* take Langesford from my family."

The bare forearm beneath his rolled-up sleeve was warm when I touched it. "Then turn the tables. Billy likes to say turnabout is fair play. Focus on *his* secrets.

"You mean the drugs?"

"No, we don't have proof of that, at least not yet. But there is one thing that won't be received well and can be proved." *I hoped.*

"Barbara's Bungalows." I said.

"Barbara's what?"

"Bungalows. Jeremy says Billy wants to turn Langesford into a suburb of cookie-cutter bungalows, likely complete with mini-malls and drive-in theaters, just a stone's throw from the charming little town of Jeffers. If he wins, I'd lay odds he's got a developer ready to go as soon as the ink dries on the new deed."

Disbelief gave way to understanding, then horror, and finally anger as Patrick missed the point. "He can't do that!"

"Property has been taken through less-likely scenarios," I explained. "The land market is hot now and the South's anti-miscegenation laws have a limited life-span. If he waits any longer, he'll miss his chance to sue for ownership while the state still supports the law. The only way to stop him without proof about the drug running is to expose his part in a development that will ruin local businesses and destroy the very landscape that makes Jeffers a top tourist attraction."

He pulled away. "Why are you doing this? Is it still for the story?"

That stung more than the sudden tears in my eyes. "Billy used me, and I fell for it. I want—I need—to make this right before I leave. Right now, Jeremy is looking for Billy's investor, and the FBI is looking into the drug theory."

"Theories," he said. "That's what this whole thing is about. Billy's theory about my family and now this…Barbara's Bungalows. And last I checked Jeremy was on Billy's team."

"Not anymore. It's a long story, but he's probably our best asset. Land developers are a skittish group. Any hint of trouble and they'll move on to the next small town. Local businesses and long-time residents won't like the competition and congestion of a suburb. Until we know for sure about the drug running and money laundering, it could be the leverage we need to shut Billy up."

I knew from his scowl that he didn't like stooping to Billy's level, and I'd agreed to do things his way. I held my breath as he considered his last chance short of a miracle to both win the election and save his plantation.

"What about the FBI?"

"Jeremy told me Billy didn't trust accountants and kept his own books. He gave me copies and I sent them to Glory to pass on to…someone she knows at the FBI. They may find something in there connecting him to a drug cartel—or even tax evasion. Remember it was the IRS that got Al Capone—by following the money."

"How long will it take to put together either option?" He sounded receptive to the strategy.

"Until the Town Hall," I said with more confidence than I felt.

CHAPTER 30

Hal advised Patrick not to complicate matters by attending Charlie's hearing, claiming it would shift the focus to politics. He called us four hours later to say that based on Leroy's testimony, Charlie's negative alcohol test, and Hal's ability to browbeat Evan into admitting he threatened Em, the judge acquitted him.

Great news for Charlie and Em, but that didn't mean Jeffers would welcome them. Patrick called his friend in Flint, Michigan, who offered Charlie a job working with his brother George. The weekend was filled with joy about Charlie's freedom, mixed with sadness for his upcoming move, and anxiety about the Town Hall meeting.

On Labor Day, off-duty employees supported Patrick by cutting their holiday weekend short and putting on their Sunday clothes for a trip to the Court House. Dani wanted to go, but I convinced her Em needed her company before she and her daddy left.

Jeremy called me early in the morning. Assuming Billy was furious with me for not providing his fake evidence, I told him I couldn't talk.

"You don't have to," he barked. "Just listen. Billy is livid with Hal for getting Charlie's hearing moved up. He was Billy's law and order platform. And now that he's been found innocent, the folks Billy talked into visiting Langesford that night want him to pay their fines. All he's got left is the race card. You have to give it to him, Laura."

"Give him what?"

"The proof he hired you to find."

"I quit Billy. At the cabin."

"Nobody quits Billy. Barbara and I can attest to that."

"What do you mean? Did something happen to you?"

"I, uh, had a little accident. I'm okay though. Just a broken nose, and some cracked ribs. Billy wouldn't kill family."

"Oh, my God!" I gasped. "When? Where are you? You need to go to the —" Oops, Jeffers no longer had a sheriff. "Hal."

"I did. I'm safe, at least for now. But I'm warning you, give Billy something he can wave around that shows he's right—for the moment. Do it before he does something crazy!"

Billy defined crazy. And now he had egg on his face. Someone had to pay. Maybe he wouldn't kill Jeremy, but while I didn't worry about myself, Patrick, Glory, or even Dani, could be in danger. If I could convince him Glory was working on his fake evidence, maybe I could buy some time.

"I'll see what I can do."

"Everything okay?" Patrick asked from the doorway.

I hung up the phone. "Oh, that? Another reporter."

He took a deep breath. "Time to go."

As expected, the Court House was packed. And already hot, despite fans in front of every window. Billy was noticeably absent amid the chaos of setting up, but for him to be a no-show after Charlie's verdict was too much to hope for.

He arrived with only moments to spare, again prancing his way down the narrow aisle of a packed building, waving and shaking hands. He nodded toward the bathrooms at the back of the building when he saw me, and I knew I couldn't dodge him forever.

"Where is it?" he demanded.

"It's coming." I cleared my throat to soldier on with as much truth as I could muster.

"You were right. Glory found someone who could *correct* the birth record. She'll send it as soon as it's done. You'll have it in plenty of time—before the election. Why not save it as insurance?"

The sly lift of his mouth told me he wasn't buying it, so I appealed to his ego. "You said you didn't need it to win. And even after the Klan fiasco, you're still ahead in the polls. The verdict releasing Charlie may even help you win the red-neck Klan crowd."

He squeezed my arm painfully and leaned close, his hot breath moist against my ear. "Don't play games. Get me that document by the end of the week, or I plaster the state with that damn note—in English. The People can decide if it's true."

He pushed me away, jamming my back into the crystal knob on the Ladies' Room door. I dared not show how much it hurt. It would please him too much.

His snarl became a smile at the sound of voices coming down the hall, and Billy tipped his straw hat. "Happy Labor Day, ladies," he oozed to matrons who beamed at his attention. "You're looking lovely this fine day."

He handed them his, 'New Blood' campaign buttons and they happily pinned them to their dresses, next to Patrick's bland, 'Two Centuries of Service' pin.

At precisely two o'clock, Mayor Andy stepped up to his microphone. Unlike the 5th of July, his opening speech was brief, followed by the Methodist minister's equally brief prayer. Even the crowd seemed different this time. Interested. Engaged. Serious.

Each candidate had ten short minutes to summarize their platform. I stood along the back wall, sketching the crowd: women wearing Sunday hats, farmers in overalls because their work didn't stop when someone declared a holiday. And factory workers in ill-fitting suits from second-hand stores. As usual, Negroes stood in the back, near the exits.

Two hours into it, with no end in sight, it was going well for Patrick. He wore his trademark white linen jacket and a dark blue shirt that complimented his eyes. I was glad he took my advice to leave the tie at home.

"It's a town hall meeting," I'd told him, though it was a risk. Dr. King Jr. was rarely seen in public without his black suit and tie. "It's informal. A dialog between the candidates and their constituents. You want to look like you're talking *with* them, not talking *down* to them."

I touched the base of his throat as I unbuttoned the shirt's collar button. He turned away to face the mirror, smoothing hair now a little less James Garner's Maverick, but not quite Sean Connery's James Bond.

"I know, image is everything," he muttered.

"People vote on more than words."

Two hours into the debate, Patrick's thick hair, without the Brylcreem gel Billy used, absorbed the perspiration on his forehead to gleam under the dangling globe lights. His open collar caught the air from the fans, while his dark shirt and white linen jacket absorbed his perspiration without showing a stain.

Conversely, a buttoned-up Billy sweated through his gray, pinstripe suit, dark circles rimming his underarms. And on either side of his red tie, his light blue shirt turned navy. His face flushed and sweaty, he looked like one of the greasy, bug-eyed, tent preachers scattered around the county in summer. He was losing, and he knew it.

Patrick fielded every question from the moderator and audience with clear-eyed deliberation and logic, explaining his limitations within the law and his well thought-out short and long-term plans. But most of all, he addressed people by name if he knew it, and asked for it if he didn't. He must have learned that from his father.

Billy only knew the names of those who had bought Cadillacs from him. A handful, at best. While bragging that people came from all over the state to buy cars from him, he ignored the farmers, mill, and textile workers in the room, evading their questions with meaningless gestures and empty promises.

Those sharing the wall with me already knew the futility of asking questions.

But even Patrick had to straddle the fence now and then. I held my breath at a question about how school integration would affect the quality of education. I let it out as he agreed that every parent, regardless of race, wanted and deserved a safe environment and a good education for their children.

My blood pressure spiked near the end, when he asked the pool of nervous white voters, "What are you afraid of?"

Silence reigned for three-beats, until he asked the people in the back and along the walls, "What are *you* afraid of?"

The answers blended like a chorus. "Bein' killed. Losin' my job. Losin' my home. My kids bein' hurt."

He looked again at the good white citizens of Jeffers seated in front of him. "Are their concerns so different from yours? Are we willing to deny *all* our children a quality education because a dark-skinned child may sit next to a light-skinned one?"

At a few mutters, he raised a hand. "No need to answer." Then he paraphrased John Kennedy. "Our success depends not on what our government *tells* us is right, but on how we *do* what's right."

He stepped down from the stage for his summation. "Change is hard, but it's also constant. If elected, I will do my best to see that change is *managed* so that it builds, rather than erodes, our district's opportunities for growth."

Then he explained how he would do it. "Reducing the cost of running our schools by consolidating districts, even with bussing, will allow us to hire high-quality teachers and materials to ensure a labor force that will attract new businesses and create new jobs. It's that simple."

He returned to his podium amid mixed responses.

Billy was apoplectic at the approving nods. His eyes bulged and sweat ran down his temples. He glared at his audience, then turned toward Patrick screaming, "Liar!"

They stared at each other until the humming fans were the only sound in the room. My stomach lurched, but Patrick winked at me and left his podium to face Billy.

"How so?" carried to the back of the room and hung in the humid air.

"You're a goddammed Negro!" bounced from wall to wall.

I prayed the collective gasp from the good citizens of Jeffers was due more to his profanity than his accusation.

Billy waved his arm, ranting, "All of 'em. The Langesfords. The O'Gradys. All liars, thieves and traitors—and Niggers!" Spit flew from his mouth as he shouted, "This man is the spawn of a Negro murderess. Great-grandson of a woman whose traitorous illegitimate son ran off to Mexico with a wagon load o' gold that woulda won us the War." With a wild stab toward Patrick, he added, "And the namesake of a Yankee spy."

Then he turned sly. "But many of y'all know that. So, here we are now, with this Patrick O'Grady, who is afraid to admit his tainted blood. I ask you, do you want a liar from a long line of liars and thieves to lead you through these troubled times—when everything you've worked for is threatened by the very race running through his veins?"

Amid confused mutters and sadly, some agreement, Billy's gold eyes sparked with hatred. "For more than a century, his family has illegally claimed ownership of the best land in this county. Land that can be used to build good schools and businesses that will bring prosperity to everyone in this proud district."

When he paused to wipe his brow with his sodden tie, Patrick raised a hand to silence the murmurs rumbling through the room like an incoming tide. He took one step toward the sweating, trembling lunatic in front of him. "We're kin, Billy," he said loud enough for everyone to hear. "Our families had differences over the years, but when the need arose, we stood together as brothers in arms. In the Revolution, the War of Northern Aggression, two World Wars, and Korea. This is not the time or place to bring up old grievances and wild, *unfounded* accusations. It's a time to move forward. Together."

He turned back to the audience. "My family history is well-known in this district, and this state. Indeed, in the country. Everything we've done has been for the best interest of the district, the state, and indeed, the country. But if ancient history is important to you in this election, I will proudly say that a hundred and twenty-five years ago, my ancestor, Anthony Langesford, *may possibly* have married a woman of mixed-race.

A collective gasp seemed to suck the air out of the already suffocating room, but he persisted. "If, after two centuries of service and sacrifice to this country and district, that possibility makes a difference to any of you, I say exercise your right to vote—for my opponent."

His voice lowered as he again faced Billy. "But know this. No one, and nothing, will challenge my ownership of Langesford—especially The One Drop Rule."

CHAPTER 31

Though the Town Hall meeting had turned into a circus, Patrick was the undisputed victor. The only reporter at the fiasco was Jacob Strong from the *Jeffers Gazette.* But I knew it wouldn't be buried for long. You couldn't buy publicity like that.

I was surprised at how little losing another headline story meant to me. For the moment, all that mattered was the stone-faced man sitting next to me on the way back to Langesford. "I didn't congratulate you," I said, as we approached the overlook.

He hit the brakes and I screamed as he yanked on the wheel, skidding to a stop in front of the new fencing. "Do you really think it'll stop here?"

"What do you mean?"

He glared at me, his jaw set. "You're off the hook. Billy doesn't need his proof anymore. I just confessed it—to more than a hundred people—in my hometown. By tomorrow morning it will be out to the state. And by evening, on the six o'clock news."

"You didn't say it *was* true," I qualified. "Only that it *may* be true."

I jumped when he slapped the steering wheel. "Holy Mary, mother of God, Laura. Around here, what *may* be true usually is. And I told them if they didn't like it, to vote for Billy. Some will, some won't, but that's not what's bothering me."

"What is it?"

We both stared for a long moment at the house below us. It looked sad under the cloudy sky, signs of neglect showing in peeling paint, bare spots in the lawn, and a few missing gutters. Finally, he said, "You conned Billy, didn't you? Told him you had proof, so he'd go off half-cocked."

It was too late for excuses. "Yes and no," I admitted to his rigid profile. "Glory has the registry showing Danielle as white. It may not be true, but it's legal. Billy wanted me to have one forged saying she's Negro. I stalled, hoping he'd lay off until we had more information about his drug business."

He pulled away when I tried to touch him. "I didn't think he'd go crazy —or you'd confess it in front of God and everyone."

The truck engine roared to life. I again thought of Danielle's journal entry. *One day our children and theirs, will pay for our sins.*

"Maybe you should take Dani out of school for a few days," I suggested when we bounced over the dip in the road to Langesford.

"Why?"

"Well, kids can be mean. If people believed Billy, they could call her names."

His laugh surprised me. "Do you really think names bother me? Or my daughter? Besides, you assured me the bloodline can't be proved, except in Billy's mind. Or has that changed? It's getting hard to track the truth."

I knew he didn't expect an answer. When we got out of the truck, he said, "I'll talk to Dani about Maw-maw Danielle, in case somebody mentions it."

I hoped he was right about Dani's ability to withstand ridicule. But because of her father, and her friendship with Em, the Dani I knew was more likely to land a punch than turn the other cheek.

~

Billy laid low following the debate, and I again fielded calls from some of the major newspaper syndicates. As I suspected, none of them cared about Billy's claims of century old crimes against his family, or the wagonload of lost gold. They wanted to know about the bloodline. I responded honestly that Patrick had a certified birth certificate and registry attesting to his white ancestry and welcomed Billy's proof otherwise.

Patrick left on Tuesday for a five-day damage control tour, returning on September fifteenth. While he was gone, I worried more and more about

Glory. She still wasn't answering her phone and her office would only say she wasn't in.

I called Edwin on Sunday afternoon, demanding, "Where is Glory?"

"Right here," he said. "She's safe. Now."

"Now? What do you mean? Put her on the phone. Please."

"Hey, Laura." Her breezy voice didn't fool me.

"Where were you? I left messages at your home and your office. Why haven't you called me? Did something happen?"

"Calm down," she said. "I was in New York for a conference with the new Student Nonviolent Coordinating Committee, about the deaths in Mississippi. I stayed over Labor Day with Vernon. When I got back, I had a minor accident."

Her voice was too high, too cheery. "Vernon of the FBI? Accident? Tell me everything."

Her voice softened. "He's amazing."

"I'm sure he is, but what's this about an accident? I won't stop asking until you tell me."

"Okay." She sighed. "I got back on Tuesday night. My light was out. Somebody smelling like sweat and cheap whiskey came up from behind and pushed me inside."

I gasped. One of Billy's drug running goons.

"I told her to call the police," Edwin shouted from the background.

"Go iron something," she shouted back.

A door slammed, and she went on with her story. "He said he wanted the proof I had about the, 'Negress'. I told him to go to hell, and we tussled."

"Tussled? What? Glory you could have been killed! Why didn't you give it to him?"

"I did give…something…to him. But it was clear he wanted…a tip. I refused and we knocked over a few lamps. My neighbor pounded on the door, threatening to call the police. Then he left."

I let go of the breath I was holding. "Thank God for nosey neighbors. Did he take the original?"

"Yes, as well as the black registry from the same period. I was going to copy it and planned to take them both back to the Cathedral in the morning."

Her voice broke. "They were priceless, Laura. Original rag paper, from linen. Irreplaceable historical information. The guy stuffed them into his belt like a movie program!"

"But you're okay. That's all that matters."

If Billy didn't have the documents already, he would soon. A good forger could insert an entry into the Negro registry, copy it and destroy the original, along with the White one.

"I'm so sorry," Glory moaned.

"Stop beating yourself up, sweetie. It was my fault. I shouldn't have involved you. I should have walked away as soon as I found out what Billy was trying to do." S*hould have could have. But didn't.*

"How long are you going to be at Edwin's?"

"Not long," she answered too quickly, and Edwin shouted, "Give me the phone."

"No," Glory argued, followed by what sounded like a scuffle, until Edwin huffed, "My sister left a few things out."

"What things?"

"Like before the thief left, he tossed her out a window."

"What?"

"I'm fine," sounded weak. "The balcony on the floor below me broke my fall."

"Yes," Edwin overrode her. "But it broke her leg in two places."

I couldn't breathe. Glory was helping me. It was my fault. No, *Billy* did this, and he had to be stopped. But I had to make sure she and Edwin were safe. It was a four-hour drive to Atlanta, and it looked like I'd be staying in the backroom of the dry-cleaning store after all.

"I'll be there tomorrow." I hung up before they could argue.

Patrick surprised us by returning before supper. He looked optimistic. His new slogan, "Courage, Loyalty and Service," had been well-received. It was Tammy's idea and I agreed it described the family—and the man—perfectly. Surprisingly, Billy's rantings about his thinly-mixed blood hadn't caused him any noticeable harm.

He smiled, saying, "I told you. It's hard to throw a stone at an old Southern family and not come up with mixed blood. Nobody wants the finger pointed at them."

I let him have his victory, but knew it was only the lull before the lawsuit. I told him about the attack on Glory and the theft of both original birth registries. "I have to go to her."

His cooler head prevailed. "What can you do for her that her brother can't? And won't your presence in a Negro neighborhood do more harm than good?"

"But she's in a cast and her brother has a business to run. She needs me," I whined. "And it's my fault. She was just trying to help me help you."

"Yes, you were trying to help. You're always trying to help."

"What do you mean?"

"I mean you never give up."

He stepped behind his desk. "Before you go, I want you to know I haven't been idle either. And what I have may change everything."

He opened his briefcase. "After the accident, I had my father's Lincoln towed to a barn near Morningbird Stables. When I went to Atlanta after the Klan visit, I hauled it there in one of our trailers. An old friend of mine from Emory runs the crime lab there, that includes vehicles. His experts confirmed the brake-line was damaged before the accident. Not enough to break right away with normal use, but a sudden stop could snap it and kill the power to the brakes."

"Could, would, or did?"

"No way to tell for sure," wasn't what I wanted to hear.

"But if they had to brake fast, the line could have fractured and sent them into a spin. Depending on the speed, road conditions, or incline, if the driver didn't have time to use the manual brake, it could be deadly."

He raised a hand when I tried to interrupt. "It's probably not enough to make a case for sabotage, but they found one other thing."

"Don't make me beg."

He pulled out two photographs. One showed a round hole in the driver's side rear tire. The other showed an odd-looking bullet next to a ruler. It was about a half-inch around, with three ridges circling the flat end. The conical head was barely flattened.

"It doesn't look like any bullet I've ever seen. What is it?"

The grief in his eyes broke my heart when he said, "Proof of murder. This bullet was in the tire, lodged against the wheel assembly."

He reached into the envelope again, pulling out a plastic sandwich bag. "It's a minié ball, from an old muzzle-loading rifle used in the War. American history buffs collect them to target shoot at re-enactments. Billy was at the Chickamauga event in September, last year. The committee invited me to join, but I don't celebrate lost causes."

My mind raced. Did Billy have Randy damage the brakes and then pull the trigger himself? I held the bag with the little lead ball that had made a four-thousand-pound, Lincoln Continental spin out of control. There was no doubt in my mind that Billy was capable of murder. "Can you prove it?"

"About as much as he can prove my bloodline," he confessed. "Circumstantial at best. There are hundreds of re-enactors in Georgia, all using the same type of ammunition."

"I see, so it's a Mexican standoff. A duel of unprovable accusations," I said.

"Maybe." He pointed the tip of his pen at the photo. "You see that little notch there?"

"Barely."

"It's caused by a flaw in the mold. Though re-enactors use blanks for the staged battles, most make their own live ammunition with original molds and use them for hunting, competitions and target practice. While they can't be matched to the gun like modern bullets, they can be matched to the mold."

I remembered the old musket mounted above Billy's fireplace. "So, you *can* prove it?"

"First things first," he said. "The FBI can't get a warrant to search Billy's apartment and cabin without cause. If we can get Randy to confess to damaging the brake line, and name who paid him to do it, we may have a strong enough link for a search warrant."

"Will Randy cooperate?"

His eyes narrowed into a, 'what do you think' squint. "Not likely. Billy's temper is legendary. Randy may be a Neanderthal, but he has a family. All the FBI can do is try."

"Maybe Jeremy can help us with that," I said. "He lived in the cabin. He may know where the mold is."

He shook his head. "Too risky. I heard about Jeremy's so-called accident. And there's your friend in New Orleans. It appears Billy knows our weak spots."

I thought about Dani and nodded when he said, "Maybe we should step back and let the FBI handle it. Didn't you say Glory had a friend in the Bureau?"

CHAPTER 32

Mattie took over seeing Dani off to school and Patrick stayed closer to home while I spent two weeks with Glory at Edwin's. I drove her to doctor appointments and physical therapy after her surgery to repair the multiple leg fractures.

Billy was strangely silent after his threat to blanket the state with his 'proof'. Perhaps he hadn't found anyone skilled enough, or willing to alter the registries, especially after Father Barklay at the St. Louis Cathedral reported them stolen.

Hal couldn't find a legitimate explanation of how, while in his early twenties, Billy managed to come up with $25,000 in cash to buy Smitty's old garage—and a few years later, more than four times that for the struggling Cadillac franchise and cabin renovations.

But I did. I took the stone I'd found in the saddle bag to an Atlanta gold dealer who confirmed that it was gold—smelted gold. He estimated the weight of the bar it came from and prices at the time Jeremy found them. The two bars alone would have been worth more than a hundred thousand dollars.

Hal sent Billy's records to Glory's friend, Vernon Thomas. He forwarded them to the FBI's Forensic Accounting Division. He also paid a visit to Randy Logan about the repairs on Edward O'Grady's car. Randy's cockiness was no match for the tall, muscular black man who Glory said looked more like Sidney Poitier than a cop. Still, it took Vernon's offer of a plea bargain and dismissal of the Klan charges to loosen Randy's tongue.

He confessed to accepting a thousand dollars from Billy to take a few shortcuts in his maintenance on the congressman's car. Sadly, it would be his word against Billy's.

Ironically, a week after arriving in Atlanta, I'd just stepped back from a blast of steam from Edwin's twenty-year-old ironer, when Glory hobbled in on her crutch. I wiped my forehead, and stepped in front of a fan, glad for the break.

"I just talked to Vernon," she said. "He was a rookie cop in Atlanta as a student at Morehouse College. He looked through his old files and came up with a slippery runner known as The Kid. He made the Atlanta run from the port at Brunswick, through the Okefenokee back country, to Atlanta. Mainly methamphetamines, and a little speed.

"They suspected more but couldn't catch him. He cut back sometime in the early fifties. Word was he only used the lanes when he had a hot client. Then he disappeared entirely—right about the time Billy became Big Billy."

"Billy. The Kid!" we both shouted.

She dropped her crutch to hug my sweat-drenched body. I removed the pair of trousers from the ironer and we went back to Edwin's kitchen/living/dining room.

"Does Vernon have any more information?" I asked. "A description? Anything more than, 'The Kid'?"

Her smile faded, showing the lines of pain and fatigue from her harrowing experience. "No, he was a ghost. Young enough to move fast, smart enough to blend into the woodwork, and mean enough to scare hardened drug dealers into keeping their mouths shut."

"Sounds like Billy."

She nodded, sending the hooked end of a mutilated shirt hanger down the gap between her cast and healing leg.

"Damn thing itches," answered my disapproving frown. "And it's starting to smell."

I took the hanger from her. "You'll hurt yourself and end up losing the damn leg. And I'll be stuck on Edwin's ironer the rest of my life. So, what do they think happened to The Kid?"

She threw me a mean look. "Leads dried up and other dealers took his place. Cops figured he was killed somewhere in the swamp between New Orleans and the coast.

I thought about Billy's threat that I wouldn't be the first body buried on Negro Island. "His territory extended as far as New Orleans?"

"Yep. The French Quarter. If it's true, and Billy still has contacts there, that's probably how he found out where I live. Vernon's making some calls, but Creoles are tight-lipped—and don't like cops of any color."

That only left the bullet and the missing mold. Could they even get fingerprints from a semi-squashed minié ball? And if they could, would it be enough to charge Billy with murder?

I called Jeremy. "I need your help. Can you still get into Billy's cottage?"

"Of course. He didn't fire me, he reprimanded me."

"Tough reprimand."

"Could have been worse. At least I got a second chance."

"What do you mean?"

"You're only allowed one mistake with Billy. I hear Patrick's doing better in the polls and Randy's on the hot seat for the car accident," changed the subject. "You should back off and let the Feds handle it."

I didn't seem to have a choice. We were at a stalemate. Election notwithstanding, Billy couldn't invoke the One Drop Rule without his fabricated church register, and we couldn't put his finger on the trigger the night Edward and Thelma O'Grady died.

After asking Jeremy to check the cabin for the mold, I left Atlanta for Jeffers. I arrived just past two o'clock to find two State Police cars and a gray Chevrolet Impala parked in front of the mansion. *FBI*?

"Please, God, no," I prayed. *Not Patrick.* A state trooper blocked my way until Mattie pushed him aside and collapsed in my arms, sobbing. "Dani's gone!"

"Help me!" I shouted to the gawping officer. "She needs to sit down."

We supported her back up the steps and onto the old settee. "Gone where, Mattie?" I pressed. "Where is Dani? Tell me so I can help."

"Haven't you done enough already?" Patrick's voice came from behind me, accusing me of something I had no idea I'd done.

I faced his bloodshot eyes. "What do you mean?"

"I mean Dani's been kidnapped. We called your friend in Atlanta, but you'd left. How did you know?"

"How did I know what?" Then I screamed without caring who heard me, "Do you think I had something to do with this? How can you? I love that little girl as if she were mine." There, I'd said it. "When? How?"

He ran his hands through his hair. "At school. During lunch. By the time her teacher noticed she was missing, he could have been half-way to Tallahassee. Where would he take her, Laura?"

Billy's voice taunted me. *Don't worry about Dani. I'll take care of her.* My lungs emptied until the room began to fade and all I saw was Patrick's accusing stare. I choked on bile and tears. "You mean…Billy? How? Why?"

"Good questions. And I have a few for you." He grabbed my wrist, tugging me to my feet. "Come with me."

"What's wrong with you?" I shouted, trying to free my arm and looking back at Mattie who was sobbing into her hands. "Are you blaming *me* for this? How could you?"

The more I struggled, the tighter he held me. It was follow him or be dragged through the house. Behind closed doors in his office, he released me. "Don't move," he ordered, reaching for a crumpled piece of notebook paper on his cluttered desk.

"This was in Dani's lunch box, addressed to me."

I rubbed my throbbing forearm. "What is it?"

"What do you think? Billy's ransom note."

I barely recognized Patrick. He'd become the man capable of beating someone to a pulp in front of an open grave. Still staring at me, he read it aloud, "An eye for an eye, Paddy. You took what I loved and have what's mine. Turnabout is fair play. In twelve hours, the healing begins."

"What does that mean?" I asked.

"You tell me."

"I don't know! What do you want from me?"

"The truth!" He returned to the note. "Don't worry about Dani. Laura knows I'll take care of her. We had some great pillow talk about you. As always, you're welcome to my left-overs."

I stumbled back into the chair by the fireplace, too shocked to even cry. But he didn't give me time to recover.

"Where is she, Laura?" blasted against my ear.

"I don't know," I sobbed. "How could I know he'd do this? And he's lying. We didn't talk…" I gasped, realizing I'd just confessed to sleeping with Billy.

Shock, followed by anger, then betrayal, hardened his features.

"So, it's true." He looked at his watch. "What *did* you talk about—in bed —with Billy."

"Nothing! It was just once, before I knew what he really was—or you. I'm so sorry."

He paced the room, the sound of his boots on the wood floor surrounding the Persian carpet, the only sound in the room. He stopped at the window and looked out at the cloudy sky. Then he took two long strides to lean over me, his arms forming bars on both arms of my chair.

"I don't give a rat's ass what you did with Billy!" blew hot and loud in my ear. I shook my head, my tears falling onto his hand before he pulled away.

"Where is my daughter?"

My whole body shook in fear and confusion. But as furious as he was, I wasn't afraid of Patrick. I was afraid for Dani because Billy was a lunatic.

Misunderstanding my panic, Patrick reached for my hand. I thought he'd softened until he squeezed it so hard my eyes watered. "Tell me everything you talked about, or so help me God I'll—"

I kicked him in the shin hard enough to free myself and stand. I wiped my tears with the back of my hand, furious that Billy had used me—again. And I'd allowed him to do it. Disappointment that Patrick couldn't see how much I loved Dani—and him—kept me on my feet.

I shouted, "You'll what? Get over yourself and understand that this isn't about me—or you—you bastard. It's one of Billy's sick games. When did you get this note?"

The kick to his shin seemed to have brought back at least some of his senses. "The school called me at one o'clock."

"So, you wasted almost two hours waiting for me, and accusing me of being an accomplice, instead of out-thinking Billy."

"What do you mean?" His eyes no longer blazed with rage. Now he just looked sick with worry, bordering on grief.

The hurt—and hatred—on his face when he accused me of sleeping with Billy kept me from touching him. "I mean the FBI can eat up twelve hours interviewing every kid in her school and come away with as many descriptions of the car and the man who took her."

I waved an arm. "Let them scour the countryside for witnesses, but *you* have to figure out what Billy's note *means.*"

He glared at me. "It means what it said, goddamnit!" He waved it in front of me.

"An eye for an eye. Revenge. Took what I loved. Barbara. Have what is mine. Langesford."

What else can it possibly mean? And if I don't find Dani in eight hours, you'll never see her again, alive or dead."

"What about, turnabout is fair play, and the healing will begin'?"

"How the hell do I know? He's batshit crazy."

"No, he's crazy, but he's not batshit crazy. I'm a writer. Those last sentences don't fit. He put them at the end because they mean something." I jabbed his chest. "To you. What?"

We paced in opposite directions, the emotional distance between us growing with each step. I wondered how he could even stand. His wife had died, his rights to his ancestral home were in jeopardy, and his daughter was missing. Billy was well on his way to successfully destroying Patrick O'Grady II. I took a leap of faith. "He won't hurt her."

"Why?"

"Because in Billy's head, Dani is his child, replacing the one lost with Barbara's miscarriage. He wants you to think he'll kill her, and when they disappear, you'll think she's buried in the woods somewhere. The guilt will drive *you* batshit crazy."

"How do you know this?" was little more than a broken whisper.

I jumped into the deep end. "Because when I tried to talk him out of coming after you at the Town Hall, he said if I didn't help him, he'd bury me on Negro Island—but not Dani, he said. He told me he'd take care of her."

I stepped back when Patrick's fists balled, but the blow never landed. "Another thing you neglected to tell me. Good God, Laura, whose side are you on?"

I risked touching his arm. "Yours, Patrick, always yours. I thought it was crazy talk, a threat to force me into giving him a fake birth certificate. If he'd wanted a child, he wouldn't have beat Barbara when she was pregnant."

"Well you thought wrong. Billy doesn't make idle threats."

His comment stabbed me like a knife, and he was right, but we can't change the past. All we can do is survive it. I picked up the note and repeated what was probably the most important sentence. "Turnabout is fair play. That's it!"

"What?"

"Didn't you do riddles as a child?"

"No, get to the point."

I took a deep breath. "Okay, an eye for an eye is about inflicting equal or equivalent pain on an enemy, but turnabout is retaliation by reversing the outcome of a situation."

I dropped the note on the desk and turned to him. "He's thrown the gauntlet for a duel. He wants you to find him, so he can beat *you* to a pulp. Then *his* healing will begin—by stealing someone who belongs to you."

He stepped up close to me, his lips set in a thin, angry line. "The clock is ticking and you're talking in riddles. Just say what you mean."

Why couldn't he see it?

I tried again. "Billy lives in a fantasy world where his family *replaces* yours. He's a re-enactor, with all the equipment, and used the Confederate rifle to shoot the tire on your father's car. Kind of an unreliable weapon for an assassination don't you think?"

His head cocked. At least he was listening.

"Turnabout." I repeated. "The first murder Billy ranted about to me was when Nathan Berens was killed by Danielle's horse. Did your father ride?"

"Not since he broke his hip ten years ago."

"So, throwing him from a horse wouldn't work. But being thrown over a bluff in an expensive car could fit the bill. Turnabout number one."

"I'm listening."

"I can't do all the work. It's your turn. Of the laundry list of ancient sins Billy claims your forebears committed, which is the most painful to him?"

Understanding finally lit Patrick's eyes. I'd given up hope for forgiveness, but respect was fine for the moment. He answered, "His Great-grandfather, William II."

"Wait!" I shouted and ran to the box of Billy's documents, tossing papers onto the desk and floor. "It's in here somewhere."

His hand covered mine. "Stop. What are you looking for?"

"Look at this mess," I said. "Billy doesn't live in the present. He's been collecting it for years. Reading it over and over, plotting his revenge. There's something in here that will tell us where Billy is. Where Dani is. There was an article about William II's death attached to a Wanted poster for Sean."

I shoved my hair back. "I think it said where his body was found. Damn!"

A tanned, work-scarred hand again covered mine. "I'm pretty well-versed in my own family history, at least from the first Patrick's time. A namesake gets curious, you know. They found Billy Berens II on the other side of the Sand Creek ridge, where he tried to rape Elena Santiago, Alvarez' great-grandmother. It's the border between Langesford and Berens land. A small bluff with a hot spring at the top."

"Then the healing will begin!" I shouted, fighting the urge to hug him.

It was nearly four o'clock. It would be dark by seven-thirty. I yanked out one of Billy's old maps. "Show me where it is."

"Too old," Patrick said. "Landmarks have changed."

"Because of the dam?"

"Among other things," he muttered and left me for the Treasure Room, returning with a framed map dated 1861. A red line showed the Langesford boundary, with the Berens property outlined in blue. He found a Sherlock Holmes-style magnifying glass in the desk and made a tiny blue dot on the map with his fountain pen.

"That's it. Paw-paw Clay told us stories about a mineral spring that bubbled like a tub of hot water in the winter. Runoff from the river cooled it in summer. He called it a paradise, but the only way to get there from Langesford land is through a cave on the side of a rock ledge, or up a bluff covered in kudzu. No one's been there since the—incident, as far as I know. Nearly a century."

"You never explored?"

"I'm not fond of small, dark, about-to-collapse caves home to bobcats, snakes, and rabid racoons. And old Sam and Cyrus Berens were very protective of their property line. Rumor was they ran an old still by the spring."

"That's it!" I said. "Billy took Dani there to recreate the scene between William II and Sean. He wants to reverse the results by killing you and getting the girl—Dani."

"No!" He stepped back, then frowned. "That's a stretch. And a hike. You can't get close with a vehicle, and there's no telling if the cave is still open. The only marker back in the day was an old Juniper pine. It's likely long gone by now."

"But Billy didn't have to use the cave," I argued. He had access from his own cabin. "It makes perfect sense. I feel this, Patrick. She's there! And the clock is ticking. Can we get there through Billy's property? Jeremy would help."

He shook his head. "Revenuers shut the still down decades ago and I heard the trail washed out in the 1950 hurricane. Besides, Billy will expect us that way. There were rumors of land mines. And God only knows what traps he's set."

As the shadows grew, so did my anxiety. The State Police were patrolling the back roads and one officer guarded the house. We didn't have time to wait for the Federal Agents to return from the interviews. "We need to go now, Patrick. Can we get there with horses?"

A thick, black eyebrow rose. "I don't like to ride," I said, "But I can. And I'm small, if you need my help in the cave."

"I'll take a horse too," a male voice came from the foyer.

We both turned to see Jeremy approaching us. The fading bruises from his broken nose made him look roughneck. "I heard the call on my scanner," he said. "Billy's gone too. He's insane, and no matter how distant, Dani is my cousin. Let's go get her."

"But the police," I said. "We'll need them to arrest Billy."

Patrick headed for the gun cabinet. "They don't have a mounted unit anymore, but we've got horses if any of them can ride."

He handed Jeremy a carbine. My pistol was still in my purse. I'd load it on the way.

Patrick told the lone State Policeman to radio the Federal agents and call for reinforcements with medical assistance—just in case. Rolling up the map, Patrick told Mattie, "Get Alvarez on the radio. Have him saddle five mustangs for rough terrain. Fast. And meet us at the base of Sand Creek Ridge."

Jeremy opened the front door and instead of the Langesford drive, we faced the broad, immovable chest of FBI agent Vernon Thomas, responding to Glory's call from Atlanta. He'd taken a private plane and just landed. His deep voice carried the authority of the US government.

"Where you headed with those weapons?"

Jeremy and I froze, but Patrick didn't flinch. "To get my daughter. Billy Berens has her at a hot spring about ten miles north of here. Step aside, there's no time to waste."

But the boulder of a man wouldn't move. "You need the law with you."

He handed Patrick a walkie-talkie. "I radioed for backup. Tell him where we're goin'."

"An old spring on top of the Sand Creek Ridge," Patrick shouted into the radio and raised a fist toward the sky. "The damn sun'll be down in a few hours and the sonofabitch has my daughter up there." He shoved the radio back at Vernon and pushed past him. "Either climb in the truck or get out of my way."

CHAPTER 33

Vernon muttered, "God save me from crazy white men," and pulled off his suit jacket revealing a shoulder harness with a .357 Magnum in the holster. Jeremy and I filled the front cabin with Patrick in the driver's seat and Vernon joined Clarence in the bed of the old, four-wheel drive Ford pickup truck.

Rising steadily toward the ridge, the old wagon trail became a challenge, even for the big truck. Rain from earlier in the day had made the clay slick and traction difficult as the tires spit mud over the truck bed where Vernon and Clarence bounced.

We stopped where the trail overlooked a fallow cotton field and met Alvarez with the horses. Patrick unrolled the map. "We're half-way there."

"You sure?" Vernon motioned at the expanse of wilderness. "This is a wild goose chase you can't afford to lose."

Patrick's finger stabbed the map. "He's there. On the border of our properties. Billy's family had boot-leg trails all through the woods leading to it."

Vernon wiped mud from his forehead. "Then why are we pretending to be goats climbing through brush and God knows what else..."

"Booby traps." Now Jeremy stabbed the map. "Landmines. US Army surplus from both world wars and Korea, as well as good old animal traps and pits. There, there, and there, just to name the few I know about. Billy helped his pa and Cyrus with the stills. But if we try to get in from the cabin side of the bluff, he'll pick us off like fish in a barrel."

Patrick looked up. "There is no 'us'. He wants me. Alone. But I'm not stupid. I need you on the ground when I bring him and Dani out."

"Don't be crazy!" Vernon, Jeremy, Alvarez and I sounded like a bad barbershop quartet.

"That's what he wants," I argued. "A duel. But he doesn't play by the rules. He'll shoot you on sight, grab Dani and follow his drug route to either the coast or New Orleans."

"She's right." Vernon pointed to the rocky, timber-covered ridge facing us. "But it'll take a tank to get us all up there. What's your plan?"

"I won't climb the hill. I'll go through it," Patrick said. "There's a natural tunnel midway up, by a Juniper tree." He looked at the now-glowering sky. "We can get close on the horses, but we need to move fast. Take the lamps to look behind fallen trees and bushes.

"It's an old Juniper," he repeated as if Vernon and I knew what a Juniper tree looked like.

"A tall bush with needles," Jeremy explained. "The bark is rough, like an animal clawed at it. This time of year, they'll have berries that look like blackberries and they grow close to their water source, so it'll be near the spring."

We spread out. Alvarez held Dani's sweater in front of Clarence's nose and took him off the leash. The part-bloodhound was off like a shot, but it didn't surprise me when he returned a few minutes later looking as frustrated as we felt.

They didn't come this way. They didn't have to. Billy knew where the land mines were.

What seemed like an eternity later, I called out when I spotted a deformed old tree with roughened bark hanging askew along the side of a weather-worn rock. Patrick and Alvarez hacked at the creeping kudzu surrounding it to find the opening of a cave. Patrick's, "Don't!" kept me from charging inside.

"We don't know what's in there, or if it's the right place. And there could have been a cave-in." Three of us shined our lights inside. I looked around for Jeremy but couldn't see him in the gloom.

"It's small," Patrick said. "And rises. Could be the one." He crouched to go inside while Clarence strained on his leash. I stepped forward and Alvarez grabbed my wrist, holding it like a vise. A few minutes later, Patrick emerged, scraped, dirty, smelling like wild animal scat.

While I'd prayed to find Dani in it, I was relieved when he said, "Empty, but it goes a long way. Narrows at the end, but I think I can get through."

He looked at Vernon. "No way you'll fit. Where's Jeremy?"

"Went around the other side."

"I hope that suit wasn't expensive," Patrick told Vernon. "How are you at climbing?"

A big grin split his face. "The suit's off the rack. I spent two years in Special Forces and can climb like a cat."

"Great. While Jeremy's circling, you take the climb. There's rope on my horse. Keep as quiet as you can. The spring is in a clearing at the top."

He turned to Alvarez, "Stay with Laura in case Billy tries to sneak out this way."

Why would Billy sneak out? Patrick was wasting Alvarez to protect me. It pissed me off.

"I'm going with you. Alvarez can circle up the long way."

"Thought you didn't like caves. Family dungeons and all."

My fist hit him square in the shoulder. "It's Dani. I'd walk through Hell to get to her. Same as you. Besides, I'm smaller and may be able to get through if you can't."

He looked at my sleeveless blouse and asked Alvarez. "You got a spare shirt?"

The ranch manager pulled a sturdy flannel shirt from his saddlebag. It went nearly to my knees and I thought of the bloody one stuffed in the saddlebag in the Treasure Room. It seemed times hadn't changed that much.

I followed Patrick at a tediously slow pace along the slippery rock floor until he had to stoop. Soon after, we smelled the mineral pool and glimpsed light. I squeezed next to him to view what I could only describe as the Garden of Eden. Gone was the tangle of undergrowth, kudzu, and my nemesis, ragweed. Less than a football field away, a thick carpet of grass kept short by grazing animals led to a pool surrounded by ancient rocks.

I looked over his shoulder wondering if the Cherokee had cleared the trees from this plateau to create a lookout for their enemies. Did they set the stones to enter the warm, life-giving waters for purification? A sudden push sent me backward onto the slimy rock floor behind Patrick.

"Hey!"

"Quiet!" he hissed. "For once, do as I say. Stay here until it's over —please."

Then we heard it. A whimper. Like a child crying. "Dani," I gasped and lunged again for the opening.

His arm blocked me. "Stay!" he ordered as if I was Clarence. Then he stepped into the light. "Come out, Berens. Where's my daughter?"

"You mean *my* daughter," Billie's voice bounced from the water and rocks, making it impossible to tell his exact location. "Put down your weapon."

"Daddy!" Dani's voice was weak but clear.

"Dani," Patrick called, "I'm here." He set the rifle down inside the cave and stepped toward a nearby oak, jumping back when a shot rang out, hitting the ground inches from him.

I held a hand to my mouth to keep from screaming, then stepped back and picked up the rifle. I'd never shot at anything alive but wouldn't hesitate to shoot Billy if I had the chance. Breathing in through my nose and out through my mouth, I steadied the butt of the unfamiliar gun against my shoulder and quietly released the safety. Ignoring everything on either side of the sight, I waited for Billy to step onto the stage for the final act of his life.

Dani cried, "Daddy, I want to go home."

I blinked tears aside and flexed my index finger. Could I be as brave as a six-year old?

"Be still, sweetheart," Patrick told her. "We'll be home soon. Mattie baked a pie. But you must stay quiet. And don't move, no matter what."

No response. Was Dani hurt? Drugged? Or obeying her father?

"Is this how it ends, Billy?" Patrick called to his unseen assailant. "You brought me here to replay the night your worthless great-grandfather got caught trying to rape an innocent girl? If you touched a hair on my daughter's head, I'll only keep you alive long enough for you to beg for death."

The savagery in his voice didn't surprise me. I supposed everyone had it in them when it came to protecting their child. Billy took the bait. He stepped out of the woods wearing his Confederate uniform, carrying the ancient rifle that had caused the deaths of Ed and Thelma O'Grady. He was closer than I thought. An easy shot, but Patrick was in my line of fire.

Move! My mind screamed. *One of you, JUST MOVE!* But they stood like two cowboys on a dusty Western street: one unarmed, the other aiming a musket at his chest. "Get ready to meet your maker," Billy crowed like a movie bad guy.

Patrick laughed. "That's it? You went through all this trouble to shoot an unarmed man? My God, you're pathetic. You could have taken a shot at me any time—or as you prefer, hired someone to cut my brake line or shoot the tires on my truck. Instead, like the coward you are, you use an innocent little girl as a shield."

What was he thinking? Dani would be destroyed if he was killed in front of her. But again, it worked. Billy leaned his weapon against the tree where Dani was tied. He was finally in my sight, but Dani was next to him. I couldn't take the chance. My arm ached under the weight of the rifle, but I kept it on target as Billy pulled a hunting knife from his boot.

"That's better, Billy Boy," the unarmed Patrick taunted. "Is that your dead, depraved great-granddaddy's knife? Or did you steal it like you're trying to steal my land?"

Billy flipped the knife in the air to show his expertise. "You mean like you stole mine," he growled back, inching toward Patrick. Hatred thickened the air as the humid, evening gloom settled around us.

Billy had stepped away from Dani but was now blocked by Patrick. If somebody didn't do something soon, they'd be fighting under the moon. Given the clouds, I wondered if we'd even have that.

Billy lunged. Patrick dodged. They circled, parried, and thrust a few more times until Billy did a razzle-dazzle leap and threw the knife. It hit Patrick in the shoulder, taking him down. I flexed my finger on the trigger, but the damn tree shrouded them both until they were little more than dancing wraiths in the dusky shadows. Dani cried from behind the tree, hearing, but not seeing what was happening.

The clouds finally moved, showing the early evening half-moon. Patrick was on his knees, one hand pressed against his shoulder, the knife in his bloodied hand. Unsteady on his feet, he approached Billy, who circled his wounded prey like a wolf, another, smaller knife in his hand.

My rifle was useless with them moving around so much. And Dani was wailing.

"Dani, I'm coming," I screamed and ran for the tree. Billy turned toward my voice and Patrick lunged. Billy fell forward, toward the musket, reaching for it just as a dark streak tore from the cave behind me and a howling, jaw-snapping, Clarence clamped onto Billy's arm. Trained to catch, not kill,

Clarence tugged and pulled at Billy's bleeding arm like a puppy with a chew toy.

With Billy screaming and Patrick stumbling toward him, I untied Dani and pulled her into my arms, covering her ears.

"Release!" Patrick called, and Clarence obeyed. With my gun lost somewhere in the deepening twilight, the two one-armed men continued the fight, stumbling more often than landing blows—until a rifle shot called it a draw.

Billy went down, and Patrick collapsed. I screamed, crushing Dani against my chest as a man's silhouette rose from a crouch at the crest of the hill on Berens land. Then it moved toward us, weaving in and out of the shadows as it descended.

I saw Alvarez coming from the cave behind us, and shouted, "I've got Dani! Patrick's hurt. Help him."

"Is he dead?" came from the cover of the trees. Jeremy. But his voice was different. Deep. Cold. Emotionless.

"No," Alvarez called out and pointed at Billy, limping toward the woods with a twisted, bloody arm.

Jeremy walked toward Billy and I wondered about the change in him. He'd come through the Berens minefield. He could have led us right to Billy! Was his shot meant for Patrick?

I couldn't accept that he was like his cousin. Not after Billy beat him only a short time ago. But he'd told me loyalty was how his family survived. Was the Berens fealty that twisted?

Alvarez ordered Clarence to sit and ripped off his own sleeve to bandage Patrick's wound. Vernon finally crested the hill, his clothes ripped by brambles and thorns. Alvarez called out, "Patrick's alive but he's lost a lot of blood. We need to get him off this hill."

"This way," came from above us as Jeremy reappeared, prodding Billy with the business end of the carbine. He didn't sound happy when he said, "He's bit up pretty bad, and I nicked him in the calf, but he'll live."

Dani clung to me, sobbing while I stroked her hair and rubbed her back. "Don't worry, darling, Billy is going away and won't ever hurt you or your daddy again."

She raised her head, ancient eyes glittering in the shifting moonlight. "Are you sure?"

I shivered from more than the cooling night air when a wolf wailed somewhere in the distance. Vernon handcuffed Billy, and Jeremy jammed a rag into his mouth, muffling his screams and curses as we followed Jeremy's flashlight."

He pushed Billy toward the old minefield and Patrick leaned on Alvarez while I carried Dani and Vernon carried Clarence toward a fallen tree at the head of a narrow path interspersed with neatly placed flagstones. It would have been a walk in the park if Jeremy had told us. What *was* his angle? I caught his arm. "Why didn't you tell us about this?"

His dark eyes glittered with an emotion I couldn't identify. Then he picked up a rock and tossed it at one of the flagstones. It exploded on contact. I jumped, Dani screamed, Clarence howled, and Patrick swore a string of oaths I'd never heard in one sentence.

"Cyrus told me where a lot of the mines were, but not all," Jeremy warned. I got lucky coming in. Now, step *exactly* where Billy does on the way out."

"Move it!" Alvarez ordered. "This man needs help."

With Billy cursing us all, and Jeremy's flashlight fixed on his feet, we followed their steps over the explosive brick road toward the cabin.

We called an ambulance first, then Vernon called the State Police. They were on the way. We put Patrick in the bed, covering him with the bear's paw quilt, Dani curled in a ball next to him. Clarence lay on the rug, snoring softly after nearly pulling a man's arm off.

Billy was on the couch. My medical expertise included band aids and aspirin, not stitches and pressure wraps, but Alvarez expertly tended both men, using Billy's expensive scotch as both anesthesia and antiseptic. He closed their wounds with towel strips and duct tape.

"Medic in Korea," answered my open-mouthed gape.

A half-hour later, the sound of sirens and boots stomping up the porch ended the two-hundred-year-old feud between the Berens and Langesford/O'Grady families. But I thought of Dani's question about being sure Billy couldn't hurt them again. A sudden rush of goosebumps made me wonder if I should have taken the shot when he dropped his gun.

CHAPTER 34

The uneasy feeling that Billy wasn't finished with us faded after he was charged with a laundry list of crimes that would keep him in jail for several decades. While Billy insisted on campaigning from his jail cell—and got some votes, Patrick was a hero,

I stayed on until Dani's nightmares subsided and she went back to school, but every time I met Patrick's eyes, I saw the knowledge that I'd slept with Billy. Worst of all, I saw the pain I'd caused him by withholding key information that put Dani in danger. I wished with all my heart I'd told Winkler to shove his smear-campaign, but what was done, was done. It was time to move on with my life.

Saying goodbye to Dani was the worst part. She presented me with the embroidered shawl from the Treasure Room and I gave her my music box saying, "It used to play *The Tennessee Waltz.* I loved it when I was your age. It doesn't work now, but maybe someone here can fix it."

She hugged it close, promising, "Don't worry, Daddy will make the music play."

McGill offered me an exclusive contract to write the story as I saw fit. I declined because I was too close to it and there was nothing political about it. Instead I wrote an editorial about the American tragedy called the One Drop Rule.

I sent it to Patrick before it was published, and he wrote me a letter thanking me for not turning his family tragedy into a soap opera scandal. It was so formal, I wondered if his new secretary had written it. If so, I couldn't blame him.

The article was nominated for an editorial Pulitzer. I wondered how David Winkler felt about that, especially after Mr. McGill fired him for his part in the Berens debacle. I took no joy from his humiliation. In his day, he was a hell of a reporter.

I stayed with Glory and Edwin until I found a place in Atlanta. My lack of ironing skills notwithstanding, I was accepted by the Old Fourth Ward residents and Mr. McGill helped me get access to jailed protesters. Sadly, shortly after Dr. Martin Luther King won the Nobel Peace Prize, someone threw a Molotov Cocktail through a window in Edwin's business, igniting the cleaning solvents. It was gutted before the fire trucks arrived.

He and Glory moved to New Orleans together and opened a law practice with his insurance money. Her leg never healed right, and I commissioned a walking stick like Camilla O'Grady's to help her make her point in the courtroom.

After they left, I wrote a series of other well-received articles on the anti-miscegenation and other discriminatory laws still in effect throughout the South. I was finally doing the work I'd come to Georgia to do, but without someone to share the passion, it seemed hollow. Still, my Pulitzer nomination redeemed me in Father's eyes. When the invitation came for the annual Stainsby Christmas Ball, I figured it was time to face the last of my demons.

Snow had transformed the old city into a post-card illusion of purity and peace. I entered through the kitchen and after a tearful reunion with Nanny Irene, hustled up to my old room to prepare for my audience with my father. It was oddly comforting to sit on my old bed, surrounded by faded movie posters for *Rear Window, White Christmas,* and *Gone with the Wind.*

Tears welled in my eyes at how much Langesford looked like Tara, but I'd only come for the holiday and to say goodbye to my old life before considering an offer to join Smith College's new journalism education program.

While visiting Glory, I succumbed to her advice to buy a new gown for the event. She insisted, "You need to knock the girdle off every Yankee bitch there."

When I reminded her that *I* was a Yankee, she chuckled, "In name only, Chère."

I settled on a simple pale rose Grecian-style silk sheath with a silver shoulder ribbon, a perfect accent for Dani's shawl. Too bad it made me want to cry.

The holiday dinner was a small affair, only twenty of the most important Washington politicians and their spouses—mostly Democrats, given Lyndon Johnson's overwhelming victory over Barry Goldwater. Another sixty people would be arriving later for cocktails, music, and awkward conversations.

I played the role of my mother, smiling, nodding, prodding people to their assigned seats above or below the proverbial salt at the table. As the only single woman in the room younger than fifty, I declined introductions to bachelor, and newly divorced sons, brushing them off with, "I'm only in town for a short time." My patience waning, I answered one pimp request with, "My girlfriend is waiting in Atlanta."

It pissed Father off. At least he wouldn't push me to stay through the New Year.

The orchestra finally began, and I counted the hours before I could crawl upstairs, climb into bed and sleep Christmas away. I'd danced with nearly every seventy-year-old politician when someone tapped my shoulder. "Merry Christmas, Laura," came from a familiar voice.

Patrick. I turned and met the eyes I dreamed of every night, and the smile that heated my blood. I fought the urge to slap him and turned away, found the shawl, and ran upstairs.

At the landing, I leaned my forehead against the wall. How could he—they—Father and Patrick, do this to me? It took nearly three months for me to be able to even think about him and Dani without crying. I planned to pack my bag, grab my rental car keys, and head back to the airport.

I turned toward my room and reached for the doorknob, stopping when I heard music in the room next door. *The Tennessee Waltz* sounded tinny and high pitched, missing a note now and then. My ballerina music box? No. The cruel bastard couldn't—wouldn't—have brought her here. Then I stepped inside and saw Dani sitting cross-legged on a four-poster bed, looking at my picture of Mary O'Grady.

"Dani?" I whispered.

Bright green eyes opened wide and we reached for each other, nearly upsetting our tiny orchestra and dancer. I held her close, kissing her cheeks, her eyes, her hair; while she giggled, hugging my neck so tight I could barely breathe.

Then we danced. When the music stopped, we wound the key to the box again and danced some more. I closed my eyes, wanting to remember every note, every movement—for the rest of my life.

"May I cut in," killed the dream.

"Daddy!"

Dani dropped back on the bed and I turned. Patrick's arm circled my waist, pulling me so close I felt his heart beating fast and looked up at tears shining in the eyes that had captured my heart in front of the Jeffers Memorial Library.

"I was such a fool," he said.

"Yes, you were," I agreed. "Me too." Our lips met, and the music played again. In the box. In my heart. And in my soul.

THANK YOU FOR READING

Did you enjoy this book?

Tell the world and leave a review at the site from which this book was purchased.

DID YOU KNOW THAT LEAVING A REVIEW...

- Helps other readers find books they may enjoy.
- Gives you a chance to let your voice be heard.
- Gives authors recognition for their hard work.
- Doesn't have to be long. A sentence or two about why you liked the book will do.

ABOUT THE AUTHOR

A Michigan Native, **Doris Lemcke** has enjoyed living in Pennsylvania and Florida. She is fascinated by historical journals and letters that tell the "real" stories behind history, the variety of ways the truth can be told, and the consequences when lies told often enough become the "truth". *Legacy of Lies,* and *The Langesford Legacy Series* illustrate the price of lies, the power of truth, and the roles both play in the rollercoaster of life in America.

For more information:
www.dorislemckebooks.com
Doris@DorisLemckeBooks.com

Eager to hear what's next for Doris Lemcke?
Join her mailing list!
www.dorislemckebooks.com/contact.html

facebook.com/Doris-Lemcke-Author-177898622282712

ALSO BY DORIS LEMCKE

WITH SATIN ROMANCE

The Langesford Legacy Series

Rebel Treasure

White Mountain Spirit

Champagne Promises

The Story of a Lifetime

Love, Lies and Family Secrets Series

Legacy of Lies

Made in the USA
Columbia, SC
04 April 2021

35055467R00174